WHISPERS OF THE PENDLE WITCHES

KAYLEIGH KAVANAGH

Whispers of the Pendle Witches

Second Edition 2024

Published by Oriana Neoma

Insta: kayleigh_kavanagh

Tiktok: kayleigh.kavanagh

Facebook: facebook.com/kayleighkavanaghauthor

Other works by the author

Getting Caught Up

Sugar Sweet and Whiskey Sour

Secrets of Olde: The Hades Interview

CHAPTER ONE

Her joints cricked and cracked under the weight of the day. At almost four-score years on this earth, Demdike should have been living the twilight of her years (or already long in her grave). However, there was *'no rest for the wicked'* as the old adage went, and she hadn't enough money to rest on her laurels. Her family barely had two pennies to their name. With winter fast approaching, the luxury of rest was one reserved for the rich.

The aged woman leant back on the grass behind her. Demdike purposely chose the spot (as she did every week) because it was on a slant and enabled her to sit against the natural slope of the hill. Helped with taking the stress off her weary limbs and meant there was less for her and her grandchildren to carry back home once they were done.

Similar to the stall, she was desperately clinging to her limbs. Sadly, throwing a nice cloth over her didn't make her look any better these days. Not enough to fool people about the broken frame beneath. Because of her increased age, people were impressed by her wares, hoping her longevity and wisdom as a cunning woman might infuse their lives with some vitality.

The stall before her was a wooden log, chopped up and nailed together with more rust than iron. It wasn't anything special, like some of the other stalls around her. Someone had expertly crafted the oak table across from her, selling one of those could have fed her family for six months, at minimum. However, this little broken bit of wood had lasted her the past few years and was better than a simple sheet on the floor. Plus, she didn't have to bend up and down as often, and it enticed more people forward when the goods were closer to eye level.

Unfortunately, this also meant everything was at hand-level and she had to keep a keen eye for sticky fingers. The hammer next to her was not just for decoration, but a warning to those thinking they might take advantage of an old woman.

To the left side of the table there was a rickety metal frame wedged up to allow various things to hang down, again to grab people's attention and make them more willing to part with their coins. Not a fancy stand, but it did the job.

The contents of her stall annoyed some people, but she always sold out of her trinkets and gems. Most of the people of the area were traditionalists. As the local wise woman, many counted on her for the old world's cures. The concoctions she created.

The little decorations forged from twigs, flowers, and little scraps of cloth also attracted attention. Many a young girl snatched up her pretty objects, hoping to catch the eyes of the boy who filled their dreams. Or young men attempting to curry favour with the pretty lady they were trying to woo. She had several creams for softer skin, protection pendants and scented waters (perfumes) which the ladies loved. Demdike was happy to share all the little beauty tips she'd utilised in her youth—and used to hold the attention of several young males—though it hadn't done her much good.

A good marriage was useless when the man died not even a decade into their '*happily ever after*', and she'd still been one of the lucky ones. At least she hadn't died in childbirth like so many of her friends. Women who popped out sprog after sprog until their bodies gave up or their innards tore and could no longer be patched back together. She'd been lucky to only have two children. However, the boy had long since left, pretending he held no connection to the beggar woman and the shame he saw her as. Men, they had it too easy and judged too harshly. Women were better off without them. Harsh to think about her own son, but she had all the family she needed in her daughter and grandchildren.

Demdike never remarried. No man wanted an impoverished woman who'd already been wed once before. Well, they might have *'wanted'*, but for nothing more than a roll in the hay. As a young mother, she'd refused more than one wandering hand. Luckily, her reputation as a degenerate kept many at bay, and her threats to curse them ensured those brave enough never attempted more than once.

'Eyes of thunder,' her daughter claimed. Her daughter, Elizabeth (Lizzie), swore to have seen Demdike's eyes flash with something dangerous whenever she got angry. Demdike wasn't sure she believed the lass, but if it kept unwanted attention away, she was more than happy to use whatever was at her disposal. These weren't safe times for vulnerable women (nothing new there). Her mother warned her about the dangers of not having male protection in a man's world. Though Demdike didn't think she'd done too badly for herself—having reached a ripe old age—despite all the odds stacked against her.

Her Lizzie technically carried the family name. A name the elderly woman once bore as well. Though she'd discarded hers early when she took up the mantle of wise woman. The world now knew her by 'Demdike'. Demdike, her nickname, her title. There were twenty-plus Elizabeths in their local area alone, all with some nickname or another. Demdike became her stage name, her brand. Even her grandchildren called her Nana Demy before they called her Elizabeth. Nana being a title as well as another word for grandmother. As though she was everyone's family.

Demdike had been her persona for so long it might as well have been her true name. The woman thought of herself more as Demdike than as Elizabeth. Elizabeth had been a young girl with big dreams and grand plans. Demdike was what life left behind. How reality moulded her from a hopeful girl into a harsh woman.

Back in the old days, cunning folk were supposed to keep their true names secret; to protect themselves from curses and the fae of the wilds. A precaution against the spirits they interacted with. If they could not name you, they could not harm you. Codswallop really, and the law meant everyone had to give their name for the records these days anyhow. Still, Demdike adhered to tradition, and this was how she was known now. People didn't ask for Elizabeth Southerns, they asked for Demdike. And Demdike gave them the show they expected.

This life wasn't glamorous, but it was honest enough work. Someone had to do it, and it'd kept her fed these many years. Enabled a single mother with no means to see her daughter into adulthood. Into her marriage. Even if her little Lizzie endured the same curse in marriage as Demdike had. At least her daughter managed a full eleven years before John Device left their world.

Demdike's eyes blinked back to the present moment. People bustled around as the midday sun warmed the earth. This year she'd added something new to the display, a group of protection bags. The travellers brought whispers of new ailments, one supposedly gripping the South. In an attempt to safeguard people from a variety of illnesses, she'd composed little bags; containing a mixture of herbs, churchyard dirt and river water.

The bags would protect either the wearer or the home from ill health. Warding away the spirits of sickness and malady. She used such herbs on her own family and they'd been healthier than most, especially given their poor pockets and many years with scraps for meals.

The stall also held a couple of her favourite poultices. She would need Alizon or James to harvest more ingredients soon. Her stock was running low. Her grandchildren were old enough to know where to go and what to get. Thirteen and fifteen seemed like babies to her many years, and both were closer to their next birthdays than she would have liked.

Adults by many's standards (something she vehemently denied in her mind). They were at least more capable than many others in the same age bracket—not by choice. Life was a cruel teacher, and the poor grew up far quicker than most. Demdike made a mental note to send them off tomorrow. The sooner she had the ingredients, the sooner she could have the poultices made up and ready for sale.

The local people might not always like her and her wares, may have scoffed at such things in polite conversation, but they were usually the first to buy them. *'Just in case'*. Their fears greater than the desire to risk their lives. She was happy to take the money, no matter where it came from.

Demdike could scarcely afford to turn away payment because of pride. She'd been poor most of her life, had been on the receiving end of their scowls and dirty looks since her father's passing. They left a crawling sensation on her skin, but this was hardly foreign after all this time. She'd learnt to take small pleasures in how they held their tongues in fear of her retaliation. She might not like her reputation, but she wasn't in a hurry to change it either. Protection came in many forms—sometimes fear was a safe place to live.

"Demdike, got any of the sleep aids?" the woman asked, her voice a little unsteady.

"Lady Bethany," she greeted. "Yes, I have them here." Demdike handed over the herbal tincture, a family recipe for inducing sleep and fighting bad dreams.

Demdike had long used the same tincture to help her troubled sleep. With age came many thoughts and countless regrets. Ones which stopped the mind from finding solace and peace in the dark of night. Like how she had outlived many friends. Or how she wasn't long for this world. Or even how her grandchildren barely knew enough to survive, but would inherit her bad name all the same.

Bethany came by monthly for the same order. She was one person Demdike was happy to help, regardless of the need for money. Bethany was one of the few people with a kind smile for her. Helping feed her family was merely a bonus.

"Thank you. I wonder if you have anything for," the woman's voice dropped, her eyes uneasy, searching for any overly keen ears, "for male virility?"

Demdike was a professional. Amongst her family and friends, she would have broken into a broad grin and said something scandalously funny. Because, despite her grandchildren's opinion, Demdike was hilarious. However, she also knew when to school her features. This woman was of good breeding. For Bethany to come to her meant the couple must have already tried the doctors. Already faced multiple embarrassments. Demdike knew to keep her mask in place.

"I do know how to aid such issues."

The woman's face brightened but immediately relaxed, remembering herself and where they were.

"However, it will take me a few days to gather all the ingredients, and one full moon cycle; full moon to full moon, must pass before the remedy is truly effective. Can you wait this long?"

Demdike knew she would. The couple would likely have been struggling for months or years already if her experience of such issues was anything to go by, and one more month would not be a huge ordeal.

"And it will work?"

Demdike wanted to answer her with the truth, but few people wanted honesty.

"Assuming there's nothing—" She paused, thinking how to put this delicately. "—broken, then yeah. I've made this many times and only once did it not work. The man in question suffered a stabbing and his innards hadn't healed, as they should've. Assuming the same is not true for your—" Demdike paused again, it didn't do well to assume. She'd had many a wife ask her, but also a few mistresses. Bethany never named her husband, and Demdike learnt better than to assume. "—partner, then I see no reason why it would not work."

"Then I will bring three silver pieces next month."

Demdike's brows rose at the price. She wouldn't have charged so much, though she was not foolish enough to reject such an offer either.

"For your silence," Bethany explained.

'Ah,' she thought. "Of course, my lady."

The woman took her sleep aid and quickly left. Funny the things she learnt about people being the old wise woman of their area. Well, her and Chattox, but the less said about that nightmare, the better. Had the gods blessed Demdike with the fortunes of good birth or an enduring marriage (or money of any kind), she could have been one of the most influential people in all of Pendle. Simply because of all the secrets she held. This was why cunning folk were both respected and feared. They knew the darkness and troubles people hid behind their polite masks and false smiles.

Her little village of Goldshaw Booth was always busy on market day, every Wednesday. People came from all over the Pendle borough to get whatever they needed. Many sellers, like herself, only sold at this market. Though in her opinion, the one in Colne was usually better for sales.

Demdike was getting too old to travel to the neighbouring areas like she once had. She was still trying to teach her daughter and grand-daughter the way of the wise women, but it would be many years before they knew all the things Demdike herself had learnt (assuming they could manage to walk the path at all). If people wanted her wares, they had to come to her here. Or her home—though the reputation of Malkin Tower kept most at bay.

The village was busy as usual, but today was different. There was a hesitancy to all the rushing. Demdike sensed this earlier but ignored it in favour of attracting custom. Now, during the lull, a sense of anticipation hung in the air. The people were all waiting for something. Their animal senses revived; the rabbit-like noses twitched in the air, smelling for whatever was nearby. However, there wasn't a physical scent, merely a pollutant in the atmosphere. Some foreign spice of life filtering in. They were all subconsciously aware of it. Picked up on the changes in the world around them, long before their eyes could find the cause of the disturbance.

As the church bells rang out, new shapes appeared along the main road. Even with the visitors from the neighbouring towns, faces were often recognisable. Families having lived in these parts for hundreds of years. New faces would pass through a few times a year, though rarely stayed long. The hills of Pendle rarely welcomed strangers. The crowd watched on as a large carriage followed the horses. If strangers were rare here, visitors with means were like a blue moon. They had little cause to traverse the harsh grounds. Few attempted the journey, and even fewer succeeded.

As a man emerged from the all-black carriage, whispers among the crowd broke out. She couldn't catch a name, but the title was hard to miss, '*Justice of the Peace*'. From Lancaster. She wondered why the hills had let him pass. The spirits who kept and cursed this land attacked anyone unknown. He must have some powerful protection on him to have made it here unscathed. A Justice. A man of the law. Recognised by the crown. To earn such a position was to be envied. But to have earned it under the new king, one who came from Scotland and united the two kingdoms? It said many things, none of which Demdike liked. Men who served the crown were rarely kind to Pendle.

From King Henry VIII's attempts to strip the church and sell every ounce of gold and silver he could get his hands on. To Bloody Queen Mary, who (fortunately) hadn't hurt them too much—given few had converted from Catholicism. However, it then made the retaliations of Queen Elizabeth even more vicious when she demanded the Church of England and Protestantism be recognised as the one true church.

In a place where tradition held more value than any church, it was the people who suffered. Stubbornly holding on to what they'd long considered a part of their culture. Even the priest was once heard saying how none of the residents truly followed Christ, they just liked tradition. None of them could argue with him. Few could read their native tongue, let alone understand Latin. The rise of the Church of England meant little when, even if the texts were now in English, most of them still couldn't read it. Never mind having the spare coin to buy a copy of this newly translated book.

Therefore, given Pendle's history, their relationship with those favoured by the crown was strained at best. A man of the law, representing the king, automatically set people on edge. Many were too young to have known the full extent of what happened. Demdike, herself, had been a mere babe when King Henry VIII's reformation occurred, but even as a small child, she'd heard many tales of how the locals won the race against the king's men and saved many of the churches' trinkets and statues.

They salvaged enough items to keep their traditions safe, but left enough gold and fabric to avoid suspicion. Decades later, several of the families still held those same sacred relics. Most returned them to the church, but after Henry's children proved to be as unreliable as him, the people decided it was best to keep certain items safe elsewhere. This left a sense of pride within the people; saving their church and keeping their traditions safe.

The locals believed this was the cause of power in their lands. The cause for the things they could all sense, but none spoke of. Many deceived themselves this was God thanking them for saving his church (and his possessions). Demdike and others knew better. The beings which blessed their lands were far older. Far angrier than any Christian God. Even those who knew refused to speak about such things. Better to remain silent and not draw the wild things' attention. There were various other spirits which played in Pendle, most far older than any god named by man.

After the gathered crowd began to quiet, the local priest, Father Trowe, stepped forward. The man was one of them. Heard their confessions. He knew how the locals saw strangers. Especially men of the crown. New arrivals did not bode well for them usually. Addressing the market, the priest performed his duty flawlessly.

"May I introduce to you the honourable Justice of the Peace, Robert Nowell."

This earned a polite clap from the crowd, but the unease was visible on their faces. The question heavy on all their minds: "*Why was he here?" "What reason did a lawman have in these parts?"* This was the thing with knowing every one of your neighbours. You knew their sins. Their stories. There'd been no murders, no thefts, no reason for someone of his status to enter their territory. For all everyone wore those strained smiles, their eyes demanded to be told why he was here.

Whispers soon travelled. About how men had come to visit, but no one knew their reasons for being here. Some claimed the man, Nowell, was here to find a wife. Others claimed the crown had come to kill them all again for not removing the Catholic church. Whatever the man's reason for being here, he'd quickly made his way to the house of Noah Smithson, the local law enforcement.

Though the man wasn't much about the law. Law unto himself maybe, but little beyond. They all heard what happened to poor Janice. How in her master's house she'd been forced to do more services than her job. The poor girl's future was ruined, but the law didn't care for the poor. Never had. Janice was just another victim. Another faceless destitute for them to ignore and throw stones at. Blame her as though she were somehow accountable for the actions of her attacker.

In Demdike's experience, the only time they punished such behaviours was when the woman who'd been attacked was of means or married to a man of influence. They viewed the crime as more of an attack or slight on the man protecting her than actual physical harm done to the poor woman herself. It seemed the 'R' word was only acknowledged when the victim was the property of a wealthy man; a daughter, sister, wife, etc. Anyone else was an expendable problem who should have known better.

Demdike had offered many a karmic curse to these invisible injured. Helped give those poor girls closure. A way to feel as though they'd retaliated without endangering themselves further. If Demdike ensured a tonic or two was slipped to the perpetrators, which would inhibit such actions from happening again, well, those were most definitely coincidences.

***

Demdike didn't ease her hurried pace until her eyes found the ramshackle building two miles away from the market. The place was jokingly called Malkin Tower by the locals. Forged of stone and wood, standing taller than many of the nearby houses. Her grandfather first built it. Then her father added to it. Her (long-dead) husband focused on the interior and the structure. Later, Lizzie's husband, John Device added a little more. Because of this mishmash of handiwork, the place looked like a child had drawn it and brought it to life. A mixture of clay, stones and various woods haphazardly thrown together and looking as though one strong wind might be its end.

High on the hill, it overlooked most of Goldshaw Booth. The people called it '*the tower*' as it was too small and compact to be named a castle, and Malkin had been her great-grandmother's maiden name. She'd been a woman of high society before coming to Pendle; marrying below her station. The locals told tales of the family being cursed because Mariane Malkin refused her father and foolishly chose love and poverty over the husband he'd picked.

Demdike once believed it to be nothing more than fiction, but after she, her mother, and Lizzie all lost their husbands early, she was no longer as convinced the tale was simply idle gossip and malicious fiction. Curses could be fickle, and ancestral wounding counted for more than most realised, but the pattern couldn't be ignored.

Unfortunately, even if the curse was real, Demdike didn't know how to reverse it. She would have to one day warn her granddaughters of their potential futures, but for now, would continue terrifying them away from the idea of suitors until they were at least twenty. Maybe even thirty if she was lucky.

At her age, a hurried pace was more like a slow crawl, but Demdike kept plodding on all the same. Her grandson James had taken the stall, as she held the stuff in a sheet over her shoulder. A routine they'd long perfected. Though he'd been twitchy about something today, so she'd sent him on ahead (unable to rush like the young boy).

Her eyes fell upon smoke coming from what was meant to be a chimney, though it looked more like a hole with black stones over it to stop the rain from falling inside. The scent of root stew reached her nose (they rarely had enough money for meat). She was home.

"Mum, you're back early?" Lizzie announced in shock.

"No, just the sun's out longer today, it seems," Demdike countered. For the autumn it had been unusually bright.

"Oh, seven hours must have flown by. How have I missed that?"

"Busy with your sewing, I'd assume, daughter mine," Demdike teased.

Lizzie squinted at her in the low light. Her daughter's eyes had been poor since she was young, but there had been little they could do about it. All the herbs and age-old treatments in the world barely touched the problem. It'd led to the little girl earning the unfortunate nickname *Squinting Lizzie*. Though compared to some of the names around Pendle, this was kinder than most.

"I'd managed to get my hand on some thread and do a bit of embroidery. I thought you could try and sell it next week."

"You bet I could," Demdike agreed, amiably, moving towards her favourite chair.

Her daughter was acting strange. Lizzie might have been a woman in her own right, but Demdike still saw the little girl she'd raised whenever Elizabeth acted shiftily like this. Her daughter was hiding something. Something which made her uncomfortable but she didn't want to speak about. Sighing heavily, Demdike left it for now. She'd get it out of the other woman, eventually.

Moving her seat nearer the fire, it was warm enough to keep the descending chill from her bones. Night wasn't here yet, but she could feel its approach in the air. Alizon came bouncing in, the girl a whirlwind onto herself. Had Demdike not checked every one of the children with iron regularly throughout their youth, she'd have thought Alizon was a changeling.

Alizon was too wild. Too detached from the world around her. This wasn't to say the girl was cold, quite the opposite. The child had a heart big enough to love the entire planet. Yet her fantasy reality held more sway than the bleak world around her. As the girl nearly tripped over the cloak stand for what felt like the millionth time, Demdike called her granddaughter over.

"Al, come sit with your nan. Tell me about y'day."

It wasn't a request. Best to keep the girl from getting underfoot. Or causing unwitting destruction as she remained completely oblivious to her surroundings.

"I saw my friends," the girl said, only half in the conversation, her eyes trailing over to her mother.

Now the family had arrived home, Lizzie would likely serve food soon, and if Alizon's watchful eyes were anything to judge by, the girl was as hungry as her. As if to confirm Demdike's thoughts, the child's stomach gave out a large call to be fed. Chuckling, she ran her hand through the child's hair, trying not to get caught in the many knots.

"You need to brush this. Bring me the comb whilst we're waiting on your mother," she instructed the girl.

Alizon huffed, but complied. As much as the girl loved having long wavy hair, she hated having to do the things necessary to take care of it. Baths and brushing chief among them. Though the wild child did enjoy coating her hair in concoctions, trying to make it smooth and shiny. Demdike couldn't comment. She'd been much the same in her youth. Especially when the rumour about bathing causing sickness had gone around. Later disproved, but for a time everyone—noble and peasant—had avoided baths. Her hair became so matted she'd had to cut huge chunks off. Demdike was glad she later discovered the wonders of soap.

As she carefully ran the brush through her granddaughter's hair, Demdike tried to distract Alizon as she negotiated knots, attempting not to yank the girl's scalp too much.

"Where's your sister?" she asked aloud, wondering if young Jennet was perhaps the cause of her daughter's earlier distress.

"In bed. Mum thinks she's caught something. She was peaky last night. Don't tell mum but we even had to cover ourselves with our Sunday best." The words fell from Alizon's mouth quickly, her eyes glancing to the kitchen, hoping her mother hadn't heard the confession. "She couldn't stop shaking. Seemed fine again this morning. But by lunch, she was falling all over herself. Mum sent her to bed."

Demdike nodded along, still trying to get the comb through the matted locks. Ignoring the *'ow's'* and *'ouch's'* as she went.

"What's upset your mum?" she asked quietly, also checking her daughter hadn't heard them.

"Jennet, food time," Lizzie called up the stairs to the missing child.

A thump followed by several heavy footsteps was heard until they reached the stairs. Alizon shook her head, not answering. Soon, two sets of footsteps were heard; James following his younger sister.

Demdike put the comb aside, letting Alizon escape as they were each handed a bowl. More broth than substance, but better than nothing. Demdike knew what it was like to go hungry. Anything was edible when you were starving. The contents didn't look appetising, but it would do.

As they all sat around, the clanking of spoons against bowls and Jennet's annoying slurping were the only sounds. *'She's still a child,'* Demdike reminded herself, so as not to snap. Distracting herself, she took in the rest of the room—drawn shoulders and pinched faces. Something was upsetting them all.

"So who's going to be first in tellin' me what's been happening here today in my absence?"

James erupted in laughter as though waiting for her to remark on the atmosphere since he'd entered the room. However, he was fast silenced by the raising of her hands.

"Daughter, you want to tell me whatever it is that I ain't yet been told about?" her body may have been weak, but her words rang throughout the little house.

"The Baldwyn's, they're claiming that we've stolen from 'em. I'm due to be summoned by Smithson at some point in the next few days." Lizzie stared at the floor as she spoke, fingers whitening around her spoon.

"And we didn't steal, did we?" Demdike looked at Jennet, silently asking if she had something to hide.

"No!" Jennet replied angrily. "I wouldn't even go near their bloody house let alone be inside it, not after that stupid Caleb tried to throw a dead frog at me, I don't like the lot of them." She folded her arms, pouting at the unsaid accusation.

It slightly lost the effect when the girl had to cover her mouth quickly to cough. Hearing the rattle in the small chest had Demdike squinting. That would need checking later.

"Good. And Smithson, is he involved or likely to do anything?"

This was troubling. Normally it would be a small nuisance, but with the Justice of the Peace in the area, they might see to make an example out of them.

"Either whip us, fine us, or make us pay back with labour. Maybe all three," James answered unconcernedly. The boy spoke in a broad Lancashire accent. They all did, but with him spending many of his days on the farm, it had gotten stronger than the rest of the family's.

"But we didn't steal it! They gave us it," Alizon muttered furiously, keeping her voice low.

"I know, but who d'ya think Smithson is gonna listen t'? Us lot, or them respectable ones?" James spat, derision heavy in his words.

The mere idea that a family so poisonous and full of liars could be respectable simply because they had money was laughable. Demdike would have to remind them of the secrets she kept.

"What are we going to do?" Alizon's tone hinted at a hope for a revenge plan, as she and James were the only two of the family prone to taking such direct action.

Demdike couldn't comment. She'd been exactly the same in her youth, but Lizzie would get exasperated with them all if ever she encouraged the children. James had taken out his wood and knife again. Whittling little pieces and statues he liked to swap for pennies and ale when working on the farm. The boy had quite the talent. Shame he had the patience of a bee in a bonnet—too angry and ready to fly off at a moment's notice—or he might've been able to turn it into a real craft.

"Well, I'm bettin' Smithson," James began before biting into a piece of the wood off that hadn't loosened by the knife. "Will demand we do a bit of labour for 'em or somert at the very least. Unless nan has a chat with them first," he hinted.

The old woman smiled. Her family knew her too well.

"I'll pay them a visit tomorrow. We need to be careful. I saw some visitors from Lancaster arrive today. The local Justice and his people. We can't afford to draw attention to ourselves when people like them are here. We know how slap-happy those kinds are at the best of times."

They all shifted uncomfortably at the reminder. All having felt the pains and humiliations of those attacks.

"The lot of ya," she said, looking each of her family members in the eyes, "keep your heads down and your actions clean. And if they accuse you, lie or run away." Not the best advice, but the only options they had available. "Now, Jennet, come here. I need to listen to that chest. Daughter, put the herbs on to brew, the ones in the pot marked with what looks like a bird's foot."

The old symbol for protection. For healing. Simple enough. Demdike might not know many letters, but there were a few words and shapes she recognised. The old tongue might have long been lost, but a few of the symbols held meaning in her work. Adding a carving to her creations made a great deal of difference. The spirits understood the language, even if she didn't.

CHAPTER TWO

"Nana Demy, we need to go before it rains," Alizon moaned.

The girl might have been close to adulthood by society's standard, but she was still too much of a child for Demdike to see her as more than the wee babe who'd once fit in the drawer.

"I'm coming. I'm coming. Oh, these weary bones." She may have been laying it on a little thick, but it was cold out and her ligaments knew there was a shower fast approaching.

Taking the gnarled bit of wood from by the door, she used it to help steady her gait. Walking had grown more difficult the greater she grew in years. The uneven ground of hills and valleys did not help. The grassy moulds hiding many dips and holes. Demdike had tripped more than once on this familiar trek. Her eyes weren't as sharp as they'd once been. The walking stick was now a necessity.

Her bones were fragile. A slight tumble could break her leg or shatter her hips. Not many made it to her age. Demdike had seen herself how after two score years, people's bodies withered away within their skin. She'd been called to aid many a broken bone and feeble frame decaying away whilst the person still lived.

She sometimes wondered if it was her connection to Pendle and its hills which kept her alive where many others had long left this plane, but there was no one else to ask. She was the eldest wise woman in the area. Well, she could've asked Chattox if she felt the same, but the old witch was her competition. A friendly adversary. Demdike scorned the idea of asking the woman.

Demdike had been honing their craft before the other woman was born. She even aided the then child through colic and teething. She refused to ask the same child (even if Chattox was now in her sixties) if she knew why they were still here. Especially when many barely saw a quarter of a century, let alone over half.

Malkin Tower was far from ideal and cramped for the bodies forced to dwell within its walls, but despite its appearance, it was sturdier than most. Demdike no longer had to fear falling asleep, to only be woken by falling ceiling slats or thoughts the house might have come down around them in the night (like she had in her youth). Despite the short length of her marriage, her husband secured the structure well. Demdike often wondered if Noah had a touch of spiritual power himself. How else did you explain the ramshackle building surviving better than the manor houses?

Either way, despite its innards, Malkin Tower was well situated. Close enough to the village, where she could flog her wares. High enough to avoid the floods, which sometimes followed the rains. Far enough away from the neighbours, they wouldn't bother her. Yet close to the forest, she could collect what she needed whenever required.

"Do you need help?" Alizon asked as they drew close to their destination.

"Could you grab my good arm, help me get through these rocky bits?"

Demdike had never been a big fan of asking for help, but pride was stupid when her body struggled. Dallying would mean they were stuck out here longer and would be caught by the rain. Neither of them could afford to fall ill simply because she'd been too stubborn to accept a helping hand. At least Alizon was gracious about lending her aid. Keen to be useful wherever possible.

They tread carefully, still using her stick to feel the way ahead, ensuring their next footsteps wouldn't fall into a boggy ditch or sink into the unsupported earth. What her eyes had lost with age, her mind had gained. The knowledge of these hills she'd trekked these many years was now as much a part of her as the wrinkles on her brow.

Demdike could feel her granddaughter hovering close by, locked worrying in her own head. Alizon had the habit of filling the surrounding space with the emotions she felt, infecting the air with whatever thoughts or feelings she was drowning in. The more the girl tried to bury them, the more obvious they became.

"So, are you gonna tell me what it is, then? Or are you going to keep me in suspense all day?" Demdike finally asked. Amused as her words woke Alizon from her own mind.

"Is it that obvious?" Alizon replied, shoulders slumping in dismay.

Using the stick again, Demdike took her next step and turned to face her granddaughter.

"About as obvious as a duck in a keyhole." She chuckled.

"Oh, Nana Demy, I don't know. It was so strange. We were just sat there."

"We?" Demdike interrupted, not that she couldn't guess, but it was fun to watch the roses bloom on her granddaughter's cheeks as she was forced to clarify her words.

"Yes, me and Peter, you know," Alizon replied, shifting her foot awkwardly.

They both knew how Demdike didn't approve of boys. Didn't want her granddaughter to fall down the path so many women had. Losing themselves to love. Alizon was nearing fourteen, courting age. The world was dangerous for young girls. Although Demdike hated it, the girl would need to try for a good marriage to have a better life. As the elder, she highly discouraged any potential activities with handsome young men. Not that Alizon often took her warnings to heart, but it was the place of the elder to offer guidance, whether well received or not.

"Carry on," Demdike ensured her voice carried a level of disapproval.

"We were sitting there cloud gazing. Y'know, seeing the shapes. And then he said to look at this one cloud, but when I looked, it wasn't a cloud that I saw." Alizon stopped speaking, a detached look on her girl's face as her mind replayed the memory.

"Then what did you see?" Demdike gave the girl a piercing stare.

A cold feeling flooded through her limbs, causing Demdike to shudder. She could tell this thing, whatever it was, unnerved the child.

"I couldn't say exactly what it was, but it looked like a face." Alizon paused again. "It wasn't a person's face, or at least it wasn't entirely human. Its eyes—they were... they weren't right. It was looking at me, trying to, well, talk. I think?" The girl's confusion was mirrored in her posture. The shrinking of her shoulders, the in-turning of her limbs, her face glazed with the intensity of her recollections.

"And what did it say?" Demdike enquired cautiously, suspecting she already knew the answer. Though it brought her no comfort.

"I dunno, it wasn't speaking English. Was the old tongue you use sometimes when doing your healing chants. I just ran as soon as I heard the words forming, but what I—no, I felt like it was warning me. Not in a friendly way, it w-wanted me to know something b-bad was coming." The small girl trembled along with her voice.

Demdike started walking again. If her guesses were right, then she knew exactly what her granddaughter had seen. She'd seen the same thing herself. Heard the same mocking warnings. For all she wanted to share her theories with the young lass, Demdike knew the impact worry had on Alizon and she held no desire to increase the child's troubles. Not yet.

"T'was likely a warning about your sister. She has consumption. If we don't get her what she needs, and soon, she will suffer and may not recover. Now lead me due east. There is a growth of herbs there. They'll be needed if we are to help her."

Demdike watched the expression on Alizon's face relax—her body uncurling as she extended her arm to help her grandmother. Alizon believed her, for the time being. They continued with their walk. Demdike now carrying the burden of what was said, and more importantly, what was to come. The image took a new visceral form each time it reached out. Though the dark message it carried never changed.

"Careful," the girl said gently, helping Demdike manoeuvre over the sharp stone.

A natural barrier to keep people and animals at bay. It took them a few minutes to make their way over and through the uneven ground. In her youth, Demdike had more than once rushed, jumping from stone to stone, bouncing over the earth as though she were some goat-like creature. For all she had sprung and jumped gracelessly over the rocky mounds, she rarely fell. Demdike half believed it was perhaps why she'd fallen more in her later years. The world demanded a balance, and she'd been spared too often in childhood to not pay it back in her cronehood.

There were certain places which were ancient and blessed. Much like the Christian idea of hallowed ground, nothing evil could enter these sacred spaces. Could not cross the natural barriers which encased them. A grove resided on the tops of the hills. A place where heather grew and wildflowers blossomed year after year. Demdike had been born near here, a surprise to her mother as she demanded early entry into the world. Rushing into life the way she'd never stopped as a child. Running as fast as possible.

Demdike felt connected to these hills. Dreamt of ancient people performing ceremonies to the old gods. Her birth gave them a spark of something they'd long been deprived of. Perhaps this was why she'd always sensed what lay dormant below the earth here. A shadow below the surface of the water, ready to awaken at any moment, but content to stay sleeping. For now.

"Wait, nana. Isn't that the patch where we went when the lady that had the...?" Alizon went quiet.

"Yeah, Al, it is." She'd brought Alizon here many times in the girl's childhood, but only sometimes did the child seem to recognise these places.

As though the spirits only sometimes wanted her to remember them and this sanctuary. The girl in question stared around, a look of awe on her face when she saw the beauty before her.

"I usually send you and your brother to the forest to collect most things, but this place is special. It hides and reappears when it wants. A safe place for the old world. But be careful, there are plenty of pitfalls and holes around the edges. Check every step. The flowers cover the empty ground below. Learned that the hard way," she muttered, more to herself than to Alizon.

"It's beautiful." By the awe in the girl's voice, Demdike suspected her granddaughter had retained little of her warnings. Though Alizon was more the type to learn the hard way. "Does this mean someone else is—?" the girl asked without finishing the full implication.

"Is?" she prompted. Demdike hated half sentences. They too often led to miscommunication, and a conversation based on assumptions led to more trouble than they were worth.

"Like the lady," Alizon answered quietly, despite there being no one around for miles. "Possessed."

"Aye, the woman had been possessed. Or at least she thought she was. I could only see wounds she'd inflicted on herself. I'd wager she was just a little off her rocker. But it made her feel better. We can heal and we can harm, but sometimes the best cure is believing in another person. Simply giving them your support."

Alizon nodded, still looking at the natural beauty around them. Demdike often wondered how much of what she said the girl remembered. Alizon reminded Demdike of herself a little too much at times, a girl not fully in this world. Daydreams were a more powerful pull than reality. It worried her. The child got too lost in her own head more often than not and reality was often cruel to dreamers.

"But why are we here this time? Do you think Jennet is possessed?" Alison was becoming alarmed again.

Her capability to go from calm to heart attack panic was usually amusing for Demdike. However, being in the middle of the hills; where one wrong footing could be the difference between toppling down a bottomless pit vs. arriving safely at your destination, they couldn't afford for Alizon to lose her focus. A troubled mind was not conducive to a safe journey.

"No, your sister is not possessed. She's just mouthing back at you, the same way you did at that age. Her sickness is entirely natural, I'm afraid," Demdike teased.

Alizon merely huffed, bending to her knees to inspect the flowers before her.

"Children can't be possessed, Al, don't worry. They're too pure." Demdike hadn't planned on sharing such secrets with Alizon, but as with everything in her craft, sometimes the only choice was to go with the moment. To flow like water and accept the world as it came to you.

"But Chattox has exorcised children? Kenneth's brother. She was there two winters back. And she travels across the county and I heard even into Scotland back in the day?" Alizon challenged.

"Aye, she does. Doesn't mean they're possessed though, just means she's providing a service they think they require," Demdike suggested cheekily.

"I don't get it. Why can't children be possessed?"

Demdike stood stationary, debating if it was even worth attempting to explain the obscure rules of the other worlds. The intricate ways in which spirits could both influence and control the actions of certain people. However, knowing Alizon to be like a dog with a bone, answering would save her from the constant nagging.

"Alright, y'little bugger, I'll explain, but don't be surprised when it goes right over your head."

Alizon nodded excitedly. Even with Demdike's failing eyes, she knew that mischievous smile Alizon wore.

"So, like I said, youngens are too pure. It's not until a person is capable of evil thoughts that they're then able to be possessed. A child is pure of mind and thought, therefore they're protected. A spirit can hover around them if they're particularly receptive to the other side." She turned and looked at Alizon, the hint heavy in her tone. Demdike may not have been a fan of half conversations, but she knew how to use them.

"As in seeing ghosts?" Alizon negotiated her footing over the holes in the field, helping Demdike as she went.

Demdike bent forward to ask the earth if it was okay to take them. Collecting a few fallen flowers and petals from the floor before replying.

"That and just sensing them, you got more senses than just your eyes, after all. I knew one lass, swore up and down she could smell whenever a ghost was near. Said they smelt like old clothes and grave-yard dirt." Demdike shrugged. She'd never been sure whether to believe the woman, but the idea brought a smile to her lips.

"Anyway, some spirits are drawn to those who can sense them. Sometimes 'cause they just want to be seen—to let someone know they're there. Some are there for other reasons. Some good, some not. Same as living people. You follow?" she asked, hitting the walking stick hard on the floor. Suddenly, several holes produced wildlife, all scattering at the presence of intruders.

"Don't wanna be tripping over a hare's tale. These dips are bad enough."

Alizon laughed, dodging the fleeing wildlife and bugs.

"I get how a child is safe 'cause they're good, but not all of 'em are good, some of them are right little so and so's." Alizon was always trying to poke holes in everything she was told. Curious to a fault.

Demdike rather liked that about the girl, though it was annoying when trying to teach.

"Aye, but there's a big difference between a child wanting to slap you and wanting to stab you." Demdike impressed her point by using her free hand to demonstrate these actions.

"I don't get it?" At least her granddaughter was honest.

"Well, by bad thoughts I don't mean a kid who's being bad and challenging an adult, or who says 'I don't like you' and 'I wish you were dead'. Because little ones don't even understand death. They say a lot of things they don't mean and definitely don't fully understand. 'Go away' and 'Go die' mean the same thing to babies. On the other hand, an adult can plan to hurt or kill someone. Once these truly evil, or ill will thoughts, are sewn, then a person can become susceptible to negative spirits.

"As I said, we can argue that children might say stuff or kick and punch, but it's usually what they've learnt from their parents, so you'd look at them or wherever they'd learnt that language or behaviours from. You get me?" Whilst explaining the deep intrinsic complications of spirits, Demdike had successfully tackled the first few burrows by herself, slowly making her way towards the patch of herbs they'd come here for.

"Like when James was spouting about how we were all 'going to hell' because the priest had told him we were bad and deserved damnation?" The girl's imitation of the old priest was scarily accurate.

Demdike vaguely recalled the incident, remembering a young James shouting at his parents because he wasn't allowed to go out and play. Would've been funny, if not for seeing her daughter's devastation. Her little Lizzie always had been more sensitive to the cruelties of others than Demdike herself.

"Aye, exactly. He didn't mean the words, but 'cause he'd been told 'em off someone in a place of power, so he thought they were true. Wanna talk about who's going to hell? I'd be pointing my finger at the man who was bullying a child. But cause he's a man of the cloth, oh no! He's a good person," she spat the words.

Okay, perhaps Demdike wasn't as at peace with such things as she'd thought.

"So, once a child is old enough and thinks evil thoughts, then they can be possessed?" Alizon's face pulled in multiple directions as she tried to process the information.

"So James or I could be possessed, but Jennet can't?" Alizon asked, voice tinged with worry.

"Eh, not exactly. Mentally, your brother's a good bit younger, an' like I said, he'd have to have a malevolent thought. And worse, he tends to come up with is 'I'll set my nan on ya'. So I think he's safe." She let out a small chuckle at the thought.

Alizon joined in with a stifled giggle. Her brother James was almost a man in being, but a child in most other ways.

"Nah, Al. James is safe. You too really. Unless you've been planning some things you haven't shared?" She raised her eyebrow in jest, but did wonder why the girl hadn't asked about her own safety.

"If anything, with all these 'child possessions', it's the adult you got to watch. Especially the one accusing them. If it's someone who gets paid for the exorcism, then I'd ignore every word out of their mouth. But often when it comes from someone who should be looking after them, you have to tread very carefully. 'Cause often they're either harming the little ones or something dodgy is up."

There was more than one case of supposed possession Demdike had to walk away from before she killed the guardians of the kids. A child covered in bruises was obvious, but in her long life, Demdike learned there were many insidious ways people would hurt those vulnerable and under their care. Those unable to fight back. She'd earned her earlier reputation for a violent temper because of a supposed child possession. Though the priests preferred to handle such things, cunning folk had long been the go-to protection against the spirit world and its many influences. And northerners did so favour their traditions.

If they were going to continue with this impromptu lesson, she might as well get comfy. Demdike cautiously lowered herself to the soft ground below. Careful to not sit on any of the flowers. Requested permission of the heather to rest her tired body on them for a short time. Nature did not talk in words; instead giving impressions, images, or energies. A warm brush of something had her finally lowering herself entirely. If the plants disagreed later, they would let her know.

"There was this one guy I knew of. A few years back now, he'd regularly accused children and entire families of being possessed. You remember hearing about Nicholas Starkie over in Tyldesley, right?"

At Alizon's nod, she continued.

"Well, John Darrell was a Puritan minister. Went around the country saying he could cure this and that. How all sorts of people were possessed. Did horrible things. Claimed he was 'cleansing them of their sins' and 'saving their souls'. All that rot. He was imprisoned for fraud about a decade ago now," Demdike added.

"Anyway, during his travels, he eventually made his way to the Starkie home and performed exorcisms on seven members of the family. How you justify saying seven members of the same family are all possessed, I don't know. In my entire life, I think I've seen less than ten real possessions, and I'm sure any priest worth his salt would say the same. This guy was taking liberties, put it that way," scorn heavy in her tone.

"Anyhow, it might have been the end of it, except he didn't know Mr Starkie was a well-connected man. Noble with a lot of friends. Oh, he knew Mr Starkie had a lot of money but didn't know his cousin and grandfather were big to-do names down in London. When the idiot threatened to claim Starkie was possessed in order to extort a load of money from him... Well, I heard he had his cousin there so fast the man was in chains and trialled before the month was out. Actually, I'm pretty sure I heard he was related to the local Justice." Demdike halted for a moment.

Was Nowell old enough to be the same guy? These things run in families. Maybe it was his dad? Something to ponder on later.

"The point, Alizon, is when it comes to possession claims, you gotta be extra careful. Especially," she dragged out the word for effect, "when it's about young baba's around two or three. When they're all behaving like little shite-hawks. Can't say in my entire life I have ever seen a child who didn't act up at that age. But this Darrell guy, he were going around, telling parents how the devil was after 'em and how evil possessed these little babes. Absolute nonsense. Then, of course, he had been charging the parents to 'rid them' of this supposed evil." She could feel her own face warp in disgust at the memory.

"His way of getting rid was to basically torture these poor kids." Demdike turned to Alizon with brimming eyes, the water pooling in her tear ducts at the memory. "I mean he would beat them, starve them, lock them up, pour hot oil on and in them, throw scalding water at them. Some of the tales I heard were just..." She took a moment, composing herself. "Well, they were sick. By the time I got wind, he'd been doing it across the country. As you can imagine, it had the people in a right state, thinking all their kids were evil and there were devils around every corner. Right mess it was." She tutted, shaking her head at the memory.

"Well, I left any supposed kid possessions to Chattox after that. We might have our disagreements, but it ain't worth my head if I end up kicking a fuss. I deal with the unfortunate girls, she deals with the poor kids. It's been our arrangement these past few decades and ain't worth changing now."

Alizon's eyes flashed in recognition of what Demdike meant by unfortunate girls. It wasn't something people liked to talk about. Whether young unmarried girls. Women with less money than mouths to feed. Or a wife who'd had an unsavoury dalliance. It was a necessary service and one which held no judgment from her.

Beginning the slow descent back down, the pair were both stopped in their tracks. The path ahead was blocked by a large deer, or more correctly, half of a large deer, sinking into a boggy marsh.

"Nana, I thought that the path didn't change for another month or so?" Alizon's eyes were locked on the slowly sinking form before them.

They couldn't risk trying to help the poor creature. Though she was mildly upset at the loss of good meat.

"It shouldn't. Must be all this freak weather we've been having, making the ground unsteady. We'll have to go take the south path. Hope it's a little drier." She tried to steer the girl in the direction of the other path, immediately feeling her resistance.

"But what about the snakes?" Alizon recoiled.

"We'll have to hope they're asleep by now. Hopefully trying to escape the weather, too." She led the reluctant Alizon away slowly.

The ground soon changed from overgrown grass to worn-out earth as they approached the main road. It was easier for Demdike to walk here; the ground was smoother. There was the odd pothole, but nothing quite as dangerous as the moors held. She could smell the bread being kneaded from a nearby house, hear the banging of a blacksmith, and the chatter of people creating the dramas of their daily lives.

Demdike had long surpassed the boredom of local people, those incapable of seeing past their own self-created disasters. She preferred her own world, her family, and the seclusion of her life as a wise woman. Nearing the Baldwyn's house, Demdike gathered the herbs in her pocket and whispered a few words.

"You wait here, Al. I'm going to go in alone." She edged up the path towards the house. Sensing the door had been opened even before her arrival.

"Demdike, we did not expect you today?" a voice said politely, but the evidence of fear ran below the melodic tones. The young girl of the house.

"No, but your parents must have. Take me to the kitchen. I need a drink." Her presence was causing unease, and Demdike would use this to her advantage.

Eyes struggling in the low light, she carefully made her way through the hallway. Her once sharp sense dulled with age. Just like the rest of her. From what she could see, these were wealthy people. The soft furnishings guided hands along the walls, making her yearn for a cloak in the same material.

The smell of fresh baking lingered in the air. Demdike's taste buds danced as each wave hit her tongue and reminded her of the decent meal she had long gone without. Being hungry made her angry (another family trait), but years of poverty meant she'd learnt to control these basic needs. The girl was taking her to the servant's kitchen, but at least it was brighter. Demdike grabbed the water from her satchel and sprinkled a little in front of her, ensuring all around her would be blind to her true intentions.

"Oh, you've spilt some," said the young girl, her tone more annoyed than concerned.

"I'm sorry, my dear. Grace, is it? You must forgive these aged hands of mine. They shudder and shake far more than they once did." Acting the part of the decrepit old woman wasn't difficult with her advanced age.

"Yes it is, and it's no matter. Here." The girl handed her a cup. Thinner and finer than any Demdike had ever held before. "Here's a little brandy for you." The girl smiled uncertainly. Her eyes looked to the door as though willing her parents to hurry up.

"You are very kind. May I take a seat, please?" she asked, indicating to a stool close to where they stood. There was a large table next to it as well. A perfect place.

"Of course, I'll go and fetch my parents." Grace hurried from the room.

There were servants still about, rustling in the corners and avoiding coming too close. Afraid of her. This was how she liked it.

Seizing the opportune moment of being unwatched, she placed the herbs on the table, gently edging them towards the centre. Vegetables kept there, both decoratively and likely to be used in an upcoming meal. Crushing the buds in her hands, Demdike let the remnants fall upon the food and allowed her lips to move ever so slightly at the corners. Her true task was complete. Now to finish role-playing.

Right on cue, the Baldwyns both entered the room. Mr Baldwyn gave off an aggressive vibe as he entered. He was not a man to suffer fools. His wife, on the other hand, was his weaker link and could easily be manipulated simply by suggestion and a sense of compassion.

"Good afternoon, Demdike. May I ask what has brought you here today?"

"Hello Richard, let us skip the formalities, shall we? I've known you since you were a lil' tyke. And y'know full well why I'm here," she let her tone become warm and friendly, as if remembering a happier time.

"I think we can both agree that time has done more than simply age us," he forced his words out, allowing a little bitterness to escape his well-mannered tongue, "Nana Demy."

A term used by all the children she'd once watched over and helped grow into adulthood. Though the words were far more terse than the small buck-toothed child who'd once greeted her with love and fondness.

"Aye, fate and fortune have definitely smiled well upon you, me lad. And I must say I'm most surprised you let it change you in such a way. But that's none of me or mine," she brushed over quickly. Glad to have gotten her little dig in.

"No, why I'm here, as you well know, Richy, is because of all this nonsense about stealing. You know as well as I do my thoughts on such. I prefer to beg, barter, and trade. To be offered food from a kind soul, not take the choice away from them. Isn't that right, Helen, our lass? Come out from behind your husband. Let me see you."

The small, younger woman stepped out from behind Richard and carefully accepted the open arms offered by Demdike. On touching her skin, Demdike could feel the softness of a lady who'd never worked. Richard had married above his station, but from the feel of the fabrics of Helen's clothes, he was supporting her very well.

"Demdike, it has been a long while since I have seen you," the young woman finally piped up

"Aye it has, Helen. Not since the birth of your little lass, if I recall? But with my age and my poor bones, I don't often get out nowadays other than the stall and when people be in poorer health than me-self. But after yesterday, and with poor Jennet being so ill." She shook her head and let out a mournful sigh.

"Oh no, not little Jennet. What's the matter with her?" Helen asked dramatically, as only a lady of fine breeding and little world awareness could.

"Consumption by the look of it. Poor lass. Dunno what we can do for her. Just prayin' the good lord helps her out."

"Oh no, here, take some bread." Helen hurried over to the other side of the kitchen, opening the cupboards to search her stores.

"Helen?" Richard opposed, anger in his voice. The man had grown only crueller with age.

Demdike didn't want the poor girl to suffer later. A man with a temper was a man prone to using his fists.

"Don't be so selfish, Richard. A young girl is very sick. Imagine if that was our Grace. We'd hope someone would give her a little food to help her if we couldn't, and anyway, we'd probably only give it to the servants," she said, scowling at her husband.

Demdike wondered if she'd perhaps read the relationship wrong, if Helen was, in fact, the dominant behind closed doors. Her higher status of birth could have protected her from any unsavoury behaviours and her father was still around, if Demdike recalled.

"But what about the sugar?" he replied, deflating where he stood.

"The sugar?" Helen asked, as though she had entirely forgotten herself. "I don't believe they even did steal it," she snapped. "And besides, we have plenty more. This is about the principle of another life, not just one about who can show their power." Helen turned outraged at her husband and consoled the (supposed) fragile old lady.

Demdike smiled to herself. Seemed little Helen wasn't as vulnerable as she'd feared. Definitely worth noting for the future.

"You're too kind, Helen, bein' married suits you. You've come into your own. But I don't want to intrude on your time any longer. I simply came to clear my family's name."

"Consider it cleared. Richard, get some cloth, and some more sugar. They might as well have some seeing as though they've been accused."

Demdike heard Richard scurry off, frustration and anger pounding in each step.

"You're a good 'en you, Helen."

"Well, I try my best. And don't think too harsh on Richard, he just doesn't like feeling out-manned." The lady laughed to herself.

Demdike enjoyed the irony of her words. When Richard finally returned, he gave Demdike the parcel and escorted her out.

"Been nice seeing you again, Richard. You made a good marriage there."

"Well, you were the one who encouraged me to go for it." He smiled, though it was strained around the edges.

Indeed, she had given him a charm to aid him on his quest.

"Aye, that I did. Knew you'd reach well. Take care." Demdike exited the property.

With each step, she was weaving the last parts of her spell. Richard should have known better; she smirked to herself as she reached the gate and an apprehensive young Alizon.

"Come on, lass, we best be getting back to y'mam."

Karma would come for the little brat she'd once been fond of.

CHAPTER THREE

Black clouds rumbled above. A growling sound echoed in stereo all around. Her footsteps, fast and fleeting, barely touched the floor. She jumped along until her legs no longer grazed the grass below. The shapes were indistinguishable. A blur of images and feelings. The only clear thing was the angry sky above. The ground trembled below as her body was pulled up towards the black miasma. Earth no longer anchored anything, the world below being yanked into the sky. Animals, homes, bricks and stones, all swirled through the atmosphere.

Roaring lashes of air crackled with energy. Debris scratched against her skin as everything rushed forward. The space between the land below and the sky above was unending. Her stomach swooped without the stability of the hills, holding her body steadily in place. The wind whipped against her ears as the sound disoriented her further. Up and down blurred. She was a piece of metal thrown through the sky towards an overpowered magnet. The sheer force was painful as it dragged her up.

There was a brief moment of awareness. This couldn't be real. The thought was gone as fast as it came, blown away by the wrathful winds. Her dress fluttered behind her. The dip of the fabric between her legs as it tried to escape the storm, but was tied to her body, unable to flee. A flag rising in surrender. The closer to her destination she drew, the more her mouth dried. Her screams never managed to escape. Frozen in her throat. Leaving a detached sense of inevitability.

This was always going to happen. Was meant to occur. She'd known. In the strange way, you sometimes know things will come to pass. An animal instinct the logical mind could never fully drown out or ignore. Warnings. Signs and synchronicities people could never completely overlook, no matter how hard they tried.

It felt like years and no time at all before she finally breached the barrier between the whirling sky and the cold clouds. Her body felt icy—wet—as she passed through the darkened sky. A momentary shock. She'd always thought the clouds resembled wool and would feel like touching a sheep, the sudden cold jarred her awareness. She tried to look around, but darkness engulfed her sight.

The static energy swamped her body from inside the blackened pools. Dark lagoons in the sky. Sweeping shapes. Beings she couldn't quite make out. Shadows and smoke swirled just out of the corner of her eyes. Her periphery gaze locked on the movement only to witness as they changed again, as though looking directly at them caused them to blur.

A memory of another time like this. Looking into the sea, where beings from the deep hid from her human eyes. Mermaids or mammals. Creatures prepared to capture her. Ready to drown her. Claim her life. Swallow her soul. It had ended before they'd claimed her, but the feelings lingered into the next world.

The water was cold, like those oceans had been. Cool against her skin. Dampened her clothes. Caused her muscles to contract and jump. Another thought almost scratched at her mind. Wake? She wasn't in mourning, was she?

The growling was louder within the dome. Her head snapped in place as her eyes scoured the shadowed space for the menacing noise.

The growls were a scattered voice trying to form words. The distance between her and this ominous presence muddied the message. Analogue sounds trying to breach a digital mind. Crashing against one another. A language too foreign. A disruption in the flow. A clash of warring energies. Life and death. Physical and spirit.

'*Soon*' was the only word her harried mind could make out.

An image. A face. Something formed and imploded on itself within the black cloud. Turned. Tumbled. A star collapsing in on itself and leaving a black hole in its place. Too dense to avoid. Pulling all life and light into its orbit. Never to escape again. Slowly, her eyes made out the twisted figure of a dog. Though no dog she'd ever seen. A gnarled version. Like something from folklore, or a demonic depiction. Eyes of blazing yellow stared back at her; lightning trapped in balls of energy, preparing to crack and rain down on the world below. Teeth as black as the rest of its form, yet somehow distinct.

"-t—soon," no more clear than the first time.

Another roar. It was angry. At her or in general? Because she couldn't grasp its message? It was pulling everything within itself. Swallowed every living thing, yet she still existed. Her life had not ended. Her heart had yet to give out. A being older and more terrifying than any she'd ever known was glaring down at her.

She was a minute bug to its magnificence. Its displeasure vibrated in the air. A taste on her tongue had her wanting to spit, a nasty habit her mother had beat out of her in childhood, but one she would happily return to remove this foul flavour from her mouth.

"It will be soon."

A shiver ran up her spine. The word *death* was never spoken, yet it screamed within her mind.

Her eyes hurt, blinking the sleep from them. Demdike rubbed the cracked gunk to help her lashes separate. Shivered at the biting cold picking at her extremities. Her arms immediately withdrew back under the quilt. A barely useful cover in this weather, but better than nothing. She took a large gulp from the cup next to her bed. The taste from her dream was still there. Mothballs coating the roof of her mouth.

The dream was slow to fade even as the details began to blur. Returning to the land of the living from the realm of Morpheus was always a jarring experience. Dreams like this weren't rare. Things reaching out from beyond the veil whilst her mind was less protected in sleep. Sending warnings or wants—the dead with unfinished business, the spirits with information, many faces, beings, beasts—all ominous in the dark.

A shadow of a spirit was nothing she hadn't faced before. But even as Demdike tried to blink away the memory, the twisted thing remained burned in her mind's eyes. The threat of death? It'd felt negative in a way she'd never encountered before. Held a weight of malicious intent. Something hungry lurked in those shadows.

Death was drawing near. Hardly a surprise at her age. She was more surprised to have lived this long already. A brief memory of earlier in the dream flashed through her mind. Of running free. Her body still able and fluid. The flying was fun, but it was the realistic memories which made her yearn for her youth. Made her miss the limber movements and strong muscles.

She'd always been slight, but decay had been setting in her skin since her late thirties. Her ankles had clicked with every step by her forties. The fusing of her arms had come by her sixties. Her body slowed down further the more birthdays passed, forcing her to feel the true depth of her age. The freedom of her mind during the night was one of the few joys she had left. Demdike long ago made peace with her passing from this realm. Though how it may come about was still something which worried her. No one wanted to die alone or in pain, but the idea of death itself stopped being a fear for her.

Demdike had seen too many people pass to worry about joining them. She was a wise woman. A person with one foot in the ether. The other side of existence had long been a welcome idea to her. It might still be a mystery, as one could not truly know the other side whilst in a physical form, but she'd accepted years earlier she was not long for the grave.

Poor and elderly as she was, Demdike was lucky to reach the numbers she had. Though it was the journey before the destination which struck a note of apprehension in her heart. Demdike did not care for how close death was—yearning to see her lost loved ones and faces her memory could barely recall—but even she feared pain.

"Mum?"

Demdike hadn't been aware of making any noise, but apparently, she must have.

"Just a bad dream. Is Jennet okay?" Her voice sounded hoarse even after a few more sips of water.

"Her fever has broken, but she's still looking peaky."

"I'll make her some of my tinctures in the morning. Make sure you smother her chest in the ointment. It'll help her breath," Demdike instructed.

"Will do. You try to get some more rest. We've got to be up early for church," Lizzie told her.

"Yeah, you too, night sweetie."

"Night."

***

The family's Sunday best were still little more than rags compared to most of the village, but they were the best the family could manage. Especially when pretty clothes were an unnecessary luxury compared to food and the thicker (less stylish) fabrics to help them survive the colder months. Not to mention how often it rained in these parts. The unending dampness of the air meant any clothes were often sodden and wore away faster than normal. Regardless of how irritatingly expensive church clothes might be, tradition dictated they had to comply with the expectations of the community.

Even if the Device family looked like most would on an average day, this was the only way to ensure their already precarious position remained steady. One little slip and they could truly become outcasts. In a place as small as Pendle, outcasts didn't last long. People would take away the already measly bits they had to beg for. Winters were harsh already with the intermittent charity.

As much as Demdike hated it, her pride had long been beaten into submission. Relying on others meant survival. Community over competition. This was how the plants in nature survived. Was how entire ecosystems supported one another. Survival of the fittest might work for the top of the food chain, but everyone else had to work in tandem to ensure they all lived to see another sunrise. They all had their parts to play. One frailty in the chain would have a knock-on effect for everyone.

Demdike might have been at the bottom of the metaphorical food chain, but she performed a vital role in the community. Her life was as tied to theirs as theirs were to hers. It might anger and frustrate her, but this was the path of the cunning folk. The folk-healers. Those who walked the line between this world and the next. Everything had its place, even her.

To bear the stares and scowls all whilst holding the knowledge these titles and positions meant nothing once they left this world was an uncomfortable cross to bear. The weight of spirit was heavy as the waterlogged clothes on her back, but there was little she could do to change the world. And in her twilight years, she no longer cared to try.

"Jennet's bloody lucky, not having to be out in this," James complained for the fifth time since they'd left the house.

"I'm sure, given the choice, she would rather be healthy and make the journey."

A lie. Demdike was quite convinced the girl would have happily accepted a cold every weekend for the rest of her natural life if it meant avoiding the Sunday service. Judging by the disbelieving looks shared between the boy and Alizon, they thought the same, but didn't bother to protest.

"Next time I'll stay back with her and mum can come instead," Alizon suggested, a little too hopefully.

"Your mum was up all night with the girl. She needs her rest as much as your sister," it wasn't said too harshly, but the two looked equally scolded by her words.

"Sorry, nana," they replied in unison.

"Nobody enjoys going to church. I bet money we see half the well-to-do lot nodding off during the good father's preaching."

Not a lie, but she hoped by making a sort of game out of it, the two would at least try to stay awake. Unlikely, but it was the best she could come up with.

The rain was bouncing off the floor as they drew closer to the River Ribble, falling with such force they needed to mind their steps. The bottoms of her and Alizon's dresses were coated in mud from the dirt. James' trousers didn't look much better. Lizzie must have finally taken the hems down after the boy's latest growth spurt. Her daughter had purposely made them longer for when the boy grew, unpicking the seams every time he shot up a few more inches. The threadbare kneecaps kept moving further up the boy's thighs.

Technically, to most people's beliefs, James would now be considered an adult. A man of his own measure. Though if fifteen was an adult, then she was definitely a walking corpse. He wasn't just a child in her eyes; he was barely born. Most barely made it to their second decade of life, let alone the multiple she'd racked up, but there was little she could do about such things. Regardless, society deemed the boy a man, and despite his attempts at trying to fill the role, the boy was too naïve, too innocent, too stunted in his development to be considered more than a wee lad in her mind. No matter how much he protested her assessment.

On Sundays, the walk through the main road of Goldshaw Booth was a little odd. The vast majority of the residents headed to the old church, but a handful walked to the newer one. The plain-looking building, built of wood and pale white paint, stood in direct contrast to the grand stone construction, with vibrant glass in multiple colours. A dazzling work of beauty built like the temples of old in honour of the God it was to worship, versus the simple hut-like one.

Demdike wondered which, if any, God might prefer. The regular worship would please most gods, regardless of what the structure looked like. But for as long as humans had existed, they'd added their own egos into the monuments they erected. To the things they worshipped. She'd heard whispers of grand structures across the world, all made to please the higher beings. People hoping to incite the benevolence of the greater gods.

Would a God who preached chastity, charity and loving thy neighbour want something grand or something simple? Would they prefer weekly worship or would they rather you stayed at home and kept them in your heart and actions every day? Demdike couldn't say. It was blasphemy to think you could speak for a God. To believe it might be your place to make demands on God's behalf. But these were questions she'd long ruminated upon.

She would soon leave this world, and thoughts of heaven and hell, whispers of Valhalla and the underworld, the Summerland and the dark dimension lingered in the back of her mind. In her craft, she'd come across many terms which implied similar ideas. A place of paradise and a place of punishment.

Would she go to a good place as death's icy breath caught on her neck? She'd tried to live a good life, to be a decent person. She wasn't perfect; had her fair share of faults. Tried to accept them in others as she did herself. Though she still acted in anger from time to time. Spewed words and performed spells some would frown upon. It was her place as the wise woman to take the strain others couldn't afford. To absorb the sins others were too broken to bear.

The path of the cunning folk had never been for the weak. It was not one of riches and happiness, nor for the faint of heart or easily misled. Only those strong of spirit and mind could do as she'd done. Worked with the spirit realm whilst still inhabiting a physical body. For all she disliked Chattox, Demdike couldn't deny the woman was a force worth respecting. It took a strong character not to crack under the pressures of the other side. Many people who were a little too attached to the ether had maladies of the mind. Would often lose themselves and fall from the path.

Even her own daughter had yet to achieve her own challenges. For all Lizzie was a good woman, she was not as strong as was required to carry the burden of death as you walked through life. To be touched by darkness and stay with the beings of light.

Cunning folk were grey. Lived in the shades of life most people turned their eyes from. Good and bad, right and wrong. The wise knew these were relative. All things which changed over time and from place to place. The spirit world was filled with both miracles and malevolence. One could easily lose themselves to the ether's influence. Become a little too happy, a little too oblivious, too open to attack. In contrast, the darkness might bog one down. The practitioner becoming a little too sad, a little too lost, until they stumbled around entirely in the dark and harmed themselves.

To have one foot in life and the other in death meant you were always dealing with the blinding lights of existence and the darkness ready to pounce. They had lost many gifted people on this difficult journey. Fewer and fewer had been attempting to learn the olde ways. The rise of supposed science and believing the olde ways to be little more than superstition best left in the past was a fast-rising sentiment. They often left the fact that people feared losing pieces of themselves to the tumultuous path out of the arguments. The conversations veered towards the irrelevance of the '*olde world*' rather than their own failings.

Demdike could hardly blame them. If the choice of healing was a few leeches or a long meditation—where the person had to confront the pains of their past and collect the lost pieces of their spirit—she would have chosen the leeches, too. Less painful. Quicker '*results*'. She'd argue their supposed efficacy, but it was a redundant conversation.

Demdike understood. She didn't like it, but she had been alive long enough to see when the tide was turning, and how things were changing. Soon she would be a relic of a bygone era. A lost sentiment of the past. As with all things, the new would absorb the old. The plain church would replace the stone ones. As those stone ones had once replaced the pagan shrines. It was all part of the cycle. Part of nature. The natural progression. All things withered away with time. Death claimed all things, even ideas.

As they entered the church, mats littered the floor. Towels were folded to the side, allowing people to dry themselves before officially entering the house of God. She rubbed herself over, trying to drain as much moisture from her hair as possible. As more people arrived, they had to hurry along. The one silver lining was they weren't the only ones who looked like drowned rats.

She took a dip of holy water, making the sign of the cross over her body. Her grandchildren copied as they followed her to the pew. She was too old to do a kneeling bow before the cross now. Afraid such an action, after being out in the cold, would have her muscles seize and keep her on the ground. However, she dipped her head forward in respect. Alizon and James did the proper bow.

More people trailed in. Some of the community elders (though she'd been a grown woman at the time of their births) came in at the back. Every week, they would go to both services. Both churches. The CofE church had changed its start times to allow them this want. They'd claimed it was to show support to both sides of the community.

Demdike uncharitably thought it more likely they were hedging their bets. If one church was better than the other, when they went before God, they could claim to belong to either congregation. Not that it mattered much to her. When she met her maker, Demdike suspected she would have more to discuss than which church she attended. She had a few choice things to say to them as well.

The Puritans were trying to inch their way into the northern territories, but, thus far, gained little ground. Demdike hoped they never would. Two churches was already more than enough.

Seeing Nowell come in with the elders had her unconsciously twitching, wanting to pull James and Alizon closer. Make them less visible. A smaller target. She turned her head fast toward the front as his eyes scoped over the gathered group. Without meeting his gaze, she could feel how it weighed and judged every person in the room.

Even with the quiet chatter, his footsteps were audible. The strong *thump, thump, thump* as he strode with purpose towards the front of the room. She couldn't hear the words exchanged with the priest, but the man had an uncharacteristically pinched brow. A few more words, a few arm touches, and the religious man was smiling once more. Whatever they discussed appeared to please Father Trowe.

Demdike couldn't see Nowell's face from this angle. Secretly relieved it also meant he could not see hers. However, from his posture and loosened shoulders, she guessed the man was happy about whatever developed. The Justice of the Peace then took a seat at the front of the church, ignoring all decorum and not performing any of the expected rituals. A few people shot him looks of disapproval. She hid her smile behind a hankie, trying to gain her grandchildren's attention.

"That's him. The Justice. Try to avoid him."

"Bit of an idiot, ain't he? Ignoring the rules an' all?" James asked, though not as quietly as she'd hoped.

A quick glance at Nowell had her hoping he hadn't heard. Luckily, it was Alizon who shushed her brother.

"I doubt he knows. Raised in the Puritan church. Or he knows he's powerful, and he doesn't have to pretend to care. Either way, the pair of you, stay away."

The two nodded. Though Alizon looked more curious than afraid. Damn, the girl's cat-like nature. As the man was joined on his pew by a few others, she had to glare at the young girl when her mouth physically dropped at the sight of a young lad. Demdike could admit he was bonnie, but she would not have the girl making eyes at the likes of him. That was just borrowing trouble. A quick pinch to the girl's thigh had her eyes back, front and centre. Though Demdike didn't miss the filthy look thrown her way first.

With Nowell unaware of her presence, she took this moment to gain the weight of the man. Larger than most, muscular. Definitely ate well and looked after his body. The stocky shoulders spoke of strength and someone who'd always had food on the table. He was slightly above average height, though Demdike wondered if the clicking of his steps meant he had lifts in his heels. The boots were good quality, dark leather, but she couldn't make out much detail from this distance. The man had dark hair, but it was peppering around the edges.

It'd been raining, but the man's shoulders looked barely sprinkled with water. A man of means who didn't have to walk far. She'd already known this from his arrival in a carriage, but this implied he was using it to travel around the village and neighbouring towns. There was a carriage which ran throughout the entire borough twice a day, for the workers mostly, but it was too expensive for most. To have a dedicated carriage meant his finances were far greater than even the richest here in Pendle. The difference of a title.

The man sat with a tall posture, as all those with good breeding were known to do. No slouching and slumping for them. She couldn't help glancing to either side. Her grandchildren were practically puddles with how they were pooling in their seats and this was without all the added rainwater.

Resisting the desire to sigh, she forced her gaze back, only to meet the darkest eyes she'd ever seen. Flashes of her nightmare came to her. Blackholes sucking everything into them. She could almost feel her mind and body being swept forward. There was something shadowy behind that cold gaze. A cough from the priest had both of them snapping to attention.

Whatever that had been, she never wanted to experience it again. Felt like her soul was being sucked out of her body and swallowed whole. The man was absent of something vital. Something human. He was a dense fog, drawing everything in and consuming all unfortunate enough to get close. A shiver racked her frame. Not caused by the draughty church. This Nowell might have been a man, but he was not whole. There were pieces missing. Somehow she doubted he would consent to a spirit walk and collect the lost parts of himself.

Demdike had only seen this once before, when a creature replaced what had once been there. Something cruel and hungry. A monster wearing human skin. Unlike possession, the thing had once been human. Simply having lost its humanity. What remained enjoyed being the creature of darkness it became.

Demdike pulled Alizon and James a little closer, pretending it was for warmth. It was, but not physically. No, she needed the warmth of family, the warmth of love. Cunning folk knew what it was to live in shades of grey, to live with one foot in the ether. Knew to keep themselves in their bodies, and their loved ones near. To help push away the lingering darkness.

She looked at the cross, a silent prayer for strength against this new threat. Nowell had been a potential problem before. Now he was destruction and death given human form. There was little protection, spiritual or otherwise, from such beings. The shades of Pendle already felt darker.

"Today we will be discussing some interesting things. I'm sure you all know the bible verse, *'Maleficos non patieris viver'.*" The priest looked around the church eagerly.

Demdike wasn't the only person who didn't understand Latin. She wasn't sure anyone other than perhaps the Justice and a handful of the well-educated folk would know even their English letters, let alone a dead language. The man's face did not drop, but his disappointment was apparent in his drooping shoulders.

"Thou shalt not permit a witch to live," the father translated.

A secondary shiver ran down her spine. Cunning folk and wise women hadn't only disappeared because it was a difficult path to walk, many died because of the accusations of witchcraft. Countless were drowned, hung, and burned across Europe because they couldn't disprove a negative. If they were accused of sorcery, there was no way to prove they were innocent. Especially, when people wanted to believe the worst.

With the rise of the scientific mind, witch trials had fallen out of favour in England—at least during the reign of Elizabeth—when people saw it was science behind herbs, not magic. This was one reason Demdike liked working with the few doctors who were open about their crafts. The sharing of theories and beliefs helped her in her own healings. Charms and spirits were as much a part of the natural world as the wind and rain. This wasn't magic as the bible named it, but nature.

"Those who do not know, witchcraft is the perversion of nature. It is an act against God. A slight to the one who gave us life and will one day grant us eternal life within his kingdom. A heinous crime."

Several mutterings broke out across the room. People side-eyeing one another. Not in condemnation, but in confusion. All wondered why the priest was discussing such things.

"Witches—" The word spat with so much hatred, a lady near the front physically flinched. "—are the devil's minions in our realm. They gain their unholy powers through an alliance with the dark lord. By rejecting God and all the goodness in the world. They chose power over God's love. They become the devil's whores. Spreading his will and his ills throughout our world," the man spoke with such conviction, Demdike almost believed him.

In her youth, Demdike personally saw people accused of witchcraft. Saw how many of them were nothing more than poor and vulnerable women who'd committed no crime besides existing and being viewed as a nuisance. These so-called witches barely knew comfrey from camomile, let alone how to brew heinous potions and ensnare men of good reputations. Men whose hands liked to wander and called the victim a harlot rather than accept their own tainted selves. Weak men who pretended to have been seduced or tricked rather than admit their own failings.

Cunning folk held no need of the devil's magic. They had nature. She was a kind and cruel mistress, caring only for balance. One did not need to beg the devil to do any deeds. They simply needed to call on karma and let her do her job. The world was in balance. Shades of grey.

Witches, to the supposed learned mind, differed greatly from her and her kind. What the peasants called witches were something else. Those like her, who used herbs and worked with the spirit realm, were quite different from the devil and demon-dealing witches the priest spoke of.

Two very different ideals which carried the same name. It's why she called herself a wise woman, one of the cunning folk. Those who walked the grey path, with one foot in this world and one in the next. One didn't easily call themself a witch when the trials of the last century were still too fresh in her memory. Even if fewer happened here than in their neighbouring countries, they hadn't been immune. As more and more eyes settled upon her person, Demdike knew these differences were lost on her neighbours.

To them, a witch was a witch. Demdike could only fear whatever falsities their minds were conjuring. Looking blankly forward, she pretended to be none the wiser. Acted unaffected by the priest's words. She'd nothing to hide. If the locals decided to twist her path to be connected to the devil, she would have to somehow prove them wrong. Demdike absently wondered if she could prove this negative. She held no pacts with the devil, but without the devil to confirm this, how did one show their innocence?

"Another thing people may not be aware of is how the devil connects with his chosen harlots. How he demands things of his people." The man took a pause for dramatic effect.

It took everything in her not to roll her eyes at the priest. This would most definitely not help her case.

"Witches have what are known as familiars. Creatures possessed by the devil which connect with the beast below and tell his minions what actions must be taken in Satan's name. These creatures can take many forms. Cats, dogs, crows, the lord of beasts is not bound like us to one form. The devil's creatures must feast upon the blood of the witch to sustain their presence in our world. Leaving upon the woman a mark known as the witch's mark."

The man was pacing about the front of the church, where he would normally preach from the pulpit. Today he was too energised to remain in one place.

"These marks are well hidden, disguised. They can appear as birthmarks, letting us know this soul belonged to the devil before was even born. An evil changeling swallowing the life of the child in the womb and replaced by a creature of damnation. Make no mistake, they are no longer human. They are not people, but demonic visions given human form. You can never feel sorry for a witch, for she feels nothing at all. Only love for her unholy father.

"Sometimes a witch's mark looks like a small teet on the edge of her skin. Others are beauty marks. You can tell a witch's mark as they feel no pain when the part of their skin is prodded. Yet more proof of their inhuman natures."

The more the man spoke, the more passionate he became. Demdike would have thought him possessed, were they not on hallowed ground. Surely a priest could resist such attempts? Though as the man's actions grew more and more frantic, Demdike became less convinced of her earlier assumption. Was this Nowell's influence? Had he spiked the father's holy water?

The paranoia of witches had long since passed. Particularly, when the country had been more concerned with which church they followed and having enough people to blame for their problems as a result. For the priest to make such a statement, when a man of death darkened these hallowed halls, did not bode well.

"When witches are near, they threaten us all. Sickness sweeps the land, crops fail, and good men fall from God's path. Witches are the devil's minions, and their ultimate goal is to take your soul to hell with them."

As the church doors flew open, a strong wind caused multiple bodies to shudder at the sudden burst of cold. Fearful eyes shot around the room. More than one person whispering, as though the devil were already here. Demdike's stomach filled with dread.

"Familiars have been well documented since the eleven or twelve hundreds. Concurrently, so was also the discovery of hellhounds. Demons who come to earth in the shape of dogs to collect souls. If you see a stray black animal, black dog, black cat, or blackbird, beware. Lucifer may have come to collect."

Chapter Four

Anne Whittle, known to most as Chattox, sat in the dark room. Her shutters closed, and the candles blown out. A necessity for her current work. Humming to herself, she fiddled with the mixture laying on her lap. Turned it over and over. Keeping a gentle pace and sound as she imbued it with her intentions. The liquid mixture slowly firming in the large bowl.

Her home was, to most people, little more than a hut. The large roots of an old tree had been dug out and walls had been thrown up around it, forming a place of shelter. Small in comparison to many homes, but comfortable enough for her. Her two daughters had left many years ago. Anne lived close by and Bessie... well, the woman was off doing whatever she pleased. Wherever she'd run off to. Bessie still appeared from time to time. Usually in the summer, as she '*hated the cold and wet of the north*'.

The girl was forever travelling the country with her husband and whichever companion they had at the time. The less said about such things, the better. As much as she accepted her daughter's many quirks, there were some things a mother didn't need to know. The girl had always been wild, even in her youth. Too much for this small borough, she'd run at the first opportunity.

A young Bessie regularly complained about the house's lack of rooms or multiple floors. Having big dreams of grand mansions and lovers who would attend to her many demands. The child had left their home at just thirteen. Too young by her mother's eye, but Chattox hadn't refused her daughter, no matter how much she'd wanted. Anne at least waited until her seventeenth summer before she, too, had flown the nest.

Regardless of Chattox's home's small stature, it'd sufficed in keeping her safe for many years. Might not have been grand, as Bessie wanted, but had stood against the elements. Able to keep the warmth in winter and the sun away in summer. Not a place of grandeur, but it was home. Her home. Chattox had lived here all but the first decade of her long life. She'd been married here, raised a family here and she would die here. Or at least she planned to.

Adding a little more water to the bowl, she continued playing with the concoction, letting the thickness dilute and dribble through her hands. Picking it up once more as she kneaded her thoughts into the mixture. It wouldn't be long before her less wild child returned and she could finally finish her preparations. Anne had always been the more sensible of their little family, but even she had her moments.

Chattox's granddaughter Marie was much like her mother. Prudent and clever with flights of fancy. A mini Anne, cute, and more cautious than carefree. At least the family hadn't had to endure another Bessie. Chattox wouldn't have survived second one.

As much as the darkness was a necessity for her actions, her eyes were well-adjusted to the lack of light. Growing up with nothing had led her to cherish the simple things. Her amazing sight definitely made the list. Especially her foresight. This was her true gift in life; aiding her with tasks both big and small. It helped her to know where to go to beg. Or where to find important ingredients. And, more importantly, who to avoid. She'd missed church today. Her morning visions were filled with haunting black eyes and cries of devil worship.

She was already three scores in age, being unwell and unable to attend would hardly be noticed. At sixty years of age, she would be easily enough excused. Her daughter would not be so fortunate. With an uneasy heart, she'd sent the woman off for the weekly service.

Seeing beyond the here and now was both a blessing and a curse. Her foresight was an ability she'd used daily since discovering it at the tender age of fourteen. The witching age, her mother called it—when those who had gifts developed their psychic intuition and began their progression into adulthood. Chattox began her journey down the cunning path then. It'd been many years since, and age only added to her talent.

For most of her life, her sight had been sharp. Sometimes painfully so. Seeing a person take a tumble and requiring her aid in advance had been a blessing—enabling her to be in the vicinity to help when called upon. However, she was rarely able to interfere. Death, sickness (animal or human), she could rarely prevent the events she foresaw. Witnessing them twice and being unable to intervene caused a great deal of distress to her younger self.

Though, with age came wisdom. You may not always be able to prevent things from happening, but it was how you reacted to them which made all the difference. Having her healing belt on hand when someone needed it could be the difference between a slight injury and a fatal one.

Chattox had taken note of how, in the past few months—when old age came and the chill of death lingered in the air—she'd felt her sight beginning to dwindle. The once crystal-clear images were now clouded. More like smoke figures just beyond her reach. Floating away before they could fully form. The details becoming sparser. Chattox wasn't sure what it meant. Though her guesses largely revolved around her age and her mind not being what it once was.

Her thoughts were less sharp than they used to be, and her memory grew less accurate. Where once she'd made this mixture with merely her own mind to recollect every step, today she'd had to check her books. The pictures of which plants were needed and when. Charcoal scratches depicting which actions were necessary.

There were words carved next to each image, but she had little in the way of reading skills to begin with. Given the age of the book, she wasn't sure it was in English. She'd seen the shapes of letters on the church boards. They were rounded and flowed. These were sharp, as though they should have been carved into stone rather than flowing over the page.

Her concerns about her foresight were partly why she sat alone in the dark. It helped to control her thoughts and open her mind's eye further. Removed the distractions of the world around her and enabled one to connect with the energies of the inner and other world. Smiling to herself, she reflected on the many enjoyments and aid her gift had brought; being able to tell the good people from the bad, who to avoid and who to bring close, when someone was up to mischief, and how to avoid those with malicious intentions.

Much of her youth had been spent wielding her tongue as a weapon and knowing when silence was the only safety. She'd been more bois- terous back then. Refusing to bow to those *'of a better station'* she likely should have been flogged more than a few times, but she'd usually escaped by the skin of her teeth.

Today, she was using her gift, alongside the teachings of the cun- ning folk. Cunning folk were spiritual balancers in the physical realm. They were expected to perform certain tasks, no matter how un- savoury, to ensure the betterment of the community as a whole. Not that Chattox was opposed to teaching this lesson. Truthfully, she may have been more than a little eager to deal out some justice. Though it wasn't her place to pass judgment, only to enable those of higher powers to move among the living and aid them in their work.

With all these thoughts battle-axing their way into her mind, she remembered the burden of knowing some things cannot be changed, and the price this would now entail for those wrongdoers. If she was gleefully awaiting her daughter's return to move on to the next step, this was something Chattox would keep to herself.

As she continued the monotonous action, imagining her energies filtering into the bowl, she continued her quiet humming. The few glimpses her foresight was able to capture made little sense. A girl running. A black dog. A wheel breaking from a wagon. None seemed particularly important.

"Mum, I'm back," called the voice she had been waiting for. "What are you doing in the dark? It's beautiful out there."

The sun was shining after hours of pouring rain. She didn't envy her daughter, having been caught in the downpour earlier.

"Anne, stop messing with the shutters. They'll come off their hinges, and y'know, I like my dark. Have you got the ginger root? This ain't gonna work without it."

"Of course I have, but I'm still not sure about all of this. I mean, he was just threatening, I bet. I know you like to live up to your Mother Chattox reputation, but this could hurt him. Is it really necessary?"

It made Chattox chuckle how her daughter would make such a determined point and end so unsure of herself. A trait she'd inherited from her father. No amount of trying to train it out of the girl had succeeded. Her daughter's confidence aside, how the girl didn't think she was worth defending against scum, troubled Chattox more than she expected. She'd tried to raise a strong woman, but society was only too keen to tear them down. She might need to try being a little kinder to the younger woman.

"Now, my little Anne, I don't care if he threatens me. I've taken on bigger and angrier than him in my time, but when he threatens to put his filthy paws on my daughter. 'Cause he couldn't have his own way? Well, he needs teaching a proper lesson. One, he isn't going to get over anytime soon, I assure you. Now hand me the root already. This is starting to form." She looked at the settling mixture in the bowl and threw the ginger in. Hoping her stern tone would have shown her daughter why this mattered.

Anne, for all she was a mother herself, had not yet experienced the fierce rage which came when someone threatened their child. Thomas (her husband), had been able to put a stop to the man's plans, but he couldn't retaliate the way Chattox could. She would ensure the cretin never laid a single digit on another woman ever again.

Thomas Redferne was a decent man. He'd been a close friend of the family since his infancy and for all Chattox had been surprised at the pair's announcement to wed, she'd been happy to hear it. She and Anne never spoken about Anne's friendships with certain women, and Chattox had no intention of starting now. It wasn't her place to discuss such things. That she had birthed two daughters with queer tastes wasn't something she'd expected, but if this was what the good lord had deemed necessary for her children, then she would embrace it—if only in silent sigil.

She accepted both of her girls as they were, but society would not. Bessie left and moved too often to draw eyes, but Anne had loved her home too much to adventure the way her sister did. Better for Chattox to plead ignorance rather than acceptance in this case. To keep her little one safe. Though she wished her girl (fully grown woman or not, she would forever be her baby girl) could find happiness and a place where such things were no longer judged. Chattox could only stand beside her in quiet support. Pretending to be blind to the overly friendly actions and deaf to stories with such glaring inconsistencies, the holes could have fit a herd of cows through.

If Chattox also suspected Thomas was of a similar nature and his best friends were more the same, it was also something she spoke not of. Thomas had more than once given her a knowing eye. But at her raised eyebrow, returned to behaving as was expected of them. The two siring a child surprised her greatly, but perhaps her daughter was more like Bessie than she'd originally assumed. Or maybe Anne and Thomas had done it to avoid speculation? Chattox didn't know (or care to ask).

Anne looked cautiously from over by the table. Unable to see as well as her mother in the dark. Though she didn't struggle with her eyesight, Anne clearly didn't feel the need to test it by strolling around and undoubtedly hurting herself. Chattox started whispering into the bowl. The words weren't fully audible, but this wasn't for human ears to hear. When she finished her work, she lifted the bowl in the air, pronouncing '*Carte dulouso*'. The spirit folk would know, would understand, and they would act.

"We're ready. Let's be gettin' outside," allowing happiness to fill her voice.

The two women ambled their way out of the house and into the field around their home. With the sunshine hitting their faces, it was clear they were related. Both mother and daughter had dark, deep-set eyes, curly, mousy hair and pouty lips. The daughter, only middle-aged, still passed for beauty. Chattox herself, however, had long surpassed such standards. A hag in her own right. She'd earned her cronehood. Was happy being feared rather than adored. Her daughter had discovered first-hand how beauty was coveted and often exploited by those in power. Chattox refused to give that man a second chance to try to hurt her child.

She placed the bowl down into the soil. They each took a piece of root, now covered in the mixture. Digging a small hole, they buried their pieces into the shallow earth. Took more of the mixture and built upon it. Allowed it to start to set, before adding more on top. Layer after layer, the two women continued this in silence until they had two clay moulds. To represent the person they were aiming their thoughts towards—who they wanted karma to chase.

"That's enough now, Anne. We should let them dry in the sun. Finish this business later. I'll make us some tea." Chattox rose to her feet slowly, feeling the weight of the world bare down on her limbs.

"That air getting heavier again?" her daughter jested.

"Watch that smart tongue, you're not too old for a hiding, misses," Chattox joked back. Ignoring how her limbs really were acting, as though the air weighed several tons rather than a feather.

"It's your tongue I'm more afraid of, mother," the woman teased, knowing full well how vicious her mother's words could be.

The locals were more afraid of a tongue-lashing from Mother Chattox than they were of being flogged. That mysterious death's seemed to follow the woman's ire—from cows going mad to grown men collapsing—was sheer coincidence. A bad word from Mother Chattox's mouth was one of the scary stories told to children to keep them in line. Chattox playfully slapped her daughter's head as they re-entered the house.

She watched as Anne negotiated her way to the table and lit a candle before using it to light several of the others spotted around the room. Chattox waited a moment. She didn't need the light to walk around the space, but did to dig into the cupboards. Even her eyes weren't strong enough to distinguish between various black pots in the shadows. Pulling out the cast-iron kettle, she set it above the stove, filling it with water and a few dried petals and leaves.

"Should only take a few minutes, camomile okay for you?" Chattox asked, not waiting for a reply. She'd already added them, anyway. "I think it helps with the mind. You need it after the past few days you've had. How was your trip into the village?"

She didn't ask, 'How was church?' no matter how desperate she may have been. Wouldn't want to seem overly eager.

They talked of the local gossip, the new courtships and the usual goings on. The village had been much quieter in recent years, people busy getting on with their lives after the upheaval of the previous century. People in these parts long held onto grudges, like herself and Demdike, but it rarely came to more than shouting matches and the odd drunken brawl.

"Richard Baldwyn has caught consumption," Anne said cautiously.

Chattox's head snapped up with the news. "And they want some healing, do they? They can think on, I ain't wasting my time on those scaremongers, accusing me of this an' that." She spat at the floor. A nasty habit, but one necessary for protective purposes.

Richard Baldwyn was someone she would have happily buried six feet under and walked away from. Maybe she'd have gone back for his teeth and clothes later (just to double-check he was definitely gone from this world). A man too full of himself and his supposed station. Were he still a young boy, she would have happily put him over her knee. If his reputation was anything to go by, the man enjoyed screwing people over more than he enjoyed laying with his wife.

She took two cups off the metal hooks surrounding the fireplaces, then proceeded to pour them both a drink. Blew on it gently, she raised it to her mouth and allowed the warm flavour to hint at her taste buds and refresh her body.

"Supposedly, he caught it after Demdike visited, and Jennet miraculously got better shortly after." Anne was implying the not-so-coincidental occurrence of these events.

"What happenstance," she drawled.

The sarcasm so thick it could have rivalled the honey she added to their tea. Chattox handed the second cup over to her daughter. One benefit of living next to, or halfway in, a large tree, was the bees. The hive was just above their home, ideal for grabbing a little sugary goodness from. A few stings from time to time were well worth the reward.

"That's what I thought. Apparently, the Baldwyn's had accused their lot of stealing from them, so she'd paid them a visit to sort it out. Then the day after, the man mysteriously fell ill. Bet she cursed them just to keep 'em quiet." Anne chuffed, taking a long sip from her cup.

Chattox watched on, saying nothing. It could be serendipitous, of course, but Demdike was all about the balance. If Jennet was to be cured, the old crone would think nothing of the man suffering in the girl's place. As much as Chattox wasn't Demdike's biggest fan, she could hardly fault the action. Chattox would've done the same. Heck, she would have done it just to get one over on the smug arse.

Chattox drank a little herself, happy with how this brew had turned out. Hopeful it would be the second success of the day. The one outside working equally as well. She would need to check on them in half an hour. Time enough to steer the conversation where she wanted.

"The priest, he spoke of witches and devils."

For all Chattox wanted to snort, she resisted. Knowing the situation was serious made the man's claims no less ridiculous.

"And I'm sure a man in King James' pocket being here has absolutely nothing to do with the strange, out of the history books sermon?"

Anne simply shrugged. "I heard tell that the king believes in such things, but given all I have seen in this very home, I can hardly deny the reality of magic."

Chattox couldn't hold the scoff in a second time. "Magic, Mother Nature, the spirit realm. They are all names for things beyond this earth we do not fully understand. But they're no more evil or the work of the devil than the wind and skies. They simply are. To account man's bad behaviour to some great evil is to remove accountability. Something these supposed good folk need more of, not less."

Her daughter shrugged again. For all Anne had taken some steps along the cunning path, the girl had neither the heart nor the stomach for it. Something she and Demdike commiserated over, how both their daughters were not committed to the old ways.

To those unaware of the spirit realm, perhaps some great evil made sense, but spirits were as neutral as people. All simply performing the role they'd been set. She was simply one cog in the wheel, helping the system keep on turning as it should. All wise women and those schooled in the cunning arts understood they were simply a conduit for the greater gods. Merely a soul within a human body walking the lines between this world and the next. One foot in Pendle, the other in the ether.

"If word of Richard Baldwyn's predicament gets around, the Justice may take notice. Remove that infernal woman from this place," Anne said with hope.

Chattox didn't have the heart to crush her. For all of Anne's brains in many situations, she often overlooked the obvious.

"Well, let's just hope this Nowell doesn't go accusing them of witchcraft or we'll have them lot at our doors as well." She laughed playfully, not wanting to spell it out, but hoping her daughter caught the serious undercurrent of her words.

Chattox gracefully ignored the swooping in her own stomach. After years of friendly rivalry and friction between her and Demdike, the one thing they knew and agreed upon was to protect their craft. If this Nowell was here for hunting (as she suspected), they'd both be needed to ensure their ways survived.

"Come back to this world, mum. We should check on the idols. Don't want some kids finding and playing with 'em like last time. Was not fun to explain to their mums. Making dolls to sell indeed." Anne chuckled as she practically pranced her way over to the door. "Come on then, if you really want to do this, we best get on."

Chattox caught up with her daughter quickly, the requirement of the job at hand overriding the physical restraints which often affected her body when moving after long moments of rest. Reaching the idols, they dug up the roots and took them into the house.

"They've set well, quicker than expected. Meant to be, clearly." Her mischievous smile slipped through the Mother Chattox persona; her smugness getting the better of her. Fortunately, it was only Anne there to witness such behaviour.

Taking Anne's idol as well, she placed them both by the fire. By the next morning, they'd be ready to use. Until then, she could continue with her weaving.

"How's my granddaughter?" she eventually asked.

The girl in question hadn't visited in the past two weeks, and little Marie's absence troubled the elderly woman.

"Fine. Healthy. We're thinking of sending her to a proper school. The lady at the church school said she showed a lot of potential, and could do well with a real education. But it's affording everything."

Chattox held in her wince. Everything came back to money. Something they'd never held in abundance.

"But it seems like a lot of hassle. Though you never know, maybe the gods will smile upon us." The woman's smile brightened, as if hoping her mother might be able to pull a few strings with the other side.

A poor attempt at hinting, but one Chattox would be happy to oblige.

"I'll see what I can do, my love. You should get off and make sure your husband is okay. I'll be fine until the morning. Get going, I won't ask you again." Watching her daughter leave, she embraced her, taking a strand of hair from the woman's shawl.

Chattox might not be able to protect everyone, but she would do what she could. Hoping they might salvage their ways at a later date. Remembering the impact of the past, destroying their way of life, and the secrets they guarded. It couldn't happen again. Steps had to be put in place to prevent such atrocities. She would take the route of sacrifice if it meant the future might be safe.

As she placed her daughter's hair amongst the gathered ingredients, Chattox noted she only needed three more items now. But it would take time before she would manage to collect them all. Come hell or high water, her greatest achievement would be the one thing no one would see coming. By the next hunter's moon, the entire play would begin. Her foresight enabled her to see things before they happened. Many events were unavoidable, but she could ensure her legacy lived on.

As the sun began to force its way through the cracks in the ceiling, Chattox awoke from her dazed sleep, still in her chair. Her body groaned as she attempted to extend her legs. In the passing years, she'd found her chair provided the right support her back needed during sleep. Rather than the hard floor covered in rags and straw vaguely resembling a bed.

The aches and pains were another reminder of how this life had been laced with poverty. Her herbal remedies were an attempt at gaining some physical comfort, but as a deeply spiritual woman, she believed suffering was simply the choice of those on the other side. The spirit world would provide what had been lost in this life.

Chattox slowly rose to her feet, feeling the full weight of her body and gravity as she pushed through the exhaustion of her tiring limbs. She managed this time, but secretly wondered how much longer she would still be able to stand without aid. Her body was growing increasingly weaker and winter wasn't far away. Autumn was already colder than it'd been for several years. To the elderly, winter was a sign of the darkness coming closer. The world whispering for them to take themselves over to the next phase of their soul's journey.

The old woman shivered at the thought. Shook the unwelcome idea from her mind, as she continued towards the door. It was time to dig up the talisman she'd buried three months previously. It would finally be strong enough. Reaching for the shawl carelessly thrown over the makeshift coat rack, Chattox wrapped it around her body and pulled open the stiffened door.

As she entered the outside world, the bright sun hurt her eyes. There was a bitter chill in the September air. The sun may have been lasting longer than was typical, but the ice was already on its way. The seasons were even behaving oddly. Something was definitely wrong, hinting that nature knew something the rest of the world had not yet awoken to.

She grabbed a stone and dug up the talisman. Once the stone hit the piece of metal, Chattox immediately wrapped it in cloth. No human hand could touch it now. It was ready. These were two important steps to the spell. Tomorrow morning, she would collect more. Everything was coming together, slowly but surely. Everything in the realm of the ether took longer than it did on earth, but patience was one virtue Chattox had honed.

CHAPTER FIVE

There was a certain irony to how peace had never been achieved through peaceful means. Violence might beget more violence, but it always had and always would occur before a time of peace. The darkness before the dawn.

This was one of the world's many repeating patterns Demdike had picked up on throughout her long life. History was littered with atrocities. The enemies of peace didn't care for others. Never blinked at causing bloodshed and suffering. They could overlook torture and torment as easily as another did a broken nail.

Such individuals could see beggars on the street and view them as a dirty inconvenience rather than recognising them as the unfortunate souls they were. The distress of another was of no concern to them. Unless the troubles touched their lives personally. Sympathies were lost on those with cold hearts.

Call Demdike paranoid, but she suspected someone bearing the title of Justice of the Peace would carry the violence with them, too. Even if she hadn't looked into Nowell's eyes and felt the darkness staring back, she'd have been suspicious. Justice meant a lot of things to a lot of people, and violence was often at its centre. Despite what the latter half of his title claimed, Demdike was already of the opinion

Nowell was one of these cold people. The ones lacking in something vital.

These people had long existed. Those who believed themselves superior to all others. Believed most people were below their notice. Why should they help the vulnerable if it meant a minor inconvenience to them? Why should they lend a helping hand when God had chosen to bless them instead of another? If this was God's will, then why should they bother to try?

The irony that these same people ignored God's decree—of love for all—was not lost on her. The messages of helping those less fortunate, or trying to make the world a better place through love and kindness, were submerged. Buried beneath their own greed. So long as they claimed to love God and attended church on Sundays, it convinced them they were doing what was expected. *A rich man could not enter heaven?* Went ignored. *Don't turn away strangers, for they could be me?* Became kill the foreigners. *Love thy neighbour?* Only if they were rich too.

It'd long troubled Demdike how those who claimed to be the most devout were only devout in ways which suited them. Very few people knew what the Bible claimed, except for what the priests preached. And given last Sunday's sermons, she was starting to wonder just how much they were taught was twisted to suit a certain narrative. They were all sheep in his flock, question were discouraged.

She was trained to spot signs and synchronicities. To read the ambient energies of the world and see what may come to pass. God's or nature's attempt at arming the spiritually sensitive with a way to understand the world. And hopefully, prepare themselves. All humans held innate gifts. Could find faces in all things. Spot patterns wherever they may occur. A sense of unease whenever danger approached. Demdike was three for three.

Faces in the shadows as they drew closer. Patterns, how people started growing suspicious of their neighbours before turning on them. She'd witnessed it once before. Watched with youthful ignorance as paranoia twisted logical minds and greed pushed the rest happily over the edge. A sense of danger: Nowell. Pendle had felt different from the moment he'd arrived. The dormant spirits were beginning to awaken, and they were not happy.

Death fast approached. Something otherworldly was circling. Nowell's soul was darker and more broken than any she'd ever sensed. She would be lucky to see next spring if her interpretations were correct. Demdike had already accepted she wasn't long for the grave, but now she feared it wouldn't only be her life lost.

***

Whispers were never quiet. If anything, they seemed to echo. Filled the space around them and distorting as they climbed from one mouth to the next. Whispers were often louder than screams. As people tried to be subtle, they drew more attention to themselves. Their bodies cried out for attention as the person tried (and failed) to tell their neighbour all they'd heard. Whilst passing along the message as discreetly as they were able, they would broadcast their intentions. In a way, normal conversations did not.

There might not have been any hiding behind hands or childish giggles, but the required closeness of bodies (unlike the usual polite distance) immediately drew scrutiny. Pulled eyes towards huddled forms. Made people curious why decorum was being put aside, and wonder what could be so important it required hushed voices. Whispers were rarely quiet, and in a place this small, they might as well have been shouts. When someone whispered to their neighbour, everyone soon heard the words.

As Demdike walked down the path near the centre of the village, she could hardly ignore the weighted gazes following her steps. The stone-filled dirt path was familiar. She'd walked it almost daily for decades. Demdike wished it was more taxing now, to distract her from their peering eyes.

Jennet bounced along by her side, entirely oblivious to the keen looks. The groups of monitoring stares from all around; attempting to catch her performing some heinous crime or dark deed. She was grateful the young girl was much better now, but Demdike desperately wanted to pull the little girl closer and force her to walk normally. Anything to detract further attention.

She'd feared this would happen. After the Sunday service. After what happened in the past century. The cunning folk and wise women were often the target of unwanted attention. The rest of the people simply looking for an excuse for their fits of anger. A scapegoat for all their problems. It started the same way back then. Though her father had still been here last time. When the rumours began circling, she'd been too young and protected for accusations to be levelled at her.

Things were different in the present times. She was the matriarch, the only protection she and her entire family held. James might have been considered a man in some ways, but he wasn't established. Wasn't wealthy. The boy still needed protection more than he could give it.

Demdike could almost see the shades of suspicion moving behind her neighbours' eyes. Their thoughts turning from general dislike to darker beliefs. They weren't afraid, not yet, but it wouldn't be long. Fear and paranoia usually went hand in hand. Were sisters and best friends to anger and aggression. If history was anything to judge by, the bitter words would come soon. When the whispers were no longer enough and fear made people lash out.

Her youngest granddaughter continued skipping along, still entirely unaware of the looks dogging their steps. Demdike almost yearned for the naivety of youth. Experience might keep you safe, might help you spot patterns and avoid certain situations, but it also left you trapped in your own mind with worry.

She could see how the surrounding people were changing. These changes in behaviour were concerning, but Demdike was painfully aware there was nothing she could do. As much as she wanted to hurry, acting out of character would merely draw more eyes and confirm what suspicions their minds were forming. Better to carry on as normal, regardless of their (so far) silent judgements.

Jennet had quickly recovered from her ill health. What would have taken two weeks to a full moon cycle to pass had come and gone within a matter of days. Demdike wasn't surprised. The healing remedy was one her grandmother created. Normally it would have been a good thing, great even. A way to advertise her abilities and help drum up more custom—especially as winter was on the way. However, with people whispering about devil worship and demon deals, miraculous healings were proof of her guilt, not of her healing talents.

Hearing her name being called, her shoulders wanted to curl in on themselves. Had they gone from whispers to shouts already? Her mind took a moment to process the familiarity of the voice. Looking towards the noise, she saw as Alizon ran, light-footed and like the fae she embodied, towards them. The girl's face was etched with worry. Though, as she paid no awareness to the people littering the surrounding streets, Demdike could only assume her elder granddaughter was untroubled by the same things she was. A secondary cause for concern? Given Alizon's eager eyes, she would likely be soon sharing whatever gossip she had learnt.

"Grace, she's fallen sick. They fear she won't make it."

It took Demdike a moment to place the name. To recall who the person the name might belong to. Unfortunately, as there were many people with the name Elizabeth, there were at least five Graces in their local community, but only one they'd recently interacted with. Her stomach dropped. This was not good.

She could see how the stacks were lining up. Jennet dancing health-ily as another girl falls ill in her place. She hadn't done it. She may have wished ill on her father, and been more than happy when he caught the sickness, but she held no desire to infect the small girl. Children were off limits, as far as she was concerned. But outsiders would see the two events and draw their own conclusions.

"Is she okay?"

"No, Jen, she's sick. Did you not hear me?"

"I heard, but there's sick and better tomorrow and then there's sick and dead. Which is she?"

Alizon shrugged, having shared her gossip, and was no longer in-vested in the story. "Dunno, Lily didn't say, but apparently she's been ordered to stay at home. Her breathing's dodgy."

'Just like Jennet's had been,' Demdike thought, though knew better than to give voice to them. "We will have to send them some of the healing balms. Hope it helps the little lass," she said instead.

Alizon and Jennet nodded, but the smaller girl looked displeased by the suggestion. As much as Demdike was curious about the girl's disregard for her words, here in the open was not the place to ask.

"Alizon, tomorrow, you'll need to head Colne way. I don't want you begging too close to home whilst *he* is still here," she stressed, rather than stating it explicitly where eavesdroppers were close by.

"Oh, yeah. Okay, Nana Demy. Though I heard he was leaving again two days from now. He's been here a week tomorrow already and according to Jonathan the blacksmith, he was only passing through.

Checking on all the places under his juris–jusridica–juri–his territories."

Demdike didn't know what the word Alizon had been trying to say was. The girl had a habit of copying big words from her more learned friends, but her vocabulary was still too underdeveloped to know how to manage them perfectly. Not that Demdike could comment. If it wasn't to do with folk work or the spirit realm, she barely knew any of it.

Nodding to the girl, she suppressed the smile wanting to stretch across her face. With Nowell being gone, people's anxieties would ease somewhat, but the seeds had been planted. They would need to be careful. Avoid drawing attention to themselves.

Her body still shuddered at the memory of those fathomless eyes. The bottomless darkness could have stolen her life and soul. That man being gone from these lands could only be a good thing. The hills had barely stopped whistling with the unending winds. Angry gods slowly awakening at the presence of a threat in their midst. The rumblings of the earth as those which dwelled below were readying to breach the surface. Demdike could only hope with Nowell leaving they would fall silent once again.

Demdike would have loved to watch the man and ensure he left, but she still was too cautious. Not wanting to capture his attention and have those dark orbs locked on hers. Rather, she would have a tipple in the safety of her own home (once he was beyond their borders). Demdike feared she wouldn't dare take a full breath until he was gone again.

"Nana Demy?"

"Yes, Al."

Both her granddaughters were walking at pace with her now, one on each side. As much as Demdike tuned out the two's sniping and snarking conversation, she could only ignore their bickering for so long. The two likely had noticed her lack of care toward their arguments. Turning to look at the girl, it surprised her to see Alizon looking around. They were beyond the main streets, and all the prying eyes, but the girl was thinking better of her actions. Thinking before she spoke. A sense of pride filled Demdike's gut. Alizon had been paying attention to her lessons. Had been taking on board her advice.

"When we were at church..."

A wave of worry swallowed the pride.

"Yes," she prompted.

For all Demdike worried about where the conversation may be heading, she'd always been the type to jump first. To tackle the anxiety and fight it at the source. Ran headfirst into trouble rather than letting nausea overwhelm her. This hadn't always been the best course of action, but her hatred of feeling worried and weak was more prominent than her fears of jumping before she should.

"When they were talking about the animals," the girl spoke quietly. They were beyond the eyes and ears of others, but she applauded her granddaughter's cautions.

"Yes?"

"Did—do—do they really do that?" the girl was close to whispering.

Like all whispers, it made Demdike uncomfortable.

"I dunno, Al. Can't say I've ever made a deal with the devil to know. To the best of my knowledge, some gods in the old tales could use animals and would appear before people to teach them lessons. So would the fae. But I've never heard about using animals to commune with the devil and drinking blood. Can't say I've ever met a witch such as.

"Many a person who works with the olde world and who walks the spiritual path, but no devil dogs. Now, that's not to say it ain't real. The good priest could be very well speaking the truth and there may be many a demon and demonic animals walking the world, but if they are, I've never crossed paths with them."

"Are the spirits not demons, though? Are you not making deals with the devil when you work with them?" The girl looked truly afraid. Though whether this fear was for Demdike or herself, it wasn't apparent.

"Spirits and olde gods have walked this world long before we came along and will still be here long after we've gone." She didn't bother to see if they were processing the words. The weight of Pendle's peepers may have gone, but her two granddaughters had stares strong enough to marvel the entire of main street. "No, they ain't some great evil. They ain't always good, I'll admit, but they're like nature, neutral for the most part," she added, answering their unasked questions.

She could see little Jennet nodding from the side of her eyes. Whether the girl understood or was simply agreeing because the words of wisdom were falling from her grandmother (a person in a position of authority) Demdike couldn't have said, but she was glad the pair weren't immediately rejecting her words.

Sunday school had filled their heads with many strange ideas. The priest and his little hanger-ons committed to '*educating*' the local folk in their skewed versions of right and wrong. Their beliefs and views of what the world was and what it should be. Young children were far too easy to influence. For better or for worse.

"You have to give them something in exchange for their help," she continued, as this was a valuable lesson and one she wanted her family to know and understand. "But it ain't your soul they ask for. And if something ever does, you shut that connection down tight. There are some spirits which demand a sacrifice of blood. The priest was right about that, but again, nothing's coming up here and feasting on a random teet. In all my years of walking the spirit way, I've shed blood less than a handful of times. And only when truly necessary. Those on the other side, they can choose to help or hinder, ignore you or attach themselves."

She'd barely taken a moment to catch her breath, launching into the archaic knowledge so few knew. For all Demdike tried to educate her granddaughter, little Alizon had been too away with the fairies, too flighty and unwilling to sit long enough to hone the craft. The girl did possess spiritual power, but Demdike had her doubts the girl would ever fully realise its potential.

Alizon was too busy living in her own world to consider this one, let alone the one just beyond this one. Only if it reached out to her would Alizon ever acknowledge it. Even then, the girl was too changing. Too quick to run away and pretend nothing happened. The girl had neither desire nor discipline to learn the olde ways. Unless something drastic happened, Demdike doubted this would change.

"Now, what the priest said about demons," she began once again, surprised to see Alizon's attention had yet to wander.

Her eyes were pinpoints entirely locked on Demdike's being. Watching her mouth as every word formed. As though Alizon hoped she might process them quicker the faster she received the information. It was a little flattering. To have that keen interest concentrated entirely on herself.

Alizon's mind was entirely focused in a way it rarely managed. The girl must have been truly interested in the subject to remain present long enough to still be hanging on Demdike's every word. Drinking them in as though the girl were parched and this information might be the only sustenance for miles around.

Demdike averted her eyes. It was almost too much, being under the unwavering stare. She wondered absently if perhaps this was why Alizon was so prone to flights of fancy, because otherwise, her intensity might have been enough to burn them all.

"Those are real." Demdike coughed slightly, trying to regain her train of thought. "Not sure if they're exactly as the church paints them, but there are spirits with only bad intentions. Malevolent beings who only want to harm. So, for simplicity's sake, we can call those demons. For all I know, they could be something entirely different.

"Deity, Deva, Demon, the words were once used interchangeably. But for argument's sake, we'll acknowledge them as demons. Evil dark spirits with nefarious intentions. Demons can be bad and do bad things, however, there are many spirits which ain't demons coming from the other side who might try to trick you. Dark fae and wild things who see humans as what is wrong with the world. This is why very few can walk the way of the cunning folk. Too many kind souls lost to the dangers of whatever is on the other side."

Jennet was still skipping by her side, before falling behind and catching up once more in big bounding steps. The little girl was paying less and less attention. Demdike couldn't blame her. Few nine-year-olds could comprehend the lessons she was trying to impart. Alizon, in direct contrast, was eagerly awaiting more. Her face open, and eyes sparkling.

"Be careful what you call spirits directly though. Many spirits would be angry to have you name them a demon. And you should never offend a spirit if you can avoid it."

A simple fact. One Demdike's mentor taught her prior to walking her way into the ether. Though she hadn't fully comprehended it until a spirit reacted in anger to her calling it by a label it didn't accept. Demdike could still feel the apprehension in her shoulders at the memory. The intensity with which the spirit had thrown energy at her. Remembered waking with scratches down her arm.

You learned quickly to be humble—almost reverent—when interacting with any spirit. To keep your guard up. To never allow them too close. Protect your body and soul. To be painfully polite. It did not do to anger a being you couldn't see, but could see you.

Many years ago, the wise woman in the next borough over had taken on a man with high spiritual power. The man tried to walk the grey path, but held more ego than talent. He'd learnt how every dream could become a nightmare when a spirit was annoyed with you. He'd given up the calling. Rightly so. With his inability to be deferential, the other side had soon claimed him. You didn't offend a spirit and not expect retaliation.

"Now, as for making deals with demons. No, I haven't done it, and I never would. Whether demons are what the church portrays them as or not. There are dark beings who want to only cause death and destruction and they're not the spirits you ever want to interact with. If you ever cross paths with something such like, you cleanse yourself as soon as you can.

"Do not let their presence linger. If they touch you, and you don't clean it, they can find you. They can haunt you. Drain you. Get you when you're at your weakest and latch on. Very difficult to get rid of them once they've made a space for themselves within your soul. It's like leaving a secret doorway only they can use. Never, ever give them the chance."

Demdike couldn't stress this enough. Too many people she tried to help had left psychic doorways wide open for dark beings to take advantage of. By ignoring and burying their traumas, the people had left a scar for the dark spirits to fester within and cling to.

"How do you clean yourself?"

"Burning herbs, like sage and thyme. Blessed water. Meditation. Those are the quick treatments. Imagine yourself bathed in a blinding light that no darkness can survive within. It's so bright it burns everything bad and negative away. Nothing with ill intent can stay when that light is encasing you. Swallowing you whole. Like water, submerging you and drowning any and all bad things. Though healing the emotional scars is the only really beneficial long-term solution."

As their home became clear on the horizon, her body unwound. Shelter and safety. Where the words of those outside could not penetrate. Not physically at least. Her mind might replay them, but she would be free from the physical presence. However, her thoughts would likely spend all night whirling with worry.

This was the first step. She'd seen it before. The way people ostracised a few vulnerable people. Whispers turning even the kindest hearts to stone. The callous words typically then followed. The actions of violence were never far behind. Her mind would try to figure a way through this mess. If experience was anything to go by (and at her age, Demdike was not one to disregard experience), she would spend many a troubled night on this problem. Her dreams filled with the images and fears that may come to pass if she didn't figure out a solution.

"Tibbs," Jennet shouted, running up the rest of the hill and finally leaving them behind.

Tibbs was the cat that had adopted them, not the other way around. Something Tibbs was happy to remind them of if they ever forgot. The black cat with white on its chest was a stray who liked to appear from time to time. Would stay in their home during bad weather, returning regularly to help take care of the rat problem. Demdike had eaten rat meat a few times in her life—in truly desperate winters—not something she wished to repeat. Rats did not improve root stew. The foul creatures were vicious. Biting and spreading their filth everywhere. She'd happily welcomed Tibbs into their home to rid them of the scourge. Keeping the cat fed and happy was merely a bonus.

Tibbs would come and go at will, visiting many homes in Pendle. Demdike had once even seen Chattox feeding the cheeky thing. The cat didn't care who it interacted with. Made its disdain known when she'd tried to herd it away from the other woman. Not returning to their house until two months passed. Demdike hadn't tried to control the little blighter again after said incident.

Cats were precarious creatures. Like children with the attitude of old white men. They were worse than spirits if offended and equally vengeful. Waking to the dead corpse of a rat, its innards ripped and splayed across her bed, was not a pleasant experience. Though for all Tibbs annoyed her, Demdike still loved the irritating beast. Hopefully, it was a good omen for Tibbs to have come after a stressful day. She could spend the night stroking and snuggling with the mercurial creature.

"Do you think Tibbs could be one of the demons?" Alizon's voice from the side jolted her back to the present moment.

"Don't be absurd," Demdike couldn't help biting out.

A ridiculous suggestion. Tibbs might have been an ill-tempered little monster, but he, she, it? Demdike had no idea what its gender might have been, but given she'd never seen it with a swollen stomach in the many years it'd wandered the hills, felt safe assuming it was most likely a 'he'. He wasn't an evil spirit, nor possessed. She had too many protections on the home for some evil beast possessing an animal or person to enter. The only vile thing able to reach her home were the bloody rats—which Tibbs kept away.

A glance at Alizon showed the girl's squinted eyes. Assessing the cat. She hadn't believed Demdike's denial. If her own granddaughter could remain unassured, it didn't bode well for those outside her home. She briefly thought about shooing the creature away, thinking it might be best to avoid any potential suspicions, but then dismissed the idea as soon as it came. If people were going to think such things, they'd already seen Tibbs coming and going from their home for years, it would be pointless. As well as unnecessarily cruel to the innocent creature.

Tibbs might be a bit of an ass, but he was an innocent cat. He'd done nothing wrong, wasn't some secret evil or cruel spirit out for their souls. He was a cat, doing what cats did. No, it would be a pointless action.

If she were damned, no actions at this point would save her. She'd long carried the glares of people for being poor and a beggar. What was one more reason for them to dislike her? It might be more serious, but her life was nearing its end, regardless. Demdike could only hope her tarred brush did not colour the rest of her family—wouldn't taint them with her very existence. Maybe she needed to be serious about teaching them and toughening them up. Winter was drawing close, and Demdike seriously doubted she would see another one.

CHAPTER SIX

The autumn air was crisp. Not quite cold, but it held enough bite she'd had to put on a shawl to protect her arms. October had always been one of her favourite months. The vibrant colours littered the earth as the plush greens gave way to burning reds and beautiful oranges.

The sounds had amused her since childhood. Even as an old woman, she would go out of her way to crinkle and crunch the freshly fallen leaves. Felt satisfaction every time her feet could create those crackles as she crushed the once buoyant life beneath her boot.

October made Demdike yearn for running through fields filled with fallen life. To stomp and jump. She missed the sense of freedom which gave her a childish thrill. Innocence. Something playful and fun. There were no (or few) consequences to such actions. She might dirty her shoes and skirts, but it was okay. She remembered feeling powerful as a little girl, destroying those crisp pieces of colour. Twisted her feet from side to side as little dead pieces of plant dissolved into dust beneath her unyielding pressure. She'd loved it.

Although December and Christmas time was well known for sharing histories and stories of times since passed, it was autumn, and October in particular, which gave her the strongest sense of nostalgia. The falling decay gave the world a tint of something, a filter over her reality. Left a sense of something missing, as though the earth itself was grieving for times long since ended.

Life faded before the eye. Reminding people how the hopes of spring and the life of summer were now gone. It wasn't quite the death of winter. Harvests were still happening, bushes bore fruit, and nuts were still in season, but it was the sense of how everything was leaving which made her miss something she couldn't name.

October made Demdike yearn for her youth in a way summer never could. She'd never been one for wild parties and indiscretion of the flesh. Instead, always having one foot not quite here. One leg amongst the fallen leaves, and the other cemented in the world beyond this one. Walking the astral plane even whilst still tethered to her body.

October was special. The veil between life and death was at its thinnest. After all these years, Demdike was convinced even the most ordinary human could sense this. Not simply her and the spiritually gifted. Something changed in even the average person. As the other side reached out to life. Stretched beyond their side of the veil and grasped at what they could. Most could sense as icy fingers brushed against their embodied souls.

As someone who'd always been more comfortable with death than was perhaps socially acceptable, Demdike loved October because it was as though the floodgates to her gift were wide open. Doors blown off their hinges by the force of the waves. It'd scared her as a child, these strange sensations. Not understanding what they were or why she felt like she was drowning whilst standing on solid land. Though eventually, she spotted the pattern.

Every year during the time of death and decay, it was as though the world gave her some sort of spiritual power boost. When she'd hit her teen years her abilities naturally increased (as was typical), but, as the years passed, it became obvious how October was something else spiritually. The changes started slightly in the first few days of the month. Would continue through the beginning of November too. Like the tide coming in and out, it wasn't only over a matter of moments, but dragged over a month and a half's span. Though always predominantly in October. Autumn. When death was everywhere. Lingering just beyond the eye line. Out of sight, but ever present.

October was nostalgia and life leaving. Demdike hoped, if she were to pass, it would be in October. Not that she believed there was a full year left in the weary bag of bones she called a body. But if her wishes could be met, she would happily pass on the day of death. When the beings beyond mortal comprehension walked side by side with them through the fields. As they jumped and crunched over fallen leaves and bodies alike. Collecting the souls and supposedly marking all those who would join his domain between this Samhain and the next.

Demdike wondered if she would be able to see or sense when the being left its mark on her. A macabre part of her hoped so. How many, even amongst the cunning folk, could say they'd studied death's mark firsthand? She'd never heard of such things. Though this didn't mean another hadn't achieved it. If she was to notice death marking her, then Demdike hoped she lived long enough to learn what it might mean. A silly dream. Likely a pointless one, but as someone who'd lived between the living and dead her entire life, Demdike wasn't afraid to pass on. Simply curious what would await her. Perhaps Alizon was more like her than she'd previously cared to acknowledge.

Death was coming for her. This she couldn't deny, but Demdike hoped she could go peacefully. Or failing this, she prayed to die quickly. No one wanted to die painfully. If death left an imprint on her soul, Demdike wondered if it might tell her the how. Share how her death might come about. Not to avoid it, but to ensure it was quick. Burning or drowning were two ways she would like to avoid.

Flashes and memories of her childhood flitted through her mind. Those had been unpleasant experiences. She had been lucky to escape them. Demdike long-held fears of roaring flames and large bodies of water. Though she also had anxiety around swords and sharp things in general. She knew she'd never been stabbed, not in this lifetime. Yet, on her stomach, there was a small birthmark which looked like a slice mark.

Her grammy once said how birthmarks were the soul showing on the new body how it died during its previous incarnation. Demdike wasn't sure she believed this. Her worry of someone stabbing her seemed more common sense than a past life memory, but whether she had died this way in her past life or not, she'd like to avoid it in this one. No stabbing, burning or drowning for her, please. If she could submit a request to death, this would be hers.

The one problem with October, with the thinning of the veil, was how the many spirits of Pendle decided to rise and cause havoc. The ancient beings were still slumbering, thank goodness, but Pendle played host to many creatures of the olde world. Fae were known to grace their lands regularly, and particularly when the veil was thin. They enjoyed causing mischief and mayhem. Brought wild magics with them to spread over the lands.

Her teacher once shared how the fae restored the earth in order to ensure the next harvest would be bountiful, but in payment, they would cause all manner of problems. Slats falling from roofs and hitting passersby. Glasses shattering and leading to cut soles. Milk souring before it should. Her mentor taught Demdike how to avoid the creatures, but to never try to stop them. Their mischief was the difference between a few people getting hurt and the entire county starving.

A small price to pay, though it didn't alleviate her irritation. The problem, at least for Demdike, was how the fae liked to hide her things. She wasn't going senile. They'd been doing this for years, knowing how much it aggravated her. They enjoyed taunting her. Knowing she couldn't react. Even with iron fillings and blessed water, she couldn't throw it at the little blighters. No matter how much she craved to. For a moment, she genuinely considered it. This was her last year on earth. She wouldn't be here next Halloween, likely wouldn't live to see the next harvest. What would it matter to her if the harvest failed? It wouldn't affect her.

"Mum, have you seen my ladle?" Lizzie shouted from downstairs.

It was an ice bucket over her head. She might not see another cycle, but her family would. With this stark reminder, she pushed the thoughts from her head. Ignoring the sense of amusement dancing in the air. Maybe she could get them back when she was on the same side of the veil next year.

"Were it just me, I'd be happily poisoning the lot of ya," she said to the room, ignoring the giggles she heard in return.

"Look in the most ridiculous place you can think of. The fae are about!" she shouted down the stairs to her daughter.

"Nana Demy, why is Mummy looking through the cinders?" Jennet asked from the door.

The girl didn't hear the peals of laughter from the vicious beasts just beyond her sight. Another downside of being part of the spirit realm, you saw and sensed things normal folk never could. It had the annoying consequence of making you look a little looney if you spoke aloud to the spirits. The fae were gaining great enjoyment at her expense.

"The fae are causing a mischief," she said flatly.

The girl nodded, leaving Demdike to her stewing. Chuntering away to herself as she searched for the things she would need for later in the night.

The list of the restless dead was growing. Spirits coming to visit and complain. Though Demdike ignored the vast majority of them. They were uninteresting and died centuries ago. There were a few with interesting tales, but mostly they just wanted to be heard. To connect with the land of the living once more. Demdike didn't overly mind communing with them, but when out and about, she had to keep herself as closed off as possible. It wouldn't do to add to the gossip circling.

In recent weeks, the people had laid many supposed crimes and deaths at her and Chattox's feet. Many who died long ago. Robert Nutter had been nowhere near Pendle when he passed. However, people saw them argue a few weeks prior to his death and were now drawing conclusions. The argument hadn't been over anything important. He'd wanted her to do some work, she'd asked a fair price, he hadn't wanted to pay. The matter was settled with the two parting ways and agreeing to disagree. Yet somehow, years later, the death was now being blamed on her. Stupid. But Demdike knew if she tried to deny it, they would assume her refusals as part of her guilt. Ridiculous, but as were people.

Sir John Southworth had died the following year. Demdike had never interacted with the man, and yet her name was still being bounded about with the other potential suspects. Christopher Nutter died a year after his brother, claiming bewitchment and foul play. Again, her name was chief amongst the accusers, because, of course, she'd killed one, she must have killed the other. Truth did not matter to the rumour mill.

She was mildly appeased to see Chattox's name was being dragged through the dirt as well. Hugh Moore had died over a decade ago, and they blamed it on Chattox at the time, she recalled. But in the *'your actions made him sick'* not in the *'you used witchcraft'* way. Now, however, after the more recent deaths of John Moore senior, junior, and his wife, all having passed within a year after annoying Chattox, it'd become incredibly suspect. Even Demdike was hard pushed to deny the potential there.

There were other, less substantial rumours, like how John Nutter's father lost a cow after an argument, which was a coincidence at best. Or how Anne Nutter, after laughing at Chattox, died days later. Actually, were it not for the threat of the noose, she suspected Chattox would have happily capitalised on the free publicity. Not that Demdike herself had also thought about doing such things... making money off people's fear and the dead. Definitely not something she would do... at all. Not until Nowell was gone for good, at least. She wasn't foolish enough to draw his ire currently.

Even her grandson was amongst the list of guilty names. The same James who could barely keep two thoughts in his head at once and was more likely to hug a person to death than actually hurt them. Okay, maybe she was exaggerating a little. The boy wasn't entirely stupid, but he lacked common sense and was unfortunately prone to arguing with people.

Demdike had no place to talk. She'd been as fiery and headstrong in her teenage years. Telling him off for things she'd also done felt a little hypocritical. However, she did have to tell the boy to shut his mouth when he'd been bragging about her accidentally turning milk into butter. It wouldn't do to add fuel to the fire when people's paranoias were reaching new heights.

All the mysterious deaths—Richard Ashton, Thomas and Jane Lister, James Robinson, Thomas Dodgson, the Walshman's babe—were being laid at various Pendle residents' feet. Demdike suspected her argument of only using curses and karma when she was paid or when the person had harmed her and hers would not benefit the situation, so she'd kept quiet. Held her head high and turned a deaf ear to the words following her steps.

Halloween had always been a big celebration in Pendle. Death and the dead were remembered with the revelry of life. A reminder of how life was short and people should enjoy it whilst they were here. Though all the simultaneous messages about God, the devil and temptations, felt a little contradictory to her.

"Why do they do fortune tellings if the priest said knowing the future was connected to the devil?"

Alizon was old enough to spot the same idiosyncrasies Demdike did, though the girl was too curious to keep the same observations to herself. A dangerous pattern, but one she'd tried and failed to stop the girl from continuing. Had they been blessed with money, Demdike suspected the girl would have gone on to be a scholar or philosopher. The child's take on the world was intrinsically different from those around her. Even Demdike, for all she recognised their similarities, felt the young girl was oftentimes simply a little too odd.

"Fortune telling is fun," was her simple reply, immediately wincing. When had Alizon ever accepted such a brush-off?

As she gathered together her stones, each carved with a symbol, Demdike wondered if she could move fast enough to escape the conversation. But the girl had always been overly persistent in trying to comprehend the things she couldn't understand. Picking up the cards, Demdike immediately put them back down. It might have been tradition, but the devil card was there. She might know the meaning was different, but others didn't, and this wasn't something she wanted to be attributed to her right now. Not after people's fearful glances had yet to alleviate.

"That doesn't make sense. Why can they say it's bad, then do it for fun?"

Demdike couldn't have held her chuckle back if she tried. The young girl had unknowingly hit the nail on the head. Wasn't that the question? Why did they do this? Or perhaps the inverse should be asked, why did they decide everything fun and potentially pleasurable had to be bad?

"Because of control."

"What?"

This was not a conversation she wanted to have with the girl. It would be easier to divert the train of thought.

"Fortune telling has been a part of Halloween for centuries. It's steeped in history and although most don't know the why, they enjoy the fun of doing it."

She picked up the pouch with the bones in it. A mixture of rat, chicken and pigeon bones. Great for scrying, but for all they fit with the holiday, it might be a little too much for the locals. A bowl with water or a mirror would be the better option.

"I don't get it," the girl crossed her arms stubbornly, blocking Demdike's path from the home.

Sighing for what felt like the thousandth time this week alone, Demdike looked directly at her granddaughter.

"People don't generally care about the histories behind celebrations. They're there to have a good time. They don't want their joys to be ruined by the darker realities which led to their frivolities."

"We live in a place obsessed with tradition," the girl argued.

"Yes, the traditions, not the reasons behind the traditions."

Her granddaughter still wasn't moving. Throwing the bag over her shoulder, Demdike reached for her walking staff. A stick, really, but it gave her the look of a wise woman, the perfect image for Halloween night. She should get more than a few coins for this. She silently hoped Chattox would have fallen down a ditch so there would be little competition for the eager festival goers. Though Demdike knew she was unlikely to get so lucky. Looking at the girl keeping her from leaving, she decided on Plan B.

"We carve turnips to ward away evil spirits. To protect our homes and keep away the tricky spirits who would cause us mischief or harm. However, most children have no idea why they are doing such things, only that the carving is fun. Then later we light them and leave them outside our doors before going to the festival. It's fun. Some of the adults, especially those of a more superstitious nature, know what they are doing and why, but few care beyond the fact they get to have an entire evening of revelry."

"I understand what you're saying, but people love Halloween. They enjoy having their fortunes told and being given hope for the future, so why does the church call it evil?"

"We can discuss it on the way," she said, grabbing the girl's arm and manhandling her out the door.

Curiosity was one thing, but keeping Demdike from her coin was not something the old woman would take lightly. She'd have beaten the girl with her stick if she thought it might do some good. But Alizon was as stubborn as James was dim. The pair were rarely able to see beyond their own noses.

Perhaps this was simply the folly of youth? It'd been many a year since Demdike had been the same age. Maybe she'd been the same and was simply forgetting. Although her grandparents wouldn't have thought twice about giving her a good kick if she'd been causing any issues, so perhaps not.

The broken road of worn stones and slippy mud was another irritant to add to Demdike's long list of complaints. Once they reached the cobblestones, it would be better. However, until they did, her stick was as much for digging into the earth as it was supporting her body. Balance was a tedious requirement when the earth below might become a boggy marsh of sinking mire at any moment. The Borough of Pendle had not been marshlands in centuries, but every so often it was as though the earth remembered what it once was and tried to return to its previous state. Nostalgia.

Alizon had been asking countless questions, which, although a chore, did make the journey shorter than normal.

"Is communing with spirits the devil's work, though?"

"If it is, I'll be strung up in days," the woman muttered, more focused on keeping her footing. "Isn't there some stories about Jesus talking with spirits? Pretty sure he wasn't in line with the devil."

Alizon shrugged. Demdike wasn't sure either. It'd been a long time since she'd attended Sunday school. When the peppy lady leading the group told them a bunch of fantastical tales which sound far more like magic than anything Demdike had ever managed, but two or three cannings had been enough to stop her voicing their lack of logic. The church didn't do well with pointing out its flaws. Like most people, she later learnt, but it had been a sharp lesson for little Elizabeth. As Demdike, she cared less, but knew when to hold her tongue.

"I know there's one about possession and being legion," Alizon shrugged.

Demdike vaguely recalled it. How Jesus had cast the demon out. This was the base for many of the Catholic exorcism rituals. Though she couldn't claim to care too much. She took many of the supposed holy messages with a pinch of salt. However, if the man decided to come to earth and change the water to wine and made one loaf of bread feed five hundred, she'd be more than happy. It'd surely help them survive the coming winter. But time and life had laid such childish fancies to rest years ago. God had allowed his own son to die. She doubted he cared all that much for her old bones.

Despite the storm cloud threatening to turn all her thoughts to darkness, Demdike refused to let them ruin her night. Halloween had always been her favourite holiday. Long before her cunning work or walking the spirit path, before Demdike had been brought forth in her consciousness, little Elizabeth had been obsessed with the traditions and drawn to the darker subject of death.

Her soul knew her life's calling before her journey began. Back before she'd learnt to embrace death in order to live. Before she became a wise woman walking the path of the grey. Back when the idea of robbing graves and eating rats were horror stories, not life experiences.

Halloween had been fun. Before it became a time of psychic expression and spiritual increase. Her younger self enjoyed making masks of the most horrifying things her childish mind could conjure. Many looked like the next-door dog—probably should have been a hint the bloody thing was feral. Though luckily it'd been shot before its teeth had managed to lock around her arm. Another memory she flicked away. Nostalgia and buried traumas were in full flow this evening.

As a child, she'd loved making scary masks, carving turnips and eating sweet treats. It wasn't much different to Christmas except for the scare factor. Jumping out at people. Telling spooky stories. Listening to the howling of the winds as mist covered all of Pendle. Every year on Halloween, those hills became coated with a thick blanket of fog.

Melancholic memories plagued her mind as she and her granddaughter finally reached the heart of their village. There was already music playing and multiple small fires burning. To keep the cold at bay as much as to keep the ghosts from walking among them. An old Celtic tradition which held strong roots in their little slice of the county. Pendle held onto its traditions like clawing it from them might result in the deaths of them all. You could take their traditions from the cold dead corpses and even then they would still hold on tight and refuse to let go. No matter where a tradition came from, once it had woven its way into the fabric of their home, it was there forever. Bonfires, scary masks and fortune telling, this was a true Pendle Halloween.

The music was soft with a burst of tempo. As though reminding the residents they were there. As people unknowingly swayed and followed the soothing beat, they were regularly reawakened to the world around them. The burning herbs and scent of burnt sugar helped to lull everyone into a place of compliance. Spotting Lizzie at one of the stools, she watched as her daughter gave a reading to an unfamiliar woman. Another thing about Halloween, it was the only time the natives weren't hostile to outsiders.

"Bessie?" The surprise was clear in her voice.

"Nana Demy?" The woman rose from the chair, embracing her gently.

It was perhaps the ultimate irony that little Bessie (also originally named Elizabeth), and daughter of her biggest competition, had become a sort of friend over the years. Bessie was the wife of a merchant, who travelled the length and breadth of the country. The girl had shared many tales of her travels over the seas and to far-off lands whilst acquiring their many gains.

"I didn't know you were back?" she asked, hoping the '*why?*' didn't sound too insensitive.

"We were meant to be going to Lancaster, but apparently the local Justice was here, of all places." She laughed.

A shiver ran down her spine at the reminder of Nowell. She'd yet to see him again since church, but his foul presence was like a stench in the air she couldn't ignore. It made sense for Bessie's husband to be acquainted with a man of stature such as Nowell. Especially as Michael (said husband) was one of the main importers for all of England. It made sense, but it did not make Demdike feel at ease.

The man had left and returned to Pendle several times since his initial arrival, supposedly planning to continue the pattern for the foreseeable future. The Sunday services were getting more and more extreme. Rumours of hidden evils being fueled by his presence each time. Bessie being here might be a bright spot, but it was shadowed by that man's darkness.

"You don't like him?" the woman asked, having always had a keen eye for reading people.

"I get bad vibes from him. He ain't here for any good reason."

"Well, I won't say he's a good man, won't lie to you like that," the other woman ribbed, "but I doubt he's here for more than taxes and reminding people he's the big bad."

Demdike hummed. She didn't agree, but she wouldn't argue either.

"You're getting your fortune done, then?" Demdike asked instead, pointing to the table her daughter sat at.

"Aye, thought I'd stick it to mum by giving you my pennies. You fancy giving me one? Not that I doubt your gifts, Lizzie," she said quickly to the woman still seated.

Lizzie laughed good-naturedly. "Nah, between my mum and me, I'd pick her too." She waved it away, rising from the chair and offering it to her mother.

Demdike happily complied. Taking the stones from her bag and a cup to jostle them about in.

"You happy with the runes?"

"I prefer the bones, but given the crowd." Bessie winked mischievously.

She was another wild child. Demdike once wondered if the spirits had swapped Bessie with a fae. Before her own granddaughter was born. Alizon and Bessie were never to meet, the two together would cause catastrophe. Her appearing here tonight of all nights felt more like fate than chance.

Demdike read several fortunes over the next few hours. Only three stone readings. Quick and to the point. She could have done more in-depth readings, but it wasn't worth spending long lengths of time when most people only wanted to hear they would have a great future filled with love and wealth. There were the odd revelations such as people going on journeys she hadn't known about or family members coming to visit, but with Christmas not far away, this wasn't as much of a surprise. It was good to see their shock when she told them things they hadn't yet shared with others. When she held information before the rumour mill did. A petty sort of superiority, but it made her happy to see she still had her gifts.

It seemed for all the scorn and belief she was a serial murderer, people had no issues putting this aside for one night and keeping to tradition. Demdike doubted most of them believed the nonsense, anyway. People died all the time, regardless of the arguments they may have had in the past. But gossip was entertainment, and Pendle—for all its beauty—was not a place of excitement. Other than the interpersonal squabbles and romantic scandals, there was little to discuss. Of course, potential murder had garnered this much traction. It was like these readings, a fun tradition the locals loved to indulge in.

Nowell, being here, had simply given them a direction to aim their wayward thoughts. A target for their excitement. It being malicious and hurtful hardly mattered, as long as it was entertaining. As much as Demdike wanted to feel repulsed, she couldn't blame them. There was a reason scandals happened regularly. Human nature. The problem was how gossip planted seeds and seeds typically bore fruit. For now, it was harmless entertainment, but soon it would turn to genuine fear when their biases were confirmed by some odd coincidence. When they would be able to say '*I was right*' because they'd briefly suggested as much months earlier.

"Nana Demy, guess what? Guess what?"

She turned to see Alizon bouncing towards her. The stool across from her recently cleared. The girl plopped down in the seat opposite.

"There's a guy here giving apple peel readings," the girl announced eagerly.

Demdike raised an eyebrow at this. Apple peel readings were complete trash, not even a fortune-telling technique.

"Really?" She didn't bother to hide her disbelief.

"Yes, and the peel is supposed to form the letter of the person you will one day marry," the girl continued, oblivious to her grandmother's scepticism.

"Ah," she began, "and does it begin with a 'C' then?" she asked, wondering what shape a peel would naturally make.

"No," the girl replied, scandalised. "It was a 'P'. Why would it be..." The girl paused. "It was 'P'. Do you think it was for Peter?"

Demdike's eyebrows would have been in her hairline if she could have raised them any higher. Talk about wishful thinking. Reminding herself such things were simply for entertainment and nothing with even an ounce of truth. She pointed to the stones.

"Do you want a real reading?" She tried to keep the condescension from her tone, but by the look of resentment from Alizon, she likely failed.

"Fine." The girl huffed.

Shaking the cup, Demdike laid out three runes. Thurisaz, someone stubborn, definitely Alizon, obstacles in their path. Would the girl be getting in her own way? Or was something going to happen? Demdike wasn't sure.

The second rune was Raido. A change of direction. It reminded her of the tower in tarot. The rug being pulled from under her. Demdike almost hesitated to look at the third stone. Pertho. Mystery, unpredictable event, gambling. To receive the fate rune on the night of death—not a good sign.

"What is it?" the girl asked curiously, staring at the stones as though by staring at them she might suddenly divine their meaning. Which, given the girl would soon be coming into her own psychic powers, probably wasn't a big jump.

"Things are going to change. You'll go on a journey, whether physical or spiritual, and it will change your fate." Her throat squeezed out the last words.

"Huh. I've no real plans to go somewhere. Maybe if I get married, my honeymoon might be somewhere far away." Alizon laughed.

"Yeah, maybe," was all Demdike could say, putting the runes away. The sinking sensation was back. Death was here, and it wasn't planning on taking just her.

***

Later in the night, they arrived home to find a scared young man waiting in front of their door.

"John?" her daughter asked.

Demdike relaxed a little. Seeing her daughter knew this half-hidden figure.

"What's wrong?"

The boy, man really (he must have been in his early twenties at least), opened and closed his mouth several times. The words refused to part from him.

"Why don't you come inside and have a little something to drink? Warm you up a bit," Lizzie instructed, rubbing his arms.

Demdike looked to the children to see if they had any ideas, but at their bewildered expressions, she guessed they were as clueless as she was. As Lizzie led the young lad into the house, they all followed suit. Each was more curious than the last as to what brought the frightened young man to their doorstep in the middle of the night.

They'd been at the festival until the bitter end. Goodness only knows how long the boy sat there freezing in the dark. For him to have endured it—to have not left and returned at first light—was troubling. Few were desperate enough to seek her out like this. Not without leaving and returning, or going to her competition. She keenly wanted to ask what had the man so terrified he'd chosen to sit freezing in the night rather than return to his home?

These actions spoke of desperation. Of someone with no other choice, or so few choices, this was the only one worth suffering. But what could be so terrifying John would face death on the night of the veil rather than going back to the warmth and safety of his home? Shelter from the elements as well as the wandering spirits of this dangerous night.

As the boy sipped his warmed ale, they each had a small cup. The children were more than happy to indulge in the rare treat. Lizzie held some issues with giving children alcohol. Demdike never discovered why. She'd raised the girl with the stuff, the same way her parents had.

Heck, they used the stuff in place of medicine for all manner of ills, but her daughter was stubborn. Even when they had mead and ale to spare, she refused to indulge her children. They reserved such things for special occasions, and like now, after long, frosty nights exposed to the whims of nature.

As they each slowly warmed, she could see the colour returning to the boy's cheeks. Looking at him closer, he did look familiar. A lot like Christopher, if she wasn't mistaken. Though it'd been many moons since she last crossed paths with the man. He'd been a decent enough sort of folk, though overly apprehensive around her. Demdike remembered thinking he likely had some extra sense or another, able to feel there was more about her.

Most were troubled by her reputation, but Christopher hadn't been unduly afraid. His troubles felt more knowing. As though he feared being pulled into her orbit. Perhaps the smartest thing he could have done. Deny his gifts. This path wasn't for everyone, and the man had been respected and financially secure enough it wasn't worth him endangering himself to the spirit world.

"Now," she began, her Demdike persona in full swing. "What brings you to our door?"

"I—you see—it's..." He shut his mouth again before muttering, "God, it sounds crazy."

Demdike kept staring at him, waiting for the words she knew would soon come spilling from his mouth.

"I don't know what it is. Strange animal. Ghost or demon. But there's something. Something in our home, trying to hurt us. We need your help."

CHAPTER SEVEN

"Jane."

She swivelled in place, but found no one. Jane tried to pretend she hadn't heard anything, continuing with her chores. Before jumping again when she noticed the floor. The waterlogged earth was the perfect plaster cast for the large prints, unmistakably an animal. Similar to a large dog, but the distance between the tracks was too far. The animal must be close in size to a fully grown man.

Her head snapped back and forth, unable to locate the source of the noise. An animal this big would not be overlooked, even in the low light of the evening. Another sound, somewhere between a bark and a growl, came again.

Her nose twitched at the scent of iron. Blood smears coated the patchy grass, now more mud than greenery. Or reddish brown, with this new addition. Feathers stood up from the dirt on their own, a mush of flesh and a few small bones mixed in. The mysterious beast had fed on a chicken. Annoying. They didn't have money to feed the local wildlife. Could it have been a large fox? Wolves hadn't been seen in over a hundred years, but they were the next logical assumption.

Was this an omen? Jane heard tell of such things before, and this was All Hallows Eve. The night of the dead. The local legends were littered with the terrifying creatures which roamed the world on this night. She'd put little stock in the tall tales, but what animal could have left such imprints behind? Tugging at her collar, she racked her mind for what a dead chicken scattered over the broken earth supposedly foretold. Nothing came to mind—the murky memory just out of reach.

A loud barking broke her internal thoughts. Followed by a warm breath on her neck. She turned on her heel with a burst of speed, but there was nothing there. Nothing met her gaze where the warmth must have come from. There was no large body or hovering animal as she'd expected. Could it have been a strange breeze? She stretched her arms out in front of her, trying to feel for what her eyes might have missed. The little hairs on her arm stood to attention; capturing what her eyes could not. Something was close. Something dangerous.

"Jane," the growl of her name came menacingly from behind.

She looked again, turning to where the voice seemed to have come from. Stumbled as her foot caught in the uneven ground and forced her backwards. Sludge painted her dress. She sucked in a sharp breath as her wrist scratched against something hidden in the dirt. A broken bone from the devoured poultry. Her own liquid added to the boggy mixture. Jane instinctively grabbed her wrist, putting pressure on the wound.

Her hair moved. A visible curl lifting itself over her shoulder. As though a child was playing with it and threw it forward. She'd have blamed a breeze but the rest of her head was unmoved. The intangible creature had tousled it. Her feet moved before her mind knew what was happening, fleeing the invisible threat.

Her home was only a few hundred yards from where they kept the chicken coup, but no matter how quick her steps, the distance seemed to stretch. Her fiery hair danced in the wind as she unwittingly searched her surroundings. Strands of orange and red added to her distorted view. She ran at a pace she hadn't achieved since her youth. Had she not felt the pounding of her heart and the burning in her lungs, she might have been impressed. Even as a child, she hadn't moved so swiftly.

Adrenaline fired through her system. She no longer sensed the threat, but still struggled to catch her breath. Doubled over, her vision was clouded for several seconds until the oxygen returned to her limbs. Still cradling her wrist, she used her elbow to slam the door behind her. The safety of home let her take stock of her current appearance. A mess.

The long sheet of reflected silver was a wedding gift. Kept near the doorway to check if they looked presentable whenever leaving the home. Jane was startled at her current reflection. Blood dripped from her cracked lip. She must have bitten it in panic. The taste of metal stayed on her tongue as her breathing finally returned to normal. How would she explain this one to her husband? He would undoubtedly be worried she'd hurt herself on purpose, again.

Though that was many years ago, after the birth of their son, it was something he was always cautious about returning. Now she was simply prone to ridiculous accidents, but the look on Christopher's face every time he documented a fresh injury left an unpleasant sinking sensation in her gut. She'd unfortunately grown more accident-prone in recent years; dropping things and tumbling over her own two legs,

'It has to be my age,' she reasoned internally, followed by a jolt in her stomach as her instincts disagreed.

Jane's body shuddered. The voice couldn't have been real, but she liked the alternative even less. She couldn't be going over to the dark place again. Jane felt mentally stronger in her forties than she had her entire twenties. Her inner demons having left long ago. She prayed to God and all his angels she would not spiral again.

"Dar-*ling.*" The sing-song voice came from beyond the front door.

It took her mind a moment to process this was not the creepy voice from earlier, but a familiar candescence. The small man in stature but big in personality. Returned home from the fields. He wasn't a field worker by trade—his main trade being carpentry—but he'd been asked to assist with the post-harvest fertilising of the ground and like the decent man he was, had been more than happy to help his fellow countrymen. If said countryman was also his cousin, Henry, who liked to pay her husband back in drink, well, it'd become a yearly ritual for the pair.

"Christopher Bulcock!" she snapped.

He finally appeared before her, carrying the smell of manure deep within his clothes. It would take weeks to rid the cloth of the stench, Jane knew from experience. Wrinkling her nose, she pulled the man through their doorway, no longer afraid of what may be hiding in the shadows. Life always seemed a little less scary with her husband by her side.

"You need a wash. Get in the house," she ordered, noticing his walking. "You've been drinking haven't you?"

His stumbling was clue enough. After the fright from earlier, anger came quicker than worry.

"I have, my lovely," he said, steadying himself against the furniture he looked at her with a broad smile. "My Jane. I have worked hard, and I have reaped the reward in pennies and ale." He chortled in his giddy way, attempting to kiss her.

Moving her head away from his attempts, she pushed him playfully with her elbows. "I swear, God would forgive me for slapping you silly," she half-joked. She wouldn't deny she was tempted to hit the drunken sod, but her anger wasn't aimed at him, not really.

"Oh, my beautiful wife, you are too pretty to be angry." He smiled at her and stumbled towards the kitchen.

Annoyed though Jane was, he was a sloshy romantic whilst in his cups. She watched him make his way to the food on the stove.

"Don't you even think about touching that before you have washed those filthy paws, to the bath with you," she barked, directing him to the small metal container filled with water. No longer the piping boiled heat it had once been, but now a tepid warmth.

She had to help undress him in his inebriated state. He repeatedly grabbed at her as he tried to get her into the water too, causing her to stumble more than once; though luckily avoiding getting wet

"Now, Christopher, you behave," she playfully admonished. "I have spent all day making this supper and I will be damned if I don't get to eat it. Now scrub up before our son arrives."

She ignored his mutterings and what sounded like '*It's just John,*' coming from her grumpy husband. Though as he was soon giggling in the sloshing water, Jane assumed he was soon happy enough. '*More like a second child than a partner,*' she thought, rolling her eyes at the display.

Jane stepped back, moving the chairs into the middle of the room. The entire downstairs was one room split by their furniture into set areas. A great way to save money, but she missed their once large house. Their current kitchen was at the back of the room, with the stairs to the left going up across the back wall. The kitchen tables extended out slightly, with wooden furniture that could be split apart to double their length.

Her husband was a carpenter by trade and his experiments always ended up in their home for testing first. This particular invention had been ingenious for moving and altering the layout of their smaller space. Especially useful when they moved house. She was still a little annoyed about said relocation even several years later. But when their son, John, moved out, and this house became available, her husband had stressed the benefits of downsizing. She suspected the penny-pinching had more influence than the man admitted, but this smaller home served them well.

After what must have been over twenty minutes, she returned to check on her drunken other half. The man half asleep, longing over the frame of the tub. She did hit him this time.

"Up! You big lout. John will be here soon, and his Alice is coming too."

The pair were in the courting stages and the girl's parents would be dropping the two off at their house. She'd invited them to stay, but was secretly glad they'd declined. As much as the young couple needed chaperoning, the house didn't have enough room for four extra bodies. Her son and his potential fiancée would be more than enough.

"Is that tonight?" he asked sleepily, stretching as the water fell from his frame.

She threw a towel at him. "Yes, it is tonight. Clean yourself, get some decent clothes on and be getting ready, or I will send you to bed with no food." She definitely sounded more like his mother than his wife.

Heaving a heavy sigh, she made her way back over to the meal she'd spent most of the afternoon preparing. Jane tasted the juicy meat and checked the vegetables. She'd purchased fresh bread from the baker and even a cake. Today was a special day, after all. Putting the final touches to her table, she felt everything was ready, all except her husband and the guest's arrival, of course.

***

The banging started. Quietly at first. Three little knocks over and over. Initially, she thought it was in her imagination, but slowly, they had become more audible. The pots clanked in the kitchen. She shoved her husband until he awoke, dazed.

"What?" he grumbled. "I was sleeping and having the best dream. I was in a river of ale." He laughed, kissing her cheek.

"There's something downstairs."

They sat there quietly, ears perked, listening for the noises. The meal had gone well and despite her husband's state and the odd snarky remark from her son, they'd had a pleasant evening. All retired to bed at a decent hour with plans to spend more time together tomorrow—when John and her husband both had the day off work.

"It's probably just John getting some water."

"No, he'd have to come past our room and the floorboard would squeak," she argued.

At her husband's raised eyebrow, she continued. "I might want to trust our John, but I'm not so foolish as to ignore this would be a golden opportunity for the young couple to sneak around."

He hummed, clearly remembering their own youthful indiscretions. "Could it be the girl?"

"Alice? No, I set a bell outside her door." She chose to ignore her husband's snickering.

A noise came again. It sounded like the wind was trapped, squealing in an attempt to push through an object.

"What is that?" Christopher asked, rising slightly and looking a little more awake. "Sounds almost like a voice, doesn't it?"

Relief flooded her (she wasn't crazy). Jane nodded.

"I don't know, but you should go look." She gestured to the door he had been slowly creeping toward.

"Why don't you go look?" he said in such a childish manner she wanted to slap him across the back of the head (the way she used to their John when he was a young boy).

She got out of bed with a sigh, taking the candle from her bedside. A few candle marks had passed since lighting it, and she guessed the time was close to midnight. The house was warmer than it should've been. Whether they were still on the last day of October or the first of November, this was unseasonably warm. Especially given the fire had died down to embers faster than it usually would have. Whatever the cause, this was something different, potentially unnatural. She almost wanted to feel around for a fire. Could the lower floor have caught aflame?

Three more bangs. Jane picked up the poker from their bedroom fireplace and held it in her other hand. Ready to swing at any intruders. Christopher grabbed the small shovel. Whatever was down there was not attempting to hide its presence. Opening the door slowly, they were careful not to have it creak and alert the uninvited guest to their waking.

They descended the steps slowly until they could see into the living room, but the kitchen was behind the stairs and beyond their sight. As Jane turned onto the bottom floor, her eyes met nothing. Eerily similar to a few hours ago, no physical person stood there. The couple turned to one another in confusion. The moonlight shone in, illuminating the entire lower floor. If there had been someone there, they could not have hidden.

Christopher checked between the furniture all the same. His steps were cautious, inching forward between each potential hiding place. A shovel braced in his left arm, strong grip ready to swing at anyone he found. Each time he inspected, Jane watched as his shoulders sagged a little more in relief. Empty. Jane checked the door, still secured—to keep the cold out—as they'd been before bed. She gestured to her husband to check the windows. None were broken or damaged; all still sealed. Neither could make sense of it.

"John?" Jane hissed in fear.

What if the person had snuck past them and climbed the stairs? Their son could be in danger. The married couple clambered up the stairs and burst into their sleeping son's room. The scene was the same as the rest of the house. Nothing was disturbed, broken, or open.

"What's going on?" the groggy voice of an annoyed young man asked.

"We heard a lot of noises," she answered. "We can't find anything to see what it was. I could have sworn someone had broken in," Jane voiced.

Her husband's agreeing nods helped her calm a little. She didn't imagine this. This wasn't like before. She was not crazy. If Jane said the words enough, maybe she might actually start believing them.

"It's probably just the wind," their son said, his voice croaky as he reached for the water by his bedside.

"It was not the wind," her husband protested.

It was her turn to nod encouragingly. Those sounds had definitely not been the wind.

"Have you checked outside? A chicken might have gotten loose. You know what they're like for making noise at all hours."

She watched as Christopher's shoulders dropped at the logical suggestions. Hers, however, remained rigidly in place. Jane wouldn't outright dismiss her son's idea, but a chicken in the kitchen would have been incredibly obvious. Christopher checked the entire downstairs, searching for an intruder. Had one of those winged devils made it inside their home, they wouldn't have been hard to find. The screeching and feather-ruffling alone would be enough to locate the beast within a matter of moments. But she wouldn't rule out one having managed to free itself from the cage.

The noises could've been coming from outside. Maybe. She'd been sure the sounds were inside the house, but a chicken banging against the outside wall or door could explain some of what they heard. She hadn't checked if the enclosure was damaged earlier, but she'd planned to do at first light. If something had broken the structure—whatever was eating one of their livestock—another hen might have been able to get out and start making a ruckus. Jane didn't believe this was the cause of the noise, but she couldn't discount it either.

"I'll check outside. Dad, you hold the light."

Her two boys left her in the doorway as they went to check around the home. It was too dark for her to see beyond the small ring of light her candle cast. Barely a metre in front of her. As much as she instinctively looked at the perimeter of their home, she couldn't have seen if a battalion of men were standing there in the pitch black of night. Her eyes tried to form shapes. Tried to find the familiar landmarks just beyond her light line, but it was all swirls and shadows.

The wood of the frame she was leaning against looked distorted in this low light. The chips and broken pieces, aged and weathered, were like tiny, ugly faces glaring back at her. Her mind conjured and created images Jane knew would no longer be there when she checked again tomorrow in the daylight. Candlelight had a way of twisting the images it flickered across. In this wind, it was even more unreliable. Unevenly illuminating the surrounding space.

A crash from the left side of the home made her jump. Automatically extending the poker she had yet to relinquish. Her heart was rushing in the same way it did earlier, as though this jump in place were equivalent to the run. Her ears strained against the blood running through her, drowning out all else. It took Jane a few moments to calm her heartbeat once again. She couldn't afford to lose her sense when there was a potential threat close by. Listening again, a second clattering could be heard, though this sound was followed by mutters. They were too far away to make out the words, but these voices were ones she recognised. Her boys. The two men were still beyond her light, but she could hear them discussing something.

"Jane, you shouldn't be standing out here in the cold," her husband's voice spoke in the dark.

He must have been able to see her, but she couldn't see him return.

"I wasn't going to sit in the house when my two men were outside and might need help," she rebutted.

Honestly, it was as though her husband saw her as a fragile flower rather than a capable woman. Sweet sometimes, but generally a little chaffing to be constantly underestimated. She ran the household, and had raised their child despite all her issues. The man really should have more faith in her by now. After twenty-three years of marriage, they'd seen each other through their highs and lows. In sickness and in health. If he still didn't see the strong woman she was... it went beyond sweet and bordered on insulting.

Particularly when he would take away sharp knives and things necessary for performing daily tasks simply because of a few episodes she'd had the year following their son's birth. Surely almost a full score years since should weigh more than the eighteen months she'd been a little less than stellar. But no, not for Christopher.

As the two shapes finally emerged from the darkness, she saw her husband carrying the no longer lit candle. Her expression must have been curious enough, because her son soon answered.

"Father forgot to shield it from the changing wind when turning around the house corners," bitterness seeping into his tone—she gauged the pair had likely argued about such stupidities on the return walk.

"I'm guessing you didn't see much then?"

"Nothing beyond the moonlight when the clouds shifted."

She looked up into the sky, noticing how the front of their home wasn't being illuminated at all. She hadn't noticed, too occupied with the worries of what might be out there. Why wasn't the end of the path clear to see? What was blocking the moon's rays from stretching that far? She tried to search the air, but her husband was leading her inside once more and she could hardly say she wanted to check the roof without causing the man to freak out.

"Everything was okay, then? The crashing?"

"That was us. Someone forgot he left a barrel outside." John's brow drew close together as he threw another unhappy look towards his father.

Jane simply sighed. Christopher, for all he was a good man, was not the brightest. She accepted his flaws, even his overbearing nature, but she'd seen how, over the years, the same patience waned in their child. John was now much closer to her than he was his father, often berating the man's foolish nature. The constant drink didn't help matters either.

John wasn't opposed to the occasional tipple, but he'd more than once voiced concerns over his father's drinking habits. Fortunately, the man in question wasn't a violent drunk, but even Jane had to admit it caused her some level of concern. However, when every man in Pendle was the same, all of them deep in their cups night after night, her son seemed to be the exception and his father the rule.

This left an unspoken tension between the two. John was annoyed at his father's controlling nature, and how he was towards herself. Jane found it sweet how her son wanted to defend her so vehemently, but it didn't aid the situation; merely causing strife between the two men in her life. Christopher was too set in his ways to entertain change, and she had become resigned to her lot in life. At least she had a man desperate to protect her. She was one of the lucky ones.

Women knew to avert their eyes to the bruises and broken bones many unfortunate wives bore. For all his faults, her husband had never struck her. Never hurt her physically. Never forced himself on her. Jane was not blind to see she'd been blessed.

It wasn't worth John getting angry and causing a wedge between father and son. She was proud to have raised a good man. Despite how their relationship may have started. Her body had been convinced the baby in the crib was not hers, and something had replaced it with some foreign being. Back when she couldn't hold him for weeping and when her teets refused to produce milk for the thing it wanted dead.

Jane was eternally grateful Christopher prevented her from doing anything drastic in those dark days. And she was beyond relieved—now with her uncompromised mind—that she'd turned to hurting herself rather than the child. As a result, she could never forget how her husband had been her rock during this time.

It hurt her. To see John getting angry at the man who ensured his survival when she couldn't. All the same, she understood. John didn't remember his first few years of his life. Didn't remember his mother's rejection. How it took two winters before she could hold him without flinching. He didn't recall her behaviours back then; he'd only ever seen the consequences between her and Christopher. She told him, of course. And she could see he understood the information, at least intellectually, but he couldn't comprehend the sheer devastation which had rocked their little family to its very foundations.

John couldn't know the heartbreak, the screaming matches, the way she once thought it better to be dead than a danger to a child. Even if it wasn't her own—as her body had remained convinced of for many moons. She'd been lucky. Many mothers in her place would have been sent to a facility, or locked away somewhere. Probably beaten and broken until they learnt to behave as expected rather than as their minds demanded they should.

A dark time. One Jane would have happily left forgotten. Buried amongst the dead, as she would have happily killed that version of herself if possible. She remembered Christopher scraping together enough money to have her see the doctor, only to be told this was normal. How some women's bodies and brains went haywire after giving birth. They never had another child, not willing to risk the same thing potentially happening again. John was their pride and joy. Jane felt they'd earned every right to brag about their miracle child, who'd survived her dark episodes and his father's stupidity.

This was why she hated to see the pair argue. She could be frustrated for herself. She could tease and cajole her husband until she remembered she was no longer the same woman who'd worn her face, but John couldn't understand the bond between the two. Perhaps when he married, he might begin to fully comprehend what it meant to have to work with another person. For better or worse.

"Mrs Bulcock?" A sound from the staircase had all three of them jumping.

"Oh, Alice, I've told you, call me Jane. What are you doing up?"

"I heard noises."

"Sorry, love, that was probably us. Some animal or another outside making a ruckus. You head back to bed. You as well, John. We'll be retiring again soon. We've had quite enough excitement for one day." She could see John was going to protest, but shook her head, pointing for him to go upstairs.

A second nod in the girl's direction to tell him to ensure the events did not trouble her. Luckily, Alice must have slept through most of it. Her window had been on the side of the house where the two men had stumbled over the barrel and had likely woken from this. Jane saw as his eyes darted between his father and the girl he was courting before he finally followed the young woman up the stairs.

"We can give them a moment before checking they're definitely back in their own rooms," her husband said, sitting himself at the table. Sometimes the man had his moments of wisdom.

She nodded. Moving to the stove, she would need some warm milk to help her get back to sleep. It had been an odd evening. Even by Halloween's standard. The meal had been pleasant, at least. And she was glad her son had found a woman he was interested in marrying. She'd worried for a moment he would find no one. More interested in his sums and learning than people in general. But it seems young Alice Tisburn was his exception.

It eased a mother's heart to know he might find true happiness. Her little boy deserved this. No matter how many years had passed, she would forever feel guilty for those first few. When she needed to learn to love her child. It seemed ridiculous now. To think there'd ever been a time she hadn't loved him with all her being. He owned her heart, could have carved his name in it like a tree, and she would have thanked him. Perhaps she overcompensated a little, but she'd become unduly grateful for the precious child she once rejected. And when they knew it wouldn't be safe to have a second, he became her world.

Between her husband and her son, she had a happy life. For the most part. She couldn't say things were always been easy—particularly with Christopher's and John's issues—but she loved them both with everything she was. There might be a lot she would change about the past, and things she might wish were better, but she was truly content with her life. Sure, they could use more money, and she would have liked a bigger house, but she had a good husband and an even better son. Jane knew to be grateful.

Yes, she knew to be grateful. So why then could she not shift this sense of gnawing cold in her stomach? Why did she feel as though she were the prey and the predator was just beyond her sight? Those hairs were raised on her arms again. She could have blamed the cold of night, but there was a need to keep looking over her shoulder. To check every shadow and potential hiding place. To run from the room even when she could see there was nothing wrong. The sense refused to abate.

Jane had learnt to doubt her instincts. With what happened after John's birth. When her body told her, the child she pushed from her body was not her own. She experienced first-hand how instincts could be false. How the voice shouting in the back of her mind that something was a danger could be entirely wrong.

Jane learnt to doubt her instincts, and yet, she could feel her pace hurry as they went up the stairs. Seeing her son and his love standing in the hallway. Arms barely touching. She remembered how electric such things had felt before marriage. How every skin-to-skin contact had felt like a delicious sin waiting to happen. As she and Christopher came to stand beside the pair, she didn't get to voice a thing before a large crash came from downstairs once more. Much louder than earlier.

The three knocks came once again.

CHAPTER EIGHT

It had been a long day. He'd woken on Halloween morning with a churning in his stomach so intense it could have easily turned milk into butter. This was the first time his parents were going to officially meet the woman he hoped to marry.

They were only in the courting stages, but he and Alice always held a strong connection. They'd met over half a decade ago and remained purely friends for most of this time. John hadn't been interested in marrying, despite his mother's many hints. Plus, Alice had been a few years younger, and not ready for such things. Her father had suggested several suitors, but the girl rejected them all.

Alice later confessed she'd been hoping he would eventually recognise the potential between them. Giggled at how blind John was about something incredibly obvious to others. Even her father had been unsubtle with his hints by the end, basically telling John he would be courting his daughter or the man would prevent the friendship from continuing.

Initially blindsided, John hadn't known what to say. He hadn't considered Alice for marriage, not because there was any fault with her, but simply because he hadn't considered marriage at all. When Christian Tisburn sat him down and told him to buck up or move along, to say he was shocked would be an understatement. John had sat there with his jaw unhinged for many moments. Demanding to know why Christian wanted John gone when he'd only ever been a good friend and never done anything untoward. He'd been rather angry, thinking the man was accusing him of potentially behaving inappropriately with his daughter.

"At this point, I'd expect she will get tired of waiting, sooner than you ever having the sense to try anything."

Christian's words had blown his mind. The man was giving his permission, or strongly advising John's course of action. He hadn't voiced these thoughts, but it was the only conclusion his mind could form.

Several days later, it clicked. He did care for Alice, and the idea of having to sacrifice their friendship because she needed a husband was an uncomfortable revelation. The idea of Alice lying with another never bothered him (beyond the idea of it being unsanitary), and he held no desire to lie with anyone himself. However, the thought he might lose the love the two held for each other, was a bolt to the heart. He couldn't lose her. If the solution meant marrying her, then so be it. And so, the courting began.

John couldn't say he would be a great husband. Something within him seemed broken to the other men. He held no desire to discuss or take part in behaviours of the body. Had no want for ale or nights blacked out by too much drink. He was seen as weird by many. Yet John knew no other way. It wasn't as though he couldn't love, or couldn't have a good time, it was simply his idea of fun differed greatly.

John enjoyed a single glass of something whilst reading a book in front of a fire. He liked doing things which tested his mind. Loved riddles and things which forced him to think of things differently. He'd learnt to read by pestering the retired priests. Whilst other children had been running through fields and roughhousing, he'd been learning his letters and numbers.

It wasn't typical for someone of his status to learn such things, but he was tenacious and refused to prostrate himself before the societal standards. Just because others hadn't learned, didn't mean he shouldn't. And when he had promised to clean the old priest's home in exchange for lessons, he finally won the man's acceptance.

John had been thought of as odd by many of the other boys. Why was he learning to read and write, did he think himself above his station? More than one beating was the result of this false notion. John just couldn't explain how something within him craved to know the written word. To understand the strange symbols. It was an obsession he couldn't ignore. Had the priest said no, he would've found another way. Reading and writing seemed as key to his existence as the breath in his body, and the blood below his skin.

A young John couldn't put into words how reading eased something within his soul. How he would've felt as though he were missing some vital piece of himself without it. Similar to when his mother tried to describe romantic love; the aching longing which made you want with your entire being. John never yearned for a person like this, but he desired those yellowed pages and calculations like something within him would wither and die without them.

This wasn't unnatural to him. It was a way to worship God and be a better man by learning as much as was available to him. There were so few books in Pendle, even fewer for enjoyment. But the scientific scrolls and the bible were wondrous texts he held as sacredly as others did their children.

To John, the idea of lying with his friend made him cringe. However, the idea of treasuring her as though she were one of those books, this he could understand. He might not be able to be the best husband, lacking things others appeared to have, but he could be a good man. He would never lay a finger upon his friend—and not simply because her father terrified him. He would never try to control Alice the way he'd watched his father do his mother. John might be lacking in some ways, but he could love, honour, and cherish her. He could give her a good life where they were partners as well as friends.

If said marriage also stopped his mother's unending suggestions for finding a wife, then this would simply be a secondary bonus. He loved his mother, he did, but she failed to understand he didn't behave the same as others. She saw him as perfect despite his many flaws. Carried a guilt which wasn't hers to bear.

Jane Bulcock pushed (like all mothers), despite his wish she wouldn't. His mother tried. Respected his want to learn and better his future, but she hadn't understood his desire to write books. Couldn't grasp how he wanted to share the stories of Pendle Forest with the rest of the world. Wanted the world to know their odd little land.

She'd grown up here, and thought everywhere else was the same. Didn't recognise the strangeness lingering like fog over their land. His mother couldn't comprehend how their stories and superstitions would be of great interest to those of learning elsewhere. Though no matter how learned he became, he couldn't afford the many parchments and inks it would take to write one book—let alone several. It was a dream. A silly one. But one he held in his heart all the same. Dreams were like this, burning bright in the face of the world regardless of how well you knew they would never come to be.

His marriage to Alice was a new dream. Though it wasn't yet certain. Which seemed strange given the two families knew one another and the pair had been friends for years. But courting had to happen. He had to prove himself worthy. That the two could work together as a unit and prove to others the things they'd been doing for years. It made little sense to John, but then so did many of the social rules he needed to follow. He learnt it was often better to simply go along with such things. To abide by the expectations in order to make life easier for oneself at a later date.

He went to work as normal that morning, doing the accountancy for the local Peacekeeper, looking over the taxes and monies of all the local businesses. It'd originally shocked him how these people paying money to the crown had no idea how much they were supposed to give. Had he been a lesser person, it would've been easy to exploit their ignorance. All too easy to skim off the top. He suspected others had in the past. But John tried to be a good man. He might not have been a devout Christian, but he did learn words and numbers through a man of the cloth.

The elderly priest often gave him sermons to read, and scrolls he held from his previous occupation. Such teachings influenced child John. Helped form his moral compass. Taught him how to interact with the world and how God was aware of all things. If the magistrates didn't catch him performing such abhorrent actions, God surely would. Wasn't worth indulging such temptations. Such was the work of the devil, and John would not fall to the serpent.

After work, he'd changed his outfit. Nothing too fancy, but dressed enough to show he was respecting both Alice and his parents. Mr Tisburn (Christian) and his wife Claire were going to the Halloween festival, John was sad to miss it, but today was the only evening he and his father were free. It'd already been almost two moons since Alice and he began courting. The meal and official introductions were long overdue. The sooner they completed the necessary steps, the sooner they could be married.

John heard many to-be husbands were impatient to reach the altar, however, they held different motivations. He merely desired to no longer have to act distant. There was a barrier between him and his friend as long as they were only courting. He hadn't realised how often the pair hugged and touched platonically until society frowned on such behaviours. He would have no one accusing his friend of impurity or wickedness by acting unsuitably, but it'd been an uncomfortable revelation—to realise how his every action was now a reflection on his friend. The good and the bad. He couldn't hold her close or swing her about the sky without raised eyes and casting aspersions upon their union any longer, he hated it.

Some of what his mother once said made more sense now. Men who drank excessively were the norm here, and she claimed if his father didn't indulge, it might lead to people gossiping about them (and her in particular). John had thought she was trying to excuse his father, and it'd angered him further. Apparently, his father tried to help and protect his mother. However, Christopher did this in odd and stupid ways, such as taking sharp objects from her when she needed them to perform basic tasks. Or how he would tell her to stay home and away from others—claiming it was for her protection—yet then the man spent countless hours in the tavern, ensuring his mother was left alone for hours on end.

To John, his father was merely locking her in the house without using a key. He was already doing everything to protect his future wife. Why was his father not extending the same courtesies to his mum? Instead, doing the reverse by spending their money on ale, whilst leaving her home, lonely and vulnerable.

John would not copy his father when he became a husband. He would respect Alice as she was. She was a great friend, with an intelligent mind and a caring soul. He would do whatever he could to preserve such traits, not curb and control them. He would not claim protection whilst hiding commands. John refused. He might not know how to be a great husband, but he had seen plenty of examples of bad ones. He would have to simply do the inverse.

When they arrived at his parents' home, John was hopeful for a pleasant evening, but seeing his father was already drunk, his expectations threw themselves down a sinkhole and surrendered to the inevitable mess that was likely to occur.

***

When later the two men found themselves stumbling around in the dark, John had been half tempted to leave his dad out the back of the house to freeze. Though the image of the upset on his mother's face, if he returned without the drunken wretch, halted such plans. He hauled the other along. '*Accidentally*' letting the man crash into several other things before pulling them both back toward the front of the house. Not caring for the noise they were likely making.

The closest neighbours were half a field away, and he gained some small amount of pleasure watching the other man experience some consequences for his actions. Without the candlelight and the clouds thick above them, the area was almost entirely hidden to the night. Every so often enough of the moonlight broke through for John to figure his way forward safely enough, but it was incredibly frustrating given all his father had needed to do was shield the freaking wick.

Moments like this were why John was ridiculously happy he moved out. Financially, it might've been better to stay in the family home, but more time spent with his father merely meant more opportunities for the two to butt heads. John wasn't innocent. He knew he was as much the instigator of their many verbal battles, but he hated watching his mother become less and less each year as the man drank more and more. John wasn't a violent man, but his father made him want to use his fists.

As they turned back toward the front of the house, his mother was illuminated in the doorway. Like an angel guiding their path with her flickering light (if you ignored the poker slung over her shoulder). At least his mother had the common sense to shield the little flame from the elements. John supposed he should be glad it wasn't raining.

"Jane, you shouldn't be standing out here in the cold," Christopher said next to him, still hidden in the shadows despite the two being centimetres apart.

With a sigh, he followed his now skipping father as the man hurried over to his wife, guiding her inside like the woman was some invalid and not a proud, capable person. John largely ignored their bantering. Throwing in a jab at his father's stupidity when not protecting the candle. He could practically see his mother mentally forming the many excuses for the man. Typical.

"Everything was okay, then? The crashing?"

The question took him by surprise, seemed she wasn't going to excuse the drunk. As much as he wanted to ask what must have had her mind preoccupied to not do so, he sensed it wouldn't benefit their situation.

"That was us. Somone forgot he left a barrel outside." John may have forgotten to mention he'd walked the idiot into it on purpose, but what his mother didn't know, she couldn't disapprove of.

His father made some inane comment, or maybe it was just drunken chuntering, but John desperately wanted to bite back. Moving closer, John noticed the man was swaying against the chair, close to falling all over himself. John wanted to hit his father across the back of the head. Repeatedly. Until it either knocked some sense into him or he stopped moving altogether.

"Mrs Bulcock?" A sound from the staircase had all three of them jumping.

"Oh, Alice, I've told you, call me Jane. What are you doing up?" his mother spoke kindly, moving swiftly over to the stairs as his friend slowly descended.

"I heard noises," her voice was soft in the night's quiet. As though afraid of being too loud, and waking the dead. It was Halloween night, anything was possible.

"Sorry, love, that was probably us." His mother grimaced.

John wasn't overly keen on his mother apologising for them, or his father specifically, but he also didn't want Alice feeling uncomfortable, particularly with the animosity between him and his father. John held his tongue, following his mother by moving nearer to the girl.

"Some animal or another outside making a ruckus. You head back to bed. You as well, John. We'll be up soon. We've had quite enough excitement for one day," his mother instructed, cutting off his protests before he could even voice them with a shake of her head.

A second nod in the girl's direction told him to ensure Alice was okay and not frightened. Finally, and with much silent protest, John followed his friend up the stairs. As much as he wanted to stay and put his father in his place, John's focus needed to be the woman he planned to marry. Proving he was better than his father started by showing the right priorities. Even if he hated leaving his mother with the man in such a state. Christopher Bulcock was more like his cousin than most realised.

Henry Bulcock was well known to be a wife and child beater, but it was largely ignored because he owned the biggest farm in all of Pendle. John's cousin, George (Henry's eldest), bore the brunt of the man's rage. As the oldest and the one set to inherit, John had patched George up too many times to continually turn a blind eye. That Peter, Mathew, and little Liza all seemed to have blue and yellow scattered across their skin was something he couldn't pretend to unsee.

Christopher had only beaten John a few times, but the rage in his eyes was the same one he'd seen in Henry's—when John had stood between the man and his children. Henry might be his uncle, but John held no respect for someone who regularly hurt his family. He received the hits that day, but John didn't regret it. Except for after, when his father told him off for interfering, as if he were somehow responsible for his uncle's violent temper. Perhaps this was when he started losing respect for the man he once called dad.

John wished his mother would stop making excuses for her husband. Saying '*he didn't hit her*' and how '*he was better than Henry*' was no justification for the man being irresponsible. Someone doing the bare minimum for someone they claimed to love was not to be cheered. That a situation could be worse did not make the current one better.

He looked to Alice with a sigh. Her warm eyes reminded him of the earth, the fertile grounds ripe for a harvest to grow in. Partly why he believed she was such a kind soul. She was filled with everything good in the world and John planned to protect this. He never wanted his friend to say a life by his side was better than being beaten; he wanted to see her genuinely happy.

"What is it, John?" Alice asked. Her voice lowered as she glanced down the stairs. His parents weren't there, but she knew him well enough to likely guess they were the cause.

"I just..." He let a slow breath escape him.

He wanted to pull her close. To feel the warmth of her body pressed against her. Alice's hugs were healing.

"I don't know how to talk to them, either of them, sometimes."

"Your mother seems nice."

He smiled, noticing how she kindly hadn't mentioned his father's state. He shared with her several times how he feared for his father's dependency on drink. Alice hadn't fully understood. Mr. Tisburn never had more than a glass of wine with his evening meal and was a man of means. Her father would never compromise the safety of his family by wasting his savings on drink and barely providing enough food in favour of nights in the tavern.

The only saving grace was John hadn't (yet) heard any rumours about the man visiting the whore house. For all his father loved his drink, it seemed he valued his vows. Deep down, John believed the man did love his mother. Christopher just didn't appear to have the best ways of showing this, and was too preoccupied with getting his next cup to realise how his actions affected others.

Alice outstretched her arm, offering a quiet comfort. He let his body loosen a little. Not the same as a hug, but more than they'd managed since the courting began. Why such innocent touches were frowned upon, he still couldn't understand, but he was appreciative of her attempts to offer solace. The stairs creaked as his parents made their way up. Though they all stilled when a loud crash came from downstairs.

"What was that?" he couldn't help exclaiming.

He almost missed the three knocks following the crash. Was some-one outside? Rushing down the stairs, all four of them had been expecting to see some form of destruction. Perhaps a broken cabinet with pots strewn across the floor. Maybe the table snapped from its legs. Or even the rear door broken open. However, to John's great sur-prise then when he saw nothing out of place. Looking at his parents, he noted the shock on both their faces. His father inspected the room, looking for the potential cause of the noise.

John strode over to the cupboards, wondering if some form of wildlife or another had become trapped within and was trying to escape. Rats were a constant issue in old dwellings like this, with aged panels of wood in need of replacement. Field mice were often in search of warmth too. Even the odd ferret had managed to make its way into the home. It would hardly surprise John to find one of his parents' dumb chickens in here. Those menaces were always causing trouble. John hated having to care for them in his youth. They were organised devils. Could take down a fully grown man if they'd wanted to. If something was in here making mischief, it'd likely be one of those feathered demons.

He couldn't see anything. Searched through each section. Not even a shadow of something moving, as he pushed the candle inside to see properly within. Nothing was there. Or if it was, it was well hidden. Slamming the doors, he cast an eye over the surfaces and the bags of grain. Nothing. Or nothing visible in the low light. He would check again tomorrow, but so far John could find no source of the loud noise they'd all heard.

"Nothing's here," his father said, having looked over the sitting room.

"Nothing to have caused a crash that loud," he agreed.

A nod was shared, a rare moment of camaraderie between the two. That it was brought on by confusion was weird, but John supposed it was a nice feeling, regardless of the cause.

"Hello? Anyone there?"

"Jane," his father hissed.

John resisted rolling his eyes. Whether at his mother's attempts to lure a potential intruder or his father immediately trying to squash any actions the woman took, he wasn't sure.

"What? I want to know if someone's there."

"I think we would be able to see them if they were."

John stayed silent, unwilling to agree with the man when he was putting his mother down. The temperature dropped, rubbing his arms, the goose pimples were fully risen. It was autumn, he hadn't noticed how warm it'd been until his body shivered with the return cold. He'd walked the entire ring of the house and barely felt a chill, but now the room was more seasonable. Bitter and biting. Made him want to return to his bed, and bury his body beneath layers of blankets.

"What was that?" Alice asked this time, looking around herself.

"What was what?"

"I thought—I thought I felt something," her words whispered by the end.

"Something?" He hoped he sounded more sympathetic than simply curious, but judging by the look his mother threw him, he'd missed the mark.

As she was going to reply, the girl jumped forward, squeaking. "Something–something touched me."

Given he could see there was nothing and no one behind her, John was ready to dismiss her and blame an overactive imagination. But Alice wasn't the type to be easily rattled. Especially not by a few bangs. He pulled her closer, just in case. Hopefully, it was something negligible, like a stray draft or a spider. He eyed the back of her nightdress but saw no possible explanation. As a growl reverberated around the room, they all jumped in unison.

"Not again." If he'd been further away, he would have missed his mother's words. Horror painted her face.

Scratches came from somewhere. Rats were common enough John would normally ignore such sounds, but these moved. A single claw dragged over the walls, not the scurrying of rodent feet. The sound altered, as the thing moved across the wall; over the uneven boards before the entirely different wood of the door frame. The sound distinctively changed from the drag of the walls to the smooth beams which framed the kitchen from the dining area.

The issue being, if it were rats, the smooth wood didn't extend into the walls. It was mostly decorative. Adding a little extra structure. What he'd assumed was in the walls must have been moving along them. Right in front of him. Directly where he was looking. Yet John could see nothing.

"What is going on?"

Another growl came. Closer this time. Like it was standing near by. Among them.

"Ow!" he couldn't help exclaiming. Turning his head to see what he had caught himself on. Expecting to see maybe a jutted-out nail or a low-hanging hook.

When he found nothing, he was more confused than anything. Extending his arm over his shoulder, he felt for where he experienced the pain. The burning sensation. He was glad when he withdrew his hand and it wasn't stained with red, but this only led to more confusion. It hurt. John thought he'd caught himself on something. Enough to split the skin or leave a visible welt.

The sensation came again, like a burn dragging down his back. Unlacing the top of his nightshirt, he looked to where the sensation was coming from. Caught himself in the mirror as he idly watched three claw marks appeared on his skin. Travelling over his shoulder and trailing down his body.

"Jesus, John?"

"Christopher, language," his mother snapped.

"Not the time, Darling. Where did that come from?"

He opened his mouth, but words refused to leave. John had no idea. Logically it shouldn't have come from anywhere. Nothing physical could have done this.

The growl came for a third time.

The scratching sound started again. This time going in the reverse direction. John had the strangest sensation they were being played with. Like a snake keeping its prey running around in a trapped circle, waiting for its meal to tire itself out. Then strike. As the invisible thing moved closer to the front door, he heard as it reached the mirror. It must not have been satisfying to scratch though, as they heard once more three knocks. The entire thing moving to the right. John had helped his father put that mirror up. Had taken the pair of them thirty minutes because they could barely move its weight between them. What was this thing who could move the silvered glass like it was nothing more than a hand mirror?

"Jane."

His mother squeaked. The disembodied thing calling her name.

"Who's there?" his father demanded. "Whoever you are, we don't want any of your nonsense. I've–" He paused. "I've got a gun and I will use it."

John's eyebrow raised. His dad having a gun was news to him. The man refused to let anything potentially dangerous be near his wife. A shadow moved to their left, making Alice jump. The girl clung to him. John wasn't sure what to do in this situation. Instructions for protecting your potential fiancée had not covered invisible threats. When the growling came again, he felt the air on his neck, letting out a noise his mother would have been envious of.

The kitchen cupboards flew open behind them. John was glad he wasn't the only one to scream as things around them began to shake. The rattling of the pots, pans and tableware were an unholy symphony, announcing this thing's joy. John could have sworn he heard the cackling amongst the screech of iron against iron.

"Jane–play–" The words were distorted, but whatever was here, it had an interest in his mother.

His mother dashed forward into the kitchen. Grabbing a bag from the kitchen before emptying it. Throwing salt all around them. His mother had a glint in her eyes that made even John want to hide the knives.

It took a few moments, but the room came to a standstill, all the air stagnated as everything waited for what might come next.

"Jane?" his father asked this time.

"I heard it wards off spirits. Didn't know if it was true or not. Worth a try when that thing kept coming at us."

His father scoffed. "My wife, the secret witch."

It was said in jest, but John noted the flinch his mother gave.

"Do you think–?" Alice asked quietly.

"Well, we couldn't see it, but the room certainly feels different."

"We need to do something whilst it's stopped."

"Like what?"

"Do we need to get the priest?" his father asked, trying to regain some sense of control over the situation.

Not that sitting at their kitchen table surrounded by a circle of salt could ever be seen as a controlled situation.

"It's too late. He'll be long retired for the night," his mother pointed out.

It was likely gone midnight now, or he hoped as much. Midnight was a powerful hour for the spirits he'd read somewhere. Probably in one of the old priest's religious texts. Or was it three a.m. which was referenced? If so, they might be in for a second showing in a few short hours.

"Do you think it's gone?" Alice said, more to him than his parents.

John paused, not wanting to lie to the girl, but afraid to give sound to his thoughts. "The thing, it felt like it was toying with us. Enjoying our reactions. I expect it will return simply to have us on edge. To keep us thinking we aren't safe."

Sometimes, John deeply disliked his own honest nature. The way Alice's entire body seemed to curl in on itself—as though by burrowing in on herself, she might be protected from this potential reality—was agonising to witness.

"The witches?" Christopher sounded genuinely desperate (John could relate).

His father wasn't on bad terms with either of the local cunning women, but he always took to avoiding them. To keep a few yards of distance between them and him, even when it would make more sense to pass them by.

John remembered thinking it was as though the women held some invisible force field and his father was trying to avoid crossing into it. He himself never sensed such things, but his father's continued avoidance was hard to ignore. For him to consider inviting these women into his home, spoke of just how rattled the man truly was.

"They'll have to do. We don't have much choice." His mother, ever the voice of reason in the storm of life.

"Right. Yes. John, go to Old Demdike's. Chattox is half blind in the daylight, and Malkin Tower is closest. Go. Make that batty old wench come and help. I'll give her three days of drinking money if she comes tonight."

From his father, that was a big promise. John didn't need to be told twice. As much as he wanted to take Alice away with him, exposed to the elements, she'd be as vulnerable outside as in. At least the salt was doing something for now. Or maybe the thing was still playing. Either way, he needed to get help. Taking a candle, he ran out into the dark. The moon was covered once again by the clouds. He could only hope they kept the water in the heavens. He did not want to be drenched on top of everything else.

Nowhere was safe on Halloween night. Especially Pendle's rolling hills. John was willing to risk the wrath of the wild folk rather than return to that house. A few tricky spirits were better than one demonic entity any day. The potential dangers of bottomless pits and shifting sands were nothing in comparison to having your soul feast upon by one of the devil's minions.

CHAPTER NINE

Negotiating the hills of Pendle was difficult enough in daylight, but in the dark of night, it was nigh impossible. Not without help. Demdike debated which of her family to take along with her. Apprehensive for each of them. Lizzie was too afraid to be much use; the woman was jumpy and prone to overreaction at the best of times. James was easily distracted and would be more likely to try to befriend the being than realise any potential dangers. Alizon was close to coming into her powers and a spirit (demonic or otherwise), attaching itself to her now could be especially detrimental to the child. Then there was Jennet, who looked like she was ready to keel over at any moment. The child had barely turned nine and at this late hour was too tired to keep her eyes open.

Despite the potential dangers, the only real option was Alizon. Even if the girl might earn the interest of the spirit, she was the least likely to cause any problems during Demdike's work.

"Al, I need you to get the bag under my bed. Lizzie, I need some of the sage, salt and iron. James, you and your sister get to bed. You have work early and she's dead on her feet."

She could see the boy wanted to protest, but at the mention of his job, had agreed.

"John, are you okay to walk us back to your home?"

"Mum's house. Not mine," the boy-man croaked.

He looked so young, not in age, but in spirit. Reverting to a child-like state when forced to face beings and creatures, his innocent mind could not fully comprehend. Demdike had witnessed such things happen to those walking the grey path when first encountering a dark spirit with malicious intent. Seen how, when the person returned to themselves, they were too shaken for their logical adult minds to process what they'd experienced. This was where many gifted people left the craft. Not able or willing to regularly interact and do battle with such negative beings.

Demdike never shied away from a fight. When she first encountered true evil, she had not been shaken. Rather, it invigorated her. The warrior in her soul rose with the challenge, ready to do battle. Such aspects of her inner self had kept Demdike alive through the darkest days. When others crumbled and succumbed, she stubbornly endured. Pushed forward. Refused to give ground or give in.

You could not back down against a spirit. They would use any and every potential weakness, showing no mercy. Demdike quickly learnt she needed to meet them blow for blow. You couldn't show kindness. Or allow any form of leniency. This only gave them the ability to stay clawed into their victims.

Demdike knew to always uproot everything a spirit might latch onto. Destroy every attachment they tried to form. She'd burnt many dolls, paintings and physical remains in her career. She wondered what they would need to destroy today. When Alizon returned with her bag, and her daughter handed over the other necessities, she guided the boy back to his feet and out of the home.

"Tell us everything on the way."

Demdike would happily have returned to her bed. Going out to a spiritual fight whilst tired and having spent hours giving readings was not ideal. Were there any other options, she would have told the boy to wait until the morning. However, by the look on his face, she was needed immediately. Her third eye could see the hook on the boy's back. Where the darkness was trying to latch onto him. She would need to deal with this, too. But better to wait and see the scene before taking action. Best not to tip the being off as to her abilities before the fight started.

As John began his story, Demdike was mildly worried about Alizon's keen interest. Hadn't they been discussing such things a few days earlier? She truly hoped the girl wouldn't try to ask the thing questions. It would be just her luck to keep James behind, only for Alizon to do the exact same thing Demdike feared he would.

Fortunately, John's stuttering sentences kept Alizon from asking too many invasive questions. Though Demdike made a mental note of how much the man appeared to fear for his mother and friend but barely blinked at any potential dangers toward the father. Cracks in families were hardly rare, but spirits capitalised upon emotional tears. Places for beings to sink their hooks into and whisper violent words whilst they warped the minds of their victims.

By his description, it could be any manner of beings. Definitely sounded like the thing was toying with them. Many spirits didn't care for humans. Enjoyed playing with them for their own amusement. It wasn't necessarily done with malintent, but simply because they could. Many spirits didn't like people. Didn't want them on their land. The attacks were an extension of this discontent.

The fae enjoyed irritating people, as they had been doing with her earlier. Then there were ghosts who were not always aware of what they were doing. Some were intelligent and enjoyed causing reactions, whereas others were unaware they'd even passed and were either going about their day as normal or attacking the people they saw as the intruders. Not malicious, but a situation of crossed wires and confusion. Poltergeists were usually human souls turned malevolent. Or maybe they'd been evil before death and losing their body simply allowed them to act without fear of repercussions. If it was one of them blighters, she'd be in for a long night.

The description of scratching along walls and being mistaken for rats, though, gave her a clue to the most likely suspect. Shadows and shaking could have been any manner of beings. But something which toyed with its victims whilst scratching and banging. The fae were more subtle than this. Ghosts were not so powerful. She couldn't rule out poltergeists, but there was a more likely option, demons. Or what people now labelled demons.

Demdike really, truly hated these malevolent entities. They were a nightmare to clear out. Like an infestation. Whether rats, ants, or flies, 'demons' were the same. You had to find the nest—where they had entered and set down roots—and destroy it. If not, they would find a way to return. Exhausting work (and often dirty).

The church bells were audible in the fields between her home and the Bulcock's residence. Two gongs. Later than she thought. No wonder Demdike's body was crying for rest. The elderly woman needed to hurry, though. They didn't want to wait until gone three. The beings of darkness drew power from that hour. Demdike didn't know why, but couldn't ignore the pattern she'd noticed over the many years. Three in the morning, whilst the veil was thin, could only mean bad things.

She fought the mildly amused smirk, trying to break free at the corner of her mouth, as she entered the house. Three grown adults huddled in a circle of salt. Clutching at one another. This spoke of a harrowing experience—one she should not laugh about. No matter the image they painted. Demdike was surprised they would know of salt protections. It was common knowledge in certain circles, but she hadn't expected the Bulcock's to know this. Normally, it was better to layer the salt around the entrances of the home. Though with it already being inside, this would have been a little redundant. Someone in the room knowing this made her brow raise.

The air vibrated with discomfort. Tangible, as though Demdike could have reached out her hand and grabbed the threads binding the people. Chains to their troubles. Whatever was here, it relished in their fear. Talking with Jane and Christopher gave Demdike a few more context clues. Something dark and wild was here. Definitely not a poltergeist.

"And then it hurt John's shoulder," the father said, pointing to his son.

She wanted to smack the boy. Why hadn't he mentioned the thing scratched him personally? This explained the dark miasma she could see, but it would've been nice to know the why. Their story—combined with the energies she could feel—confirmed her suspicions. This was most definitely malevolent in nature, something evil, what most would label demon.

Many dark spirits were called demons because they weren't nice, regardless of their true natures. Demdike believed most so-called demons were various species of spirits. Not a singular type. However, her philosophical wonderings had no bearing on what she was here to do. What most would call demons were powerful malevolent hauntings which enjoyed taunting humans, consuming energy and mocking anything the humans held sacred. Such as the church and all its beliefs.

Whatever dwelled here, no matter what name she gave it, meant to harm. To cause strife to the living souls. She would need to keep her wits about her. Demdike instructed the others to stay within the salt circle as she began to work.

Opening her bag, Demdike placed several items on the table. Specifically, telling Alizon to stay with the others. She debated telling the girl to stay quiet and not to engage with whatever might happen, but her granddaughter had the annoying habit of doing the opposite of whatever she was told.

Sadly, it wasn't even malicious. Demdike noticed this years ago. If you mentioned something to the child, it was as though the seed was planted. Whether or not you told her to do something, it was as though her brain ignored the '*do*' or '*do not*' aspect and spent time merely ruminating on the concept. Kept the idea until the child burst with the need to do or say whatever was mentioned. Again, regardless of whether she told the child to '*yes, do this*' or '*no, don't do this*'.

It was handy when Demdike wanted to hint at (politely manipulate) the girl to do something important. But if you told the girl not to say something, you could guarantee at some point within the next hour, it would be spilling from her lips. Thus, Demdike said nothing. Didn't tell the girl not to speak with the demon, despite how much she wanted to.

It wasn't long before the activities started and the spirit made itself known. A few gusts of wind were easily overlooked at first. The odd knocks could be excused as someone moving without realising. Alizon's restless legs definitely caused one or two of the sounds, but not the others. When the growls came, even Demdike struggled not to jump. Instinct demanded she find the cause of the threat and remove it.

Demdike knew there were no canines in here, and yet, her eyes still expected to see some dark-furred creature on four legs when she turned around. The blank space was not a surprise as much as she half-hoped there would have been a physical presence. Give her a physical threat she could stab any day.

When the scratching on the walls started, Demdike knew it was time to step up. She wished the thing could have waited until tomorrow morning. When she would have had a good night's rest and been recharged enough to do battle. Though life rarely gave the luxury of fitting into a preferred schedule. One thing she and Chattox agreed on; events happened as they happened. It was how you reacted in the moment which made all the difference. She kept her bag always packed for just such occasions. You might not be able to plan when these things happened, but you could ensure you were as prepared as possible.

Raising the wooden stick, she imbued it with her spiritual power. The light of the astral plane which travelled through her body and into her weapon. Some might call her stick of hawthorn a wand, others a focus item. Didn't matter what label they attached to it, merely its purpose. A battle sword against the other side, a powerful weapon against attacking spirits. Taking a second stick of rowan wood, she made a cross with the two.

Not the cross believed to be Christ's death, but the real one, which looked like an 'X'. Some of the cunning folk believed it linked to the runes and had older origins, but she cared less about the histories than she did the results. Hissing soon followed. Malevolent entities would respond negatively to positive energies and anything perceived as spiritual or holy. From the rising noise, she could tell it was angry.

"Get thee gone, spirit," Demdike spoke sternly.

She moved the cross back and forth in the air. Eventually, she would walk the full floor, but to start with she remained stationary, testing the strength of her opponent. Other than a howling outside, which she hoped was simply the wind, it seemed to have quietened. Were it not for the assessing gaze she could feel burning into her body, Demdike might have thought it gone. The thing was weighing her up as equally as she was it.

The creature was enjoying itself. Entertained by the house's residents' responses. It hadn't expected her presence, but the threat of a fight didn't put it off. She was simply as a new toy to play with. Demdike never cared to be underestimated.

When a loud bang came from the kitchen, she spun around to face it. There was a breath on her neck. Turning directly back around, she saw the others were all still within the circle. There was either more than one being here—which was a possibility, infestations were rarely singular—or this being was significantly more powerful than your average haunting. Demdike didn't like either option.

Hauntings were like wounds. Once infected, the more germs gathered. This general rule would have confirmed her thoughts of there being more than one spirit here. However, the Bulcock's had already stated nothing occurred before today. If this place had been open enough to be infected by multiple spirits, there would have been signs prior to this night. Halloween alone couldn't account for all this increase in activity. Something was off.

Demdike couldn't have transcribed her instincts into any human language. The best comparison she could manage, was like when you're asleep and it feels wrong, even if you don't yet know you're dreaming. As though everything was tilted slightly to the side, or the furniture had been moved a few centimetres to the left, everything still appeared the same, but you kept tripping over details because something wasn't right.

When a growl came from beside her, Demdike chose to act as though there was only one spirit. If there were more she could deal with them another time. There was a big bad here, and it was ready to play. She threw blessed water about the room and heard the hissing once again. It wasn't technically holy water, but water she'd channelled spiritual power into. A concoction blessed under the light of the full moon and in which she'd steeped multiple herbs. Demdike might even (not-so) humbly claim it was more powerful than most holy water.

Half the priests barely believed in the God they claimed to serve—the money and the power of more interest than the book they spouted from. Men who held no spiritual power and could barely make real holy water even with the scriptures to follow. Although Demdike could acknowledge the few trained exorcists she'd met were actually gifted. Either way, her blessed water was enough to weaken dark spirits, better than anything she could get from the local church. She liberally splashed it across the room. Happy to see a shadow physically move as it was hit with the spray.

"Over there," a shrill voice said behind her, pointing towards the door.

Demdike crept where instructed. This thing could hide at will. These were not simple parlour tricks. Which meant this was not some run-of-the-mill spirit. It was a powerhouse. To attack twice in one night and be only mildly hurt by her wares... This shadowy creature was something to fear.

"Alizon, I want you to burn that dried sage. Stay in the circle, but use the flint to light it and waft the smoke about you. I need to weaken this thing."

As Demdike drew near the door, her attention became drawn to the large mirror. The reflected image warped as it held her gaze. Her reflection melted like her being was spilling down the edges of a candle. Words she couldn't understand were spoken. The language might have been too much for her mortal mind, but malicious intent was something easily understood regardless of the tongue it was spoken in. She threw the water at the mirror, breaking the trance. The mirror would need to go.

This thing wanted to draw her in. Trap her. Demdike was not some little tyke. She'd trained in the art of the spirit world for decades. The creature would need to do better than soul-trapping to hold her. As a burn came up her arm, it was Demdike's turn to hiss.

"Al, John, Jane and Christopher. I need you to each take a bit of sage and salt and go to the four corners of the room." The entire downstairs was open plan so technically she meant the four corners of the house, but she wasn't overly concerned with specifics. Seeing the hesitance on their faces, she snapped at them.

"Quickly, or do you want this thing to get worse? We must be nearing three a.m. by now. And if you think this bastard was powerful before, it'll be nothing compared to what will happen then."

As though she lit a fire under the four, they each followed her instruction.

"Alice, was it?" Demdike asked.

The girl still seated looked like a breath of wind would be enough to knock her over.

"Could you keep a hold of these charms?" She handed the girl three separate objects. "When I need them, I'll ask for them, but I can't afford to have to root around for them when we're busy trying to fight this thing."

The girl hesitantly nodded. She didn't look well, her pallor more ghostly than English rose. When the four returned to the circle, Demdike splashed some water over each of them. She gave Christopher a look before the man even had time to protest. She wasn't in the mood for anyone's rubbish. Demdike couldn't afford to become distracted.

"I'm going to bless each corner now. You lot ensure the herbs keep burning."

She started with the north corner. Saying a prayer and blessing, sprinkling some of her water. Moving to the west, then south and east, sprinkling the water as she went and repeating the same process. As she returned to the table, the bangs from the kitchen began again. This creature wasn't giving up. Were she not so tired, Demdike might have enjoyed the challenge. It'd been many years since she tackled something of this calibre. However, the thrill of the fight was lost on her aching limbs and sluggish mind.

"The metal one," she said to the girl, who shakily extended the small charm.

A coin, symbolic of paying the ferryman to move the spirit along. She held it up chanting the ritual words for aiding a lost spirit. She doubted this thing was lost. But if it had gathered energy by stealing from lost spirits, this would help drain it of those power sources.

"The stone," she demanded next.

A small piece of agate, banded with many colours. Oranges, reds and browns. It had come from her great-great-grandmother, passed down matrilineally. The woman had supposedly received it as a wedding gift from a foreign merchant. Whatever its history, Demdike knew it was perfect for directing negative energies. The small stone could capture them or move them elsewhere. Disrupting the spirit's body and its power over the physical realm.

The bangs ceased as she moved toward the kitchen area. Stone extended forth in her right hand. It carried its own spiritual powers, but she regularly charged it with light from the sun and moon. Placing it gently on the counter, she finally asked for the rosary.

Demdike wasn't a priest, but God helped his children. And they needed his aid now. As she spoke the 'Our Father' prayer, the shakings of the cupboards grew more violent. Throwing blessed water, she kept up her chant. Imagined the entire house engulfed in a holy light which nothing with ill intent could remain within. Asking God to banish this evil from whence it came. She pushed her own power into the cross of her rosary and directed it toward the kitchen. The screams were unpleasant. But she could show no mercy. Give no quarter. This thing meant to harm. It was her or it, and Demdike refused to lose at her own craft.

Nobody moved or spoke for several long minutes. No one dared to break the peace. All waiting to see if the monster was playing another game and faking defeat. When, after five minutes, nothing happened, Demdike finally relaxed. Sitting back at the table. Her body ached with exhaustion. She was getting far too old for this.

"Marked by darkness, never a good thing." She shook her head.

Why certain spirits did this, she could only guess. Demdike had worked with the dead long enough to assume the reasons behind them. The physical marks were not necessary, not really. If they wanted to attach themselves to a soul, there were much less obvious ways to do so. Ways in which the attach-ee would remain unaware of.

The markings, in her experience, served two purposes: warning away other beings from their prey, and secondly, to act like a homing beacon for the spirit to find the person again at a later date. But again, the beings did not need to leave a physical presence. Therefore, Demdike formed the opinion that the physical marks were simply to cause fear and panic. A mark from nowhere would be concerning. Physical pain was unpleasant, especially when the marked didn't know where the scratches came from. It left the individual confused. Sure, some might brush it off, but most who received the scratches were fully aware they were being haunted.

"It kept saying my name," Jane piped in, the others nodding in agreement.

Demdike's face scrunched. Things weren't fitting as they should. Not as they had in her previous experience. Although there were spirits across the world she'd never encountered and knew nothing of, in England, she was an expert. Demdike couldn't know everything, but she knew a lot. A being could have come from elsewhere and settled here, it wasn't impossible, but this thing had all the marks of a demonic haunting. Yet, it still didn't fit quite right.

Hauntings generally followed a pattern of behaviour. They typically started off small and escalated over time. Building and building as the beast played with its victims. Drawing pleasure and amusement from people's fear. Why would it suddenly attack the boy who claimed to have no prior experience with the thing?

This entire situation was odd. John didn't live here, and he seemed genuine about not having experienced anything like this before. In theory, his mother should have been the one to receive the marks. If the creature was attached to Jane and interested in her, why had it scratched John? Had the boy simply been in the way?

"Well, tomorrow I'd advise you to bathe in holy water, or at least ask the priest for a blessing. I have a bit of holy water and oils to tie us over, but a priest can ensure nothing is left behind."

"What use are you, then?" Christopher scoffed, as though he hadn't spent the past hour cowering.

"There are a lot more spirits than demons out there. And most people just lump all spirits as the same thing. Which they really ain't. Think of me as a jack of all trades who can deal with all spirits but a priest as a specialist in the real nasty ones. I can cast them out and put up protections, which should work as well, but demons like to return. Like to torment their victims. If it's been once, it will come again. And my trinkets will eventually wear down. A priest can banish the thing, better than these old bones. I can ward it away and keep it at bay, but he should check the entire home."

"You're like the cleaner and he's the nail in the coffin?"

"Yes and no, with enough time and ingredients, I could do what the priest does, but I don't have the spare money to stay fully stocked for every potential spiritual attack."

Technically, she just refused to go down into the foundation of the home. Her knees were too old for such things. The priest could do that. She'd banished the thing for the time being. He could do the rest. But she didn't want to come out and directly do such things.

"So it's about money?" Christopher scoffed.

"No, it's about me being old and exhausted after a long day and the priest being rested and ready in the morning," she spat back.

The man flinched, lowering his head. Demdike wanted to say more, but she was genuinely exhausted, and something still was not sitting right with her.

"It is strange, though. Well, it is unusual," she corrected herself. "To mark one but call another, typically ghosts, poltergeists or demons are attached to a place or person. Sometimes a physical object. This haunting is strange."

"Why?" John asked, holding the girl, Alice, in a protective hug.

"Well, hauntings can happen in families, it's true, but this here was just." She paused, searching for the right word. "Odd."

"Why?"

She could see Mr Bulcock's frustration when asking, but Demdike was struggling to connect the dots herself. Like a piece of the puzzle just beyond her mind's eye.

"Why, because it's after John." A small smirk twitched at the side of her mouth in the face of the other's building anger.

"But why? Why would you think this was strange?" Jane asked this time, much more politely.

"Because John doesn't live here. It chose tonight. When he was here."

"But, Nana Demy, it was Halloween. Maybe that's why it did it tonight?" her granddaughter, ever the insightful, piped up.

"Maybe, but it doesn't feel right."

"Feel right?" Christopher didn't even bother to hide his discontent at her reply.

"Aye. It feels purposeful. Like Halloween just gave it the strength to do what it planned all along. Lke it's been lying in wait. That tonight is All Hallow's Eve—or All Saints Day since its past midnight—feels entirely secondary to its motivations."

"You can sense that?"

"Aye." She couldn't have put it into words. It was like when someone was angry at you but kept a blank face. Or when someone stood behind you, but you hadn't seen or heard them. Some deeper sense of knowing able to pick up on the energies a person wasn't consciously aware of processing. "Not 'cause it was Halloween, but because he was here. I wonder why." She spoke more to herself, not acknowledging the others in the room.

"Was there something special about tonight? I didn't see you at the festival?"

Demdike hadn't thought about it earlier, but now she looked back. The family had been absent from the event. Jane always came for a reading on Halloween. She hadn't noted her absence during the night, but now she looked at them, waiting for an answer.

"It was our first time meeting young Alice. Properly at least," Jane said, pointing to the girl.

Demdike had almost entirely forgotten her presence. The girl was silent as a shadow. Everyone knew everyone in Pendle and from gossip; Demdike knew the son and Alice had been friends for years. Rumours of their recent change to courting were confirmed, but was it important to tonight?

"Quite the welcome," she couldn't help but joke.

The young woman gave a breathy smile. Not a scoff but as close as was polite.

"So, John comes home for the first time in months, with his sweetheart and this being decides to play up? Hmmm."

Demdike was confused. There were spirits who were possessive of humans. Beings who claimed humans as their own—whether through obsessive love or the desire to destroy them, and who were often damaging to the chosen person—but this didn't have the typical signs.

"You've definitely never been haunted before?" she asked John again.

Could the boy have been oblivious to something such as this?

"No. Nothing like this has ever happened."

Like this—*like this*. The phrase caught her attention. "Like this?" she prompted.

"No banging or scratches. Things going missing, or noise, but nothing that couldn't be explained away or didn't have a cause."

She nodded. Everyday events. Nothing to raise any immediate red flags. Which brought her back to the '*hurting Jane*' theory. Looking at the woman, she could see how her shoulders were pulled in on herself. The temporary theory she formed about John being attacked because he was important to Jane held some weight. The attack would keep him from the home and lead to further isolation of the woman for the entity to latch onto. Demdike wasn't discounting the theory, but she wasn't entirely convinced either.

"Jane, do you have a warm drink? My old bones could do with a little warming," she requested, leading the other into the kitchen away from the others.

"Aye, my love, a cup of warm milk and a drop of whiskey," Christopher called after them.

She did not miss the twitch John gave at the request. Interesting, but not relevant. When they were away from the others, she gave the woman a sharp look. Communicating '*spill*' without opening her mouth.

"You have to understand–"

Demdike fought not to sigh. If she received a coin, for every time she heard those words in her career as a cunning woman, she would have actually been able to retire many years ago. No, she did not need to understand. She didn't care. It wasn't Demdike's place to judge. She held her tongue her entire life. Never shared the many secrets she'd discovered. But of course, few knew this, because the people she held secrets for wouldn't tell others she was a great secret keeper.

"Peace, Jane. You will find no judgment from me. I simply need all the information."

"Many years ago, I was sick," the woman stressed.

'*Sick*' had many connotations. Waiting for the other to continue, Demdike leaned against the counter, keeping her face polite and her body language open.

"I love my son, I do. But back then, something went wrong. The doctor said it was not uncommon for new mothers to have negative reactions to their babies." Despite the words, Demdike could hear the shame the woman still held.

"Aye, it's common enough. One in twenty women I've helped have strange reactions. Some refused to let another person touch the child, and others physically throw themselves away so as to not touch the babe."

Jane took a long, slow breath. "I was the latter. In my mind, in my heart, I did not think my son to be my child."

Demdike nodded. They must have kept the secret pretty well for her to not have heard about it. That or they'd called on Chattox, though this wasn't the time for thinking about their rivalry.

"What does this—"

"I learnt to not always trust my mind. During this time, I saw things, heard things, felt things. Things others did not. Things which were not real."

The image was forming before her. Demdike had to hold in the sigh. A person with a history of a broken mind was often a favourite for the beasts. Playing games with them as the people feared they were reverting and doubting the realities before them. At least things were finally making a little more sense.

"John, he doesn't remember, thank God, but it has left scars. Scars on me, on the relationship with my husband. Between the two men as well."

A torn family in an already tense situation, with a mother trying to compensate for the child's infancy even now. The puzzle pieces were slotting together. Hurting the child when it was what Jane still feared would cause the woman great pain. Especially if she felt responsible once more. As much as Demdike wanted to say '*The spirit is using your guilt to anchor itself*', she'd played this game long enough. People who already felt guilty didn't simply stop because you told them to.

"We will do what we can to ensure it does not return, but Jane, you must keep yourself safe. Can you move in with your son for a few days? Getting away from the home might help with protecting you both from the beast."

A lie, but if the woman was more focused on keeping her son safe, it would help her try to remove the anchors. She would have the priest tackle the home, but would need to work directly with Jane. Away from her family's influence.

"What about my Christopher? He won't be safe here alone."

Honestly, Demdike hadn't thought of the man. He was more than capable of taking care of himself. The darkness had little to no interest in him.

"He could go with you," she suggested gently.

"I doubt John would like that."

Demdike would not scream. She was a fully grown adult. She would not. No matter how tired or frustrated she might be, she was a professional. A cunning woman. She would maintain her mask. She could scream on the inside, like all good adults.

"After the priest has been, come to Malkin Tower. We don't want you being vulnerable, especially if alone."

This at least had the woman nodding.

"Will John be okay?" it was asked so earnestly, Demdike couldn't have snapped no matter how tempted she might have been

"He will be fine. I'll rub a balm on his shoulder to heal the skin. And give him a charm to wear to protect him from anything attaching itself. I've already thrown some holy water over the mark, but ask the priest when you see him. He'll ensure nothing is able to return."

Demdike didn't like having to keep discussing the priest option, but it would help reassure them. The priests were the known protection from such things, and Demdike had learnt over the years how this helped them all. The sufferers, the priests who would otherwise scorn her work, and herself, as they, working in symbiosis, helped keep them all safe.

She would need to ensure neither she nor Alizon brought anything supernatural home with them.

CHAPTER TEN

Yule was a strange time in Pendle. Long-held traditions were mostly pagan in nature, not Christian. However, if asked, every resident of their little settlement would have claimed themselves as good god-fearing folk. Perhaps not devout Christians, but most definitely good ones.

Yule and Christmas were terms used interchangeably. *'Merry Yule', 'Merry Christmas'. 'Have a great Yuletide', 'Have a great Christmas'.* These were sentiments, blessings, shared happily between the locals. Most even meant the words they said. Wishing their fellow (wo)man a pleasant Yule. Hoping they would be happy and healthy when they all went through the darkest days of the year.

Yuletide was odd because it was a mix of the old(e) world and Christianity. Filled with traditions which had been a part of their little isle for hundreds, maybe even thousands, of years. Burning the Yule log had nothing to do with Christ, and yet it was done in every home to ward away bad spirits and ensure they protected the home through the coming winter.

Pies filled with dried fruit and sugar had little to do with the birth of a God onto the human plane and were more reminiscent of the tree kings swapping their crowns. But they didn't speak of this fact outside of plays and entertainment. *'Mince'* pies were a seasonal treat, alongside a cake that was only enjoyed at this time of year. Cake and treats were a rarity for all. Christmas cake, or Christmas pudding, was mostly reserved for the wealthy. Yet even the poorest of families indulged in sweet treats and these small luxuries in the dark days because it was a reminder of celebrating life whilst still living.

For all Samhain was about celebrating the dead and the two worlds being at their closest, Yule was the time you were most likely to die. Of natural causes, at least. Eating something sweet wasn't simply a pleasure. They served them as a reminder of life getting better, of knowing how, although they were living through the hardest times right then, the good times would come again. Spring showers and summer sunshine would always return once more.

Yule was about bringing brightness and hope to the dark times. They hung up bits of twine and coloured cloth around the home. Used twigs and scraps to represent stars and angels. Anything to make the world look brighter and prettier than it was in these months. With the lack of flowers and foliage, the world was dark and depressing, the hanging ornaments and decorations were a way to remind everyone to keep their spirits up. A way of silently celebrating even when people were busy performing other tasks and continuing on with everyday life. A constant reminder to try and stay positive.

Demdike in her many years on this planet had long thought of Yule as the worst and best holiday. The day the wheel turned, and the world was at its darkness so they might once more return to the light. *'We turn from darkness back to light.'* The words she whispered over the burning hearth every year on this day.

As she watched her granddaughter speak the sentiments—the ones the girl had seen her perform previously—it filled the aged woman with a strange melancholy. She wouldn't get to see this day again. Demdike knew it in her bones. Like she knew the rain was coming and the storm would pass. The future was playing out before her, and she would not be around to witness it.

As a young child, she'd loved Yule. It was the day her family made the best food. Meat was always guaranteed, and sweet treats were a must. Money and food hadn't been in scarcity back then. Though her father hadn't been a wealthy man, he'd been a well-respected person in the local community. No one would even think of denying to pay him for any labour he'd done. They weren't wealthy, but she hadn't known the pains of hunger until after he passed.

Demdike had been barely older than Alizon when her father left this world. Without a man's support, a younger Elizabeth soon understood all the dangers she was in. One of which being how difficult it could be to put food on the table when you didn't have a man to stand as your protection in a male-dominated world. Her mother and extended family did their best, but even at that age, she'd understood the vulnerabilities of not having male protection in a patriarchal society.

Demdike had still married for love, still been happy, but it hadn't lasted. She'd had to harden herself as the world demanded. Couldn't afford to be soft and gentle. Hadn't the luxury of weakness. The world forced Demdike to sharpen her edges. Become a jagged stone. She'd been unrefined as a child. Wild and curious, but still painfully naïve. Sheltered in ways she'd never known. Only once that security was gone did she realise the dangers of the world in which she lived.

A younger Demdike had remained outspoken, quick to anger, and oblivious in ways she was, to this day, surprised they didn't beat her for. Life was a hard mistress, and it'd beaten her in other ways. Forced to face the harsh realities as a young widower and single mother. Forced to see how those happy Yules had been a rare blessing, not the standard.

Just thinking about it angered her. How things had once been rosy. She went back and forth, wondering if it was better or worse to have had that taste of a better life. Her grandchildren expected little because they'd never known more. For all she struggled to improve their lives, there were too many roadblocks—too many people who wanted to keep them in the dirt—to let them truly escape.

When James lost his job a few days prior, she hadn't even pretended to be surprised. It devastated the boy, asking what he'd done wrong. She hadn't known how to tell him it wasn't him. It might have been her, and people's paranoia ramping up—something she wasn't out ruling—but it was more than likely the people at the top wanted to keep them at the bottom. If James did well, and had money, he could pull his family up with him, something they would never allow.

When her Lizzie got some work over at the mill, Demdike held her breath. Little Grace had succumbed to her illness. Richard Baldwyn had been no friend to them before this, and with Helen in mourning, the man had become crueller than ever before. Demdike felt no surprise when a few days later her daughter had come to her, head bowed and watery eyed, declaring how the man refused to pay. Tears then streamed as Lizzie told her how she'd laboured away, worked herself to the bone, and came away with nothing to show for it. Demdike had gone to see him. The man calling her a witch and a whore hadn't been pleasant, though she'd blasted the man right back.

"Aye, maybe I am. Curse your bloody useless hide and let you rot in the grave you've been digging with that wicked tongue of yours."

Wishing she could lay a true curse on the man, but he was in mourning. As angry as she felt, as unjust as the situation was, Demdike couldn't bring herself to wield that level of malevolence in his direction. Oh, she was sure the fury would come, eventually, but for now, she was too tired. Too exhausted with existing to keep fighting these useless battles.

When Baldwyn called her a witch, it unsettled her more than Demdike was willing to show. Not in front of her daughter and definitely not to him. Step two, when the whispers became words spoken in anger. When the accusations would start. They often used witch as a derogatory term. A way of calling a woman something lesser. Something foul. Like a whore or a harlot. '*Witch*' was another way of calling a woman promiscuous and damned.

Demdike had been called a witch many times in her life. She would typically bat away the words, shouting something equally condemning in return. Normally, she'd have laughed it off. However, this accusation felt loaded, as though he were trying to call God down to judge her soul. He likely would have refused to pay, regardless, but after Grace's death, the man was laying his loss and misfortune at her feet. Baldwyn was calling her the thing that'd brought ruin to his family. He was casting the first stone.

This hadn't been a simple word spoken in anger. It had been a pointed comment. An accusation. The old woman hadn't expected step two to come this quickly, and yet, as much as it shocked her in the moment, she wasn't surprised. Not of the words and not of the source. It was a strange mix of relief and worry to know this was happening.

She was angry. The man was hurting her daughter, hurting her family, unjustly, but to him, he was simply returning the favour. He was taking a small dose of revenge. Demdike doubted it would end there. The man wouldn't simply spit a few words and deny a few coins. No, this was a personal vendetta. The eyes of Goldshaw Booth had become burning gazes every time she stepped outside her home. Where usually Yule was a time of generosity and greater charity, goodwill to all men, their begging had yielded little result.

Sending Alizon over to Colne had been a saving grace. She'd gotten enough money and fruit to see them through Yule, but it left a sour taste in Demdike's mouth. The only consolation was how Chattox did little better. Troubled gazes landed on the other cunning woman as much as they did Demdike. Not much of a consolation, but it was something. Better to bear the weight of the scorn equally.

Chattox had been smug for all of one day until people turned as cold towards her as the winter weather. Demdike was somewhat mollified it knocked the smug smirk off the other's face, but by the third day of nothing, the two had silently nodded to one another. A silent decision to go elsewhere and avoid the prying eyes. Until those analysing gazes had lessened. Until the paranoia passed. Demdike wasn't entirely hopeful. Though she couldn't help but pray, for her family's sake.

Things had been off since October. Since Nowell stepped into their little corner of the country. The turning of October to November still sat uneasily within her. The haunting of the Bulcock family. Demdike tried to help Jane since then. The woman coming to their home once a week, but it was slow progress. Demdike and Christopher rarely got along. The man wanted to hover while she wanted the man far away. Hoping to heal the woman without interference.

It'd been a few weeks until her subconscious recalled the dream she'd had, leaving her to wonder if the malicious dog-like being had been the same creature she fought Halloween night. It would make sense. Though the entire situation sat like a splinter of wood in her thumb. It fit, but not right. Demdike had gone round and round in circles, eventually deciding to put the matter aside for the holidays and the sake of her sanity. Hopefully, whilst she wasn't consciously thinking about it, something would shake loose from deep within.

Yule was supposed to be a good time. Though it rarely had been for her. It was a yearly reminder death was near, and this year, Demdike understood she would greet the primordial soon. From the ice on her neck, to the chill in her hands (which refused to ease no matter how often she tried to warm them), life let her know death was coming. Seeing her family try to keep up their spirits as they lit the Yule log and gave wishes for the coming year, all she could think was she hoped her family survived when she was gone. Or if not, that they would come with her. Quickly and painlessly.

Many fell asleep in the cold of winter and never woke. If they were to follow her on her final walk into the ether, Demdike could only hope they went easily. A long life wasn't worth much if it was filled with suffering. She knew how often death could be a kindness.

Demdike drew before the log, wondering what intentions she wanted the burning wood to carry to the spirit realm. All she could think was how, if she wasn't here next year, she hoped her family remained safe without her. She'd lived a long life. Her family deserved a good one. Perhaps her death could be a sacrifice—an exchange of energies—her life, for theirs. It was a price she would happily pay.

Yule had a nasty habit of bringing up her darker thoughts. Of showing the shadow self and forcing Demdike to see the dark reflection she tried to keep at bay. Yule was the time of facing your own darkness. Her grimmest thoughts and saddest wishes. The things you normally refused to think about in fear it might give them leverage to enter the world. Yule had the nasty habit of shining a black light on her buried thoughts and illuminating them. Forcing her to face them.

"We turn from darkness back to light," she whispered over the log. Help them. Save them. Let it be quick. If she was to die—when she was to die—she hoped it was fast.

***

The graveyard was unusually cold, even for a winter's morning. As though death himself had walked the land and left his icy chill on the world. The days following Yule and Christmas were quiet. People stayed home to keep warm. Huddled by the fire and avoiding the harsh world beyond the doors. Many of the poor lost their lives in this season, but even those with money were not spared the harshness of winter.

There were hints it was going to be a sunny day, breakings in the thick cloud covers as the sun fought valiantly for its place in the world, but the frost which refused to bow to the sun's repeated attempts at warming the land. Her path was clear, and in the limited light, her actions were hidden. As were many of the things required of the cunning folk. The darkness was a blanket to protect them from prying eyes and judgment.

The carved stones before her claimed only the best of the deceased residents. Demdike wondered if hers would soon be littered amongst these long-gone members of their village. Families with no one left to protest her actions. Wouldn't do to be digging up someone's ancestor or a recently passed patriarch. She worked with both the dead and living. There was a necessary level of respect required in all her actions. Digging up the recently deceased would not have gone over well. Though it seemed not everyone held her level of care.

The rushing of a bitter chill had her believing there were other forces at work here. Nowell might have left the area again, but there were already rumours of his return. He'd gone home for Christmas, but he'd not yet achieved his reason for coming here. Not that anyone had any idea what his reasons might be. But where there was no concrete proof, people let their minds wander with ample possibilities. Demdike held a few theories of her own, each less pleasant than the last. She could only hope her head was making outlandish nightmare scenarios and not anything which could come to pass.

Demdike had approached the graveyard early, knowing these old remedies received a frosty view from the locals. Though they never failed to sell. People might have frowned upon their origins, but they were the old wives' tales, the legends, the things people had grown up knowing and believing. As a cunning woman, it was her job to ensure people had access to such remedies. This was why the cunning folk were often looked down upon. They did the dirty work no one else would. Went to the place angels would have fled in fear of.

Cunning folk made deals with shady individuals with dubious morals. The hand of a hanged man; a great protection from evil. The liver of a dead virgin; perfect for hammering to the wall and warding away all manner of evils. The brains of a newborn animal, put them in a jar and it would protect your mind from withering and decaying. A particular favourite of the elderly.

Others might have frowned upon the origins of the ingredients, but they needed them for their own good health. Hypocrisy at its finest, but Demdike learnt to bear their scorn with grace. Money was money. Survival was key. She had mouths to feed and no husband to work for her. You did what you had to.

Six feet down, she extracted five milky pieces, the only pearls she desired. Wrapped them in two cloth bags before hiding them in her robes. The gold and riches had long since been scavenged from these bones. Graverobbing had been a big issue in her youth, bandits and travellers passing through, but not before they'd stolen all the valuables from the local dead. She couldn't judge. Were there any gold left, she'd have taken it herself. But in her more privileged youth, it'd been quite the scandal.

A young Elizabeth couldn't have comprehended why anyone would disturb the dead. To perform acts of such sacrilege on bodies put to rest under the earth. Of course, she later realised such niceties were the luxury of those who had enough food to eat and no extra mouths to feed. Still, she could recall the horror she'd felt when first hearing the news. How she'd hoped such nasty people would meet a bad end.

It was, in part, why Demdike didn't get too angry at other people's reactions. She remembered being just like them. Naïve and innocent. Untouched by the darker aspects of the world. Back before she became one of the grey. Seeing life and death as black and white. Good and bad as straightforward, simple. Nothing had challenged her worldview back then.

She hadn't yet felt the sharp pangs of hunger after a week with no sustenance. Hadn't seen how greed—both physical and metaphorical—could change even the best of souls. She might not have made a deal with the devil, but she could understand why some might. The world was not a kind place for the vulnerable. Elizabeth might have been horrified by grave robbery, but Demdike was simply annoyed others had gotten there first.

The grave robbers might not have left behind any riches, and the cloth and clothing the corpses had been buried in may have been eaten away by the earth and bugs, but there was something only the cunning folk would find of great value here. A short time later, she emerged from the hole and threw the broken earth back over the lifeless creature, fleeing the scene uncaught.

Leaving no apparent trace of her presence. As though she'd never visited the abandoned graveyard or done such deeds. It wouldn't do to be caught. Someone (and she suspected who) had been messing with fresh corpses in the still-used cemetery. If anyone caught Demdike here, they'd assume those actions were hers as well. Regardless of proof or alibis. Another of life's hard lessons she was well-schooled in.

What someone might be doing with fresh bodies, Demdike shuddered to think. She understood robbing from the dead, but many of those dug up had been too poor for any finery to have been included in their caskets, and all the locals knew this. In fact, many of the exhumed dead had been too poor to afford coffins. They'd been buried in rags and thrown into graves with multiple bodies. An end which most likely awaited herself.

Demdike wasn't precious about what might happen to her body once she left it, but the idea of someone using her remains for nefarious purposes did leave an uncomfortable churning in her stomach. Who knows what someone like Chattox might do with the body of a cunning woman of her power?

Demdike's long-standing feud with Chattox was well known throughout all of Pendle. Their shared animosity was no secret. Their shouting matches were the cause of much entertainment to the locals over the years. Truthfully, the two had fed the rivalry as it helped their businesses and kept their names in people's mouths, and always on their minds. If anything happened, the other residents would think of them first. A direct way to funnel people to them.

Not that the issues between the two were entirely manufactured. No, there were many years of friendly and not-so-friendly rivalries. Decades of anger and resentment layered on top of jokes and competition. When the difference between the pair's successes often meant the other's family being able to feed or not, desperation fueled many of their fights. That the other woman might be able to do all sorts of untoward things with her corpse left a lump in Demdike's throat she couldn't swallow. An unpleasant realisation. Death at her age felt more like freedom than doom, but she was a spiteful woman, and she'd rather her body be burned than any part of her be used to help her competition.

Demdike suspected it was Chattox messing with the newly dead. Not simply because she didn't like the other, but because the cunning folk held a darker path. Darker arts. Ones reserved for only desperate times. They weren't much use, given the level of preparation. Where most of their craft took a few months on average, these darker spells took years in the making. Some even decades. Demdike never had the patience herself. Never wanted to lose herself to the darker side.

Cunning folk walked the line between the two extremes. They were grey for a reason. To slip into the black path was not recommended. They taught it to all, as a '*last resort*' type of scenario. Or to protect from those who had fallen. But even after a lifetime of walking the way of the spirit, Demdike couldn't see why anyone would embrace that level of depravity.

She remembered, though. Remembered the steps. Knew the spells. Recalled what could be done and what it took. Demdike knew, and of all the people in the Pendle borough, there were only five possibilities. Herself and her daughter, Chattox and her daughter, and the woman they spoke not of or to. The five of them, this was it. And Demdike knew she wasn't doing it.

Her Lizzie definitely wasn't. The girl barely went a few steps down the path, she didn't have the power for something this dark. The same for Anne. She might've been Chattox's daughter, but the woman only managed a step more than her Lizzie. The other, the lady with riches and a name of respect, was unlikely to damage her pristine reputation. Demdike mentally crossed her off the list. This only left one choice. Chattox.

Well, one choice if the person doing these things was a spirit walker. There were all manner of people on the earth, and for as long as she'd lived, Demdike heard many tales. Many stories of people who liked to lie with the dead. Of those who liked to consume them. Of those who wanted to learn about the workings of the living by exploring the bodies of those passed on. Considering there was a doctor who recently arrived a few towns over, he could be another potential suspect.

People were already looking at her with guarded eyes and angry auras, it wouldn't do for this grave robber to point to her. To bring the full force of the borough's grieving families to her doorstep. She might have been somewhat feared, but grief made even the most logical of people turn to attack. Just look at Baldwyn and his recent behaviours. Demdike had to swallow the bile threatening to rise in her throat. Hoping against hope little Grace was not amongst the bodies being interfered with. For all she and Chattox didn't always get along, she didn't think the woman would cross such lines. If she had, Demdike would curse the woman herself. Some actions were unforgivable.

There were many potential reasons why someone might have been digging up the recently deceased, but Demdike wouldn't be worth her salt if she ignored her intuition after all these years. You didn't earn your cronehood, didn't gain the title of wise woman, by ignoring those gut feelings. The seasick sensation of her midriff had Chattox written right through it. Everything within her was convinced: her counterpart was the perpetrator. The guilty party.

However, even if her suspicions about the 'who' were correct, this didn't automatically mean the 'why' was as well. Chattox could be upturning bodies for a variety of reasons. Maybe she was becoming paranoid in her old age, or maybe the encounter with Nowell had affected her too. Demdike feared she was becoming as suspicious as everyone else. Whatever the reason, she needed to uncover what was happening.

For all Demdike couldn't be certain of many things, she was certain of this: if it were Chattox, she would stop the woman. Whether by hook or by crook. If the other woman was responsible, she would hear her out. Listen to the possible reasons, but if necessary, she would claim her life. The cunning folk did the dirty work others would or could not.

If Chattox had chosen the darker path, become devoid... It might have made her a little more difficult to deal with than the average person, but Demdike also had twenty years of experience on her colleague. She would remind the woman why her name was feared throughout all of Lancashire.

Demdike sighed, heaving her body as she walked the worn path leading back towards Malkin. At her age, she should have been spending most of her time resting. Should have been spending days lounging at home and in her bed. Yet another luxury reserved for those without money troubles. She'd sleep when she was dead. Hopefully.

CHAPTER ELEVEN

A lizon held the tears in as she ran from the scene before her. She could cry in her room at home. The man had been unnecessarily cruel. She'd stood petulantly, chin raised in defiance, denying his petty accusations. When Peter had disappeared inside his home, neither arguing against the man nor defending her, she decided it wasn't worth sticking around for. If he was willing to bear his father's foul tongue, far be it from her to intervene, but when the man lashed out at her, Alizon didn't have to take it. They'd thrown a few choice words before she stormed away. Henry Bulcock wasn't her father; she didn't have to endure his abuse.

Peter had said many times how his dad was an arse and wasn't a pleasant man to be around. Shared his hopes to escape and get away. The pair of them dreamed up plans to flee to the other side of the country before anyone realised they were gone. They were childish fantasies. They both knew they could never afford it, but it didn't stop the hopes they carried.

Peter, as the second son, wouldn't inherit the farm and would need to make his own way in the world, and she, as the daughter of the beggar women, would be lucky to make any match, let alone a half-decent one. It was why Nana Demy ensured Alizon kept herself chaste.

Threats of whore houses and liberties being taken were real-world horrors Alizon could end up experiencing if she wasn't careful.

She would ask her grandmother later about how she might retaliate. Maybe burn Henry's name or shadowbox it. Anything to alleviate the stewing rage. As much as she wanted to run all the way home, it wouldn't be safe with the sodden earth below. It might not have been currently raining, but the land was still slippery from the previous night. She sighed for what must have been the twentieth time since starting the trudging walk home.

'What a woeful world it must be to be a small girl with such big feelings.' Nana Demy always laughed whenever Alizon got a little too irrational in her anger.

The elder woman spoke the words in sarcasm many times, mocking her fragile feelings. Looking back, Alizon could admit she had been working herself into a frenzy. Being a brat and expecting everyone to move to her wills. The world didn't work this way. If it did, she would be wealthy and free.

The words may have been originally said in jest, but her nana hit the nail on the head. The errant statement clung to Alizon's consciousness like a sticky willy would after running through the wild fields; leaves refusing to leave her skirts or skin no matter how hard she tried to peel them from her. Goosegrass, her mum called them, but everyone called them the other. The thought stuck to her mind like those irritating leaves. Swelling and circling, refusing to abate. Forced her to face the idea. The idea she was a small girl with feelings far too big for her little body.

Alizon often wondered how she hadn't drowned. Her feelings were like a tsunami, totalling everything in their path, including her logical mind. She was nothing against the weight of her emotions. They didn't care for how, in another moment, Alizon would act differently.

They demanded all her energy. Swarmed her with unyielding intensity and forced her to act and react as they wanted, regardless of her wishes.

Alizon often felt like a slave to her emotions. As though they were another person, or being, dwelling within her. She knew this wasn't true. She'd had Nana Demy check, but it didn't stop her from thinking such things. Didn't stop her from wondering if a demon might have possessed her during childhood and hidden within one of these emotional scars her nan always talked about.

It was a woeful existence. To be so ruled by waves which rose and receded. If they either stayed or left entirely, it would be easier. Whether the logical lack of emotions and her colder thoughts, or the raging storm that made her mind burn and act like a wild animal instead of a person. A woeful life to be eternally tilting between the two extremes.

One moment, calm and collected. Happy and laughing. The next, embodying the storm as she spread vitriol and hatred as easily as warm butter on toast. Let her malicious emotions into the air and gave life to the dark thoughts she normally held tight within. Poisoned the world around her. She sometimes feared herself. Asking why she went from one extreme to another, was she cursed? Why else would her emotions be this volatile?

Her grandmother assured her it was normal for someone her age to be swayed by emotions, thoughts and feelings they could barely contain. Like a pot ready to boil over at the slightest change. Alizon didn't argue, but she knew she'd been just as emotional as a child. Before her monthlies. Before her body went from girl to woman. As a child, she'd cried and screamed as easily as any animal.

Tibbs had the annoying habit of yowling and never being quiet about his annoyance and she'd been the same. Her mother told her how children learn such behaviours were not allowed and stopped those actions. But even when she no longer screamed her daily frustrations at the world, this didn't stop the feelings. She might be more prone to losing herself now, easily swallowed by the waves, but she could barely recall a time when this hadn't been her norm.

Her body was a balloon too filled with the things she couldn't say. With all her wants and fears. Filled with the screams, forced into silence. Her intermittent rages were a way to avoid daily breakdowns, but Alizon hated them. They might have saved her mind from caving in on itself. Might have prevented her brains from exploding and covering those around her in the bloody mess that would be left behind, but Alizon could hardly claim to prefer the alternative. It was horrible to lose herself.

She was still a little girl in many ways. A child in a growing body. She might have felt the temptation of flesh (never indulging, she was still a good girl). Her nana made no secret of how she would murder Alizon otherwise. But for all her body was growing into an adult, a part of her feared she would never grow enough. Feared her emotions would always be bigger than her frame.

Her dreams were also too big for her little world. Her friends and family never had any issues telling her as much. Telling her she couldn't become a butterfly and fly away. Or be a tree and watch the world from on high. Couldn't become a fish and swim away either. When she wanted to change this, they also said she couldn't be an adventurer. Couldn't scour the globe for faraway lands. Couldn't join a ship and sail the seven seas. Something about being a woman.

The world refused Alizon her freedom. Told her every dream was impossible. Because she was a girl. She'd briefly thought about pretending to be a man and escaping, but the plan had fallen flat when she saw how James was treated despite also being male. Her problems weren't solely because she was a woman, but also because she was poor.

Poor, female, and a dreamer who had no idea how the world beyond the Pendle borders worked.

Alizon was a woeful girl with big feelings and bigger dreams. A step out of time with everyone around her. They were dancing to the same song, whilst no one bothered teaching her the moves. The music in her heart sang a different tune. She was the wild child. Labelled fae. Witch. Whore. People threw harsh words and cruel insults at her, but none were as diminishing as her inner voices. This didn't help with convincing Alizon she wasn't possessed. Surely, it wasn't normal to be so at odds with your own body and heart? A cruel reality. A despondent life she was forced to live.

Imbolc was fast approaching. Her fourteenth birthday. It didn't mean much to be a year older, but her nana kept dropping hints about how Alizon would come into her abilities. *'An important age for any spiritually gifted individual,'* the elderly woman would say. Alizon remained unconvinced, but she would humour the old goat. Psychic visions and chats with the dead were not Alizon's idea of a good time. As much as she respected Demdike and the work she did, Alizon wasn't keen to join her.

Her mother had done little on the path. Told Alizon how, even though she respected the spirit world and all it could do, it scared her. Elizabeth Device, or Squinting Lizzie as most called her, had been happy to leave the cunning work to her mother. Alizon suspected she wouldn't be quite so lucky. Nana Demy was old. She'd been old even before Alizon was born, but another decade and (almost) a half turned old to ancient. The woman's body was breaking down before their eyes, and although her grandmother refused to bow down to old age, it was clear the woman wouldn't last much longer.

Most of their family's money came from odd jobs and begging, but the cunning work was what had seen food on the table regularly throughout Alizon's entire life. If they wanted to keep above water, someone would have to take on the mantle. She refused to let old Chattox have it. That witch was the reason her daddy was dead. He'd stopped paying protection money to the wicked hag and keeled over on his way home three weeks later. Nana Demy thought it was a coincidence, but she and James believed otherwise.

Their mother, knowing some of the cunning work, had created clay faces with them of Chattox (and the man who had threatened to take their home). Though they'd had to move in with Nana Demy, and Chattox was still alive, so the spells must not have worked. Her mother said it was likely because it'd been too long since their daddy passed, though Alizon wasn't sure. Mother Chattox was feared for a reason.

Instead, Alizon and James gained small bouts of revenge on the old hag; dumping rotten food in her yard or throwing foul-smelling things into the tree above her home. It'd been a year before anyone discovered it was them and they were told to stop. They'd been small actions, but it made her and her brother feel better. Demdike had been highly amused. Though her nana was often encouraging them to do the things their mother frowned upon.

Her mum wasn't a bad person, not by any stretch, but she was a cautious woman. Overly cautious in Alizon's opinion. Always afraid some big bad or terrible catastrophe was just around the corner. Her mother lived a hard life, and it left scars. When things often did go wrong, it proved her mother's fears right. It had become a vicious cycle. The woman was barely able to be happy because she was constantly waiting for the bad to follow, the other shoe to drop, the next thing to knock them down.

Alizon couldn't really argue against it. Her mother must have been born under a bad star. Take the other week; they'd managed to receive several donations whilst begging in Colne, only to return to discover

Chattox's daughter had stolen linens and oatmeal. The woman had denied it, of course, but the neighbours had seen Anne near their home. She had no reason to be near Malkin Tower and no one else in Pendle would be stupid or brazen enough to steal from Demdike's own house. Bad things did seem to follow good.

Alizon couldn't fault her mother for her troubled nature, but growing up around it could give a girl a complex. Having a parent who jumped at shadows and both under and overreacted to the most obscure things was incredibly draining. She never knew which version of her mum she would meet on a day-to-day basis. Which, thinking about it, might explain some of Alizon's own emotional reactions.

Though Elizabeth Device was usually worried about something, it was how she reacted to these worries, which kept Alizon on her toes. The woman danced between copying her own mother (Nana Demy) and acting like a meek, subdued individual who was willing to bear the weight of the world on her shoulders. It got confusing. Her grandmother's comment about woeful girls fit Lizzie more than the adults seemed willing to accept.

Between the two older women in her family, it was no surprise they often accused Alizon of being some fairy-flighty creature. Why would anyone want to languish around in dreary the monotony of the world when in her mind she could escape to far-off places filled with bright colours and creatures she'd only ever heard vague stories about? They could hardly force her to stay in reality when the world was filled with such suffering.

Malkin Tower came into view. The trees between her path and the house were obscuring most of the house, but it was settling to know she was close to home. An invisible weight left her shoulders. Her body began unwinding the nearer she drew to safety. Not that she felt unsafe in the wooded area, but there was simply something about being home. Being close to her family, where she lay her head each night. It was always madness, always something or another happening, but it was hers. Home might've been where the heart was, but it was also where every exciting and strange thing happened. There was never a dull day at Malkin.

Alizon watched as her mother was jumping around holding a broom was a weird sight to come home to. Odd sights were far from a rarity in this house. With a grandmother who was barely in the same world and a mother who was the epitome of a headless chicken. Forever running around. Busy. Doing many, (un)necessary things which are always urgent meant the woman must rush from place to place. Weird was nothing new.

The... dance? Was tiring to watch. Her mother looked like an animal with a broken leg, hopping and jumping around. Alizon vaguely recalled her mother making her and her siblings join her in such dances when she was younger, but that was usually something to do with rain. She searched the sky. The clouds were thick and grey, but it would likely be a few more hours until they dropped their bounty onto the earth below. Looking back to her mother, Alizon tried to parse out what the woman was doing, or attempting to do.

"It's to encourage crop fertility and growth," her mother answered the unasked question.

Though it simply generated several more. The most obvious being: why? Why now? Not in spring or summer. Why did she think mirroring a limp chicken would help? Just why?

"You dance with the broom and hope the crops will follow this example." Her mother jumped up and down a few more times, from bent knee up into the air, looking more like a child trying to figure out how high they could jump, but Alizon charitably did not voice this observation.

"Mum, I think people are more likely to think you're trying to ride the thing than grow crops."

"Alizon!" came the woman's scandalised squeak.

Alizon couldn't help but laugh. "What? I meant flying. What did you think I meant?" she asked in her most innocent voice, tilting her head to the side to mimic confusion.

Moments later she ran laughing into the house, ignoring her mother's spluttering protests. One good thing about her mother's absurdities, they made her easy to tease.

Alizon entered her room. The one she shared with her sister, Jennet. The girl was absent for the moment. Likely making mischief down by the river or playing with her friends elsewhere. The child was always off somewhere, coming home covered in mud and slime. Alizon wouldn't have minded so much, but when she got the dirt on their sheets, it made her want to lock the brat out in the nightly downpours. Or push her into the river and hope the girl came back out slightly cleaner.

Dropping dramatically to the bed, she let the world-weary sigh escape her. Her anger had cooled on the walk home, but she was no less frustrated with the situation. She wanted to demand the water return to her ducts as it slowly descended her face. At the angle, it was mostly moving toward and landing in her ears, but it still felt like a betrayal. Her own body defying her wants and wishes.

Hitting the bed, she wanted to bite, claw, scream, something. To fight. Fight what? She wasn't sure. Wasn't like she could take Peter's father in a fight. Plus, the man had guns. It would just be plain stupid. Maybe she just wanted to punch the world in the face for making her live a life like this. So filled with emotions, she could barely process.

Accepting the tears would not stop, she let them come more easily. Remembering the hunch of Peter's shoulders and the way his face turned from her. Rejection? Felt like it. The quick, sharp stab to her heart as he walked away from her and towards the angry man. Alizon remembered eerily thinking it was as though he were walking to the gallows. To his own doom. He'd looked so defeated. Although she was sympathetic to his situation, she couldn't help seeing him as a kicked dog. Resigned and accepting his fate.

It'd been an eye-opening situation. One where she, who'd been kicked and spat upon all her life, stood up to the man with little effort. Whilst Peter, the supposed man, was the coward. Maybe she was being uncharitable. Alizon didn't live with Henry Bulcock. She had her own family and shelter to return to. She wasn't stuck under the same roof. Didn't have to rely on the abusive man for survival. If her mother and grandmother turned abusive, would she be more like a wounded animal? Alzon hoped to never have to test the theory.

All she knew was it hurt. Hurt her to be on the receiving end of the man's ire. Hurt to watch Peter become despondent and a shell lacking life. Hurt to feel him turn his back to her. Those dreams of running away together and escaping were clearly just that—dreams. Ideals for escapism. Like her many fantasies, where she could fly with the birds, or swim with the sea creatures. They were nothing more than beautiful illusions, shattering in the face of real life and real people.

At her mother's call for food, she wiped her eyes. Hoping they weren't puffy. As much as she wanted to show her upset by stomping down every step, it wouldn't help endear her family to her situation. Instead, she dropped to the floor with a loud thud.

"Henry Bulcock has accused me of bewitching his child," she announced to the room.

The accusation hadn't overly bothered her, not really. Alizon heard such ridiculous things before, but this didn't stop the sting of the man's words. Didn't stop the feelings of frustration and shame swaying through her. She had thought she'd calmed down, but among her family, the anger felt safe to return.

"Which one?" James asked unconcerned, more interested in his whittling.

Alizon hesitated. She'd been so incensed by the accusation she hadn't actually stayed to hear the full details. Her mind had simply connected the dots, which made the most sense to her. She'd thought Mr Bulcock had meant Peter. Peter, her friend, and potentially something more. When his father cried bewitchment, she'd automatically assumed he meant the feelings the pair shared. The secret caress of lips they never spoke of. Scandalous if others discovered such actions. However, now that she thought about it, Henry never mentioned Peter directly. Never named the boy.

Henry hadn't explicitly said it was bewitchment in the form of love. Many people had been accusing others of bewitchment, usually when someone fell ill. Peter hadn't been unwell. Had Mr Bulcock meant it in another way? Seemed a little foolish now. She shouldn't have fled. If someone was accusing her of a crime, she should get the details.

"I thought he meant Peter–" She ignored James' amused scoff. "–but I didn't stick around to find out. I might have actually cursed the man if I had."

"Bit stupid," her brother muttered, whittling away again.

She wanted to shove him, but learnt not to do that when the boy had a knife in his hand. There was a scar on her leg as a permanent reminder. Though he had one on his thumb too, so that fight hadn't been a complete loss.

"I just wanted to punch him in his ugly little face. Thought I'd better leave. Before I was tempted to try to hit him."

"Being courageous isn't about facing wild beasts and gods on a vengeance," the old woman said from the corner.

Alizon almost hadn't noticed her. Nana Demy spoke in that voice which usually meant she was about to impart something she saw as great wisdom. It wasn't always wise—often just plain out there and deranged—but it always led to some interesting stories. Old people always had weird tales about when they were young or all the strange things they believed. At least the old woman kept them entertained.

"No true courage is about facing yourself. Your devils. The lies you've shrouded yourself in. The blocks in your mind you've constructed to deal with whatever darkness you hold within."

"Mum." Lizzie came into the room carrying a tray with their food on. Her voice held a warning tone.

"What? When we get angry, it helps to know why."

"That's not what you were saying and you know it," her mother returned.

"The girl's nearly fourteen. Better for her to know now," her nana mumbled.

"No. Now eat your food."

Her grandmother sighed, accepting the bowl, her face resigned until she saw the content. Alizon literally saw the moment her nana realised what was in the bowl by her comical widening of her eyes. The grin which followed made the young girl twitch uncomfortably. It wasn't normal to look at food with such intense desire.

"Meat?" the elderly woman asked in delighted surprise.

"Yeah, if your teeth can even handle it," her mother jibbed at the older lady.

"Oh, hush, there's strength in this old carcass yet," the woman took a large spoonful, winking at Alizon as she did.

Alizon wasn't entirely sure about the half-conversation between her mother and grandmother, beyond the psychic stuff, and how turning fourteen was important. She'd ask later. They rarely got to have a decent meal like this. Would her mother be right, though? With something good, would the other shoe soon drop? Hopefully, this was a reward for the bad thing that had happened earlier. Maybe her mother was wrong, and the reverse was right. Good things followed bad, not the other way around.

She'd speak to Peter the next time she saw him. Friends argued. Maybe this was all normal.

CHAPTER TWELVE

J ames could accept he wasn't the brightest candle in the church. He'd been born with a cord around his neck. His breathing unable to begin until his nana pushed the air into his lungs. For those first few moments, the world wanted him for the grave, greeting death before he'd even known life. The good book said life began with the first breath. Said the soul flew into the body when it became one with the world. A little James had wondered if this made Nana Demy his personal God.

She was definitely powerful. A creature he would fear crossing. Even without her cunning work and label of wise woman, his nana would be a terrifying thing. With grey, wiry hair, eyes that seemed to look through you rather than at you, and lips thin enough to slice another open. She was scary. Especially when she let her tongue loose from within them. A razor wire capable of claiming heads and cleaving hearts in two. Were she not his grandmother, she would scare him.

As her grandson, people's fear of Demdike was a blessing and a curse. Some were keen to avoid her anger and, by extension, his. However, it also made friendships difficult to form. No one wanted to be connected with their kind. Even in his youth, when people believed in magic but not malice, he'd carried the taint of his family. Boys wanted to throw stones at him rather than welcome him into their games.

Alizon hadn't had it much better, but she barely seemed to notice other people's ill will. *'Too away with the fairies'* as nana liked to say. Jennet seemed to be the only one spared such actions. Though maybe this was because he'd stood threateningly in the background, so if they had lobbed things at her, they would know he'd throw something back.

As a child, he'd shed tears at others' hatred. Wondered why he wasn't good enough. Why they would extend a hand to others, but never him? Wanted to know why did people want to hurt him when he'd never hurt them.

"Fear and bad words from their mummies and daddies. Makes even the kindest person become a black heart. Don't let it get y'down, lad." The words made little sense to a five-year-old James, but a decade later, he understood what his nan had been trying to say.

She wanted people to take responsibility for their actions. Though in his experience, most shied away from the concept. Eventually, he learned to throw things back at the other kids. To kick and bite and punch. To never take it without a fight. This made many of them stop, and a few were even curious enough to befriend him, but then the parents started warning kids away from him as he was *'violent'*. People throwing rocks at him had been fine, but James throwing them back made him the bad guy. James might not have been the brightest, but he wondered how stupid you had to be not to see the giant flaw in that logic.

He'd been fighting all his life. From his first breath, to earning the few friends he managed to keep, to getting a job. Everything in his life had been a battle, and he refused to take this latest loss without giving some form of retaliation. James had loved working on the farm. Loved how it was honest work he was good at. He'd been proud to help support his family. Help with putting food on the table, or Jennet keep in clothes (as the girl began growing like a weed). Even helping his nana not have to go out begging as often. She was as old as the grave already, she needed the rest. The woman had been joking about dying more and more recently. For James to have noticed, it must've been a good few times. As though the woman were trying to gently prepare them for the inevitable.

James enjoyed working as it let the old woman spend more time in their home. He'd never been late to work, despite the five a.m. start time. Particularly difficult in the cold of winter. Regardless of the previous day's events or the weather, James was always there, bright and early. Happily grafting away. Looking after the animals, cleaning up after them, making sure they had food. They were clean and well-groomed. Heck, he'd even milked the cows a time or two when the milkmaids had been short-handed and couldn't afford to miss a delivery. James went above and beyond because he was proud to be doing a good job. Happy to be making an honest wage.

Being fired surprised him. The boss barely gave him a reason, even tried to shortchange him, but James hadn't been afraid to use his fists to correct the mistake. The man wasn't a gentleman or one of the gentry. Wasn't overly wealthy as farmers were ten-a-penny round here, but he had been in better standing than James himself. So, when he threw James to the curb with no reason beyond, he was *'bad for business'* James was stunned. Mere days before Christmas, and he was unemployed.

Three months had since passed, and he was still struggling to find work. The dark shadow which stopped him from making friends had now extended to him getting a good job. He didn't want to be angry at his nan. She'd done nothing wrong. The woman worked hard to keep them all afloat over the years. It'd been the same job these people scorned which they all demanded whenever anything went remotely wrong.

At least his nan didn't demand protection money. Though he was starting to think maybe she should. Demdike was always there whenever people needed her, always helped in whatever way she could, but the judgemental bastards were only too happy to have someone to blame all their problems on. His nan had been right; you needed to take responsibility for your own actions. These people were not the wolves, they were the sheep, happy to blame others for their own faults.

His nana said half her work was catering to the stupid things people believed in, no matter how much proof you offered them to the contrary. He might not have been the brightest, but even James could see how often the people in Pendle blamed his grandmother and others for their own stupidity. He'd temporarily managed to get work on another farm. The owners barely paid enough to keep their livestock fed, let alone clean and healthy. When a cow had died, they blamed it on Chattox. James hated the old hag, especially after she killed his dad, but even James admitted he doubted the woman had anything to do with the death.

The grain had been mouldy. Even starving, James would've hesitated to eat it. Rye when it turned, messed with your head. He'd seen it when his nan got sick years ago. She'd been crazy, chattering on about impossible things and seeing shapes and strangers where there were none. It did take them a little while to realise something was wrong at first. The cunning woman often being aware of things they could not sense, but when the elderly woman confused James (running about with a stick) for a soldier coming to slay her, they'd taken notice.

They'd believed she was on her deathbed, losing the last of her mind. When the woman recovered, his nan didn't remember the incident. They'd been careful about accepting spoiled food after this. When the cow went crazy and died, it didn't surprise James. The owners blamed Chattox—rather than admit the shoddily run farm was the problem. He'd openly scoffed into his water and ignored their stupidity, but when the same owners refused to pay him for his hard work, well, James was ready to fight back once again.

He doubted the family kept much money. The man and his wife spent any coin as soon as it reached their hands. James decided liberating one of their animals was fair recompense. Plus, it would be kinder to the poor thing. James doubted he could steal a cow, as useful as that might be. The milk alone would be a great help to his family, but cows were stubborn at the best of times, and wouldn't flee with him.

He'd thought about taking a pig next, but those things could eat you out of house and home. It would be like having three extra mouths to feed. The meat would not be worth it in the end. Plus, with their low body weight, they were as difficult as cows if they decided they didn't want to cooperate.

This left one option. There wasn't much use for sheep outside of their wool and meat, but it was more than the pigs. Also, the thing could graze around Malkin Tower so it'd be easy enough to keep alive. Made the most logical sense. Sheep were easy enough to carry and curious enough not to put up much fuss. If he could lure one to him and away from the others his plan should work.

The field the livestock were let into had a broken fence, one the owners were too cheap to fix. Even if they realised what he'd done, James could argue he found the sheep wandering the fields far away from their farm. How could James have known this wild-running sheep was theirs specifically? A great plan, if James did say so himself.

When approaching the field in question, he noticed one of the farm workers nearby, putting a bit of a dent in his original plan. Though he wasn't one to back down from a difficult situation. He crawled along the grass, keeping out of the other man's eye line. The ground below was moist and it was going to leave marks on his clothes—his mother would have his hide later. He needed to steal the sheep simply to stop her tirade about having to get the stains out of fabric.

As the lookout was distracted, he climbed the broken fencing. Moved as silently as possible. Crept forward like a wolf. As swiftly as possible. When he neared a pack of three sheep closest to him, he was forced to dive behind one as it began bleating. James refused to rescue the traitor purely on principle. Checking to see the man hadn't spotted him, James was relieved to see the other hadn't even moved his head.

Sheep made noise at random. Even he'd learnt to tune it out on the job. The animals bleating about anything and everything. He could have sworn one had been shouting up at a cloud once. Maybe confusing it for one of its herd?

He felt a strange sensation. Turning his head, it snagged on something. As his scalp felt damp. "Oh, for–"

The brat was chewing on his freaking hair. His mum may have compared it to a bush once or twice, but James hadn't taken it literally. Stupid sheep. Something this dumb needed to be put out of its misery, and as the thing had chosen him, James felt no guilt in liberating it. Removing his hair from its mouth, he grabbed it by the middle and ran back to the fence.

"Hey! Hey, what do you think you're doing?" he heard someone call from behind, but James ignored the man's cries.

Fleeing as quickly as he could. Hopefully, Tommy, or Timmy, whatever he was called, wouldn't recognise him. Though having a sheep at Malkin might be a little suspicious now. Either way, James didn't care, he was simply taking the payment they owed him. When the sheep started chewing at his sleeve, James decided it was best to ignore it. The action kept the beast quiet, enabling him to keep running. He giggled all the way home. Unable to stop the sounds escaping his chest. Luckily, no one was around to hear him laughing like a little girl. Except for the sheep, but no one was going to believe old Gerty. She was a sheep, after all.

"Really?" had been his mother's unimpressed tone when he had presented her with the results of his heist.

Gerty had answered for him, bleating at the woman in a matching unimpressed tone.

"Oh, don't be like that, Gerty. Mum means nothing bad by it," he said, stroking the sheep like a pet.

"Gerty?"

"Short for Gertrude. She needed a name, after all."

"How do you know it's a she?"

James paused. He'd just assumed. All the cows they kept had been female, and the chickens as well. He supposed he just made the same conclusion when it came to the pigs and sheep.

He shrugged. "Gerty could be for a boy too, not like it matters. We now have wool for clothing and in a few months, she should be fat enough for some decent meat."

"And how do you expect us to feed another mouth between then and now?"

James looked confusingly at his mother, before pointing to all the surrounding grass.

"God, give me strength. Your nan can deal with this. It was probably her that gave you the idea."

"I thought of this all by myself, thank you very much," he responded indignantly.

James hadn't so much as given a whiff of his thoughts to anyone in his family, more afraid they'd want to tag along and cause mischief than talk him out of it.

"And the fact your nan did the same thing with a pig and bunch of chickens in her heyday had absolutely nothing to do with this, I assume?"

James sometimes forgot how he and Alizon gained their sarcastic natures from her. Though his mother's also came from Nana Demy, so really all blame went back to the old crone in his opinion. Sparkling at this new tidbit of information, James couldn't help bouncing in place, putting Gerty down when she complained about the jostling.

"Did she really?" he could hear the awe in his own voice.

"Oh, goodness. That was not a challenge for you to steal more," his mother bemoaned, smacking him across the head.

As much as James would have loved to accept the challenge, he noted the moment she caught the mud and grass stains across his body. Ducked before she could wallop him again. Why were people always hitting his head? He held delicate thoughts up there. These attacks didn't help his candle burn any brighter.

"Get those rags off and into the basket. And get in the bath before I decide to lock you out in the rain and deal with you that way."

Hurrying inside, he fled up the stairs, more than aware the woman would make good on her threat. When he returned to a freezing tub of well water, he knew better than to complain about the lack of heat. The woman used the soap nana made to scrub him clean. At least she hadn't made him go down to the river in this weather. Spring was coming soon, and with it his birthday, but his mother wouldn't care about such things if he left a trail of dirt through her home. Though for how cold the little tub was, he might as well have been at the lake.

He'd hated baths as a child. Always too cold and made his skin itch with how hard his mum would scrub. That and his hair was always flying everywhere the first week or so after. Every strand seemed to be drawn to his eyes. But no matter how annoying and unpleasant, it was better than facing his mother's anger.

He used the half-hole-filled rag to dry his skin off before leaving the tub and putting on fresh clothes. His mum already using the leftover water to scrub the clothes. He would offer to help, but the woman was very particular about how to remove stains and he'd earned more than one smack when trying to help her in the past. Best to let the woman work the frustrations out on the fabrics rather than his head.

"What happened here?" Nana Demy voiced from the doorway.

"Your grandson followed in your footsteps and started stealing livestock."

He watched as his nana processed the words, before throwing her head back and laughing. "And here I thought it was Alizon who was going to be following my example."

He knew what she meant, Alizon showing promise in the cunning arts from a young age. James wasn't useless, but he just didn't have the same spark for communing with spirits. He could make the potions and poultices easy enough, but he was more like his mother, able to do the easy stuff, but not holding enough spiritual power to manage more. He understood his nana's meaning, and yet it brought a warm feeling to his chest to hear the words.

If a younger James wondered if his nana breathing breath into him made her his God, this older James wondered if she'd simply shared some of her traits. How the air might have contained pieces of her essence and it'd forced them into him. Whatever the cause, he liked being like her. A mixture of the people who raised him, his grandmother's impulsivity, his mother's snark, and his dad's love for a hard job well done. Pendle might choose to see a dark cloud hanging over his family, but James saw only people to cherish.

When Gerty tried to ram the front door, he let her in from the rain. It was only fair. She was a member of the Device family now, too.

Chapter Thirteen

Wednesday used to be one of her favourite days. The market busy and people buying things from her. It had seldom generated her great riches, but it was a consistent income these many years. Demdike stood outside, in all weathers, getting whatever coin she could. Today, however, the fish were barely biting. She'd sold all of two things after five hours of standing (leaning) there.

Low sales weren't entirely unusual. Any stallholder would tell you how there were ebbs and flows. Times when you hadn't enough stock to meet demand and others when you wouldn't sell a single thing all day. No, these lulls weren't unusual, but it was when she could see the want in people's eyes as they passed by, before checking no one had seen their yearning.

It was as though there was a barrier around her preventing people from coming forward. An invisible wall pushing everyone away. Even the people walking along the street were taking great pains to avoid her section. She'd checked several times if she stunk (more than normal), she didn't. Whatever this invisible obstacle was, she hoped it abated soon.

When Bethany was careful to cover her face before coming forward, Demdike knew this was more than the normal decline in sales. Since the whispers of witches began, things had steadily been getting worse.

However, this was the first time it became this obvious, keeping people away even amidst the bustle of the market.

If the hushed words had been bad, the many glares felt like a thousand slow cuts dosed in salt. When her regular customer scuttled away, polite, but barely speaking two words to her, Demdike resigned herself to a long day of foul looks and not-so-quiet taunts. Had she been the same woman as in her youth, Demdike would have demanded they come and say it to her directly. Face her fists. However, age hadn't only tempered her anger, it had weakened her muscles. She might still manage a good, swift kick or a slap if someone wasn't expecting it—the shock as painful as the hit—but punching had to be left to her younger years.

The sun had broken through the intermittent spring showers. Drying her clothes a little. At least her feet were dry. Demdike hated soggy feet. She could be entirely drowned and keep a smile so long as she had dry feet. The reverse was also true. Her entire body could be dry, but she'd be miserable if her boots and socks got wet. She hoped the sun breaking through the grey might be a sign of the day improving.

"You don't seem to be selling much," the impersonal voice could have made the dead shiver.

She startled. Looking up, Demdike was met with familiar dark eyes. She was starting to think the universe was mocking her. Is this what happened when you were marked by death? Everything you once knew turned on its head? Those endless voids were ones she'd hoped to never see again. As deep and devoid of life as they'd been in the church.

"I'd heard you'd left?" The words tumbled out of her mouth before she had consciously thought of them.

Demdike had hoped to never see the man again. She stood straighter, trying to hide her wince. Nowell raised an eyebrow in amusement. The man could have commented on her supposed insubordination—speaking too directly to a member of the gentry—they'd whipped her for as much in the past. The supposed fine people with egos as large as all the hills in Pendle, offended to be spoken to on equal ground. Luckily, or unluckily, he did little more than quirk the side of his mouth, lips twitching slightly.

"I've been given an important task. It has brought me back to Pendle once more," the mocking in his voice was well hidden.

Had someone overheard them, it would have sounded like a civil interaction, not one filled with minefields Demdike felt forced to dance around. This man was powerful, and so long as he appeared to be behaving reasonably, it wouldn't draw any unwanted observations. Not that people here would have supported her—especially not against this man—but the niceties had to be observed by individuals of his station. People had to act as was expected of them and this thing (wearing the skin of a man) could act better than most.

"You must be a well-respected man to be working for the king," she replied, watching for any reactions.

The twitch near his eye was answer enough, but he verbally tried to side step his unconscious reaction. "The king would not trouble himself with the useless ruffians and those of low birth, such as those found here."

Demdike hoped people heard this. The man, whilst trying to impress her lack of importance, basically said everyone in Pendle was useless. Her jab about the king must have landed better than expected. She could only guess why. Kings and queens. Nobility, and gentry. It was all beyond her wheelhouse of awareness. None of what these people did made much sense to her. They claimed to be protecting everyone, but were never there when thieves and bandits were about. However, the minute taxes were due, you couldn't shake them.

King James wasn't as loved as his predecessor, but Queen Elizabeth had been raised to an almost divine status. A hard act to follow. Plus, James was Scottish. Many Englishmen were not happy with such developments. Then there were the rumours about what he got up to in the bedroom, things not discussed in polite company, but somehow everyone had heard about. It mattered little to Demdike, past the taxes and the latest man in favour—peacocking around and expecting the locals to worship him by proxy of the crown. Absurd.

"Will the king be visiting the area, like Elizabeth did before him?" She was poking the bear, but no one had ever accused her of common sense.

The man looked like he was ready to slap her silly and beat the stupid out of her.

"Watch your tongue, witch, or you will lose it," the man hissed through grit teeth.

As much as she wanted to reply and argue about him calling her a witch—it was one thing for an angry neighbour to say it and another entirely for a man of the law to throw out such accusations—it'd been a perfectly reasonable question. Other than how she'd subtly asked if the man was insecure after being snubbed by the *new* monarch. The king who would've been on the throne a decade next year (not so new anymore).

Nowell was not as high standing with the royals as he wanted them to think. Demdike couldn't decide if this was a good thing or not. Amusing for her, but when a man's pride was hurt, they lashed out. Became desperate to prove their worth. Looked for any way to climb the ladder. Demdike would normally watch on as he made a fool of himself, but this man had a level of sharp cunning. He might actually manage the feat.

Nowell came here planting seeds. Slowly sewing distrust and working the locals into a frenzy. He hadn't come in guns blazing, which would have made locals immediately turn him away. No, instead he'd been the invisible hand, moving the people with respected voices to puppet his words and intentions. Returning just often enough to keep people afraid and thinking. Where others would have been subtly excluded, he was wearing a groove, being welcomed by the rich and poor equally. People were smiling at the sight of his face, as though they couldn't feel the darkness this man was built by. The death and destruction he radiated.

Where normally Pendle rejected strangers, Nowell was being accepted as one of them. Being from Lancashire wasn't enough, people had to prove themselves in some way. A task he'd managed. His voice gained traction with every return to their little borough. Calling her a witch now served a two-fold purpose, showing everyone he believed her to be one and implying this was why he'd returned. Mentioning the king obsessed with witches was a misstep on her part. A pit grew in her stomach. She may have unconsciously just handed him the keys to his next step up the grubby ladder of social climbing.

Despite knowing logically this was not a good situation to be in, there was a small part of her which filled with a sense of success. Even if she didn't win the war, this battle was most definitely a draw. Rage seeped from him, whilst the Justice couldn't act as he wanted. The violence promised in those black lagoons would have made a weaker woman weep. She'd originally planned to taunt the beast a little more, fake apologise whilst poking his fragile ego, but it was no longer worth the risk.

"Apologies," she said in a small tone, the one she had perfected in her childhood on the rare occasions her father had shown disappointment in her. "A lowly old woman like myself doesn't know as much about such things as the whispered words one hears."

Okay, she couldn't resist a small dig, but she'd given a submissive enough reply to curb the man's desire to inflict pain.

"You should be careful, Demdike," he spat her name. "Your wicked ways can only protect you for so long." He strode away from her stall at speed.

A generous person would have said with haste. She thought it resembled someone who was fleeing whilst the hounds chased them off. Demdike suspected this was another aspect of his ongoing play. To act as though she'd done something. Or maybe he was genuinely afraid? She doubted it somehow. A predator could always spot another one. But she was the fox to his snake. He was lying in wait. She'd spent her life being sly and running from danger, where he slowly laid the trap around his victim, caging them in, until they could no longer escape.

Unfortunately, recognising these things and being capable of stopping them were two very different issues. Demdike wasn't the smartest woman, but she was far from stupid. This isolation and ostracisation was building to something more. Seeds of suspicions slowly gained life. Growing with every slight paranoia, adding to the overwhelming sense of fear. The average person becoming more riled up, looking for someone to point fingers at. People to blame for every bad thing that came to pass.

She watched on hopelessly as people's strings were pulled, entirely unaware they were being manipulated to fulfil the agenda of a greedy monster. Because Nowell was. Beneath the polished surface, he was a demon, given skin. A black hole walking among them waiting to suck them people into his orbit and swallow them body and soul. Demdike had been aware of demons for many years, of their evil. She still doubted all of one species was inherently bad, but when faced with

Nowell, she could think of no other word to describe the hatred and malice colouring his aura. She would need a bath tonight. In blessed water.

***

It'd been a while since she and Chattox crossed paths. The two often frequented the same areas, and there'd been one point where they would have an argument a week simply because they were constantly getting in one another's way, but that was when the two held more energy and vitality. Demdike could admit her common sense went straight out the window where the other crone was concerned.

The two had spent almost their entire lives bickering with one another. A hard habit to break. It'd been a few months since she'd so much as shared a glance with the other woman, let alone a cross word. A strange occurrence. She almost missed their antagonistic relationship. This wasn't why Demdike was currently making her way towards Chattox's home. Not at all.

Demdike didn't care if the other had gotten sick or broken a bone and this was why she hadn't seen her since Christmas time. No, those were groundless fears, and she had several very real fears to discuss with her counterpart. The other wise woman. The one who may or may not have taken steps down the dark path. Banging on the door, Demdike could hear a few clanks and shuffles from inside before the wooden slat slammed open.

"You took your time getting here," not a greeting.

Chattox, having such keen foresight, had long irritated Demdike. She could read the ambient energies, interpret them, and even had prophetic dreams. Demdike was no slouch, yet she was practically a novice to the other woman's gift. The strength of Chattox's ability had been a point of contention between the pair for years. Though not solely due to envy, as the other assumed. Demdike was frustrated by how heavily the other relied on her prophetic gifts. Often to the exclusion of common sense and any intellect. Just because you knew some of the puzzle pieces before they formed did not give you the full picture. She'd more than once had to school the other on such oversights.

How someone able to see the future was so blind to multiple possibilities always confused her, but Demdike had learnt it was better to hold her tongue and let others make their own mistakes. The other being right as often as she was, hadn't helped with their tense rivalry. Even now, Demdike would hesitate to call it a friendship. Yet there was a camaraderie which came with age. Living and surviving through the same events, meeting the same people, watching the same catastrophes. Left a sense of understanding. A quiet settlement where words were barely necessary. Were the two not so often in competition, they might have been able to be true friends. Not in this life, but she held out hope for the next.

"Afternoon, to you too," she replied, not waiting to be invited inside.

"I put the water on already. You can pour yourself a cup." As much of a welcome as could be expected from the other.

Demdike let the leaves stew, before adding a little sugar. The other preferred honey, and she added a spoonful to her cup. Chattox refused to admit her eyes had been failing in recent years, and Demdike was kind enough not to call her a daft cow for trying to ignore it and not adding more light to her home. Surely the other knew straining her eyes in the dark was making the problem worse? But again, Demdike knew it was best to hold your tongue over certain arguments.

She took a seat on the opposite side of the fireplace, handing the cup to the other. They'd done this many times. When consulting one another on hard cases, when formulating plans to drum up more business, or for simple catch-ups. They'd also convened for what they jokingly referred to as a war council on several occasions. When they were aware of an imminent threat and needed to work together to survive it. Nowell was the reason for this meeting.

"Death's marked ya," the other woman croaked, even after several sips of tea.

Perhaps Demdike's worries about the others being sick weren't unfounded.

"And you," she replied casually.

They were both old. Death was not a worry for them.

"And others." Chattox smiled, her mouth having gaps where decay had claimed the once pearls.

Demdike nodded. She'd feared as much. Despite checking since Halloween, there'd been no visible mark to show death was closing in. Even in the ether's realm, her soul showed nothing out of the ordinary, and yet she could sense it. A slight chill which couldn't be warmed, no matter how hard she tried. Demdike believed even if she were to burn, this chill would linger in her body. It wasn't a physical presence, and yet it felt as though it were.

"He's made no secrets of his game, for those who know how to spot them," Demdike said instead. There was no need for complicated explanations, the other could fill in any blanks her words left.

"For those who have seen these things before. You forget, most are not as old as we are. Many are lucky to reach their first score, let alone a third and fourth."

Demdike couldn't help laughing at this. Those sixteen years between them had been a point of contention many times. A young Elizabeth already thought herself an adult when the other was born. With hindsight, she could see she'd been nothing more than a babe herself, but believing yourself wise was one of the many follies of youth. Though she still enjoyed reminding the other, she was walking the grey path before the other was able to walk at all. It was more of a joke these days, but she still pulled rank more than once. Not that Chattox ever listened. They were more like siblings, or perhaps contentious cousins, by this point in their lives. Both community and competition.

"And if we point it out to them, we will be the bad guys. Spreading falsities and weaving our wicked spells." Demdike couldn't help scoffing at such things.

Chattox hummed, taking a slow sip of her drink. Demdike removed her eyes from her fellow crone, staring into the flames. She tried not to do this too often. The spirits of fire were great guidance in times of hardship, but they were too fast, too volatile. They didn't help her already impulsive nature. Better for her to scry in the calm water, her natural opposite, than to be led by the flames which already burned within her soul. The oranges and reds made her gut clench before settling.

"He's a clever one."

"Have you met him?"

"No, I have avoided his path, but he has been trying to search me out."

"Is this why I have barely seen you?" Demdike couldn't help questioning.

"Partly. Though my spell required more time and concentration than I'd expected."

There it was, the other reason she was here, or at least had initially intended to come. There were several important topics, though this was the most pressing. As she relaxed back into the chair, Demdike could sense this would be the last time she would ever be here. The punch to the gut told her what she'd already suspected.

"The dark path," Demdike was surprised, her words sounded more resigned than accusatory.

"Darker. But mostly within the grey,"

"Really? And using fresh corpses?" there was a little more accusation this time, but more shock than anything.

"The last of the line spell," the other replied flatly.

Demdike felt as though someone had stolen all the air from her lungs. "Anne and Bessie?"

"Bessie will be fine, but she is barren."

Demdike hadn't known this, though given the stories the younger woman shared, it shouldn't have been a surprise. Such activities would have guaranteed most girls would have been caught. A bun in the oven long before now.

"You should do it too. Or add yours to mine."

There had been a few occasions in Demdike's life where she recognised fate using another person as a mouthpiece. She'd been her hand on earth before. Saying words and performing actions not her own to aid the higher beings. It was an odd experience, leaving most questioning their minds when they spoke things they hadn't intended to say. As a person half in this world and half in the next, it'd only been odd to deliver messages the first few times. After decades of following the path, this was as much a part of her life as the clicking joints and achy knees. Didn't happen every day, but often enough.

Chattox, being a mouthpiece to deliver a message to her, filled Demdike's veins with ice. She'd hoped Alizon's reading was wrong, that she'd interpreted the signs incorrectly. Hoped they would spare the children. Fate had confirmed her worst fears. Her death would not come alone. There was hope for little Jennet, but not much beyond her. Their two youngest granddaughters would be the only hope for ensuring their blood survived. The gifts carried from generation to generation would live on after they were gone.

Demdike could feel her stomach wanting to part with its contents. She handed over a piece of cloth. One Jennet had given her earlier, as a hanky. The only thing she had to hand which the girl had touched. A horrible realisation, or maybe acknowledgement might be the better word, to know her greatest fears were not only well-founded, but soon to come.

"What can we do?"

"Besides curse the land and every person on it?" a dark joke, but the desire was there.

"Other than that?"

"I honestly don't know. Other than hoping our abilities live on and can ensure future generations aren't left vulnerable to the many spirits which would do them harm? I have no idea. Nothing that wouldn't involve going dark. And if they plan to claim my life and break my body, I'll be damned if I let them have my soul as well."

Demdike could feel the spite waving off the other woman's body. The anger and injustice Chattox felt. Would normally have been right there with her, but after the shock of a few moments earlier, all the woman felt was tired. As though her age had caught up with her all at once and those long hard years were showing no mercy. She needed to rest, an eternal rest apparently.

"Aye, we might not be able to stop them, but we can at least make it difficult for them."

"That Nowell, what were your thoughts on him?"

"Evil given human form. Dark. Death follows him. Not someone I would choose to be near."

"Could he be working for the higher beings?" Chattox challenged.

"The only thing that man would worship is himself."

"Can we use this against him?"

"His pride? Maybe. Though I don't think he cares enough about anyone or anything other than his own position and reputation, and there isn't much we can do about either. He's basically untouchable, and he knows it." Demdike sighed.

"Perhaps we can plague him with nightmares. Curse him to never having a good night's rest again," Chattox suggested with a gleam in her eyes.

"Do devils have fears?" she asked in jest.

Demdike absently wondered if sending the man nightmares about being drowned in holy water would do much more than feed his ego and have him believe he was doing God's work. She would put little past the man.

"Maybe have him live our deaths over and over."

"A karmic curse? Might be our only option, but it will do little good when we'll already be dead and he'll have succeeded in his task."

"Which is?" the other asked eagerly, sitting up in her chair.

"To find favour with the king, of course."

The other hummed once more, calming with disappointment. "Then we make it so he doesn't. Witch hunting fell out of favour as the men of science rose. We make him a laughingstock, an embarrassment. The person others look at and think lowly of."

"And of our neighbours?" she asked cautiously, not truly believing what the other had said was possible, but refrained from pointing this out.

"Easy. We make them fear who will be next. You remember how it used to be. People were afraid of every shadow because it soon turned from who were the witches, to who would be called a witch next? They might not remember the last witch hunts, or gone to Scotland and seen theirs, but many families lost someone to the reformations and how messy those became. People pointing fingers at everyone. We let the maggots feast on themselves."

"All for the small price of our families."

Chattox sighed. "You're welcome to try to stop it, but you know as well as I that this is bigger than you and me. The old gods themselves are involved here."

Demdike wanted to pull her hair out in frustration. Didn't matter how much she might understand this logically—how after years of walking the path, she knew certain births and deaths were inevitable—it made her no less angry. Made her no less desperate to try everything in her power to ensure such realities did not come to fruition.

"And be careful of your Alizon. That girl has carried the mark of the other world from the moment she was born."

Demdike couldn't help but flinch at the words. "She isn't a fae. I tested her."

"Her soul isn't human, though. Even you cannot deny this."

Demdike said nothing as she placed her cup down gently and gathered her outer robes.

"I suppose the next time I see you will be at the gallows?" It was supposed to be a joke, but felt a little too poignant.

"No, we'll be going on a long walk before that."

Demdike decided it was best to ignore the other's comment. For sanity's sake.

***

The house was settling in the early evening. Creaks of the wood grunted throughout their home, as the last of the sun's rays were leaving. Fingers of pink and purple clawed into the hillside, as though the sun protested its leave. Unlike the rest of the world, there was no guarantee it would return tomorrow. Not when the north was famous for its thick grey skies. Bessie had once told her it rained more in the northwest of England than anywhere else on the isle.

Demdike had thought the girl likely to exaggerate, and had taken her statement with a pinch of salt, but it wasn't the first time she'd heard travellers declare how the rain here poured and bounced back from the ground with such a vengeance it were as though the gods of old were angry here.

Today, however, weather-wise, had been beautiful. As if the world itself had granted her one last good day as a backdrop to fate's cruel declaration. Ever since returning from Chattox's home, she couldn't look her family in the eyes. Knowing, or at the very least suspecting, the fatal reality approaching. Had she not been a wise woman, or a member of the cunning folk, she could have gone about her life happily oblivious to the changing tides around them. Now it was as though they'd gone cockle-picking and the water changed ahead of time. They were trapped, but the others didn't know yet.

Demdike could almost envy them their peaceful ignorance. But this was a cost she accepted when first walking the grey road. Sometimes in life she would know things before they came to pass, and there would be nothing she could do to prevent them. It was a harsh truth, and one she'd endured many times, but the cost never felt as heavy as it did now.

She watched James and Jennet playing about the living room, chasing and tagging the other. Where soon her family's presence in the house would be mere shadows left behind. Demdike could almost see Jennet turning around, to find them all gone.

A harsh burden to leave upon a young girl. To leave her the family's legacy. As cruel to her as it was to them. To wither away from this world long before their time was due. For the vibrancy of their souls to be candles blown out by the hurricane Nowell. None of it was fair, and yet, Demdike couldn't have said who she pitied more. James, who was to be cut down before even reaching his prime, or Jennet, to be left to walk this road alone. Bereft of all those who loved her.

Demdike debated warning the young lass, but her tongue refused to move in her mouth. The spell had already begun; the die was cast, and now fate would place the pieces wherever they were meant to lay. Walking the grey road made a person understand the ether in ways other souls could not. Demdike didn't fear death because she'd already accepted it as being the next step on the soul's eternal journey. However, acceptance didn't mean she couldn't worry.

Whether she were to depart for heaven, or one of the other philosophical counterparts, she couldn't say. Though she hoped against hope that whatever it was labelled: hell, Tartarus or the underworld, she wouldn't find her soul trapped there. Whichever religion might be right, they all held one constant, a good place for good souls, and a bad place for the bad. Demdike prayed she'd racked up enough good karma for the former.

Demdike was a part of the '*needs must*'. A necessity for life to continue. Even if the crown tried to kill all the cunning folk, they would not die. It was a calling, something which spoke to the soul. Those who walked the physical world but had never truly left the land of the dead. Call it reincarnation, call it psychic ability, call it yearning for a home you cannot recall. The label didn't matter, so long as humans as a species existed, so would those who walked the barriers between the worlds. With one foot on either side.

Didn't matter what gods they believed in, what cultures they were raised in, or the colour of their skin, this was a matter of soul, not body. The cunning folk couldn't die. Their gifts, however, those could be lost. Such as Chattox's gift of foresight, or Demdike's own ability to heal ailments. Ones most couldn't even dream of managing. Their gifts came from the higher powers. Whether from the old gods of the land they lived on, the realm of the dead, or somewhere so beyond human awareness, Demdike couldn't even guess.

The *where* didn't matter. A gift was only as useful as the one who wields it. If cunning folk ignored their abilities, they would be no more of use than the average person. The *where* might not matter, but the *what* did. What gifts they had blessed you with, and what you did with them.

Demdike hoped Jennet could allow the bloodline to flow, or the world would lose some of its most valuable healers. Goodness only knows what could happen if the natural healers were gone. If the last defence between the physical world and spiritual sickness were torn down. People would start falling in droves.

It took a special something within the soul for one to walk the path. A resolution of knowing who you truly were, and being able to bear the burdens of the higher beings. Even when they seemed unnecessarily cruel to those on the mortal coil. Demdike now struggled with such weight. She had hoped, when death began to circle, he would come and claim her alone.

She'd lived into the twilight of her life and beyond. Been lucky (or unlucky) enough to experience this much life. Both its greatest joys and darkest atrocities. Walking the path felt like a blessing as well as a curse. A blessing to know what others could not, and a curse to be looked down upon for something you couldn't help. There were those who ignored the call of course, and there were those who began the path and had to abandon it, but for all it had given and taken away, Demdike felt, on balance, it had been worth it. However, faced with the latest and greatest challenge, she was no longer as convinced.

Though for all her worrying and doubting, fate had already spoken. Demdike could plan and scheme, rage and scream. It would make no difference. When Alizon burst through the door, face almost purple in rage, an iceberg could have sunk in her stomach. The girl wore green about her body. Not physically, but spiritually, fate had already begun weaving her thread into the tapestry of their lives. There wasn't even one hint of gold. It was the green of a bog, dark enough to be close to black. Poison. Death. It was time.

"And he refused?"

Demdike hadn't heard the start of the tale, but soon caught up with the rest of what was being said. Alizon tried to buy some pins from a peddler, had her coins ready as proof, and the man refused to sell to her simply because he thought her too low and not worth his efforts.

It was one of the few things which darkly amused her, how no matter how much people scorned them, they would still happily accept their money. This was new. The man wasn't some member of the gentry refusing to consort with peasants, or some merchant on a deadline who could ill afford to stop a cart for fear of thieves. It'd been a lone person, perfectly capable of selling her the goods, and he'd refused. A petty act. Likely someone who'd heard the hurtful rumours about them and their family, and the man embarrassed a young girl simply to feel his own sense of superiority. What other reason could there be? Alizon had the money.

Fate was lining up her toys before she knocked them all over. Chattox's words from earlier came back to haunt her. Had the woman foreseen this incident as well?

"I hope he sits on the chamber pot and falls in," James declared passionately.

"I hope everything he eats tastes like ash in his mouth," Jennet added eagerly.

The children didn't understand curses. Didn't know how words could cause spells. How, by projecting them into the air, the spirits might listen and act upon them. Though the beings seemed to favour the malicious ones more than her many requests for food and money. They still didn't know, and as Alizon declared her final hope, Demdike could almost see the magic taking shape.

"I hope he falls from his high horse and learns what it's like down here in the dirt. The pompous ass."

They weren't terrible curses. Jinxes at most, not even close to hexes. Or they wouldn't have been—normally. James once threatened to put pins in the eye of one guy who'd looked at his sister too long. She'd threatened to tan hides and break bones of anyone trying to force themselves on her and hers. Even Lizzie, with all her gentleness, cursed and said she would happily bash the children who'd once thrown a rock at her baby with those same stones. They'd all said worse. Venting their frustrations in the privacy of their own home, but this was the first time Demdike had seen those wishes take shape. Her own tongue still refused to move.

"But old mould heels gave me a little cloth, so it wasn't all bad."

Demdike could practically hear the spirits whisper how '*no good deed goes unpunished*' bad things weren't coming. They'd already begun.

Chapter Fourteen

S pinning the wheel was as passive an action as breathing. Dying the wools and monitoring their progress took a little more concentration; having to ensure they were coloured equally and didn't turn brittle and break. Airing out the cloth and cutting them to precise sizes, she could have done it in her sleep. As was normal of any action you'd done day in and day out for years on end. Often, even in her dreams, she performed the same monotonous tasks.

All these jobs had taken great skill in the beginning, but it'd been over a decade since Katherine had wed her husband, Oliver Hewitt and he inherited the business from his father. When all the tasks of acquiring, running and selling fell to their shoulders. As her husband had a great head for business and deal-making, but less for the day-to-day operations, it became her role to ensure things ran smoothly.

The daily tasks took up such a large part of her life that even her unconscious wouldn't allow her an escape. She didn't begrudge her husband his constantly changing schedule; having to wear many hats and travel from place to place all the time, but she did wish for a little more variety in her everyday routine. It was always the same: wake up, have a warm drink and eat a little, go to work, come home, sleep, repeat.

She made each day slightly different in how Wednesdays were specifically for dying clothes and Fridays for collecting the wool, but these were more because of deliveries and their business partners' schedules. However, even if it meant there were different tasks from day to day when it became week by week, it was all the same again. Not to mention month-by-month and year-by-year. The only excitement they ever got was when some local lord or lady was throwing a big party and needed a large order, but those were the rare exceptions.

Upon her marriage, Katherine had been entirely new to the clothier business. A steep learning curve for her. She'd made mistakes, of course, but it'd all been too fun to dwell on the little problems. What did a few torn threads matter when these new ways of colouring the cloth had just been discovered? Why care for a few broken pins when she had entire barrels of fillings to be sorting? It'd all been new and exciting and she'd wanted every day to always be the same. Be careful what you wish for.

Pendle had been a nice place to move to as well. She hadn't moved far. A few towns over, from a neighbouring borough, but the locals had regarded her as nothing more than a stranger, an outsider, for several years. Eventually, she'd become as much a part of the community—of the furniture of their little home—as everyone else, but it had taken work.

This was partly why she'd been obsessed with ensuring their business survived. She hadn't wanted the locals to look at her with disdain for yet another reason. The people could be incredibly cruel without any conscious thought. Excluding people simply because they were different.

It might have been years since, but she remembered the pain. Of having no friends and little support. People might have called her a cow and not liked her now, but this was once they knew her. People not liking Katherine because they knew her personality and decided she wasn't for them was fine, but disliking someone because they were new to the area or an outcast? Having nothing to do with the individual in question beyond how the rumours circled? This annoyed her. She'd learnt to pay the whispers of Pendle little heed. People with small minds and little to do all day needed something to stave off their boredom, and bringing others down seemed to be their favourite pastime.

Maybe she was being a little unkind. Katherine had many great friends across Pendle. People who hadn't been outright hostile back then. Though the avoidance and cold stares had been hard to bear when it came from everyone in this small community. Her friends may have apologised since then, but Katherine made a pledge to be different from them. She refused to judge based on the words of others. She chose to observe the actions, then form an opinion.

Unfortunately, she spent most of her life working on their business and saw little of people beyond market days and when she needed to go out and about for stock. Deliveries were mostly dropped and collected here at the workshop, but there were always reasons she needed to get more. Items broken in transit. Things not working out as expected. One time a worker had knocked a bowl, and they'd lost an entire day's worth of work, meaning she'd had to go over to the next town to source the same materials and complete the order on time. Little things, which, although annoying, couldn't be helped.

Therefore, for all she did go out and about, usually travelling between Rough Lee and Colne, it was mostly work-related. She wasn't listening for the latest gossip—though if she sometimes stopped for a quick brew and catch up, it was simply to be polite. The point was, she didn't get to observe many people and often the rumours were her only awareness of one person or another. Katherine might have wanted to be a better person, but she was as flawed an individual as anyone else.

When she came across a young girl crying on her way back from town, her first instinct had been to look the other way. Every woman knew the shame of being found whilst having a cry in solitude. However, this girl didn't seem to be aware of much beyond her mission to keep pushing forward. Katherine automatically checked the girl's clothes for signs of anything untoward. It would hardly be some great surprise. Men of means taking liberties with the younger ones. Luckily, the patches on her clothes spoke of the girl's poverty, but not any potential attacks.

When the red-cheeked youngster spotted her, she froze like a wild animal. One who'd noticed a threat and was hoping the other remained oblivious to them. Katherine almost wanted to smile, but smiling at someone who was crying could easily be interpreted as taking humour from their distress and she didn't want to accidentally aggravate the other.

"Are you okay?" Katherine asked, keeping her voice gentle, unthreatening.

The girl's eyes darted back and forth as though waiting for people to spring from everywhere and attack. Katherine recognised this skittishness. She'd seen it in the mirror many times, particularly those first few months of moving to the area. Whoever this girl was, she wasn't used to kindness. Katherine's actions were making the little mouse mighty suspicious, if the girl's tightening frame was anything to judge by.

"I just got some ale from the market. Might you join me in a glass, at least until your cheeks are less red?"

At the acknowledgement of her predicament, the girl wiped her face. A scowl replaced her distrust. Though to Katherine it looked more like a little hamster—puffed cheeks, rosy red, trying to be intimidating. She kept her calm countenance, and pointed the way, letting the girl follow her at her own pace. When they made it to her office in the workshop, she handed the girl a cup with a small splash of liquid in it. It didn't take long for Alizon, as she learned the girl was called, to share her entire harrowing experience.

"John Law is a joke of a man," Katherine couldn't help adding.

Having dealt with the man many times in her trade. He was always bemoaning the quality of their fabrics and trying to haggle for a better price. She was convinced it was that annoyance who started calling her '*mould heels*' because of their linens. They were the best quality in the area, but they lived in a constantly cold and damp place. Today's rare patch of sunshine aside. Keeping the mould from the cloth was a losing battle, and he knew this, but he was an entitled ass and a charlatan. The man would have been good for the stage, a great actor but with little substance in the real world.

As the two commiserated over their other run-ins with the man and with the many faces of Pendle, the girl had gone from weepy to angry. Venting her many frustrations at the world. Alizon had dreams of escaping. Of a great love and adventure, though the boy she'd thought was her future was no longer certain. Whether he was to stand by her side or not, she was resolved to leave their little neck of the woods. Convinced the world beyond would be kinder. Katherine hadn't had the heart to tell her how few places were kind to strangers, especially ones without a great fortune, but she didn't want to shatter the girl for a second time in one day.

At parting, she gave Alizon a few of the scraps of fabric. They were usually donated to the church or to the farms anyway, and the little one deserved something to brighten the personal storm cloud she seemed to be carrying around. Katherine hadn't realised the girl was the granddaughter of the famed Demdike until several days after.

A blessing, for had she been aware, Katherine feared she would have been more reserved with the child. Although she tried to be good, she wasn't immune to the fears Demdike generated. If one believed the rumours, Katherine wouldn't have seen what a kind and funny girl the Device child was.

Going to the local tavern with her husband the following Sunday was a part of their routine. After church, they would get a meal and have a cup or two with friends, nothing out of the ordinary. What was unusual, however, was how the building was almost buzzing with the latest gossip. From the moment they walked in, it was obvious by the way people were going from group to group, like children eagerly sharing every tidbit they'd learnt.

Between them finding the table and ordering, three separate people, asking if they'd '*heard the news*', visited them. Within a few minutes, she'd heard multiple versions of the same retelling. Soon enough, the entirety of Pendle would be ripe with the sharing and twisting of this story. Altering as it jumped from person to person, distorting what had supposedly happened to John Law. Poor unfortunate John, targeted by the wicked witch.

The most recent tale went like this:

John had been walking the hills on his way here, readying for the next market, when he came across a crazed Alizon. When she demanded he sell her his pins, he refused the wench. Declaring her a liar and a thief and he would not open his sack so that she might steal from him.

(Katherine noticed there was no mention of the coins she'd seen with her own eyes.)

When he'd walked away, the girl had shouted curses after him, wishing him ill and announcing he would be harmed by her craft.

(Again, Katherine doubted this was the entire truth. Alizon likely shouted something unkind after the man who'd been rude to her, but the rest sounded like idle fiction at best. Though the rumour mill was already absorbed in the drama of Alizon's potential declaration.)

Upon reaching the inn, John Law had managed a meal and a drink, before falling over and becrying witchcraft, declaring the girl had cursed him and in her bewitchment of him, meant his death.

The story kept altering to him crashing through the doorway and collapsing in a dramatic fashion to others where the man fell down on the road and never made it to the inn at all. How he was then lying upstairs in one of the beds, seemed to have escaped everyone's notice. How would anyone have even known to bring him to this inn, let alone been able to carry him? However, the gossip mongers didn't care for logic.

The story was far more entertaining if the man had fallen down just as Alizon cursed him out in the fields. Katherine wanted to point out how the girl and supposed '*thief*' would have then had ample opportunity to claim the pins she wanted, but again, logic didn't make a good story.

Katherine also wanted to say how the others had been with her during this time, but her voice was lost to the sea of people, guessing what might have happened and adding their own spin to the story.

After all this, John—despite supposedly being at death's door and unable to move—had sent a note to his son. Abraham Law (said son) was due to arrive three days hence. Everyone was on pins waiting for the next instalment of the drama. Twitching every time, the door opened in case the man mysteriously arrived ahead of schedule.

When Nowell came through the door of the inn, he held a sense of glee about his step. His face looked calm and collected, but there was something beneath it, like when the men were hunting a fox, and they'd finally found its burrow.

Katherine was almost relieved on Monday to go back to spinning yarn and dying clothes. Far less exciting than unnecessary drama. Though in her mind, silently where no one else could hear, she wondered. If she hadn't met Alizon herself—had she not seen the distraught girl as she'd walked her way home heartbroken after such an encounter—Katherine wondered (feared), if she would have been another voice in the crowd, adding to the drama of what occurred. Speculating what happened that day. And more importantly, what was to happen next?

CHAPTER FIFTEEN

The scent of rain weaved its way through their home. Of damp earth and unsettled foliage. New life swathed in decay. Spring was in full bloom, and yet it hadn't reached their house. The wildflowers of the forest held enough scent to dance along the breeze and tease them, but despite a few warm days, it still felt like winter at Malkin Tower. Or at least it did for Demdike. There had been no warming with the seasons this year. Only a chill which refused to leave.

The cold was nothing new. Since last Hallow's Eve, it'd endured. Today, however, there was a strange addition to her usual frigid frame. A shivering not caused by cold, but by the ice in her stomach. Since waking in the afternoon (rather than at first light), Demdike couldn't shift this unease. She didn't feel *sick*-sick, but neither did she feel well.

It wasn't a cold, as there was no cough or runny nose. She wasn't reacting to the seasons as some did; when the flowers spread across the earth and the trees danced with their blooms, causing many to have itchiness around the eyes, nose and mouth. Demdike hadn't a temperature or the flu; Lizzie checked earlier. She hadn't thrown up or needed to visit the chamber pot—all the typical signals one might have caught something foul—were absent. Yet she still didn't feel right.

Her body's tiredness was hardly something to judge her health by, as a constant state of being. Though Demdike had been happy to note, she was still much sprier than many of those even half her age. Still, Demdike felt wrong. The world moved around her whilst she remained dizzy in the centre, feeling every turn but barely moving in place.

It reminded her of a moment in her youth. When the travellers passed through. Playing their music and dancing for the entertainment of the locals. They were the only strangers welcomed here, mostly because everyone knew they would soon leave. Like visiting family, they regularly reappeared but were never there long enough to wear out their welcome. On one of their visits, there'd been a boy. He'd seemed like a man to the young Elizabeth, but to Demdike's grand age, he'd barely been born. Seven and ten summers, at most. Back then, anyone a few years older felt incredibly grown up.

The boy played a song. His instrument of wood and string created such a mournful sound, it haunted her for years to come. The melancholy melody he'd strung with his fingers felt like the grave come early. Chased the living and left behind a cold so deep it ached in a person's core. Demdike never discovered what caused the young man to play a tune filled with so much sorrow it brought tears to her eyes, but she'd never forgotten it either.

The cold of his music was eerily similar to what she was feeling, but this ache today left her wondering if he'd known death was stalking him. She wondered if his skill enabled him to put a sound to what he'd been sensing. There was the funeral march of the church, but even those didn't come close to the intrinsic fear of knowing death was coming and it wasn't coming quietly.

It took Demdike a few hours to recognise the feeling. To recall the foreign cold he'd conjured. Years passed since she'd felt this way. Helpless in the face of something much bigger and more frightening than her. Though logically death shouldn't frighten those with more friends and family on the other side than in this world, her animal instincts still rose in alarm.

As a mother, then later grandmother, Demdike knew this confusing sensation well. Love as a parent, as a person responsible for another, was never just love. It was always bundled with worry. With constant concern about what may happen the moment they were out of sight. The two emotions overlapped completely. There was never love without worry and never worry without love.

This was why it took her hours to parse out what she was feeling. Demdike had little to fear over the years, beyond the general troubles for her family. Worry had been tinged with love for so long it became synonymous. The two lived simultaneously in her heart for most of her life. She'd forgotten what it meant to feel one or the other separately. The churning of her stomach could've made five pails of butter in one afternoon, then cleaned all their clothes for good measure. Anxiety was both a constant and entirely foreign experience. She almost didn't recognise it.

When death staked its claim, she knew this wasn't good, but it hadn't frightened her. When she looked into Nowell's eyes and felt the world being sucked into his cavernous blackness, she'd been troubled, but it'd all been abstract. Leaving an awareness she should be afraid, but thinking how, having lived for so long, death would be a welcomed friend.

Like all people, she feared pain and didn't want to experience starvation or burning in particular, but there had been a subconscious level of removal to the *how* it might happen. She would die. As someone who walked alongside the dead for most of her life, this was nothing to fear. Just another thing which would come to pass. The sun would rise, the grass would grow, and one day, she would depart the mortal plane. Demdike accepted this and waited for the inevitable. It was not a cause of concern in her head or her heart.

In all things, there was a distance. When you'd racked up as many years on the earth as she had, and survived as much as Demdike endured, it was easy to overlook or ignore certain fears. Easy to recognise a threat but not feel it. Now the safety barrier was torn away, and she felt everything once again. Demdike didn't like this, already missing the calm consistency of her previous emotions. Or lack thereof.

"Where's Alizon?" she eventually put words to the cause of her unease.

Jennet had been playing games and going about her day in the carefree way only a child could manage. James popped in briefly, whittling away with a new piece of wood. Determined to earn a bit of coin whilst between jobs. Lizzie had come and gone several times, enforcing how Demdike needed to rest and returning regularly to check her mother was following these orders.

Demdike would have normally protested she wasn't an invalid and was more than capable of pottering around the house and still resting, but her daughter was in a foul mood and honestly, she was too tired to fight pointlessly when her body was this jumpy. She wouldn't speak it aloud, but something had opened the floodgates on her emotions. Left her struggling to stay afloat amidst all the crashing sensations.

Every shadow felt like a potential threat. Demdike wanted her entire family here. All of them under one roof. She needed them here. Away from the dangers. Away from the outside world as it encroached further and further into their territory. Something was coming.

Every sound was a prelude to the song from her youth. Impressed onto the world. Embossed itself onto the surrounding reality. A filter over the life she knew; distorting her view and colouring this average day. Safe no longer. The sound crept in. A haunting tune like a gentle stream flowing over everything and leaving a sheen behind. Difficult to ignore.

Demdike often fought with her words. Struggled to articulate the things she knew instinctively. How does one explain a reality others don't know? But now, as darkness came closer, her mind quickly found a thousand ways to describe the experience. Yet she still couldn't push them from her mouth. Her tongue froze to its roof, as though the frosts of winter held the thing in place, sticking it to the roof and preventing her need to scream.

"She hasn't come home yet," was Lizzie's almost snappish reply. At hearing her own tone, the woman flashed a sheepish look.

"James, go and look for your sister," Demdike instructed the boy.

When the smart ass pointed to little Jennet, Demdike had no qualms about hitting him across his head. Ignoring his over-exaggerated '*ow*', she hadn't hit the brat hard.

"Go find Alizon," she repeated, giving the boy a stern stare alongside it.

With a huff, James put down his whittling, making no secret of his discontent. She would've hit him again, but the boy had little sense he could afford to lose. Tempting though it was.

It was a long couple of hours before the boy returned. She sat by the fire, knitting away. Demdike had never been a big knitter. A skill she learnt out of necessity, but it did help her mind settle. The repeated patterns, the monotonous movements, kept her hands occupied and her brain focused on other things. She'd spent many a night communing with the spirits whilst working the large needles and thread.

It was cheaper to buy twine or wool and make things than to buy ready-made clothes. Thus, knitting had become a staple. Her huge aversion to wet socks and living in one of the wettest places in the country might've also been a secondary motivator. She'd taught all the others the skills too, including James. There were no male or female jobs under her roof, just work which needed doing. The boy having a talent for whittling had been mere serendipity. Alizon was better on the spinning wheel, but theirs had broken years back and they didn't have the spare coin to replace it. Lizzie was the sewer, turning their scraps of fabric into wearable outfits. Jennet had yet to come into her own, but no doubt she would develop some ability in time.

When James crashed through the door, she had calmed herself, mostly, but upon seeing him alone her heartbeat picked up pace.

"Couldn't find her." He shrugged.

"Did ya even look?" she couldn't help snapping at the boy.

"Of course I did. She wasn't by the farms, in the village, by the river, near the churches, or by Peter's place. No idea where else she could be," he griped back, clearly unhappy at her accusation.

Demdike took a breath, reminding herself not to be angry with the child. The situation wasn't his fault. Seeing the sweat on his brow and the heavier breath, it was apparent he'd been running about, trying to find her before the light faded. As the last of the sun's rays reached their home, and the darkness fast approached, it seemed like yet another sign. The churning in her stomach reappeared with a vengeance.

"What was that?" Lizzie's voice came from the other room. Panic in her tone.

"What was what?" James asked before she could.

"I swore—I could have—I heard…" The woman was looking around as though searching for something.

Demdike and James naturally mirrored the woman, trying to find the source of the noise neither of them heard. When Jennet came in the door, having grown bored with playing outside and likely chilled by the dying sun, she looked equally as perplexed.

"There was growling," Lizzie finally finished.

For all her stomach was swirling, it soon dropped through the floor. There was only one reason a person would hear growling that others couldn't. How had such a thing made its way into her home?

It was then a long night, as she burnt sage and blessed the home multiple times, but the growling never came again. There'd been nothing to indicate it'd ever been there at all. Had she not seen the fear and confusion on her daughter's face, Demdike would've never known about its presence at all. Had it been here before? Did it follow her, or Alizon, home? Had it come with Jane during one of her weekly visits and stayed? Demdike couldn't answer these questions.

The entire situation of the haunting still felt wrong. Different. With both death and fate playing games, Demdike was feeling her age. The weariness which came with not knowing your opponent and what move they would make next. She was being toyed with, and whether by demons, angels, or gods, her death was guaranteed.

When Alizon still hadn't returned the next day, Demdike was ready and raring to go. Despite the exhaustion she carried and the sickness refusing to subside, she couldn't shake the sense that trouble was afoot. Something bad was happening. Collecting her stick, she and Lizzie were out the door as soon as the sun came up. James and Jennet a step behind. The two planned to go east whilst they went west. Wherever their lost family member was, they were going to find her. Demdike only hoped the girl was unharmed when they did.

She'd warned Alizon many times about the dangers of men. Of how she'd seen more than one unfortunate woman be sent to the whorehouse because a man took liberties and her family threw her out. With no choices, it left the girl (who'd already been violated) to face a repetition of the same harsh fate. Demdike wouldn't allow those pains to befall her granddaughter. Better a life in poverty or death than one where your every freedom and soul was stripped away piece by piece.

The hills were filled with the scent of life. Plants spread their cheer across the land as everything came awake. Bright and beautiful, whilst her heart remained stuck in the dead of winter. Demdike could hardly appreciate the pinks, greens and yellows littering their path. Couldn't think of how it would be ideal to pluck them for her future poultices and potions, not when her mind was entirely focused on their lost duckling and where the girl might have gotten to. Her eyes found the bright reds of the petals and could only think of how they reminded her of fresh blood, fighting images of Alizon painted the same.

It wasn't long before they crossed paths with other residents. People avoided her eyes, but were more than happy to stare. Where she might have bristled previously, now she used it to her advantage. Approaching each of them, asking if they'd seen the missing girl. Whilst some looked affronted, most looked guilty. Her hackles rose. It wasn't until the seventh person that she finally learnt what had transpired.

"She did what?" her voice had risen so loud that all those in the vicinity stopped to stare. Demdike might have taken a quick note mentally, but she was too incensed to react to their keen interest.

"She confessed," the woman repeated steadily. A look of disgust aimed at both Demdike and her daughter. As though this woman might catch whatever foul thing she thought them plagued with.

"No. No," Demdike protested. "Our Alizon might be a bit out of touch with reality sometimes, but she ain't stupid enough to confess to something so bloody stupid."

Witchcraft was not something people confessed to. It didn't matter if the hunts fell out of favour during Elizabeth's reign (with her focus on the rise of science). So long as the law existed, you kept quiet. Everyone knew, no matter how ridiculous the charges, you never confessed. Not to witchcraft. Not to anything. Even if they caught you red bloody-handed, you denied and denied. You never, ever confessed. That was a guaranteed walk to the gallows.

"From what I heard—" Jane had appeared out of nowhere by their side, a look of worry etched onto her gentle face. "—she had little choice. He hunted the girl down and dragged her before his father. Made her confront him and confess her sins."

For all her sympathy, the woman didn't look as though she thought the girl innocent of her crimes, simply sad about the brutality of her treatment. As much as this made Demdike's insides curl, it was more understanding than the other witnesses showed.

"A strange man—" she started slowly, hoping everyone was still listening.

By the way, some were almost rising on their toes and straining their ears to listen, she assumed so. Keeping her voice low and even, Demdike continued.

"—Alizon didn't know hunted her down and dragged her away whilst no one helped her? And you're surprised she said whatever she had to freaking escape?" As much as she wanted to shout at the end, she instead let the incredulity rise in pitch for her.

There were a few whispers, but nothing more. When a man came forward, John or Jack or something, Demdike, was already on the brink of screaming at everyone gathered there.

"But she confessed?" he said, like nothing else mattered.

To him, she supposed it didn't. This wasn't his granddaughter in danger. Just another woman to feed the gossip fodder and bring amusement to their boring lives. Demdike wanted to scream. How stupid were these people? If the same thing had happened to them, they'd have said whatever to get to safety as well. However, as usual, the sheeple were too convinced by the gossip, too entertained to think beyond their own delight. Demdike wanted to hit them.

"Plus, everyone knows you and Chattox are witches. Why would it be a surprise your granddaughter was one as well?" it was spoken so nonchalantly that it took Demdike a moment to fully process what had been said.

"There is a big fecking difference between the cunning folk who work with plants and the spirits, to those who work with the bloody devil!" this time she did shout.

Demdike knew some locals were idiots, but surely they couldn't—she didn't even bother to finish the thought. No, of course not. She'd seen this before. They did this last time. All logic and knowledge went out of the window. The people who weren't affected didn't care, and those who were affected simply wanted someone to blame. Somewhere to funnel their anger and pains.

For all, she wasn't surprised. The slow slinking of her innards was a shock. Demdike knew this was coming. Had seen the patterns before they even fully formed. She'd known. And yet, when faced with the reality, she was still disappointed. It'd been over half a century since the supposed taint of witches had been upon their land, since science had become the new '*it*' thing, and yet, here they were again. Looking for shadows and hidden evils. On some level (despite all logic to the contrary), she'd expected better of her neighbours—of the people of Pendle.

"We need to find her," was all she could say in reply.

For all a part of her wanted to argue, wanted to point out all the ways they were wrong, Demdike knew a pointless cause when she saw one. And the longer they dallied, the more danger Alizon would be in. It wouldn't be long until Nowell heard, and with one confession already made, the girl was in greater danger than she could possibly comprehend.

When the man pointed south, stating the inn with the tavern attached was where Alizon had last been seen, she and her daughter began at pace towards it. Hopefully, they could retrace the girl's steps.

CHAPTER SIXTEEN

Only a few months had passed, not even a full turn of the wheel. How did everything change this fast? When did the long days of small smiles and lingering touches evaporate like summer rain? How had the face of her friend, her heart, turn as cold as his father's? Looking back was easy when the happy days were already gone.

Alizon thought them bad at the time, but those secret moments of relief—where they escaped the stressors of their lives and hid away from the world—were memories she now clung to. Every moment had been a solace to their souls. Amidst the unending fear and pain of their lives.

Him with his home life, he refused to speak about. Though there were more than enough clues; she'd patched him up enough times for guesses to be confirmed without words. Her with her family problems; worries about food, money, and avoiding the many pitfalls of existing in Pendle. Things had seemed too big for them.

Alizon would never have guessed she would miss those times. Miss their lives. But even with all the pain, there were happy times. Bright golden rays of happiness weaved through the tapestry of grey and darkness. Without those golden moments, it left her without a life raft. Constantly ready to drown. Isolated from the surrounding people.

She might've endured it. Might have simply ignored their vile words and scorn, had her heart still been filled with love and hope. With dreams of escape. She could have carried on. But when he'd turned away from her. When his father's tongue became as hitting as his fists. The boy she'd hoped to one day meet at the altar, walked away from her. Like he'd never known her. As though they'd never shared their darkest secrets and greatest hopes. He acted as though he didn't know the stupid rumours were nothing more than idle gossip. Behaved as though she truly were something foul. It hurt.

Alizon hadn't known her heart could break and she would still live. How could it still beat when it ached like this? Alizon wouldn't have believed it possible, and yet here she was. Putting one foot in front of the other. Pushing forward. Trying to reach safety before her eyes became too swollen to guide her path. It seemed Peter inherited his father's cruelty, after all. She'd simply been too in love to see.

Nana Demy was right. You couldn't give your heart away. Couldn't afford to let love guide your actions. Alizon was only glad she hadn't given him what he wanted. And didn't that sting? For all they had shared, he may have truly only been with her, for one thing. With an agenda on his mind.

Even as she thought this, her mind rejected the idea. Peter wasn't that good of an actor. He couldn't have been playing her this entire time. Though she couldn't shake the nagging doubt. Had their every moment been false? Every memory felt tainted, as though his farm hands left muck across everything he'd touched. Those golden shades muddying in her mind.

***

"You're such a tease, Miss Device, and I refuse to chase you, because all the boys do, and they can never catch you. I've watched you weasel your way out of their grip countless times." His brood-

ing voice and folded arms showed he was no longer playing games.

It was false, there had been a few games of such, but her grandmother would have her hide if Alizon generated such a reputation. Running from the boys was as much a safety precaution as it had been a game.

"Okay, Peter. If you can capture me in the first five seconds, then I will stop, I promise," Alizon teased, pouting her lips at him.

She pretended as if she were about to run, but instead laid back down on the grass, this time hoping her meaning was clear. She wasn't going to run and make him chase her anymore. He was the only boy she would allow to win.

Peter moved closer, his body shaking. Eyes darted back and forth, as if wondering if this were another one of her games. She couldn't blame him. The boy hovered above her, waiting for her to turn away. When she didn't, he finally claimed his prize, one soft kiss upon her mouth. The fluttering bounced between her stomach and chest. The thrill of knowing this wasn't acceptable behaviour, but simple physical desire. Their lips only touched for a few seconds, but it cemented the first real stage of their young relationship. They shared a smile together, as he regained his position on the grass next to Alizon.

"We should play kiss-chase more often," was all Peter said.

They lay side by side for hours. Their hands almost touching, but never quite connecting. In their field, on their hill, both stared back up at the sky as if the moment had simply been another daydream.

***

Could this have been fake? Alizon thought she'd been the one in charge. The one leading him. But could she have missed something?

She hardly had any education beyond copying what her friends imparted, or what her nana and mum shared. The way to use herbs and make healing balms. They were good things to know but had nothing to do with managing people. Peter hadn't much book learning, just enough to do orders for the farm, or so he'd claimed. Could he know more than she'd been told?

Alizon was no longer as convinced as she'd once been. A second son wasn't usually worth much in terms of investment. They were the spare. Educated just enough, in case the first son died. Though Alizon had no concept of how far these learnings extended. Could confusing a poor girl of no learning be a lesson he'd received?

***

They laid side by side, describing the images they saw. Passed hours and days away in this comfortable cocoon cut off from the world beyond. A diversion from the tension bubbling between them. Things they gently tiptoed around and away from. They spoke of their hopes and fears. How he worried his brother wouldn't live and he would become the heir. Or worse, he did live and Peter would be left with nothing, expected to make his own way in the world. Alizon shared her fears of her nana passing and the family having even less than they had now.

When they were brave, they would even discuss a possible future together, but they kept it to possibilities, nothing ever truly planned. How they could leave Pendle, how they might make money elsewhere, where two people may be welcomed. It all held a level of hypothetical thinking. Of how, if such things came to pass, two people might make their way in the world beyond Pendle's borders.

Nothing was carved in stone, but there was a silent understanding of 'if'. If certain events came to pass, they could both flee. Together. Until then, this place between the sky and this hill had become their home, staring at the clouds and creating stories where they both lived happy and wondrous lives. Free of pain and hunger.

"A tree." The adolescent boy smirked, tilting his head towards her.

He was always checking to see if she was staring at him. Alizon found it sweet. Though she refused to fully turn her head in his direction, peeking out of the corner of her eyes. Her dark hair was spread across the grass as the daisies weaved their way in and out of her waves, the ringlets caressing the soft petals. He'd once said It was as if she had sprung from pools of Mother Nature herself. Alizon had flushed so hard she felt the purpling burn on her cheeks.

***

Peter was always sweet. Not like the other boys. Soft in a way others were harsh. He wasn't weak. Years of working on a farm prevented such things. But his eyes and voice had been gentle. This gentle strength which first captured her attention. His eyes reminded her of the trees; growing strong and silent, weathering the storms of the world and remaining as they were. Kind in a way so few of the people were to her. Had it all been a lie?

In one of their many conversations on their hill, Peter shared how her eyes were the reason he'd noticed her. Looking to the sky as he voiced how he'd thought she looked like a fairy or some other woodland dweller, earthy and hypnotic. She always wore earthy colours as well, greens, browns, and creams. To most people, her clothes were a sign of poverty. There were no reds, blues, crisp whites or night blacks, but to Peter, they were a sign of her being different, being more than just another girl.

Alizon had heard the fae comment before. Something her nan and others said many times. Yet, from him, it brought a fluttering in her stomach. A sensation Alizon hadn't felt before, but one she'd immediately wanted more of. Maybe those seemingly innocent comments were not so sweet after all?

***

"Where?" Her eyes followed the direction of his pointed finger. "Peter, you idiot, that's not a tree!" Alizon hit him lightly, laughing in false outrage.

"Go on then. What is it to you?" Peter smirked, awaiting her answer.

She stared intensely at the sky, chewing her lip as she decided what the image might be. "A strange animal, with a bushy head and four legs," Alizon said, nodding her head in agreement with herself.

Her mind could see oranges and yellows where her eyes couldn't. She purposely pushed down the words her nana shared about second sight and the mind's eyes. She was not a cunning woman. Hoping to convince herself she didn't have the gift.

"Of course, it is." Peter scoffed. "Because there are loads of animals like that in existence." He didn't even attempt to hide his laughing this time. "You should get someone to write these things you come out with. They'll make you the town fool, you're that witty," he continued in amusement at his own joke.

Alizon's face burned with his words, trying not to huff and argue with the other. "Well, that's what I see. It's definitely not a tree," she returned strongly.

She hadn't been sulking. If her voice had risen higher in frustration and embarrassment, it was purely coincidental. She turned her entire body away from him in protest.

"Oh, don't go getting upset with me." He wrapped his arm and leg around her dress, pulling her closer to him. *"Y'know, I'm only playing with you."*

She pushed the blonde hair away from Peter's face as it fell over his eyes. Gazing at him as if he were the cloud, and she was trying to understand this perfectly formed image.

"Get off of me." She pushed him away. *"I don't want people talking. Let's go back to playing the game."*

As if responding to a command from a priest, he threw his body away and regained his previous place on the grass.

***

Had it all been fake? Games? Schemes and scenes she hadn't known she was a part of? It felt real, but Nana Demy warned her, time and time again. Men who used young girls' hearts to have their wicked way. Just because Peter was only two summers her senior didn't disqualify him from this pool of people. But if this was true, it would be callous in such a way she could barely even contemplate. He'd been her friend long before anything had grown between them. Had his dark intentions been hiding the entire time?

It wasn't possible. Couldn't be. She knew him. Alizon loved him. Surely she could not have fallen for someone with such a black heart?

***

"Oh, Al, look at that one. What do you see? Looks well weird."

They'd both watched as the darker cloud moved swiftly across their field of vision and turned all the other clouds the same murky colour.

He looked back at her expectantly. "Are you alright, Al? You look unwell?"

Alizon stared, as the cloud took on a new form, faster than any of the other clouds. She often saw things in the clouds, images close to reality. Had Alizon been the type of girl to believe in signs and omens (which she was, but denial was often healthy for one's mind), she would have thought the clouds told more than childish stories.

***

When she'd first started cloud watching, it hadn't taken either of them long to notice how the things she'd said in jest came to pass in her life. After months of cloud gazing and dreams which told her secrets no human should know, Alizon wondered if the clouds were a way for Mother Nature to communicate.

Or perhaps it was simply because she only watched clouds when he was by her side. Her dreams only changed when he was in them. Peter was her happy place. Her calm in the storm, and the world beyond them. Her heart beat for his, her thoughts returned to him, and maybe, just maybe, her abilities were centred around him, too. Had what she'd taken as proof of them being meant to be merely been a warning all this time?

***

This cloud didn't bring with it the light, wispy happiness. Even when a storm was coming and they turned dark, they never reached this shade. Alizon could feel the atmosphere alter. The animals disappeared, fleeing the oppressive warning. Even the trees cowered away from the sky. It wasn't just darkness; it was sinister. Sunk the light of day into its grasp, claimed the whites of the sky and tainted them with its force.

The primitive image formed an almost human face amidst the shades of grey and black. What was left of the white sky became the hollow eyes, glaring down upon Alizon. The black eyebrows were as clearly defined as those of an elderly man. There were even thread-like densities where they appeared wild and uncontrolled. The rolls that naturally formed in clouds emerged as wrinkles, adding another level of reality to this figure.

It shifted once more. The mouth became a snout. A dog? The top of the face still appeared human, but the mouth... the sharp teeth... this was something else. The clouds were still moving, but this face now stayed stationary, fully formed and eyes unwavering in their intensity. The being was aware it held Alizon's attention. Its crooked snout, an arrow pointing down directly at her. Forced Alizon to stay rooted to the spot and hear its message.

A growl erupted through the gritted teeth. Alizon doubted her eyes. If the yellows and oranges of earlier had not been there, who was to say this thing was there either? The mind played tricks in the darkness, and as the sun was swallowed from the sky, it made a strange sort of sense. She tried to move her head or even her gaze away from this shape. At mouth level, it appeared more animalistic than human, and the noises it was generating only supported this thought.

"They're coming," the malicious tone took great delight in saying the words.

Had its eyes not been the pale white Alizon would have sworn they'd sparkled. The message could have been completely innocent, but it was how it was delivered which crushed any hope. The thing was too joyous in its malevolence, like a judge delivering a sentence of death.

"Alizon, are you okay?" Peter asked.

His words had broken Alizon from the hypnotic state the thing caught her in. Looking at the boy beside her, she remembered where she was and what had been happening. Turning her glance back to the sky, Alizon saw that the image had broken up, and now all the clouds were the grey of a heavy storm.

"Yeah, Pete." She was still stationary. Her eyes hurt from being open too long. "I've gotta go. You should get back. It's about to rain."

Alizon ran down the hill and towards the wood. As she left, the first raindrop touched her face. Then the rest came all at once, changing what had almost been a happy summer's day into another dark Pendle evening.

***

She'd quickly buried the event. Alizon had been happier to think it was a moment of temporary insanity rather than the alternative. When they went to Jane's house on Halloween night, it'd taken everything within her to not mention how familiar those growls sounded. How she'd maybe (just maybe) encountered the being before.

Now Peter had shown his true colours—or perhaps caved to his father's wants—he was no longer a person she could rely on, or share such secrets with. Alizon questioned how much her previous beliefs were valid. Had her intuition been warning her all this time? As the entirety of Pendle became a place she no longer wished to be, Alizon considered if she could convince her family to move. Goldshaw Booth was a small village, and Pendle was a small borough. Perhaps beyond its borders, they could all find happiness.

Her throat dry-swallowed. Peter called her a witch. Spat the word like poison. He'd led that man directly to her. To their field. Their safe place. With one action, he broke her heart, her trust, and the last remnants of safety she'd felt.

Their field had always been her happy place. Even when Alizon struggled to sleep, her mind would cast itself back to sunny days lying side by side, staring at the world above. Whether sun, showers or stars, she'd felt a sense of peace there. A little piece of the world carved out just for them. It was safety and serenity. She associated with some of the best moments of her life. This was why seeing Peter approaching with an aggressive man made something drop within her.

Betrayal. An unfamiliar sensation. Not when you were used to expecting the worst from people. Trust didn't come easily to her. The world tilted slightly as the picture before became clear. Yet it was off, obscured, by the wet trails running down her face. Tears. Alizon wasn't a big crier. For all her emotions were larger than life, she really only ever shed tears in the safety of her room. Bottled them within herself, a storm held within her body, until it could be safely allowed to explode. Her family didn't judge her for spewing salt water.

Safety. She'd associated this hillside with safety. Maybe this was why the tears fell freely now. She'd only a few moments to wipe her face before the man she thought would be her forever, and the well-dressed aggressor, reached her. Even before he opened his mouth, she knew he had nothing good to say. No one who looked at another person with such loathing could hold good intentions. This man meant her harm, and Peter brought him directly to her. Invited him into their sacred space. She could survive the stranger's ire, but her heart shattered with Peter's look of shame and disgust.

A small vindictive side of her felt vindicated by the boy's discomfort at his obvious guilt and upset, but it wasn't enough. This wasn't just hurting her—for no apparent reason—but betraying every happy moment they'd shared here. It wasn't exactly a hidden place. Anyone could technically have found it. Yet in the three years they'd come here, they'd never seen another soul. There was no way for this to be a coincidence. Peter brought the intruder here. Purposely led this man, filled with fury, directly to her.

Were her heart not tearing in two, she might have launched herself at the boy. To hit, kick, bite. To inflict damage. The wild beast she kept tethered within her soul rose in anger and anguish.

"You're the Device girl, yes? The little witch who cursed my fa-ther?" the man sounded almost bored as he spoke the words. If it weren't for the red of his face and twitching of his brow, she would have thought him indifferent.

The way his shoulders were tensed, like a boxer preparing to hit, spoke of his less-than-calm intentions. This man wanted to attack her the same way her inner animal wanted to claw at the boy behind him. It took her a moment to process the words, *'little witch'*, she'd been called such before. Having a cunning woman as a nana meant many accused her of such things. Especially the past few months, as the entirety of Pendle seemed to fall under the spell of anger and paranoia. If there were any witches here, the ones like this person meant, she would have assumed them to be the culprit of the sudden changes she'd seen.

Nana Demy had not-so-subtly implied it was Nowell. Stated they were to avoid the man at all costs. Though the woman also said this about all men. Not much different from the many other lectures Alizon heard. But even Alizon couldn't deny how people changed recently, just as her grandmother's rants predicted. Nowell was a man to be feared, but so was this person standing before her.

"Abraham Law," he introduced, unprompted. "And you are com-ing with me. You will be faced with what you did to my father and forced to face the consequences of your actions." One hand on the piece at his side, he stretched the other in her direction.

Alizon couldn't help the cry that escaped her as the man grabbed her hair. She hadn't time to run. Too afraid of the weapon on his hip. The gun. James always wanted one. But when the family had to make choices between thrice-used fabrics and food, a weapon was pointless. Now she wished she had one. The threat of a large angry man towering over her would've been reduced if there was something to defend herself with. All the ways she'd learnt to escape another's grip were useless when the man held no qualms about shooting holes in her.

As he dragged her through the hills, the man kept silent. Despite her repeated struggles, people simply watched on. More interested in the drama than the present danger she was in. The tears were coming once more. Burned a track down her face as the hairs on her scalp remained taught in his grip. The man kept a pace she could barely keep up with. The scuff marks and scratches on her legs showed he had no issues with dragging her along. Her neck ached with the angle it was forced to. She almost wished he would have thrown her over his shoulder. It would've been humiliating, but hurt less.

The man kept silent except for a few grunts. Refused to address her, as though she were some unruly dog and not a young girl he'd kidnapped. She tried screaming, but his free hand had been enough to stop her from continuing. His punches carried far more force than her own. Biting and scratching had been batted away as though she were some irritating kitten. Peter followed them until they reached the main street. Departed with a nod to the man and not so much as a glance in her direction. She wanted to cut him. Had she a gun, she'd have happily put a bullet through him.

She'd asked the boy, her friend, why. Why was he doing this? Why would he betray her? When he denounced her as a witch, her body froze. Surely, of all the people to know the truth, Peter should know she'd never made a deal with the devil. That she was not what they proclaimed. Her struggles ceased as the weight of what was happening caught up with her. If Peter could turn on her, was there anyone she could rely on? By the turning of blind eyes as the man carted her through the village she'd grown up in, her neighbours looking on idly, Alizon realised it was a resounding 'no'. No, they would not.

He pulled her toward the inn. She started struggling afresh. The man, Abraham, had said it was to face his father, but she had no guarantee of his words. Once she was locked inside, he could do anything to her. This was exactly as her nana always warned.

As he threw her into a small room, it was too dark to see much. A candle too close to the end of its burn to give much energy. Her breath was coming fast. Her chest was heavy. Exertion and fear caused her heart to beat like a drum. As the other man came in behind her, she was relieved to see he kept the door open. Might not mean he wouldn't attack, but it left one potential escape route. When several people were visible from the doorway, all peering in eagerly, she wanted to flash her teeth at them. Act like the wild animal she was slowly being reduced to.

"Look at him," Abraham announced, his voice strong. He was still close to the doorway, not quite blocking it, but keeping between it and her.

She looked over, seeing he was gesturing toward the bed. In the low light, it took her a few moments to parse out what was lying beneath the rags. The peddler. The one from last week. The man who'd refused to sell her pins and been rude to her.

"You bewitched him. Admit it, witch," the man was forceful in his words, a promise of violence beneath them.

Alizon shook her head. She hadn't bewitched him. She wouldn't know how. Okay, she knew a few things, clay statues and dolls with pins, but nothing she could have done which would affect the other immediately. Alizon had heard of no practitioner, witch or otherwise, who held such power. If the man had been lamed, it was by some force far greater than her.

'*Karma perhaps*,' she thought bitterly. Still resentful of the treatment she'd received.

Even as the man lay there pitifully, it was hard to feel sympathy for someone who had been unjustly cruel to her. Like father, like son.

"Admit it, and I will spare you the lashings you deserve, wench!" his voice shook the walls of the room. The wood ready to fall apart with the force of his wrath.

She shook her head again, quickly darting back as the man made for her. Ducking to avoid his ham hands, but it was no use. The room was too small. The man soon grabbed her, putting pressure around her neck as he raised her body from the floor.

"You will confess your sins, you will admit what you have done, or I will squeeze the life from you right here and right now," he said, tightening his grip as he spoke to show he was entirely serious.

Her throat burnt with the lack of air. Her heart had barely calmed from being thrown in here but was now beating double time, trying to get her limbs moving once more. As he threw her down, her back slammed against the wall. Her spine and neck ricocheted against the wood and caused her head to crack back again. A sound like a wounded woodland creature escaped her throat. It was apt. She was prey. Felt like it. The vulnerable small creature being toyed with by the larger predator. As soon as she opened her mouth, he slapped her.

"No more denials. Speak, or I will force it from you."

The words made her shudder. He may not have meant them the way they sounded, but the implication was hard to overlook. Nana had always said to do whatever she had to in order to avoid that. But confessing would be as good as a death sentence. Nowell was likely waiting in the wings, ready to pounce. Yet, her option was death at this man's hands, and whatever he might choose to do before that, or death later. Later was better. Where there was life, there was still a chance.

Her mouth opened once more. One look in those murderous eyes had the words tumbling from her lips.

"I confess."

***

The blood pooled around her. Alizon hadn't thought a little graze could have produced such a dramatic effect. She was already feeling queasy, but one drop of blood was usually enough to make her go weak. Enough to make her mind fade and her stomach turn inside out. Even when she simply heard the word blood, her body would cringe, turning in on itself to avoid the red liquid. This time, however, the cut leaking all over her clothes was not merely an idea dancing around her brain, but a wound gushing from her temple.

It'd been a near miss after the loud bang. One inch to the right and her brain could have been painting the floor. Bullets were easy enough to remove from soft tissue—according to her brother at least—but a head wound was usually fatal. If not from the bullet itself, then from the force of the impact. Wind could be as brutal as iron.

The head was the most dangerous place to get a cut, according to her nana. A small cut could bleed out completely if it were not treated, as the skin was too fragile to repair and the pressure of the blood would force it open repeatedly (as the liquid escaped the body's confines).

Alizon couldn't stay here and give up. It'd been mere hours since she escaped the room. When Law Junior had been happy to throw her in the dirt outside the inn. She hadn't stopped to ask questions, merely fled on foot as fast as her legs could carry her. She couldn't fight, but she could take flight. And flown she had. Travelling the hills of Pendle faster than she'd ever managed before.

Although bruised and winded, her body refused to stop. Too close to the dangers of the man who could have done anything to her and everyone else would have simply looked on dispassionately. Alizon wanted to reach home, the only truly safe place, but it was becoming less and less likely she would reach her destination.

Having stumbled for a third time, she rose her body slowly, equilibrium as messy as her stained clothes. Once back on her feet, Alizon grabbed a leaf from a nearby tree, spat on it, and covered the wound on her head. Would have to do. She had to actively ignore the desire of her body to hibernate, to seek low ground and shelter herself away from the world. Running was the only option for escape. At hearing another loud sound—the ringing of the weapon—her heart began increasing in fever once more. They were drawing closer.

With heavy feet pounding against the ground, she frantically tried to maintain speed. Having run many miles already, the exhaustion and excitement of the day were making themselves known. She needed rest. Sleep. Hopefully not the eternal kind. Alizon knew each rise and dip of the land better than most, but her sense of direction was becoming increasingly fogged. Her body succumbing to the loss of blood and dehydration.

The mediaeval mob, with its sharpened pitchforks, hunted her like a pheasant. She became fair game the moment Nowell heard of her confession. Declaring the warrant for her arrest. Truthfully, she'd been surprised he wasn't waiting for her downstairs in the inn. But he mustn't have got word fast enough. Or maybe a warrant took more than a few hours to legalise, even as the Justice of the Peace? This or he simply hadn't known where to find her. Had she made it home by now, he likely would have already captured her. Small graces.

The slobbering mouths and vicious eyes associated with wild animals weren't only coming from the dogs, but the men she'd once broken bread with. They weren't only performing their *'legal obligations'*, they were enjoying this. She was sport, and they were happy to play the game.

The absurd thought of *'this is the most dangerous game of kiss chase I've ever played,'* ran through her mind. Alizon would blame the blood loss for the hysterical laugh which left her mouth. She must have looked mentally impaired by this point.

"Alizon!" the bellowed screams echoed around the wooded area.

"Get back here, you little witch!" the screams of the locals were becoming more menacing.

If Alizon had been any other person, the ground would have caught her and brought her to her knees by now. Nana Demy once taught her how the earth didn't punish one of its own, but it was still a tricky mistress. As she ran, it was as though Mother Nature herself awoke, moving the tree sprigs and leaves from the young girl's path, allowing Alizon to keep her advantage over her followers.

The wind screamed its rage, blowing against Alizon's back, pushing her further forward. Rushed into Alizon's lungs, hitting hard against her windpipes and all the way down her chest. She took great gulps; drowning on land, it burnt as it entered her, but was welcomed all the same.

She kept going, even as her muscles cried for her to stop. An angry crack ripped through the sky, a lightning bolt directing Alizon towards the river. In that instant, she knew she had to follow the trail nature was providing. Giving her the advantage. Stopping meant her capture, which would result in death. Another shot of adrenaline kicked in. She pushed through the pain, her legs moved even faster. The last kick of life was known even to her.

Alizon heard the dogs quickly catching up with her. Their barks and growls were eerily reminiscent of that night. Like the demon was behind her. Chasing her through the overgrowth of the forest. These beasts, however, were trained to hunt vermin and to show no mercy. Images flashed into her mind of watching rats shredded apart with the hound's bare teeth. A trembling moved within her, at the idea of the

dogs getting their jaws around her already strained skin. The bruises
and scratches from earlier were already delicate.

Fear made her brave, and as she reached the banking of the river.
Alizon knew she had to enter it and go as far in as possible (if this
plan was to work). The water was like ice against her skin, rushing past
her downstream. Anxiously holding her footing, Alizon progressed
steadily. Water was not an element she was used to. Her sister, Jennet,
was the water bug of the family, but Alizon trusted the earth was
protecting her. She had no other choice. It was either believing what
her grandmother taught her or capture.

The further from the banking edge she went, the faster the height
of the water rose. It was already at her torso. Alizon bit her lip against
her natural urge to cry out in pain. The scrapes and broken skin jolted
at the cold liquid surrounding them. The extra weight of her drenched
clothes would slow her down, but throwing the dogs off her scent
would give her vital extra time. She could not run forever. It was time
to think strategically. Sadly, Alizon had always been the dreamer, not
the thinker.

The men knew she had no place to hide, and no friends who would
associate themselves with her. Not before today, and especially in
light of the accusations against her. To support her would be to die
alongside her. Perhaps this was why Peter turned on her. Too afraid to
be tarred as well? She shook away the thought, and the water from her
eyes. Peter wasn't here. He wouldn't help. Her hurting heart would
have to wait. She needed to think of all the places where she might be
safe and which ones might mean she avoided the mob and the dogs.

Her eyes found the great imposing hill, the one the entire area was
named after. Alizon wondered if she could get there and climb it in
time. No one would be senseless enough to go up there, not when
the paths changed too often. It might be spring, but the countless

sinkholes and shifting earth would be too dangerous for the dogs and horses to safely navigate. No one would risk it, no one but Nana Demy, and Alizon.

Pendle Hill's great presence was felt across the land; it was as much a part of the people as it was the earth. With its luscious greens, wild heather and ditches which could swallow a man whole. Pendle Hill was infamous. Not only for the old gods lying in sleep beneath it. For those who knew—those who remembered—it was where the old religion worshipped. The earth remembered.

Alizon's mind quickly concocted a new plan, one where fewer people would see her. Knowing that Pendle Forest surrounded great hill, if she could get to it, she would be safe. The forest was famed for being the home of ghosts and ghouls, but she would take her chances with the creatures of myth and legend. The monsters chasing her were a far greater threat. Several hundred yards up the river, she saw a tree branch stretching into the water. She reached towards it. Climbed it steadily out of the water.

She went across the tree rather than the banking. The dogs would search the floor for where she might have left the river. They wouldn't search the heights of the trees. Jumping to another branch, she made her way down to the stable floor once more. Her feet immediately took off again, running purely on animal instinct. Her mind had shut down in the grips of terror, and the freezing temperatures of the water, but with her senses focused on getting to the hill, Alizon continued with all the strength she had.

The flecks of green varied as she darted through the woods. The altering shades of nature varied from tree to tree. Pendle was as alive as any person. This forest as secretive as the rest of the dwellers on this land. She kept running. If they couldn't find her, would they keep trying to arrest her? Leaping into the threshold of the forest's edges, she saw the men closing in on her. Her capture meant death for more than just herself. She prayed that the men's hearts, filled with fear and blind hatred, would be too cowardly to enter.

But Nowell took a step inside.

CHAPTER SEVENTEEN

How he hated the rolling greens and dreary greys of this place. Were Nowell given the choice, he would never return to Pendle. However, this was bigger than him. Bigger than the one-sided grudge he held against this backwater borough and its tiny-minded people. Still, he'd have drowned the lot of them, given half a chance.

He'd visited the place several times in the past year, leaving as quickly as he could, but always forced to return. It burned something in his innards to keep his actions cordial and polite when he would have happily led the lot of the cursed inhabitants to the stake, lit the match and danced on the ashes after their deaths.

Nowell might have been the Justice of the Peace, but in his role, he knew better than most how often simply killing the problem was the easiest and preferred solution. The idiots here were a bunch of superstitious, unwashed, peasants. Even the supposed gentry was hardly worth noting. Too inbred and cut off from the rest of the country to be of any value. They held no true power or political sway. The only use they'd served thus far was in entertainment—as he and his men insulted them and they laughed—oblivious to the many slights sent their way.

A source of amusement in the beginning, but when the game continued, and the others remained entirely oblivious, it grew boring.

This entire place was boring. There was nothing to do. They'd thrown a party in his honour and hosted a few dinners, but beyond the odd social occasion, there was nothing else happening here. Lancaster had always felt incurably small to him, especially compared to London society, but he could never complain about his home again. At least something actually happened there.

Pendle might have been a stone's throw away from Lancaster, but it was like travelling back in time with each mile he crossed. Visually, it wasn't much different. A place filled with greenery in the north of England. However, Pendle felt different. Dirt he couldn't scrub from the skin, as though the earth itself was tainted. Likely polluted by the people who lived upon it. He wouldn't be surprised if the land itself was toxic. He hadn't even bothered to learn the names of the villages and towns, simply referring to them all as Pendle and being done with it.

At least back home, with the coast being close by, it gave a lot of options for activities: fishing, boating, cockle picking. Then there were lush fields filled with game; he went hunting at least thrice a season. The city was ever-growing, and he enjoyed its beauty, even if he might have preferred a sunnier borough to claim as his own. Though at least he had inherited something. There'd been more than one of his fellow gentry, who lost everything in the name of the Tudors.

With King James now settled on the throne, it opened a host of opportunities for progression. Everyone was already vying for favour. Being so far up north posed a few problems. Out of sight, out of mind, being a big issue. Though with Lancaster being the main hub of the north, people were always passing through. Bringing stories and tales with them. He knew much of what was happening in London, even from this distance. King James himself also came more than once on his trips to and from Scotland, so Nowell wasn't completely unknown to the monarch, merely not as established as he'd prefer.

It was one of these stories which began his plan. After writing to one of his southern counterparts he held an alliance with, they'd put him into contact with a man in Yorkshire. The War of the Roses might have been over, with red coming out the victor, but relations between the two sides of the country were still tense. However, the three nobles came together with a plan. A way to clean up their counties and win favour with the king.

He'd laid the seeds months in advance, with how much the people here gossiped he'd expected them to bear fruit earlier. Though finally, it seemed things were moving as he wanted. It'd taken months—where he'd hoped for weeks. It meant him returning over and over to this disgusting place. His frustrations and temper grew greater with each return trip.

Nowell was careful not to scrawl all over the parchment as he transcribed the information he'd heard. They kept important documents as proof. He would later have to show he'd followed procedure. Even if the king didn't care, there were plenty of circling sharks who would happily pull him down for missing a simple step. It was part of the game. He would have done the same. Though it was irritating when on the receiving end.

Nowell wouldn't allow anyone even an inch of leeway. This was his win. He would gain the king's ear and reach the heights even his grandfather hadn't managed at Henry's side. He could easily envision this prosperous future.

As he signed his signature, he couldn't help the twitching of his mouth. In the solitude of his room, he allowed the smirk to break free. This was it. His moment had come. He'd always enjoyed a good hunt. Luckily for him, his prey was willing to give him a chase. The Device girl had confessed. He was now legally within his rights to round the lot of them up and remove the scourge from his land. Witches or beggars, he didn't care. They were a problem and he would take great delight in being the hero who removed this 'evil'.

The hunt started easily enough. He was almost impressed by how the girl evaded them several times. A rat like her shouldn't have been able to outmanoeuvre the dogs and the men, but she had. Perhaps the creature was a witch. Not that he cared either way. The devil might protect his own, but he neither believed in God nor devil. Nowell believed in himself. If the gods were real, they should fear him. Fear a man with a mission and no soul to care about. It would only be a matter of time before he caught her and set the next step of his plan in motion.

"Nowell," one man called to him, pointing toward the river.

The girl was more skilled than expected, but the trails of blood and tracks she left behind were easy to follow. Using the trees was smart, but again, the broken twigs and small splotches of blood were clear to a trained hunter. As he kicked the horse to move forward, he could hear the murmurings behind him.

"She's heading toward the forest," another local man cried.

Nowell hadn't bothered to learn his name, hardly cared, and he would never have to see them ever again soon enough.

"And?"

"It's—it's filled with things. Evil creatures and bad stuff. No one goes in there."

"Clearly they do." He pointed to where the girl was showing more backbone than all the men with weapons.

He would reiterate how much he loathed the people of this place. Begging silently for the strength not to kill them all. He might accidentally start a fire when he leaves. Burn the place to the ground behind him. Ignoring the cautions of the other men, he got down from his horse. Partly for dramatic effect, partly because the trees were more compact here and the horse would be more of a hindrance. He couldn't see the girl in the shadows, but he heard her sharp intake as he stepped within the boundary of the forest.

A bunch of trees would not stop him from achieving his goal. Not when he was this close. As his hands found her shaking form, he showed no mercy, dragging her from the overgrowth of the forest and back to his horse. The girl was limp in his grasp. The blood loss too great for her tired limbs. He needed to get her back to his lodgings. Everything would be lost if the bitch died before he had obtained her confession personally.

***

"I'll ask you again, did you curse the man known as John Law?"

The girl sat strapped to the chair, glared at him with pure loathing. If she weren't less than the dirt beneath his boot, he might have thought her pretty in her anger. In another life, she might have been of some use, but in this one, she was more likely to taint him by touching her than the other way around.

Her teeth were gritted as though there was something obstructing her mouth. There wasn't. He'd checked. She resembled one of his bitches during their training; a muzzle through their mouths to stop them from biting. As though there was some invisible gag to keep her from spewing all the foul thoughts painted across her face. She was better trained than he'd thought. The girl was able to sit before him and bear his taunts with nothing more than a scowl. Though said scowl was so intense it could have peeled away his skin.

No matter how he taunted the wild thing, she held her tongue. The odd scoff and spit to the side—a foul habit he wanted to backhand her for. Though with how regularly she performed the action after his words, he soon spotted there was a pattern. She couldn't spew vitriol without endangering herself, so instead, she was literally spitting. The brat must have seen his distaste at the action and done it more.

A vague memory of a traveller woman spitting at those who aimed malice her way wormed its way through his mind. Nowell had been little more than a boy. His mother informed him it was an old belief, a way to protect the person from the words hurled at them. He couldn't recall the how or why, though. It had fallen out of favour when manners became more commonplace, though it could have been another hint at the girl's history. He made a mental note. Could be useless, but he should keep any potential avenues to exploit open.

"You've already confessed once. I don't see why you keep quiet now. Your fate is as good as sealed." He loomed over her.

Her eyes glared up in defiance, refusing to bow.

He'd lied. Without the girl's confession to him, a person of the law, it could be argued her previous confession was nothing more than hearsay. And as all of Pendle declared her family witches and nothing ever came of it before, Nowell refused to have any weaknesses in his case. Wouldn't allow any potential for exploitation from outside parties. He would get the confession. Nowell would have an airtight case, and this filthy creature would hand it to him on a silver platter. Whether she agreed or not.

Supposedly, she'd confessed when confronted with her crimes the last time. At least this was how the locals were painting it. He suspected there were other contributing factors, but he would use this knowledge until he figured out more. The girl was weak, not quite broken, but worn with the weight of the world. He only needed to learn where to apply the pressure and she would break. He could practically taste success, and this little cretin was the only obstacle. The longer she held out, the longer between him and his goals.

"Your grandmother is well known as the local witch, her and that Chattox—" A twitch of her brow. Interesting, he would have to push the later. "—are well known throughout the lands. You expect me to believe that you, her granddaughter—who is regularly seen with her—has no knowledge of her heinous craft? Hasn't followed her down the same slippery slope?"

The girl stared back dispassionately, as though bored with his presence. The monster in his chest wanted to claw at her. Rip those two earthly eyes, which reminded him of the hills of Lancaster despite the hollowed face that framed them.

At the three-day mark, he lost all patience. He couldn't beat her as he wanted. Couldn't pull the nails from her fingers or stab her with knives, but Nowell hadn't achieved all he had by being stupid. He was clever. He'd resorted to less obvious ways of keeping her in a state of pain. The chair was at an angle, which meant her legs could never fully relax. The restraints were a little too tight. He deprived her of food and sleep.

Nowell was also debating taking water away from her. He'd limited her allowance after the spitting began, but he had one more card to play before he resorted to more drastic methods. Some might argue water deprivation was a form of torture, particularly after her recent blood loss, but he ensured she had just enough to keep conscious. There were no rules against it. Waterboarding might be out, but water deprivation wasn't mentioned anywhere in the rules.

As he had the men bring the girl to his carriage, he debated having her dragged behind it. Pulling her along and letting the ground below loosen her skin and her tongue. Despite his anger, Nowell knew such actions would be considered torture and not allowed. He could consider it again after he'd coerced a confession from the rat.

The girl looked at him suspiciously as he led her to the carriage. Her entire body tense, expecting a strike at any moment. He used fewer restraints but ensured she couldn't escape. In the middle of nowhere, travelling along would be an ideal time for her to jump out. Her knowledge of the local area was better than his. Her awareness of the natural landscape could test his hunting skills.

"I'll be using fewer restraints, as it would make the journey uncomfortable," he spoke in a soft voice, hoping it sounded kind.

The girl was too skittish, with good instincts. She was more like her grandmother than most would recognise. The old woman went toe-to-toe with him in a verbal spar, the only person in this godforsaken area who could match wits with him. Nowell suspected if the girl did speak, she might be equally capable.

As he secured her in the carriage, her eyes were dewy with fear, but she wasn't struggling. Not quite resignation, but there was an air of acceptance of her situation. Wounded on an emotional level. The scrapes and scratches he could see through her torn clothes were healing, but he suspected a few might have been infected. It gave him a pleasant feeling to know she was suffering in his presence the same way he was hers. To be wasting his valuable time on someone so below his station...

His new ploy was to try and create a sense of companionship between the pair. To make himself into a confidant and have her confess to a friend, instead of a man in power. She thus far seemed more afraid of his kindness than of his harsh words and actions. Suspicious. Her eyes darted around, measuring every way he might surprise her with pains rather than escape him. It was interesting. The girl was a contradiction. Were she and her ilk not such a scourge on his county, and his ticket to moving up the ladder, he might have enjoyed prying all the thoughts from her mind. Seeing what made her tick.

When they arrived at the farm, the girl relaxed somewhat in the familiar surroundings, but her eyes still watched him from her peripherals. He unshackled her. Her arms were still bound, but her legs were needed. The men were ready in case she made any attempts, but the girl seemed more interested in keeping a distance from all of them, rather than running. Another interesting note he stored for later.

When he brought her to the fence which caused a squabble between families, he watched as she stared at it, then him, in confusion. As though he had given her a particularly tricky sum and her mind couldn't calculate the correct answer.

"The man accused you and yours of being witches." He left out the whore's part of the accusation. It wasn't relevant to his current proceedings.

"He said that as an insult. So he didn't have to pay us. Not because it had a lick of truth," the first bite of a reply he'd earned.

More than the simple '*no's*' and foul language she'd thrown at him. Interesting. She was defensive of her family, but ignored his previous taunts. In the presence of her accuser, she seemed more belligerent, not less. The pieces weren't fitting together. Why would she have confessed in front of the peddler, but not here? Was it because this was against her family, not her personally? A mother was more likely to fight or comply when her children were threatened. Could this be something similar? Arguing against those who hurt her loved ones, but not as protective of herself?

The more he watched, the less clear the girl became. A smudge of dirt over his vision. She wasn't what he expected. Nowell would normally have respected such an opponent, but this only made him hate her more. As one of his men rough-handled her back into the carriage, he saw that same skittish look return.

Afraid of men? No, he paused. Afraid of being alone with men. It should have been obvious. A girl in a vulnerable situation with no male protection. How had he forgotten such an obvious tool? He'd grown so used to women and girls of all ages throwing themselves at him, trying to acquire a good marriage, he'd forgotten what happened to the girls without protection.

Nowell had to keep the vicious smile trying to uncurl along his face inside. It wouldn't do to have her suspect anything. Once he had the little beast back in the room, he would remind her of the dangers she was in. Better to confess and risk the noose than be used goods. A girl like her couldn't afford even the hint of such things against her name.

Once she was secured in the chair again, the room looked darker than it had earlier. The bright and open of the outside had been a direct contrast to this tiny room. It was dingy and disgusting. Nowell had barely noticed it before, too focused on obtaining that bloody confession.

As she sat there once more, he looked her over before pulling the chair closer to him. The alarm immediately reared in the eyes of his prey.

"Alizon. Alizon. Alizon. What am I to do with you?" He let his eyes roam over her form.

He would be more likely to throw up in his own mouth than be attracted to someone of her station, but she didn't need to know this. And any hole was better than none.

The way she began immediately struggling told him he had finally found where to apply pressure. Trailing his fingers over her skirt and between her thighs.

"I think it's time you started speaking, or I'll have to find other uses for that mouth of yours."

CHAPTER EIGHTEEN

When Alizon didn't return for the second day, Demdike grew genuinely afraid. When she heard about what was essentially the hunting of her granddaughter, she had (for the first time ever) been genuinely tempted to turn to the darker aspect of her craft. To curse every one of those people who'd hurt her baby girl. Her grandchild wasn't some wild animal to be used for sport. Alizon was a young and vulnerable girl who needed protecting, not whatever rubbish this was.

Demdike hadn't been surprised when the men arrived at her door several days later. Their attempts to aid the girl and get her out of the jail cell had fallen on deaf ears. Most of the borough had long since turned their back on her family. She'd been tempted to reach out to Chattox, but knew instinctively the woman would be no help. The other wise woman had known all this was coming and hadn't prevented it. Demdike had known too, though she'd thought it would've been her hauled into jail, not a child.

When they came for her, Demdike barely even put up a fuss. A small resigned part of her having expected this since Halloween. Since that day in the church. Since she'd looked into Nowell's eyes and saw the endless void staring back. When they threw her into a room, it hurt her old bones. The rough treatment was only a precursor to what was to come.

She still hadn't seen her Alizon, but suspected the girl was being held somewhere close. When Nowell strolled in, a look of great happiness and superiority on his face, she didn't need any psychic abilities to know how this was going to play out.

"Hello, witch," he said. The man would have been bouncing with happiness were it not against decorum.

She scowled at him, not responding to his greeting. The passive-aggressive game already underway, and this time she didn't have the luxury of witnesses to protect her. As much as Demdike enjoyed a good verbal spar, it wasn't worth the risk. If he was going to treat her like an animal, she would act like one; flashing her teeth at him in warning. She wanted to jump from her seat and attack, but it would do her no good, not only because they'd secured her in place, but because the man was already toying with the weapon on his side in suggestion.

Torture might be prohibited, but self-defence was not. If he could prove her unruly, any measures to make her compliant would be accepted. Though Demdike was tempted all the same. If this was the beginning of the end, she wanted to go out the same way she had lived, fighting.

"Let's make things simple to begin with. We don't need your confession. We have you named, by your own granddaughter, no less. We have the entire area as witnesses. I don't need you to say a single word," the glee was clear in his voice.

Demdike stared him down. If that was true, she would be in a cell ready to be carted off to Lancaster, not in the interrogation room. So either the man was lying, or he had something else up his sleeve. With a person like this, Demdike couldn't afford to assume.

"Before you get any ideas, let me prove what I am saying is true, so you have no doubt over the validity of the evidence I hold against you."

He took great pleasure in reading Alizon's supposed confession to her. Uncurling the parchment with a dark smile as he coughed before beginning.

"The confession of one Alizon Device," he began, throwing her another look, before beginning:

"*Two years ago her grandmother*, that would be you," he added unnecessarily, not even trying to hide his amusement. "*Persuaded and advised her to let a devil or familiar appear to her, and that if she would let him suck at some part of her, then she can have whatever she would.*"

Demdike wanted to scoff. Not only was it complete tripe, it didn't even sound like her granddaughter. Alizon was more likely to say she'd tried to get her to talk to spirits or gather herbs, but of course, they didn't see such things as evil. Witchcraft was connected to the devil. According to the learned, at least. The truth would be no use to the monster before her.

"*Not long after these persuasions, Alizon being walking towards Rough Lee, in a close of one John Robinson's, there appeared unto her a thing like a black dog. Speaking to her and desiring her to give him her soul.*" He gave her a look, which Demdike thought was meant to be filled with judgment, but she too confused to care.

She'd warned Alizon many times to never open up to strange spirits and would never encourage her to connect with anything dark. Demdike wasn't surprised the entire thing was filled with lies, but it annoyed her how it was also in direct contrast to everything she had taught the girl. An insult to the injury. This entire situation was a farce. Demdike wanted to bite the bastard.

"*In return, he would give her the power to do anything she would want. Enticed in setting her down, the Black dog did with his mouth sucked at her breast or little below her paps, which place to remain blue for half a year next.*"

If Alizon had a bruise that long, Demdike would've used one of her poultices to heal it. Another insult to Demdike's actual craft as a cunning woman.

"*Didn't appear next until 18th of March which time she met with the padlock on the highway called Colne field near Colne and she demanded of the peddler to buy some pins but he refused and as they were carting the Black dog appeared.*" Nowell's vicious smile grew larger.

"*What would you have me do to him?*" His voice was deeper, in a caricature of something evil. "*What can you do?*" he recited in a high-pitched tone, switching the character in this story and as a mockery of Alizon. "*I can lame him,*" he continued in a deep voice again. "*Lame him.*" He recited with glee.

"And thus is the confession of your granddaughter." He re-rolled the scroll with a smug arrogance Demdike hadn't thought possible before this.

Were she not bound, Demdike would have launched herself at the man. Gouged his eyes out and strangled him until she could steal the teeth from his corpse. This man was foul. A foul, lying toerag.

"As I say, no confession is necessary to have you swinging from the gallows. You, Chattox and—" He unrolled the scroll at the edge once more. "—Anne Redferne, were all noted by little Alizon. The other two are being rounded up and brought here as we speak. So it won't be long until you and your old friend are sharing a cell."

As much as Demdike wanted to rebuff Chattox being referred to as a friend, she didn't want to do anything that might give this man ammunition. Alizon's confession was complete rubbish. It didn't take a genius to figure this out, but the man held leverage over her. To denounce her granddaughter could mean worse for the girl, but agreeing could bring danger to the rest of her family.

As she sat there silently seething, a ruckus came from outside. The familiar high-pitched shrill she'd heard many times throughout her life. The woman spouted colourful language at her captors. Demdike would have laughed if the situation weren't so dire. For all her plans, and ways to see how others moved across the playing field, Demdike could see no way out of this. When she caught Chattox's eye through the barred opening in the door, the woman gave a quick nod.

They'd set the spell in motion. No matter what happened here, their bloodlines would live on. The gifts of the old world would survive. It was a relief and entirely terrifying. Her life would be sacrificed for the spell to succeed. She'd accepted this reality, but Alizon being claimed alongside her still stung. Wasn't fair. Were she not afraid for her soul, Demdike would curse the man with every wicked thought she held. Would have cast him to the depths of the pit and dance upon his charred remains. She wasn't overly proud of her darker nature, but some people truly warranted the level of hate she usually managed to keep at bay.

"Ah, your co-conspirator has arrived," the void masquerading as a man spoke cheerfully, as though telling her the milk delivery had come.

Again, she held her tongue. Ironically, in this instance, he was right. The two were conspiring. Using their knowledge of their craft to see their ancient abilities survived him and his machinations, but in general, he would have been wrong. Demdike thought better of making the many catty comments primed to jump from her lips. The desire to scratch the man to pieces was too potent for her to even feign civility. Demdike was well aware of the compromised situation she found herself in.

The man watched her. Studied her like she was some fascinating specimen he wanted to take apart and store in jars. He wouldn't return her whole from the experience. He enjoyed breaking his toys too much to consider kindness. Demdike kept the sigh tight within her body. As much as she wanted to rage and scream, as desperately as escape might tempt her, she resigned herself to what was to come. When the man began his so-called interrogation, she barely kept from rolling her eyes.

"What about this Tibbs?"

The question caught her off guard. She'd been drowning out most of his words. As the man said, he didn't need her cooperation. Didn't require her confession. Her silence soon turned to daydreaming and attempting to shut out the world beyond her mind. Cauterising the wound of life from the safety of her inner realm. What did Tibbs have to do with anything? It was a stray cat half the neighbourhood had adopted and kept fed.

The man was checking a book. Demdike had never hated her lack of reading skills more than at this moment. An errant thought flashed through Demdike's mind. What if Alizon's confession had nothing to do with anything she actually said and the man had simply forced the illiterate girl to sign the confession? She wouldn't put it past this monster. He was the type to get off on playing with his food. Had likely taken the bare bones of the girl's words and twisted them to fit his narrative. Alizon would then be unable to deny she'd said the words, even if not in the way this beast later worked them into being. Manipulation was a skill this man carried in spades.

Holding her tongue, she watched as Nowell read a passage. His eyes moved along the book before scribbling something down. She could only guess he was cross-referencing something, like a teacher checking the work before it was submitted for testing. It made her blood run cold when his eyes lit up. The child-like excitement was troubling on a man like Nowell. He was far too happy for it to be anything good.

"King James wrote this book." He showed her the pages, as though the scribbles might mean more than chicken scratch to her. "He's a big believer in witches." There was a level of contempt that twitched at the side of Nowell's mouth.

Interesting. The man clearly believed otherwise. As much as Demdike wanted to comment on his true thoughts, the man barrelled on.

"The king believes witches make a pact with the devil through creatures who suck their blood."

This at least explained Alizon's weird confession. Cunning folk often worked with the animals. Could even somewhat communicate and commune with them. She'd even heard some were skilled enough to see through the eyes of the animals they'd connected with, but Demdike always took such claims with a pinch of salt. In her many years, she'd found no true proof of such tales. Though even she knew that to work with the land meant also working with the creatures which dwelt upon it. No bloodsucking though. She'd no idea where this absurdity came from.

Demdike looked at the man. He dropped all subtlety, but she wouldn't give him what he wanted simply because it suited his goals. If he wanted to play, she wanted some contingencies of her own.

"My family," she croaked out. Not aware of how dry her throat had become.

His eyes squinted at her, suspicion written across his body. "What of them?"

"Their safety. I want you to ensure their safety."

"No. I don't think you understand the position you are in."

"Oh, I understand," she argued back. "You want the king's favour, and you're trying to tailor our confessions to fit the bullshit the ignorant, inbred, two-bit son-of-a-whore believes. And we can hardly confess to rubbish we don't know or believe without agreeing with you. You can't torture us, but you can put words in our mouths through threats. You must have threatened my granddaughter with something big to have her spouting any of that tripe."

"I believe Alizon's compliance was entirely your own doing," he replied flatly, not enjoying being called out on his games.

She couldn't help the raised eyebrows at this declaration. The man was blaming her—*her*—for his kidnapping and scaring a child into a false confession. Did this man have no shame?

"How?" Demdike decided to indulge his insanity.

"We can't torture you, that's true. Not during your time in that room. But you see those cells, they're guarded by men. Good men, but weak to the temptations of the flesh. And a young girl, bound and helpless, well I can't be here all the time to keep them in line. And poor Alizon recognised this." His teeth flashed in the low light, absorbing all the light in the room and showing the monstrous animal behind the human visage.

He, this thing, this monster, threatened *that* of her little girl? Demdike wanted to be sick in her mouth. Had to force down the desire to throw out her breakfast alongside all the words she wanted to scream. Her body instinctively launched itself forward, caught by the bindings as she wanted to tear the man before her limb from limb. How dare he? How dare he! This man was supposed to be a protector of the people. She was brought back to a thought she held previously, how the men in law rarely upheld the sanctity of the covenant they were supposed to represent.

Curses. She wanted to curse him until there would be nothing but smouldering ash where he stood. Never had Demdike been as tempted by the dark path as she was in the presence of this beast. He was not a man. He didn't deserve to be considered human when he held no humanity in his heart. He was devoid. One she would have happily removed from this plane given half a chance.

"So, Tibbs. He is your familiar, yes?" it was stated as a question, but the promise of violence in his tone made it clear she better cooperate.

"Tibbs is my cat, yes," not quite a confession. She was dancing the line.

The twitch of his left eye gave her more pleasure than she was willing to admit. Though petty points were not worth earning when they came at the danger of her loved ones.

"How about this, Jennet?" He looked at another piece of paper. "Yes, Jennet, only nine years old. It would be undue to kill a child. Not anymore at least," he spoke the last part mostly to himself, but Demdike heard it like a hit to a bell.

The man sounded genuinely disappointed that the murder of children was no longer seen as an acceptable sport. Just when she thought the creature could stoop no lower, he surprised her yet again. What sort of person could enjoy seeing a mere child being hurt? Demdike was starting to think this thing was why the darker part of her craft existed, to punish the wicked beings wearing human skin. If there were any servants of evil here, it was the one standing before her, acting as the Justice of the Peace. A monster in human form.

"I will spare Jennet. Assuming she co-operates, we will not add her name to the list."

"Her, Lizzie and James," she bit back, not willing to concede too quickly.

The man scoffed. "With the number of tales I've heard about those two, there's no way they don't end up swinging beside you. Or soon following. Hear me, Demdike, I will not rest until you and I banish all your ilk from this land. The only one I will consider sparing is the young girl."

She could feel the force behind his words. The vow in his commitment to the cause. A selfish, self-serving cause, but a cause nonetheless. He was willing to do whatever it took to destroy her family. She wanted to kill him.

"Think on it. I'll be back soon. It would be a shame to have your entire family wiped out like this." He left without another word.

As much as she wanted to scream, Demdike couldn't afford to lose her temper. She still hadn't seen Alizon. Could Nowell be lying? It was the last frail hope she was clinging to. That the girl might have escaped, and be out there somewhere. Somewhere safe from all this. Logic said otherwise, but she hadn't lived this long without sheltering any small hope in her heart.

A few hours later, Nowell came back in, a jug of water and a smug yet annoyed smile plastered to his face. Demdike didn't know what Chattox might have said, but knowing from experience just how infuriating the other could be. Demdike felt a jolt of pleasure at the woman having irritated the monster.

"Chattox has implied your daughter makes clay statues, your granddaughter mentioned it in passing, too. I hadn't understood its connotations at the time, but now. You're going to confess. Or I'll be paying a visit to the girl personally. And there won't be anything left to swing from the gallows but a bloodied hole when I'm done with her."

Murder would be too kind for this beast. He deserved to have his skin peeled away layer by layer, dosed in salt and set aflame. He deserved tortures and punishments her mind could barely begin to conceive of.

She knew if her Lizzie were here, the woman would beg her, beg her to spare her daughter. That death by the noose would be better than letting her little girl suffer in her stead. As much as it broke something within her to let this monster win, Demdike had no choice. People were so afraid of death, they often forgot there were much worse fates. The body could only endure so much pain before the mind broke. She would rather Alizon die and be spared anything this man might do to her. Lizzie would feel the same. Sacrificing her own daughter felt like the biggest sin Demdike could ever commit, but the alternative didn't bear thinking of.

"Show me Alizon. Show me she's really here and safe. Then guarantee no one will touch her, and I'll confess to whatever horseshit will have you licking the king's ass."

***

"A long walk, really?" She couldn't help the snark that escaped her at seeing Chattox.

The four were equally bound, the ropes securing their hands and tying them to the back of the carriage. The other simply gave her a gap-toothed smirk.

"Aye, a long walk, before a sudden drop, of course."

Demdike couldn't help the laugh which escaped her. This woman's sense of humour was as dark and warped as her own. In another life, they might have been best friends. Perhaps it could happen in the next one.

"Lancaster," came the soft voice of Anne, Chattox's daughter. "I hear you can see the coast from the castle. I've never seen the sea."

Demdike wasn't sure what to reply to this. She'd seen the sea. Visited Lancaster and the bays of Morecambe in her youth, on holiday with her father. A nice place to visit. Her father had worked with the lawmen of Lancaster and used the journey as an excuse to have a vacation.

Even all these decades later, she recalled the journey down the River Lune. She'd wondered why they needed ships and her father refused to allow them to simply cross at low tide. It was only when she'd seen the force of the tide—a three-foot wall of water as it rushed across the river and battered against the ships—that she then accepted the Lune was a little different from the river back home. The River Ribble had never seemed safer than in the moment she saw the Lune swell, making her wonder just how many unsuspecting lives it must have claimed.

Lancaster was littered with ghosts even back then. When she was still Elizabeth and didn't know about the cunning folk or walking the grey road. Even then, she'd felt the unnatural chill of the place. The old buildings and the cobbled streets which seemed to echo with more than sound. As though you might blink and be able to see the past playing out before your eyes. It was almost cathartic to think she would lose her life in such a place.

"I hear when they hang us, it will be from a tall hill. Near the Williamson's estate, overlooking the bay. So you'll definitely see it at least once before we croak." It wasn't exactly a kindness, but a way of trying to find something good in their dire situation.

Demdike hoped she would leave this life before the noose claimed her neck. The miles before them, the sprawling hills and countryside they were being forced to walk, would hopefully see her end. Her heart-stopping or a deep enough ditch to swallow her whole. Someway for nature to claim her before Nowell would have the pleasure. One last act of defiance.

"Move it, witches. Take one last look at your home. You'll never see it again." Nowell was back to wearing his mask, but he couldn't quite hide his happiness at their situation. The uptick of his mouth betrayed his cool demeanour.

She could see Lizzie, James and Jennet amongst the other residents. As much as she wanted to hang her head in shame—having named her own daughter to the monster before them—she kept her head high. Refused to give him any more pleasure over their situation. A quick glance at Alizon made her wish she hadn't looked. The girl was filthy. Her eyes darted around. The man may not have touched her inappropriately, but Demdike didn't doubt for one second he hadn't kept frightening the younger girl with such threats.

Lancaster couldn't come soon enough. At least in the dungeons, they would be kept together. She could protect the girl better then. If only until the end.

Chapter Nineteen

Lizzie didn't know what to do. First, her daughter. Now her mother had been taken in. The men literally forced down her door before hauling off the old woman. She'd been too shocked to react. Her body frozen in place until after they'd already gone. Taking the elderly lady with them as though she were some troublesome dog and not another person.

When they heard Alizon had confessed, Lizzie didn't know what to do. It made no sense. Her mother's fury had been grounding. The woman always had a plan, but this stumped even the great Demdike. A confession was a confession. There was little they could do besides going down to the jailhouse, but no one had been there.

They heard the next day how her daughter had been hunted. How her child had been close to home, in the forest itself, before the man (the man her mother, Demdike, warned them about over and over), caught her little girl. They'd returned each day to no news and no updates.

They'd learnt the man had taken Alizon to the Baldwyn's, which made no sense. Was the man trying to get Alizon to implicate her family as well? Lizzie's mother seemed to think so. Demdike had been old for many years, but for the first time, the crone truly looked her age. Resigned to the world and all its woes.

When the men came, the old woman put up a token protest, but Lizzie knew her mother. Normally, she would have kicked and punched. Bit and scratched. Demdike hadn't seriously tried to escape. She was confused. The crone looked like she'd been waiting for this to happen; her shoulders drooped in resignation.

Because of this, it wasn't too surprising when they told her Demdike confessed. Not that her heart hadn't stopped and her mind hadn't rebelled at the idea, but shock wasn't among the cocktail of emotions she experienced. Instead, left her wondering what they could've leveraged to make the great Demdike confess. The answer was obvious, Alizon. And if they now had two of her family, it was only a matter of time before the men came for them all.

When she glimpsed her family bound in rope alongside Chattox and Anne, something in her stomach bottomed out. Lizzie wasn't sure what to feel. Numb disbelief mostly. Her little girl looked tired. Dirty. Broken. She wanted to scoop her child up in a hug and hide her away from the world. James had to keep a hold of her arms to stop her from running forward.

Demdike gave her a small grimace, which might have been a smile, but missed the mark entirely. Lizzie was lost. Her mother, for all the hardships they'd endured, had been her compass. Always pointed them through the mess and kept their family together. From the loss of her father when they were young, to the loss of her own husband and three children to raise, to the general troubles of life in Pendle. Demdike, her mother, had been her beacon lighting the way through the darkness.

To see her mother reduced like this. To see the obvious pains, the woman was hiding—her body sagged, ageing decades in a matter of days—it was painful for Lizzie to watch. Her mother and daughter were being carted off like animals. She wanted to scream. Wanted to hurt the men taunting them. Wanted it all to stop.

"We need to do something," she whispered without conscious thought. Her breath laboured with the weight of the scene.

She had no idea what they might do, but there must be something. This couldn't be it. Lizzie refused to accept there was nothing they could do. She couldn't wait to hear her child and mother were going to be sentenced to death.

"I'll ask around. Someone must know what to do," James spoke softly beside her, carrying most of her weight by this point.

Lizzie wasn't sure when her little boy had become a man, but he was showing his strength now. Holding it together when all she wanted to do was break apart.

"Who can we ask? Anyone with any law experience will be in the man's pocket," her words sounded as defeated as she felt.

"Despite everything, we still have friends."

She wanted to scoff. What friends? The people who'd avoided them like the plague since the whispers of witchcraft began? The people who'd gossiped about them in the streets like she couldn't hear the words they were saying? The people who watched her daughter being dragged into an inn by a strange man because it was more exciting to watch than it was worth intervening?

Those people weren't friends. They were despicable individuals acting like they cared to learn the latest instalment of the drama. But if she could use them in return to help her family, it would be worth enduring their snide comments and eager eyes.

She nodded to James. "Do what you think is best," was all she could say. "Jennet, help me home." She could see the child was going to protest. "Not now. We have bigger problems than you playing with your friends," she snapped.

This wasn't Jennet's fault. The young girl didn't fully understand the gravity of the situation. However, she was old enough to know it was bad, and Lizzie didn't have the patience to deal with her daughter's mood on top of everything else.

"I'll ask around. Jennet be good. You can play later." The girl shut her mouth at her brother's chastisement.

Lizzie might have, at another time, been frustrated about the girl listening to her brother more than her own mother, but she was too emotionally worn out to be worrying about something this pointless.

The unofficial meeting at Malkin Tower was scheduled for the next day. Word quickly got around, but it wasn't official in the way church and village hall meetings were. This was a neighbourhood issue, and although all were welcomed, someone of standing wouldn't be recording or overseeing it. People started arriving armed with platters of food. Were this any other time, Lizzie would have been happy to see an excess of food in their home. For all the times life forced them to beg for scraps, this was practically luxury. If it weren't for her daughter and family being in danger, she might have been able to truly appreciate it. (If she ignored the fact people weren't doing this out of the goodness of their hearts).

As everyone started settling, her home looked smaller than normal. People propped themselves against everything in the room. The few chairs quickly claimed. Soon, bodies were lining the wall with people from all across Pendle. Several families had come and gone. Offering words of false sympathy. Elizabeth could practically taste their hunger for news on their breaths. Fogging her home with their smoked words. She hated it, but now wasn't the time to alienate people. Her mother would have her hide if she didn't try and use this moment to gain some goodwill.

When those who intended on staying remained and those who had better things to occupy their time with had left, the '*meeting*' began. Though it was mostly a recap of all the local gossip, and no matter how many times she argued, Alizon was not guilty, the looks of pity at her apparent delusions were grating on her.

"The problem is—" John Bulcock began as he took his usual seat. He and his mother having become repeated visitors to their home after the events of the previous Halloween. "—they confessed." He held his hand up as she argued.

"They made her," Lizzie protested for what felt like the thousandth time today alone. The words were starting to lose all sense.

"It doesn't matter. Even if evidence comes out later that the person who confessed lied or was wrong, or not even there, the confession is all the lawmen care about. You say you did it, they need someone to pay, case closed."

The man spoke bluntly. She was almost grateful for how his eyes held no sympathy. He wasn't trying to hurt or help her, simply stating a fact. Strangely, it did help calm her somewhat. Even if the facts weren't ones she wanted to hear.

"Demdike is a well-known witch, too. There is nothing we can do to help her. Everyone always known she was what she was," a voice she couldn't be bothered identifying piped up from among the crowd.

Lizzie trailed her tongue along the back of her teeth, trying to keep the distaste in her mouth. The gossips' were here in full force, just in case something exciting happened. As much as she would like to throw each of them from her home, it wouldn't help anything.

"Can we hire someone to take their case? I hear there are people who do that?" A desperate plea for any potential avenue.

"In London maybe, and they would cost a pretty penny," James answered before anyone else could.

She felt herself deflating in the chair. The hardback caused her discomfort in the new position, but she couldn't bring herself to move once more. A part of her accepted she might just deserve this pain. Goodness only knows what her daughter was enduring right now. A wooden chair was nothing in comparison.

"Money aside," John began again, "she confessed. If she had only been implicated, if the accusation had come from another, it could be argued against. But they both themselves admitted it. There isn't a lawyer in the land who could get them off a charge they confessed to. Especially not on something the king himself will be interested in. The likelihood of anything..." he trailed off, likely having finally spotted the many despondent faces around the room.

"You're saying there is nothing?" Lizzie's voice came out as fragile and breakable as she felt. Like a young girl barely capable of speech and vulnerable to the many pains of the world.

"I'm saying this likely isn't the end, and if you don't want to be swinging with them, do not confess. No matter what they offer or threaten, because let's be honest here, we all know a fourteen-year-old girl did not hurt that man. No matter what fun the story might be to tell, we know better."

Lizzie could see there were many faces who didn't agree with the man and were they not in her house, would have had no problems informing John of such, but fortunately, in present company, they merely pulled faces whilst keeping silent.

"If anyone was a witch selling their souls to the devil, they'd be asking for riches and an easy life, not made to beg and work for a pittance," John looked around the room, as though saying, '*Does this fit?*'

Although she felt slighted, Lizzie couldn't disagree with him.

"Most of the posters show them as dirty wenches living in squalor," someone argued in return.

The second look around the room from the inhabitants did anger her.

"Make a deal with the devil and you live in squalor, but promise yourself to god and all this is a test of suffering? Don't add up if you ask me." James sometimes had his moments of insight.

"And yet, it is strangely only the poor who are targeted by such accusations," John continued her son's thoughts. "Especially after the late queen decided science was the way of the future and witchcraft was a superstition of the past. We would be fools to simply believe something because the latest monarch favours it. Remember what they did to our land with their many squabbles?"

This generated a few more nods of agreement.

"My Richard, bless his soul," an old woman began, "he said to never trust a courtier as far as you could throw them. Said they were always up to something. They still hate us for having a Catholic church, despite everything."

The face was so rarely seen, it took Lizzie a moment to realise who it was. Old Alice Nutter in her home. The widow was one of the more wealthy patrons of Pendle and barely concerned herself with any of the events of their village. If anything, she would have expected her to be among the masses, denouncing her family as witches and leaving them to their fate. She was glad to be proven wrong. Or maybe the drama was too tempting for even the wealthy widow to ignore. Either way, Lizzie was glad her words had been in support of her family and not of Nowell and his men.

The old woman's words garnered several nods of agreement. Each shared a story of the rude Justice who'd been in their homes the last few months and the many insults they'd been forced to ignore and pretend to be both deaf and blind to. In another time, she might have laughed at the absurdity of some of their stories. Not that she doubted them. No, Lizzie could fully believe a man as pompous and rude as Nowell had behaved as such, but that the tales were so outlandish. She wished she could have seen the faces of the people pretending they didn't understand or recognise the many insults aimed at their feet.

"So, the only way forward is if accused, do not confess?"

It was John's mother, Jane, this time. The woman looked around hopelessly. Jane had grown rather attached to Lizzie's mother in the previous months. Lizzie suspected, to Jane, the missing Demdike was likely like losing another parent. She would have to reach out to her later. If there was a later.

"Shame we can't actually curse them," James muttered.

"It's no use. Without something of the man's or the materials to make clay statues, which would take longer than we have anyway." She sighed. Exhausted in ways she hadn't known were possible.

Lizzie had never been good at any of it, anyway. There was a reason Alizon accompanied her grandmother rather than her. Lizzie's ability was like a puddle to her mother's ocean and Alizon's rainstorm. Nothing more than average. She wondered if the pair might curse the man from the cells. If anyone could weave the magic of the world with will alone, it was those two.

***

"What are we gonna do, mum?" James said, tidying up the leftovers of the day.

People had stayed for a while, but when no new thoughts were suggested, and the gossipers grew bored, the rabble finally left her home. Lizzie paused, considering her son's question. She had no idea. What could they do? Even some of the brightest minds in Pendle hadn't been able to come up with a solution—if they ever wanted to. There was no obvious answer.

"I don't know, son. If this was someone local, we could barter or argue, but these are people bigger than our little hills. People who don't care who they hurt or what they have to do to get a leg up. And if the king's eyes really will be on us, I fear there is little we could do at all."

A dark reality. For the first time in her life, Lizzie wished she had learnt more of her mother's craft. She hadn't realised how much she relied on her mother to sort out their problems until the elderly woman was gone. Lizzie was suddenly a small child again, afraid of the big world beyond her home.

"We're fucked then?"

"Language." She didn't say yes, but didn't rebuff him either.

***

When night fell and she heard the growls from outside once more, Lizzie could barely raise her head in protest. The thing was back. The beast that'd been circling their home and the people of Pendle for the past few months. As much as she wanted to run out the door, banging pots and lighting herbs to ward it off. She couldn't physically move. Her body refused even the slightest suggestion.

When a heavy presence weighed down her chest, Lizzie forced her eyes open. Terrified by the black creature that sat there staring at her. Studying her. A smile stretched across its broken mouth upon seeing her awake. She would have shut her eyes and hid if she could, but her body refused to obey. Forced her to watch as the thing drew shapes across her chest. Her heart beat wildly. She half expected it to force its hand through her rib cage and bring the still-beating muscle to its mouth.

The winds outside picked up, whistling as it turned around the house and to the trees. The room grew unnaturally warm, as though the creature was burning. The smell that filled her lungs was enough to make her gag. Air scraped as it dragged down her windpipe. She needed water, but the being kept her in place. Pinned as it observed her. It looked far too pleased with itself. Lizzie couldn't hear the thing, but she suspected by the way its shoulders moved it was laughing at her. Deriving amusement from her fruitless struggles.

As her fingers twitched, Lizzie focused on moving that hand. On having a free limb with which to push the creature from her body and regain control once more. It looked to the left, as though sensing her impending freedom, but did little more than watch for a few moments longer. Bending over her, the thing's face was right next to hers, those monstrous teeth close to her ears.

"Soon," its voice crackled.

Chapter Twenty

S he ached. Demdike was used to pain. Living a long life meant you became familiar with the sensation. Though usually, she could rest. There was no rest for the wicked, at least this was what her jailors told her. They couldn't afford to lose time. No one apparently considered how much time they would save if they let the four women sit in the carriage rather than hauling them along behind it.

Well, this was a lie. Their captors weren't stupid. Of course, they knew it would be quicker to not have the women walk the entire way, but then '*the witches wouldn't suffer like they deserved*'. A direct quote, when one of the younger men braved to ask why they were doing it this way.

Demdike would have said something, but every time she opened her mouth and made a sarcastic quip, they were there with the whip. Safety measures (to keep them from running). More like a legal torture device the men delighted in using. Were her hands not bound, the elderly woman would have pounced on them and ripped their throats out. Her mind was becoming increasingly feral. She didn't hate it.

The aches were bad, but it was the open sores which were worse. The long days of trekking through fields. The constant wet from both the weather and marshlands. Disgusting. The soles of her feet—barely cushioned by the rags she called shoes—were blistered beyond belief.

The sides were not better either, from the damp. The puss-filled sores opened repeatedly. Every step was agony. She tried to hide her wincing, refusing to give the monsters watching them the satisfaction.

The other's feet were just as bad. Anne had a gash up her leg from where she'd slipped. It looked painful, and although not too deep, would easily become infected in these conditions. Alizon looked ready to pass out, but the fire in her eyes kept her going. Despite their circumstances, there was a feeling of pride burning in her. They weren't giving up. Demdike always said, '*If you can't do something out of love, do it out of spite*', and that right there—that fire in her granddaughter's eyes—was spite in its purest form.

The path changed to rocky terrain. Demdike couldn't fully hold in her sounds as the four were forced over the uncomfortable path. Even if they'd been given proper foot protection, she doubted they would do much at this point. Her blisters had blisters. It hurt. Everything hurt. When the rain first came, it was a welcome relief. A break from the sun, and finally some water for her parched throat. However, after several days of water-logged clothes, she now despised the weather more than ever.

***

Lancaster Castle was intimidating to look upon. Demdike saw it as a child, but from a distance. The woman had a vague recollection of thinking it was pretty. A passing thought and recognition of the large building, but nothing her child-mind held onto. Up close, the grandeur and size dwarfed them. Looking at such a structure made her feel insignificant. She'd seen large manor houses before, but nothing on this scale.

The stone detail was beautiful. There were places where you could see painted colour, slowly losing the battle against time and fading to beige. Demdike could relate. There were sections where the limestone was damaged and being repaired. If only some patchwork would help her body. Demdike could easily believe the castle would still stand tall a thousand years from now. It'd lasted five hundred already—it wasn't a stretch to think the structure could reach out into the future. Enduring far longer than the people who built and added to it over the centuries.

As they were led closer, Demdike could feel the memories lingering in the stone. All of Lancaster felt like this; old in a way that predated humans. Like you could touch the past as easily as the present. It grew stronger the closer they drew to the castle, passing its threshold and into the enclosed hallways. A chill ran along her arms, the delicate hairs rising where it touched. The ghosts were intrigued by her presence.

Some were trapped, but most seemed to simply have nowhere else to go. The dead claimed this building as much as the living. Demdike didn't need to look over to Chattox to know the other women could sense them, too. Her entire body was a live wire with the spirits circling them. They weren't quite connecting, not yet, but they were curious. Those dead eyes were as keen as the living guards leading them to the cells.

The four were all thrown into one dingy room. There were people in there already. Twelve hooks, Demdike counted on first glance. She could only assume more people would find themselves crammed in the small space before long. They were each tied to a hook. The rope had enough leeway to allow them to move to the corner of the cell and back.

It didn't take long for her to discover why, when one of the older prisoners went to the corner and squatted down. Averting her eyes wasn't enough to keep the sounds from penetrating her mind. As much as she wanted to protest, Demdike knew it was better for it to be in one corner than across the room. Even animals knew not to contaminate their living space with their excretions. Recognising the logic, however, did not make her any happier. She would soon have to follow suit.

A curl of her lips made her want to reject the reality she found herself in, but they were prisoners. People lined up to die. They would find no sympathy for their conditions. No kindness here. As far as those in charge were concerned, the prisoners should be grateful for every day they got to live. Regardless of a trial, her death was a done deal. A foregone conclusion.

It was this same day, after a week of walking, that Demdike realised the second major cruelty of their situation. They were given barely enough food to survive on. When the plate and water were thrown in, they had to fight for the scraps. There was no camaraderie here. There was only survival of the fitness. Fight or starve. She gave Alizon some of her meagre amount of bread because the girl hadn't realised what was happening.

She was glad Chattox wasn't among the many constantly scraping for sustenance. It might be an uncharitable thought, but it was one less mouth to feed. Anne tried to give her mother some of her food, but the woman remained entirely oblivious, as though she could hear nothing happening around her. Demdike knew the other cunning woman's eyes were going, but her ears were fine. It took her a few days to realise what was happening.

Demdike tried talking with Chattox a few times, but the woman was barely present. Her mind off elsewhere. The way she would rock back and forth against the hard stone muttering to herself and entirely ignorant of the people around her, were Demdike not a learned woman in the cunning craft she would have easily believed her old frenemy to be possessed, or entirely gone in the mind. However, she could recognise the intense focus of a spell being upheld. Of magic being kept alive in one's mind despite the situation of the physical form.

Were Demdike not this exhausted, she might have applauded the other's tenacity. Enduring and continuing, despite both of their looming deaths. The other had known this was coming, and as bitter as a small part of Demdike's heart was, she could see why Chattox had walked as fate instructed, only doing the spell to ensure their bloodline lived rather than ensuring their personal survival. She was still angry, though. Her death meant little, she'd lived enough. But her granddaughter, being in this cell alongside her, wasn't fair. The girl deserved more. Should have been able to live a long life.

After a week, Demdike was overtly aware of the constant sounds. It was never quiet. Even in the dead of night, this place refused to be silent. Between the beating of prisoners; the sounds of fists and blood were easily recognisable even when she couldn't see them. The screams of women. Didn't take a genius to guess the cause of those. The wet squelch and cries to stop echoed around the stone chambers and hallways.

Then there were the ghosts, screaming day and night. The way they cried out for the help they didn't receive in life. Were she in a better place physically and mentally, she would have tried to aid them, as was part of the cunning woman's role, but it was hard to aid others when you couldn't help yourself.

Demdike wondered how long it would be until the guards set their sights on her cells. Seemed the men had a rotation of whom to torment. Specifically, who would be leaving and who would be long-term guests. Those likely to leave soon got the most of the attention. Ensuring everyone else was forced to hear. Hear and wonder when they would be next, when it would be their turn. There was no '*if*' in this scenario—it would happen. It was only a case of when. An extra layer of cruelty to the prisoners and great enjoyment for the guards.

Then there was the smell. She couldn't decide if the heat of the sun or the waterlog from the rain made it worse. The eternally changing English weather meant the intensity and note of the stench changed often enough it was hard to block it out. Like the noise, there was no escape. A constant reminder of the helplessness of their situation; how there would be no escape.

***

When her daughter and James were thrown into the cells alongside them a month later, Demdike barely had enough strength to greet them. Her heart ached to see them both. Happy she had the chance to see them and devastated their presence here meant they would die alongside her. James wore blue and black across his face. The patches of muddied red spoke of repeated beatings.

She wanted to go to him and offer comfort, but her body was slowly becoming one with the stone. Her bones, old and weary long before they forced her to spend weeks on end sitting here, were unable to move or find any comfort. Her limbs became stiffer and less mobile by the hour. The fight for food became pointless when the energy to fight was less than she gained from the meagre offerings.

"Mum," the broken whisper of her Lizzie as the other sat beside her.

She hadn't noticed the other approaching. Through a glance, she noticed Alizon had moved. Now sitting beside her brother, the two clutched at the other as though the world would rip them apart at any moment. Had she the energy, Demdike would have joined them.

"What happened to your face?" her daughter sounded broken.

Demdike only shrugged. It wouldn't help to worry the other. Saying she took more than a few hits protecting Alizon from the guards and their wandering hands would only scare the other more. She likely would see firsthand soon enough. A few hits were worth it to protect her family. To keep them safe in any way, she was able. Her body was old and falling apart. What were a few more bruises and broken bones compared to her granddaughter's safety? They likely would have turned on her sooner or later anyhow, at least she felt still useful like this. The last barrier between the world and the young girl.

"What happened?" Not that she really needed to ask. Nowell had stated his intentions loud and clear.

"They started about a week after you left. That man—" Demdike never heard her daughter speak with such hatred, but if someone earned it, Nowell was definitely the one. "—threatened you and Alizon, but we knew better. But then he set his sights on little Jennet, said he'd sell her to the whorehouse or a circus. James was spilling every sin he could think of in a matter of moments."

She could only nod, the same as he'd done with her. "And Jennet?" she asked apprehensively.

"The priest took her in. Said he'd keep her safe. Not sure how much I believe it, but better than the alternative."

Demdike didn't have the energy to make any disparaging remarks. She could only hope the idea of making a witch's daughter into a nun would be more of a draw to them than hurting the girl for the supposed sins of her family. It was all too complicated for her sluggish mind.

The warmth of her daughter's arms was gentle, but the aches and pains littering her body made her instinctively tense. The soft touches as the other pet her head, running her hands over her hair, was enough to have her body unwinding. She could have floated away. As she slipped into the land of Morpheus, she wondered how long it would be until she never awoke again. Death was circling her. She hoped he came sooner rather than later.

A cry startled her awake. The guards were attacking James as he bodily protected his sister. A fierce pride roared through her. For all her failings, she raised a strong family. People willing to live and die to protect one another. Grabbing the broken shard of a plate she'd kept, Demdike used what remaining strength she had, and stabbed it into the back of the guard's leg. Revelling in his cries of surprise and pain.

The man kicked back at her, but she could barely feel the pain. Too happy to have landed a blow on the bastard. Spitting at him, she sacrificed some of her strength to see karma mark the man. The beast who enjoyed hurting her family. It wasn't quite dark magic, but definitely grey. Bonding a person to their bad actions and alerting the world of spirit to the caster's desire for this person to be tormented. Equal to the actions the person has taken. Karma which anyone could join in repaying. The spirit world delighted in having a target for their waves of anger. The restless ghosts in this place would be unable to deny such an opportunity.

It was her last bit of fight. Her last act of defiance against the people who were hurting her and hers. Demdike had always said she wanted to go out fighting, and if this was to be her last stand, she was glad James was here to help his sister. A horrific reality, but she knew firsthand how the pain of living was often worse than death could ever be.

She could hear the cries of her family. Chattox even looked present for the first time in weeks. Her eyes honed in on Demdike. They both knew. Had known. Would always know. The grey path was welcoming her to the other side. It was time for both of her feet to enter the ether.

She could hear the desperation in Lizzie's voice. The screams of Alizon as she tried to deny the inevitable. The guards had left them. A small silver lining. Her remaining moments on the physical plane were surrounded by the ones she loved, by the family she was beyond proud of. They might have lost, but they had tried and in the end, that was all she could have hoped for.

With her last breath, she willed her energy into Chattox, powering the spell. Her bloodline would live on.

CHAPTER TWENTY-ONE

J ames blinked slowly. Then again for good measure. It didn't make sense. None of this made sense. His nana was gone. Alizon was gone. If the rumours were true, he was soon to follow. He wouldn't have normally put much stock in the local gossip. People were prone to exaggeration. A tall tale was more exciting than a simple truth. No, normally he'd have ignored them, but given how things were currently turning out, he couldn't help thinking that, for once, the gossip mill might be true.

"Jennet," he tried to whisper, but it came out louder than expected.

Luckily, their mother was busy in the kitchen. Over the clangs of the pots and bangs of the cupboards, she remained oblivious to his words.

"What?" she grumbled, hair skewed and face heavy with sleep.

It was another rumour. Something he'd heard the old biddies from church saying. Initially he'd put little stock in it, but now...

"You know what happened with Al and nan?"

She might have been only nine-years-old, but the level of contempt she managed to convey with just her face was pretty impressive.

"Yes," she drawled, making clear she was not happy to be missing sleep for this conversation.

Their mother had dragged them both up at the crack of dawn every day since Demdike left. Her way of trying to cope, keeping them busy and too tired to think. James might have appreciated a few more hours of sleep, but he understood. Jennet was less charitable. As the days turned to a week, the young girl's mood soured further with each early rising.

The pair took to trying to get a few minutes of extra shut eye in the living room whilst their mum made breakfast; it became almost sacred to the pair, and here he was breaking this ritual and keeping them both awake.

"I know. I know, but it's important."

Her face scrunched, but at least she was keeping her eyes open this time.

"I heard some stuff. People saying–" He paused, unsure how to say this. Words were never his strong suit. He was all brute force and brawn, this delicate stuff was no good for him. "They're saying we're next."

The young girl stared blankly at him, clearly not understanding or underestimating the severity of the situation.

"Nowell and his dogs, they're gonna come for me and mum next," he finally bluntly stated.

Her eyes widened, the sleep entirely cleared from her visage as the weight of his words fully woke her.

"James?"

"There ain't much we can do. We've looked for help and there ain't none. We've spoken to law people. And John, he knows some stuff, but not enough. I even heard they might go after him and his mum for trying to help us. It ain't good Jen. Bad things are happening."

"Wha–what do we do?"

This was why he started the conversation. And why he wanted to do this away from prying ears. The cord around his neck at birth made him a bit slower, but he wasn't as stupid as he let people think.

"Al and nan's confession, they talked about it in the pub. Complete rubbish. Pacts with devil animals and all this lark. All lies. But they confessed. Even if it's all nonsense, they still confessed. Mum won't let me talk about it, but Nowell must have had leverage. Ain't no way Demdike is admitting to those sins without some great threat. And I think we're it."

"I don't understand."

"Nowell threatened us, or as I heard the rumours, threatened to either save or hurt you."

The small girl shook in the chair, her head moving side to side as she tried to deny his words.

"Listen, Jen, I ain't trying to scare ya, but we have to think about this. Think proper like. He's clever, and he knows that no jury is gonna want to hurt a kid, but he could hurt you in other ways."

He didn't mention the many lectures their nan had given them about vulnerabilities and people taking liberties. Children were particularly targeted by these bad people, and she'd always made sure they knew to protect themselves, and fight back.

"But he wouldn't–"

"Maybe not that, but if things go the way they seem to be going, if you're left on your tod, he could put you with nice people, or bad people. Heck, even if we're spared, they could still say they want you away from me and mum and all our influence, could put you with a different family or one of them workhouses they keep talking about."

Apparently, they were a trend in London, one they wanted to bring to the north, a way to '*deal*' with the poor. They'd yet to catch on, but if people like Nowell got their way, it was only a matter of time.

"Better a workhouse than the whorehouse," Jennet muttered.

James wasn't sure she fully understood the statement, and was simply parroting what their nana told them, but at least she knew it, even if she couldn't grasp it just yet.

"Aye. He could put you with a good family, or a bad one, is what I'm getting at."

"I don't wanna go. I wanna be here, with you and mum."

He shook his head. Not able to say how he doubted he and their mum were going to make it to the harvest, let alone live long enough to raise the girl.

"And hopefully you will, and we'll be together forever." The lie tasted like burnt bread on his tongue, bitter and hard to swallow, but he needed to do this, to say the words. If the worst came to pass, at least he'd know she was safe.

"The rumours, they're saying you'll be taken—" He raised his hands to stop her protest. "—I'm just saying, just in case. Like nan does, telling us what to do if bad stuff does happen. Even if it never comes, better to know what to do and not need the information than to be caught with your pants down."

Her lips pursed, but she didn't argue. Mollified by his reasoning. Never was James so grateful for all the lectures and pearls of wisdom their nan was known for imparting.

"If they come for us. If there's no way for us to escape—"

"I'll break you out. Me and Rodge were speaking about it. Reckon we could dig a hole under the jail and get you out."

James paused for a moment, recalling a previous event. "Wait, is that where all the spoons went when they took Nana Demy?"

Jennet turned away from him with a sheepish look on her face, muttering something.

"What?"

"I said we could have made it, but they moved her too soon."

James didn't feel the need to explain to her all the ways in which her plan was destined to fail. Sweet though her intentions were, it was not something she could pull off in real life.

"Right... anyway." He ran his hands through his hair, trying to regain the strands of the conversation. "Right, so, the rumours, if the worst should happen—"

"Which it won't," she protested.

He held in the wince, just barely. "If it should," he repeated slowly. "I need you to be careful. I'm serious here, Jenster, I need you to play it careful. No shouting, biting or attacking, and if..." He halted, taking a steadying breath. "If I ever confess, it's 'cause they've got real leverage. Something big. Something scary. I need you to be brave for me."

Her eyes were shiny. James couldn't see his own, but he suspected the same moisture was gathering at the sides as well.

"The rumours. They say they might try and get one of us, and by us I think they meant you, to turn on the family. To discredit us and lie to the jury."

"But!"

"No buts, Jennet. If worse comes to worst, if for some reason I ever confess, you lie. You get on that stand and you lie. You say we're the worst type. You say we make pacts with the devil or whatever nonsense they want to hear. You say whatever they want. You lie and you protect yourself."

He could see the arguments forming behind her eyes. She and Alizon were polar opposites, but there were times—like this—when the fire behind his sister's eyes were so similar to that of their missing sibling, there was no denying they were family.

"It might not happen, Jen. We might get lucky and those rumours are just that, rumours. Like that time they said farmer Joseph were eaten by his cow, and he turned up three weeks later having gone to visit his family on the coast."

It worked—made her chuckle.

"Could be nothing, but like nana says, best to have a plan and not need it, than to be caught with no plan and left to pull something out your rear end."

The small girl laughed wetly.

"Promise me. Please, sis. When they come for us, because them hauling us in is going to happen. If, when they talk to us, I confess, you agree to testify against us. You keep yourself safe. Let them think you'll play along. Have them put you with a good family. If it happens, do it for me."

"It's just a plan. A stupid plan. I don't want to go, and I don't want you to go, but if it happens." She looked away. Even in this hypothetical situation, the young girl didn't want to denounce her family.

It warmed James' heart. They bickered, like all siblings, but no matter what, they loved one another. Family was everything. Their mother taught them this. They saw it every day, with their old nan trying to carry on despite her age. By their widowed mother who tried to keep them fed and clothed despite how tired she was. Even Alizon, who rarely seemed to be in the same world as them, how she would beg and work wherever she could to help keep them afloat. Their family was everything, and were he in Jennet's shoes, James wasn't sure he could do it either.

"Maybe." She hesitated. "Maybe just nan. People believe the worst of her anyway."

He nodded, grateful she was willing to consider it. If the rumours were true, if Nowell and his people were coming for them, and wanting to use Jennet, he could go to his grave knowing she was safe.

James never really showed any promise in the cunning arts, and couldn't sense the spirits the way the women in his family could, but there was a great pit opened in his stomach. An empty gnawing chasm that no food could fill. He might not have his family's skills, or the intellect of the learned people, but even James could see how the cards were lined up. His family was going to fall.

***

When they came for him, he didn't fight. He told Jennet to remember their conversation. With tear tracks down her cheeks, she'd nodded, hiding into Jane's skirt as the woman took his sister in. He was grateful, but a dark shadow clung to the woman, and he suspected it wouldn't be long until she joined him in the cells.

When Nowell threatened Jennet, he was resigned to it. Spouted rubbish after rubbish and let the so-called Justice pick whatever nonsense he wanted. Some random woman from Yorkshire he'd never met? Sure, he'd seen her. Dancing in the moonlight? His nan struggled to walk, but yeah, this happened too. And of course, they were all in league with demons, *obviously*, that's why he was here and not living rich and happy.

None of it was real. Didn't matter to him which parts the man kept or not. Jennet was safe. Would be safe. This was all that mattered.

When he landed in the crowded cell, it was both a relief and a jarring ache to see his nana and Alizon. They both looked battered and bruised. Both were thinner than he'd ever seen them, and considering how scarce food was at the best of times, that was saying something.

It was barely two days in and he'd had to physically cover his sister and mother multiple times to stop the guards from beating them. He'd likely already gained a few broken bones, but for some reason, his mind didn't process the pain, not constantly at least. The sharp pains were difficult to ignore, but the constant toothache-like ones were easier to discard. His mind detaching itself from his physical form with each new injury.

'*It didn't matter,*' he found himself thinking more and more. None of it mattered. He would protect his family, keep them safe, and then he'd go into the afterlife in peace.

When he watched his nana die, something within him froze. James believed if he ever witnessed death, it would scare him. He never expected to feel jealous. She looked peaceful—he wanted that. In the meantime, all he could do was try to be the shield for his sister and mother. Try to keep the guards from harming them. It wasn't much, but it was all he could do. All he was good for.

James came into the world with a cord around his neck. Strangled. Nana Demy once said you could never escape your fate. You might delay it, but it always caught up with you in the end. James should have died at birth. He'd had a full life of extra time. Seemed his time was up. He'd meet the noose soon enough. Fate would collect on her debt.

Chapter Twenty-Two

When the creature came into the cell, she hadn't known what it was. Her mother and Chattox both went stiff in its presence. The growling told her it wasn't friendly. She was tired. Tired in a way she'd never known. Her nan's description of being soul weary finally made sense. When days of doing nothing drained more than your body.

Her grandmother's death came as a shock. Despite their situations, some childish part of her heart expected the great Demdike to survive. To live forever. She squeezed the rope around her ankle until it hurt, trying to fight the storm of emotions which came with the memory. Recalling how Demdike smiled as the life left her eyes. It shattered something within Alizon. Made the situation real. Real in a way she hadn't fully comprehended before. They'd said over and over how the trial would lead to her death, but this hadn't been processed in her mind.

Death was an abstract concept. She still grieved her father, and it wasn't as though death had never touched her. Yet her mind had been refusing to acknowledge the reality of their situation. They were going to die. Her family was going to die, and it was entirely her fault. It hadn't hit her until she'd seen the lifeless body of her nana. This was how it would end, for all of them, and it was all Alizon's fault.

Nana Demy seemed like a timeless being, something eternal. A part of Alizon expected the woman to outlive her. Survive unendingly. The world could have imploded and shrivelled up before her nana would have left this mortal coil. To see the vulnerable human behind the impossible powerhouse of spiritual energy, to see the bag of bones the woman left behind, felt impossible.

No matter how many times she tried to blink the image away, to push it aside with the sleep that seemed to have found a constant home in the corner of her eyes—would not leave. This was real life. This was happening. Had happened. Her nana was dead. Died protecting them. It didn't feel real, and yet she couldn't deny what had occurred.

The guards had taken her body and thrown it outside like she was some dead doll. Not the remains of her precious family. Alizon hadn't been able to stop herself from attacking. Following in her nana's footsteps and fighting with all she had. When they'd thrown her back against the wall, Alizon's temple was warm. The blood poured once more. Like the day she'd been hunted.

It was daunting to be reminded of just how breakable she was. How had her grandmother stayed strong in the face of constant adversity? How had she kept fighting no matter how big or strong the enemy was? Humbled Alizon to realise how truly great her grandmother had been. What a loss to the world her death was. Even if no one beyond this cell ever realised what was gone.

No matter what Nowell and people like him said. No matter how many looked down upon them for their poverty, the jobs they performed, or how much they begged for the slightest scraps of life. Her grandmother had survived it all. In a male-dominated world, she'd seen eight decades of life. Managed without male protection. Looked after two generations of family and kept going. Alizon would like to see Nowell try to survive in such circumstances. He'd have died within the first year, she'd bet. Unable to manage the extremities of life without luxury. Without money and influence. She hoped in his next life the man knew what it was to live their way of life.

A drop in temperature alerted her that the creature was prowling close by once more. She could feel it, even if her eyes couldn't see the thing. Chattox kept chanting, to keep the thing away from her. Her daughter and even Alizon's mother tried to aid the old woman in keeping the thing at bay. It would leave and return at random intervals. Tested them. Taunted. Let them know it was stronger and could come and go as it chose.

"Alizon," the airy word whispered near her ear.

She expected to see James peering over at her, trying to gain her attention, but the boy was slumped against the stone wall, face turned towards her but fast asleep. When the sound came again, she saw a dark figure among the shadows. Her eyes were confused as to how in the dark a mound of it looked even more devoid of light than the rest.

"Who's there?" she whispered back.

"You know the answer to that, Alizon. You've always known."

A denial was on the tip of her tongue, but the shifting of her mother beside her had her head turning away to check on the other. She was still asleep and entirely oblivious to the conversation happening beside her.

"I—I don't," it sounded weak even to her own ears.

"You can't lie to me, Alizon. You don't need to pretend. Not anymore," the voice was low. Masculine, but gravelly in a way she thought must have hurt its throat. It chuckled. "They killed her."

Alizon nodded. Yes, they had. Killed her grandmother. And were going to kill her family.

"You're already being tried for making deals with the devil. Why not make one anyway?"

She couldn't help scoffing. She wasn't an idiot. Her nan had warned her time and time again to never make deals with the spirit realm, not before she was trained. And if she had to guess, she'd place her last copper piece on this thing being what her nana warned her about.

"Demons don't want to help. They like to hurt. What use is that to me?"

Its laugh was like a gentle breeze across her cheek. She stiffened, unsure when the thing had drawn this close.

"Whoever said I was a demon? There are beings much older than those. Much older than your current god." It drew closer. "And you were never a normal girl, Alizon. Never meant to live among the people. You are a wild thing. From a time long passed. Meant to run through the forest and cause mischief."

Alizon wondered if this creature would be the last to accuse her of being one of the fae. For all the times she'd been called one, Alizon never thought she could be possible to miss it.

"I'm human," she said instead, arguing against the unvoiced implication.

"For now, yes, but souls are not easily changed. No matter what body they inhabit. Nowell is a human, but his soul is darker than any supposed demon. Surely you have seen?"

She didn't answer. Nana Demy warned her of how smart and persuasive the spirits could be. Especially the malevolent ones. They didn't care who they hurt.

"You don't need my permission to cause problems. You have more than enough power on your own."

"Oh, that is true. And yet, to awaken this land, to let the olde ones return. To invite all manner of beings here and hold revelry among the ancients. A spell such as this needs the sacrifice of someone born here. Someone wronged. Someone innocent."

Alizon's entire body clenched at the last line. Innocence meant many things to many people. But given what had almost happened to her repeatedly over the past few months, she understood how this beast meant it. Untainted by the sullied men who wanted to deflower and claim her. Chastity. Of all the people here, she was likely the only one who could.

"Tell me, Alizon. Why protect them? Why care for them? When they will soon see you and yours swinging from the rafters?"

Alizon didn't reply. The being was smart, whatever it was. This thing had been circling for at least a year. Had been in the forest when she was playing. Hovering above her hill when she cloud watched with Peter. At Jane's that Halloween night. It'd been playing a long game, and Alizon was intelligent enough to recognise when she was being used as a pawn.

When the cell doors opened again, she could see as all the pieces fit together. Slotting into place and creating a picture she did not want to look at.

"If they hurt me, I can't help you," she whispered harshly.

"If you don't, you'll be hurt either way."

As the men drew closer, her heart started pounding. Could she? Could she ignore everything her nana taught her about the spirit realm and the grey path? Allow darkness to descend upon the land? As hands grabbed at her clothes and forced her to her feet, she struggled. It was pointless, but she wasn't done yet. Three of them held her. She was out of the cell before her family could wake and see what was happening.

As she was being stripped, she saw it watching from the sides. Staring the being down, she showed it her teeth. Alizon wasn't prey, she was a wild creature. They would not break her.

"Only if I am spared, otherwise we both lose."

"Do you swear?"

"Only if I am spared this injustice. If I go to my death unsullied, you may have your wish. I will cast it with my death."

Blood dripped from her hand. Dropping onto the stone below. The agreement was sealed. The old gods would awaken once more and, with it, the magic of the land. Lancashire would be the home of the ancient once again. No monarch or empire could destroy what nature had created, what fate decreed.

AFTERWORD

In 1612, the trial of the Lancashire Witches saw sixteen people found guilty and hanged for the crime of witchcraft. Twelve of which were the Witches of Pendle Forest:

Elizabeth Southerns (Demdike)

Elizabeth Device

James Device

Alison Device (Alizon)

Anne Whittle (Chattox)

Anne Redferne

Alice Nutter

Jane Bulcock

John Bulcock

Katherine Hewitt (Mould-heels)

Isabel Robey

Margaret Pearson

Though gone, these *'witches'* are remembered throughout Lancashire to this day, over four hundred years later, tales of their lives, and their untimely demise, still capture the attention of historians, occultists, and storytellers.

The Lancashire Witches, or the Pendle Witches as they're more commonly known by the locals, were a group of unfortunate souls who fell victim to prejudice and ignorance. May we remember them for the people they were—flawed and beautiful individuals just trying to survive.

Further Information

For further information, please consider checking out these resources:

https://www.pendlewitches.co.uk

'*Thomas Potts, the Wonderful Discovery of Witches in the County of Lancaster: Modernised and Introduced*' by Robert Poole

'*The History of the Pendle Witches and their Magic*' by Joyce Froom

'The Lancashire Witch Conspiracy: A History of Pendle Forest and the Pendle Witch Trials' by John A Clayton

Another book written after I'd completed my novel (but published a few months prior to mine) is '*My Mother is a Witch & This I Know to be True - The Voices of Pendle*' by Charlotte Meredith. Which includes spiritualist medium connections to the witches and other interesting facts.

Notes from the author

Demdike's Age:

The texts denote Demdike as being eighty, though some believe she was in her sixties. Personally, I believe she was likely closer to sixty due to the age of 'Squinting Lizzie' Elizabeth Device. Demdike aka Elizabeth Southerns is believed to have had two children, a boy and later Lizzie. Due to the time period, it would be more likely for her to have married in her late teens and started having children at this time.

She could have had fertility problems and had children far apart, but I feel this is unlikely.

It would also add depth to the tensions between herself and Chattox if they were closer in age. As two who grew up together and were constantly competing, their issues would make more sense. I chose to follow the recorded age of eighty, but I personally believe she was likely younger than this.

The Meeting at Malkin Tower:

I don't believe the meeting ever happened. I think it was made up to connect the Lancashire witches with those who were tried and found guilty in Yorkshire. As a way to lend credibility to both trials. I highly doubt this meeting actually happened. I still included it in the novel, but changed the purpose.

Where they Lived:

Pendle is a borough with multiple small towns and villages. Malkin Tower, and many of the witches, are now believed to have come from the Newchurch area. A town named many years after their death. During the witches' lives, it was recorded as being a small village named Goldshaw Booth.

The Accent:

After reader feedback, I used the Lancashire accent sparingly in the text. Otherwise, half the letters would be missing from sentences and it would be difficult for some to understand.

The Confessions:

The confessions always struck me as odd. Naturally, I assumed they'd been tortured and confessed what they were told to say. I was then later told by a historian that torturing wasn't used during this time period. I'm not sure how much I believe this, but I did try to think of ways Nowell could have tortured them pre-Hopkins methods of the (later) 1600s. Such as threats, making them uncomfortable and denying them basic necessities.

Diabolism was the recognised form of witchcraft in this era. There is some debate about whether the witches would have declared themselves as such. I personally landed on the opinion of paganism vs. diabolism. Those beliefs of those with an education vs. those who used the passed down knowledge and word of mouth. Diabolism believes the witches worshipped the devil. Paganism is a mixture of non-denomination beliefs based in nature, spirits and what we would recognise today as alternative healing. If they did declare themselves witches, it likely meant something different to them than it did the lawmakers.

Nowell was a Puritan. He would have been taught about witches being connected with the devil and could have read texts such as Malleus Maleficarum and King James I's book Daemonologie. Alizon (as the first to confess) however, would not have known to include things specific to what the king believed. I considered how they might have heard these details, without the luxury of an education or Nowell's coaching, and drew the conclusion of church. Church and local gossip.

I still believe their confessions were trained and without torture or leverage would not have implicated themselves, their families, and members of their community. Still, I tried to follow the evidence as much as possible.

Printed in Great Britain
by Amazon